UNTETHERED

MARCIA LYNN McCLURE

Published by Distractions Ink
P.O. Box 15971
Rio Rancho, NM 87174

Published by Distractions Ink
©Copyright 2012 by M. Meyers
A.K.A. Marcia Lynn McClure
Cover Photography by
©Philcold, ©Olena Chyrko, and ©Fibobjects | Dreamstime.com
Cover Design by
Sheri Brady | MightyPhoenixDesignStudio

First Printed Edition: June 2012

McClure, Marcia Lynn, 1965—
Untethered: a novel/by Marcia Lynn McClure.

ISBN: 978-0-9852807-8-9

Library of Congress Control Number: 2012940803

Printed in the United States of America

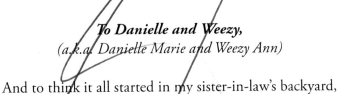

To Danielle and Weezy,
(a.k.a. Danielle Marie and Weezy Ann)

And to think it all started in my sister-in-law's backyard,
with three salt licks!
Oh, how close we've grown over the years—
melded our hearts with plungers, *Christmas Vacation* quotes,
cunning jewelry excursions, etc.
Yet in the end, the fact is our souls were always *meant* to be friends.
I love you two! More than words can ever express!
Untethered represents my heart's dedication to you both.

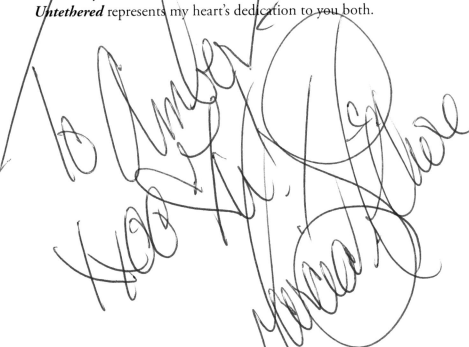

CHAPTER ONE

Cricket could see the ramshackle rooftop of the old Morgan house rising above the tree line on the horizon, and she smiled. Respite was almost hers. There were no dishes waiting to be washed, dried, and set in the cupboard at the old Morgan house. There were no chickens to be fed or cows to be milked or laundry to be hung out on the line.

She sighed, knowing that, tardy or not, there was fun and laughter awaiting her within the abandoned, dilapidated old house. And so she rushed on, lighthearted at the prospect of a lovely summer afternoon spent in merriment with friends.

Cricket's petticoat and dress felt heavier than usual, and she was sure they were slowing her pace. Yet she knew it was only impatience making her feel so irritable and weighted—her impatience and the blaze of the already hot morning sun. Oh, she couldn't wait for late summer and early autumn—when the weather softened to a comfortable temperature—when all the world was splashed with comforting colors and life itself seemed serene.

But for now, Cricket Cranford couldn't wait to meet Vilma, Marie, and Ann, finalize the plans for their Friday evening of mischief, and then race to down to the old Morgan swimming hole. As she brushed a trickle of perspiration from her temple, she decided then and there that she wasn't swimming with every piece of her undergarments on the way Vilma had insisted they all do the last time they'd gone swimming. No indeed! It was too hot a day not to enjoy the cool water to its fullest. Furthermore, her corset had been damp for days following her taking Vilma's nagging to heart and swimming in her clothes. Nope. Today Cricket would stand up to Vilma and her preacher's-daughter propriety. No one ever happened upon the old Morgan place. It was deserted, discarded, forsaken, and long forgotten by most everyone in town. No one even knew who owned the Morgan house, swimming hole, and surrounding properties anymore. It was exactly why Cricket and her friends had begun meeting there. Furthermore, the brush and trees surrounding the old swimming hole in particular provided perfect isolation. No one ever went swimming there—not since a couple of young boys had drowned in it ten years before.

Therefore, as Cricket approached what had once been the front yard of the old house that had so long ago housed a family named Morgan, she wiped more sweat from her forehead and decided to really enjoy swimming that day.

She paused a moment to study the neglected structure looming before her. The old Morgan house was a spooky place at times. Age and elements had erased any hint of whitewash or paint that might have lingered on its outside walls or trim. Thus, it stood gray and lifeless—gloomy among the overgrown brush and old trees (many of them long dead) surrounding it. Its windows were glassless and dark, and it had no doors at all.

Cricket studied the old, battered, and sadly neglected place. She imagined that it once stood white and bright against a canvas of blue sky—that happy children had played in the shade of the old willow tree that still owned a few green branches. Yet now the house looked like something dead that had had its eyes plucked out—and Cricket smiled. The spookier the old Morgan place looked, the less likely it was that anyone would venture into it—anyone other than Cricket Cranford and her friends.

"For cryin' in the bucket, Magnolia Cranford!" Vilma scolded with obvious irritation. As Cricket stepped into the dark, dusty parlor of the old Morgan house, Vilma continued to complain. "We've been waitin' a month of Sundays for you to get here."

"I'm sorry," Magnolia (or Cricket—as everyone called her most of the time) apologized, brushing a strand of coffee-colored hair from her face. "My stepmama had a list of chores she wanted finished that I swear was as long as the Bible."

"Don't blaspheme, Cricket!" Vilma scolded again. "You know good and well your chore list wasn't as long as the Bible. And you shouldn't swear either."

Cricket sighed, rolled her lovely violet eyes, and smiled at Vilma's predictably. After all, Vilma was the preacher's daughter. Auburn-haired and green-eyed—pretty though she was—Vilma was an utter pill sometimes, and nauseatingly self-righteous a good majority of the time to boot. The fact was Cricket often found herself wondering why in all the world she even counted Vilma among her friends. Yet Reverend Stanley's daughter owned a good heart—for the most part. And besides, girls of the same age who lived in small towns like Pike's Creek needed to stick together. At least to Cricket's way of thinking.

And so Magnolia "Cricket" Cranford determined to silently remind herself of all good things about Vilma and her character.

Thus, she conceded, "You're right, Vilma. My chore list wasn't as long as the Bible. I *was* exaggeratin'."

But Vilma wasn't one to let anything go without the proverbial *I told you so*. Letting a sinner repent and move on wasn't her way. She preferred to follow up repentance with an affirmation that *she* would always remember the sin.

"Of course you were exaggeratin'. You always do," Vilma sighed with barely disguised pride in triumph.

Yet, as it always did, Vilma's preacher's-daughter haughtiness tweaked Cricket's tendency toward mischief a bit too deeply to be ignored. "Nope," Cricket couldn't resist adding. "You're right, Vilma. You're right. The list my stepmama gave me wasn't as long as the Bible… only as long as the Old Testament."

The other two young ladies in the room—Marie King and Ann Burroughs—attempted to stifle giggles while Vilma glared at Cricket as she took a seat in one of the rickety old chairs gradually decaying in the Morgan house parlor. Cricket inhaled deeply. She loved the smell of the old wood, the dust, and dried leaves that had collected in the old parlor. It gave her the sense of bathing in the past. She often wondered if spirits of the departed lingered there, enjoying the quiet isolation and sharing dearly cherished memories of laughter and love.

"Blasphemin' ain't something to scoff at, Cricket," Vilma warned. Casting reprimanding glares at Marie and Ann, she added, "And you two will find yourselves dragged straight down to hell right along with Cricket if you don't quit gigglin' every time she does it."

Marie and Ann exchanged glances. It was their way—exchanging glances and somehow communicating without even speaking.

Ann nodded to Marie, and Cricket knew that some unspoken agreement had passed between them.

Marie, nodding to Ann in return, giggled, "Careful with that sanctimonious attitude of yours, Vilma. Or else I'll tell your daddy you said 'hell.'"

Cricket tried not to laugh, but Marie and Ann were always so willing to come to Cricket's rescue where anything was concerned—especially Vilma's nagging.

Marie King's raven hair and azure eyes gave her the look of a young woman of strength and determination—exactly what she was. She was somewhat the mama bear of the group—strong and protective when one of her cubs (or friends) was being threatened in any way.

"Hell is in the Bible, Marie King," Vilma reminded. "It ain't profanity if it's in the Bible."

"Now you all quit," Ann interceded. "We're here to have fun, not to squabble."

In perfect contrast to Marie's strong, determined self, Ann's sky-blue eyes and corn-silk hair offered the appearance of frailty—the misleading appearance of frailty. Ann—though the smallest, fairest, and most soft-spoken, the peacemaker and nurturer of the group of small-town friends—was as tough as new nails and twice as sturdy.

Buoyed by Marie and Ann's support, Cricket chimed, "That's right, Ann. We're here to have some fun…and we've got plans to make before we go swimmin'. So let's get busy makin' 'em. It's hotter than hell outside."

"Cricket!" Vilma exclaimed with pure as much fire-and-brimstone wrath as her father often preached with. "Do not profane like that!"

"But you said it yourself, Vilma," Cricket began, "that hell is in the Bible…and that it ain't profanity if it's in the Bible."

Marie and Ann exchanged amused glances, simultaneously covering their mouths to muffle their laughter.

Vilma simply inhaled a deep breath, shook her head with feigned disgust, grinned, and mumbled, "Well, just say hello to Satan for me when you get there, Magnolia."

Cricket smiled as Vilma's sense of humor finally showed up.

"I do not know why I put up with your shenanigans," Vilma giggled. Shaking her head, she added, "Heaven help me, because I do not know why."

"For the sake that we do the best we can to make others feel better… to leave only good things in our wake," Cricket replied. "And besides, we have much too much fun ourselves when we're doin' it."

Vilma nodded and picked up the pen and tablet she'd brought along to the old Morgan house. "Well then, let's get started," she began, dipping the pen's tip in the small inkwell sitting on the floor at her feet. "Now, what's our next order of business gonna be? Or rather, who is our next order of business gonna be?"

The fact was that Cricket and her three friends had found much more than just rickety old chairs inside the abandoned structure when they'd first decided to use the dilapidated Morgan house as their secret meeting place. Certainly a family had once lived and worked in the old home, but that had been long ago—more than twenty years. And now the old house was nothing but a vacant shell. And yet it was a secluded retreat for four effervescent young women who preferred to be about making mischief here and there as well. Among the dust, cobwebs, and dried leaves gathered and settled into the once beautiful home, Cricket Cranford, Vilma Stanley, Marie King, and Ann Burroughs found friendship, respite, and much more.

"Well," Marie began as a sulk furrowed her lovely brow, "did you hear that the Olivers are leavin' town, Cricket?"

"No!" Cricket exclaimed. "When? They can't leave town! Hudson Oliver is meant to be yours, Marie!"

"Oh, I had hoped it," Marie moaned.

Cricket frowned as empathy for her friend washed over her. Marie had been sweet on Hudson Oliver since she was ten years old. Cricket, Ann, and Vilma all knew she'd harbored hopes of marrying Hudson for simply ever. And now that she was finally old enough to perhaps catch Hudson's eye, his family meant to leave town?

"Maybe Hudson won't move with his family," Ann offered. "He's near twenty-two now, Marie. Maybe he'll just stay and make his own way here in Pike's Creek."

But Marie shook her head. "I doubt that. You know how his mama depends on him. I don't know if his daddy would let him do it either."

Yet Cricket was not so easily thwarted. She wanted Hudson and Marie to end up scandalously in love and then married, almost as much as Marie wanted it. And she figured that there had to be a way to convince Hudson Oliver to stay, to just let his family move on, to start his own way—and with Marie.

In truth, it was part of who Cricket was—"a fighter," her father called her. It seemed there wasn't a whole lot in life that Magnolia Cranford gave up on. And she certainly wouldn't let Marie give up her dream of Hudson Oliver—not without a battle anyway.

And so she announced, "Then you better make this Friday night the night you plant your lure on Hudson, Marie." Cricket smiled as Ann nodded. Even Vilma nodded with encouragement. "Today when we choose our Pike's Creek folks to cheer up on Friday, you choose Hudson Oliver...and you somehow make him know that, if he stays in Pike's Creek, you'll be here with him."

Cricket winced when she saw Marie's eyes fill with tears. Still, she was determined to see her friend happy and blissfully wed to the man of her dreams.

"Hudson needs somethin' to stay *for*, Marie," she continued. "I mean, sure...he's old enough to stay behind and make his own way. He's a man now, not a boy...but he needs somethin' to stay *for*. And that somethin' will be you. You choose Hudson Oliver as your choice for our Friday night shenanigans. You've been talkin' about doin' it for months anyhow."

"Oh, you're one to talk, Cricket," Vilma said—though without malice. Smiling and shaking her head with amusement, she asked, "How long have you been sweet on Mr. Heathro Thibodaux? Since the day his horse galloped into Pike's Creek, that's how long. And you haven't cast any kind of lure at him. But you're gonna go on and tell Marie to go after Hudson Oliver easy as that?"

"That's as different as sugar and vinegar, Vilma, and you know it," Cricket answered.

"Well, I don't see how," Vilma teased.

"I think you should do it too, Marie," Ann chimed. "It's your last chance. You've loved Hudson Oliver forever! You can't just let him walk away without tryin' to make him stay."

Marie sighed and nodded. Looking to Vilma, she asked, "What do you really think, Vilma?"

Cricket bit her tongue. It pricked her sensitivities—the way everyone always looked to Vilma for confirmation of anything just because Vilma was Reverend Stanley's daughter. Yet even Cricket had been guilty of somewhat asking for Vilma's blessing at times. She supposed it was because deep down inside everyone felt Vilma was somehow closer to the Lord because of her daddy.

Still, once in a while Vilma could display a morsel of humility, and Cricket sighed with relief when Vilma smiled at Marie and answered, "I think you *should* cast a lure to Hudson this Friday, Marie. I really think you should. Don't let him get away without even tryin' for him."

"Yes," Ann agreed. "You've gotta at least try for him, Marie. You'll regret it your whole life long if you don't."

Marie nodded. "You're right. You're all absolutely right," Marie determined. "I need to at least try for Hudson."

"You do, Marie. You really do," Cricket assured with a nod.

"So? How will you do it?" Vilma asked.

Marie and Ann looked at one another. But when the silent understanding they usually shared seemed absent, they both looked to Vilma. But Vilma simply shrugged and looked to Cricket—just the way Marie and Ann did. As was always the case when the need for an idea was at hand, Vilma and eventually even Marie and Ann looked to Cricket with expressions of expectation plain on their faces.

Cricket shook her head. "Why are you all lookin' at me? You all always think I've got the ideas. But this has to be Marie's choice. I-I don't know Hudson Oliver the way she does."

"But you do always have the best ideas when it comes to cheerin' a body up or catching a boy's attention," Ann offered with a giggle.

Cricket shook her head as a strange anxiety began to rise in her. She well recognized the sensation in her bosom. The sensation of desperation, impending loss, and fear were seasonings of empathy her heart was beginning to feel for Marie. But she also felt strength welling inside her, and she somewhat resented it—though she couldn't ignore it. She *was* the fighter of the group—the strong one—and it was why her friends always, always looked to her for leadership, guidance, courage, and creativity.

"But he's *your* lover, Marie...not mine," Cricket reminded in a futile effort to alleviate herself from the responsibility of trying to coordinate a way for Marie to capture Hudson Oliver's attention and heart.

"Lover?" Vilma exclaimed with a preacher's daughter's disapproval.

"I don't know Hudson very well," Cricket added, ignoring Vilma's aghast expression. "He's always been yours in my mind, Marie...so I've never really tried to get to know him better."

"You know him well enough," Ann offered. "You know him as well as Vilma and me. What should Marie do on Friday, Cricket? Just take a moment and think about it." Leaning forward, Ann placed her hands on Cricket's shoulders, forcing Cricket's attention to her. "Now think. What can Marie say or do to Hudson to convince him to stay? What can we do to help her?"

Cricket sighed. "Short of walkin' on up to him and sayin', 'I love you, Hudson. Stay in Pike's Creek and marry me,' you mean?"

"Yes," Ann confirmed.

Cricket sighed, relented, and began to pick her brain for an idea— some manner in which Marie might approach Hudson—some way to hint to him that she wanted him to stay with her in Pike's Creek.

"It can't be subtle," she thought aloud. "It has to be firm...even brazen maybe."

Marie, Vilma, and Ann remained silent as Cricket continued to muse. Yet even for the silence, nothing came to Cricket's mind—nothing, that is, but what to her was the obvious. The time had passed when it came to offering anything in the line of delicate clues to Hudson Oliver concerning Marie's feelings. Nope. The ox was in the mire; the eleventh hour was at hand. Cricket grinned as she thought how proud Vilma would be of her rather scriptural considerations. Still, it was true. If the Oliver family was planning on leaving Pike's Creek and taking their handsome son Hudson with them, then Marie had to act—and boldly.

"It's simple," Cricket announced. "You've got to tell him how you feel, Marie. That's all there is to it. We've lost our chance at easin' the man into it."

"What? No!" Marie exclaimed. "Have you lost your ever-lovin' mind, Cricket?"

But the more Cricket considered the idea, the more certain she was of what must be done. "It's the only way, Marie," she answered. "We don't have time for willy-nillyin' now. Hudson has to know how true and deep your feelin's are. If you want him to stay, then he has to know he's stayin' for a woman who loves him and wants to be his wife. Therefore, I propose this. We figure out how to get Hudson out of the house Friday night after dark. Maybe we can get him out to that old lean-to at the back of his father's property…say we saw a coyote or somethin' out there stalkin' the henhouse."

Cricket looked to Vilma and Ann to find both were nodding in agreement—obviously approving of her plan. It was only Marie that sat shaking her head, every ounce of pink having drained from her pretty face.

"Cricket," Marie began, "I could never just walk up and…and just…just tell him! Not right out loud to his face."

"You have to!" Cricket told her with rising desperation in her bosom. Wanting to allow little to no time for Marie to argue further, Cricket continued, "Once we get him out to the old lean-to…you just tell him, Marie. You flat out tell Hudson Oliver that you love him and want him to stay in Pike's Creek with you." Cricket inhaled a breath of courage and added, "And then you kiss him...and I mean square on the lips."

"Cricket!" Vilma gasped. "You cannot be serious! Kiss Hudson Oliver? In front of God and everything? You want Marie to kiss that man without even—"

"She *has* to kiss him, Vilma," Cricket interrupted. "And besides, God is everywhere...so it doesn't matter where they're standin' when she kisses him. God will see it." She was feeling almost frantic now, her heart beginning to break the way she knew Marie's had begun to. Turning to face Marie, Cricket took her hands in her own, forcing her friend to look her in the eyes. "Hudson has to know you're sincere, Marie. He has to know you love him! He won't know it unless you show him as well as tell him. You know how men are. Their heads are as hard as oak." She paused, her own heart aching as she studied the fear in her friend's frightened blue eyes. "Fight for him, Marie," she whispered. "If you're not willin' to fight for somethin' you love, then you don't deserve to own it."

"I do love him, Cricket," Marie whispered as tears escaped her eyes to trickle over her cheeks. "I do. B-but to walk right up to him and... he's never even once asked to come courtin' me or anything, Cricket. What if...what if he doesn't feel anything for me? What if he laughs at me?"

Cricket shook her head. "He won't laugh, Marie," she answered. "Hudson Oliver is one of the best men any of us have ever known. He won't laugh." Cricket took a deep breath and added, "And if he doesn't return your feelin's...well, then at least you'll know you tried. You won't go through life always wonderin' 'what if' where Hudson is concerned."

"Oh, this is all so easy for you to plot out, Cricket," Vilma offered. She pointed a rather bony index finger at Marie and in her preacher's-daughter voice said, "You can sit there and tell Marie to walk right up to a man, tell him she loves him, and kiss him square on the lips...but I don't see you doin' the likes. I don't see you waltzin' up to Heathro Thibodaux confessin' your feelin's and kissin' on him."

"That's very different, Vilma...and you know it," Ann interjected.

"Not really," Vilma countered.

Cricket couldn't understand Vilma. When compared with Heathro Thibodaux, Hudson Oliver was a boy! And besides, Marie had known Hudson for nearly ever. Heathro Thibodaux had only moved to Pike's Creek six months before. Hudson Oliver and Heathro Thibodaux? It was onions and oranges.

But Cricket looked to Marie. Marie loved Hudson so perfectly—and she'd loved him for a long time. The pain in her heart seemed to leap right out of Marie's bosom to be shared in Cricket's, and Cricket knew she could not watch Hudson Oliver leave Pike's Creek—not without Marie as his bride.

Furthermore, she knew what Vilma meant—what she was implying—that Marie needed strength, the strength in knowing that another person could find courage along with her. Cricket sighed and looked to Vilma. Vilma's frown revealed guilt mingled with uncertainty when she shrugged.

"Heathro Thibodaux is different," Cricket began. "He doesn't know me from a night crawler in a rain puddle. Hudson knows you, Marie. You all have grown up together."

"But, Cricket…I-I can't do it," Marie whispered, trepidation and disappointment blending in her pained expression. "I can't just walk up to Hudson and tell him how I feel. And I certainly can't kiss him! I just can't!"

"Maybe we can't ask Marie to do somethin' we aren't willin' to do ourselves, Cricket," Vilma timidly suggested. But Cricket knew the *we* meant her and nobody else. Still, what were good friends for if not to weather the good, the bad, and the terrifying with?

"Now, let's just think this out," Ann offered, sensitive to everyone's feelings and fears. "Let's just think."

Cricket released Marie's hands and slumped back in her chair, defeated. She felt entirely drained of the enthusiasm she'd known only minutes before. But she'd tried. She would always remind herself—whenever she saw Marie sad and alone, living as the spinster of Pike's Creek and still pining away after Hudson Oliver twenty years from now—Cricket would always remind herself that she'd tried.

"Well, if anyone wants my opinion, I think Cricket's right, Vilma," Ann the peacemaker ventured.

Cricket was a little comforted by Ann's sound support. She looked to Ann and smiled. "Thank you, Ann," she said.

But Ann bit her lip, wearing a rather shameful expression, and added, "But I think Vilma's right too, Cricket."

"What?" Cricket gasped.

"I mean…it's all fine and dandy that you come up with this great design of havin' our Marie just walk right on up to Hudson and confess herself," Ann explained. "But I think Vilma has a point. You *have* been sweet on Heathro Thibodaux from the moment you saw him…and I don't see why you can't just…well, I think you should choose Heathro Thibodaux for this Friday night."

"Ann!" Cricket exclaimed, feeling momentarily betrayed. Surely Ann saw the difference between Marie's feelings for Hudson Oliver and her own for Heathro Thibodaux. Again, it was oranges and onions!

"I mean…I mean to say," Ann began, "why don't you just choose Heathro Thibodaux as your person for Friday night? You don't need to confess your undyin' love for him or anything like that. You could just…just welcome him into town." Ann reached out, placing a calming, supportive hand on Cricket's knee. "You know how folks are around him. He's so frownin' and angry-lookin' all the time that no one dares to befriend him. So why don't *you* do it? I mean, you don't have to tell him you're sweet on him. You just have to welcome him to town and all."

"And you have to kiss him," Vilma added.

"What?" Cricket, Marie, and Ann exclaimed in unison.

Vilma shrugged. "Remember last month, Cricket? When we were talkin' about our most romantic daydreams? You said you'd rather kiss Heathro Thibodaux than anything else in all the whole wide world. So? Here's your chance to do it. Friday night, you walk up to Heathro Thibodaux, properly welcome him to town, and steal a kiss from him while you're at it."

"I just meant she should talk to him, Vilma," Ann clarified. "J-just welcome him to town and all, so that he knows *somebody* in Pike's Creek cares about him."

"A lot of people in Pike's Creek care about him, Ann," Vilma reminded with an insinuative wink. "Why, Widow Rutherford's eyes nearly bug clean out of her head whenever he walks by." She looked to Cricket. "Every woman in Pike's Creek—every woman in the county, for that matter—daydreams over Heathro Thibodaux as much as you do, Cricket."

"Does that include you, Vilma?" Cricket asked in a whisper. She was inconceivably unsettled. The mere thought of approaching Heathro Thibodaux struck such a nervous anxiety within her that she began to tremble a little. Add to that the wild, insane suggestion that she kiss him, and she nearly felt as if she might vomit.

"All I'm sayin' is that this is your chance too, Cricket," Vilma offered, "your chance to kiss Heathro Thibodaux the way you've always wanted to before some woman snatches him up for good. And it will give Marie the courage to talk to Hudson at the same time." Vilma put a comforting arm around Marie's shoulders. "Isn't that right, Marie?"

"I'm only tryin' to help Marie, Vilma, and—" Cricket began.

"I know. But I am too. Truly," Vilma interrupted. "Think of it this way, Cricket. This way, you both might get the deepest desire of your hearts."

Cricket tried to keep her trembling arms and legs still as she looked to Marie. "Marie?" she asked.

"You don't have to do it, Cricket," Marie interrupted. "You're right. If I love Hudson…if I want him to belong to me…then I need to do this. You're right. This was about what *I* need to do."

Cricket felt the excess moisture brimming in her eyes, for there it was—from Marie's own lips, the confirmation that her friend needed to see Cricket's bravery manifest before she could find her own.

Marie *had* to win Hudson Oliver. She just had to! Cricket imagined for a moment how wonderful it would be to attend their wedding, Marie and Hudson's. In her mind's eye, she could see little raven-haired babies at Marie's knee. Hudson Oliver had raven hair as well—and blue eyes. No doubt the babies Marie and Hudson would have together would look just like little dark-haired angels.

Furthermore (though she hated to admit it to herself), Vilma Stanley was right. Someday a woman would rope Heathro Thibodaux. Someday a woman would tie him up and own him—tether him to her porch and keep him forever. And whether it was the young and beautiful Widow Rutherford or Vilma Stanley herself, Cricket wanted to live her life knowing that she'd felt what it was to kiss him—that she'd had the courage to walk up to the handsome, ex-Texas Ranger, press her lips to his, and let the memory linger in her heart forever.

"Would it help you, Marie?" Cricket asked, commanding the moisture in her eyes to retreat. "Would it help if I chose Heathro Thibodaux for myself for Friday? If…if I find the courage to welcome him to town and steal a kiss from him…will it help you to have the courage to talk to Hudson?"

She already knew the answer to her own question—but she had to ask it, just in case she were wrong.

"Truthfully?" Marie asked—and Cricket's heart sank.

"Yes. Truthfully," Cricket answered.

"Then yes," Marie admitted. "I think…I think if I could see you walk right up to that devilishly attractive Heathro Thibodaux and steal a kiss…then I could walk right up to Hudson Oliver, tell him how I feel, and beg him to stay in Pike's Creek with me."

"Then that's what I'll do," Cricket said. She forced a smile as she nodded. "For you, Marie. I'll do it for you. I-I want you to be happy. I want to see you marry Hudson Oliver and have his babies and live happily ever after."

She ignored the just plain fatigue that was washing over her—the sense of weariness at always having to rise up and soldier on for everyone else's benefit.

Inhaling her own breath of determination, she said, "Then I'm gonna welcome Heathro Thibodaux to town." Marie smiled, and the sight of the sudden courage and hope visibly raining over her gave Cricket's heart a lift. "Yep. That's who I choose for Friday…Texas Ranger Heathro Thibodaux. And Marie's gonna lure Hudson Oliver into stayin' in Pike's Creek," she began, attempting to shift the burden of responsibility. Then, looking to Vilma and Ann, she asked, "So? Who are your choices for this Friday night, ladies?"

Vilma smiled and breathily sighed with relief. Vilma wanted Marie to win Hudson Oliver as much as Cricket and Ann did, and Cricket had to admire her insight into how to buoy Marie's courage—even if she had rather thrown Cricket to the lions in doing it.

"I'm thinkin' it's about time old Mrs. Maloney had that pretty teapot she's been dreamin' over," Vilma answered. "You know…the one in the general store? The porcelain one with the yellow rose pattern?"

Cricket's mouth dropped open in astonishment. Everybody in town knew old Maymee Maloney had been dreaming about owning the pretty porcelain teapot in the general store's front window for over a year. And it wasn't so much that nobody in town wished they could give it to Maymee; it was just that nobody in town could afford it!

"Vilma!" Ann exclaimed. "You're not suggestin' that we…that we steal that teapot and give it to—"

"Oh, land sakes, no!" Vilma interrupted. "For cryin' in the bucket, Ann! *Thou shalt not steal*—it's one of the ten. I cannot believe you'd think I would even consider—"

"Well, what is your plan then, Vilma?" Marie asked.

Cricket perked up as well, wildly curious about how in the world Vilma expected them all to acquire the teapot for Mrs. Maloney. Certainly her anxiety of Marie and Hudson was lingering about; her anxiety over how in all the world she'd ever find her own courage to approach Heathro Thibodaux was there. But Vilma's suggestion was almost more inconceivable to pull off than Cricket's and Marie's.

It was then and only then, as Vilma pulled the ribbon from her hair, that Cricket knew just how they were going to acquire the teapot. Or rather how Vilma was going to acquire it.

"Vilma!" Ann exclaimed in an astonished whisper as Vilma's normally waist-length auburn hair tumbled from the ribbon to barely reach her shoulders.

"You sold your hair!" Marie breathed, awestruck.

Vilma smiled. "I did. To that man who makes wigs over in Thistle.

He gave me so much money for my hair…bein' that the color is so vastly sought after and so likewise rare."

Cricket swallowed her mild irritation. Leave it to Vilma to do something so self-sacrificing and yet still find a way to ruin the beauty of it by bragging. Yet she knew how important Vilma's "vastly sought after and so likewise rare" auburn hair was to her. It was a mammoth sacrifice on Vilma's part—and for a very kind and thoughtful reason.

"The wigmaker gave me just enough to purchase the teapot for Mrs. Maloney," Vilma sighed with pleasure. She turned and lifted a box from the floor behind her chair. Removing the lid, she revealed the contents of the box to be the beautiful teapot Mrs. Maloney had been dreaming of owning for so very long. "I even asked Mr. Brooks never to tell one livin' soul who it was that purchased it. I figure we can leave it on Mrs. Maloney's front porch with a sweet little note attached."

"But…but you're the one who managed to acquire the teapot, Vilma," Cricket began. "I think you should be the one to give it to her. After all, it's such a thoughtful gift…and so expensive."

But Vilma shook her head. "No. I want us all to give it to her. Every one of us has wanted to be able to buy the teapot for Mrs. Maloney for months and months now."

Cricket smiled, astonished at how back and forth Vilma's moods could be.

"And anyway, I'll always know that we could never have done it without me," Vilma added. Cricket almost laughed out loud. Vilma was such a vain little thing! It was almost too entertaining to keep from giggling over. "I mean, none of you all could've fetched the price *my* hair did from the wigmaker in Thistle," Vilma added.

Ann, Marie, and Cricket exchanged amused glances. Vilma— she wasn't one to stand still and let the chance of claiming glory for something simply pass her by. But Cricket didn't care if Vilma hung the fact of the matter over their heads for the rest of their lives. She knew that Marie and Ann wanted Mrs. Maloney to have the porcelain teapot as badly as they'd ever wanted anything.

"It's incredibly thoughtful and selfless, Vilma," Cricket said—and sincerely. "Mrs. Maloney will love that teapot more than anyone else in the world ever would have."

Vilma smiled and sighed—almost as if she'd been concerned that the others wouldn't approve of her choice of whom to cheer up on Friday night, and how.

"Well, now I feel just ridiculous and pitiful," Ann mumbled.

"Whatever for, Ann?" Marie asked.

"Well, you're gonna confess your heart to Hudson Oliver," Ann explained, waving a hand in Marie's direction. "And Cricket's gonna welcome Heathro Thibodaux to town with a big ol' kiss." She sighed, nodded toward Vilma, and added, "And Vilma's gone and cut off her hair and sold it to buy that pretty teapot for Mrs. Maloney."

"So?" Vilma urged. "Is it that you're havin' trouble thinkin' of somebody to do for, Ann?"

"No," Ann mumbled. "I have the someone…but now I'm just wonderin' if the somethin' I was plannin' on is enough."

Cricket smiled. Ann was so tenderhearted and sweet. Her doings for other folks were always, always, always profoundly thoughtful and self-sacrificing. Ann didn't see her own goodness.

"Ann," Cricket began, "any good deed…any kindness no matter how big or small it may seem to you…well, you never can understand just how much it might mean to the person you're offerin' it to. A smile might be enough to lift someone's spirits up so high that all their worries just fade away for time and their heart is lightened for days."

"That's exactly right," Marie added with a nod.

"And besides," Vilma added, "what Cricket's gonna do where Mr. Thibodaux is concerned might just lift her spirits more than it will his." All the girls giggled—even Cricket. "So you see, it's just like Cricket says. No good deed is too small."

"So who were you thinkin' we should do for as your choice on Friday, Ann?" Marie asked.

"Well," Ann began, "I-I was thinkin' Mr. Keel might could use a new quilt. I-I mean, it's warm enough now, bein' summer and all. But come winter…well, since his wife passed so many years back, he's sure to need some new linens. So I-I made him this."

Cricket's heart leapt with delight as she watched Ann stand up and stride to a large flour sack that was sitting against a nearby wall. Carefully she removed a new quilt—a beautiful new quilt.

"Mama let me use any of her old fabric remnants I wanted," Ann explained as she draped the quilt over Marie's lap for everyone to consider. "I chose the brightest colors I could find...hopin' that it lends a little joy to his life."

"It's lovely!" Marie exclaimed. "Just so very lovely, Ann!"

"It so charmin', Ann," Vilma said as she closely studied the length of the quilting stitches. "You have the prettiest stitchin' in the world. No wonder you won the blue ribbon at last year's county fair."

"It's perfect!" Cricket exclaimed. "But...but isn't this somethin' you'd like to give to Mr. Keel yourself, Ann? I mean, it must've taken you a very long time to—"

"No! No, no, no," Ann interrupted. "I want all of us to leave it for him...with a note. Just like we'll leave the teapot for Mrs. Maloney."

Cricket studied the blush on Ann's pretty cheeks—the way she'd begun to wring her hands. "You know, you could take a more...a more personal approach, Ann...somethin' like Marie and I have agreed to do. I mean, we all know how handsome Mr. Keel is. There's not one of us here who wouldn't think it would be the most romantic thing in the world if you managed to catch his eye and—"

"Mr. Keel is as old as Ann's daddy, Cricket!" Vilma exclaimed with a giggle of disbelief. "Are you suggestin' that Ann set her sights on marryin' a man as old as her daddy?"

Cricket rolled her eyes at Vilma's insensitivity. She wished Vilma would fall in love with someone. Then maybe she'd have a bit more insight into what Marie and Ann were feeling.

"How old is your daddy, Ann?" she asked her friend.

"Thirty-five in December," Ann mumbled.

"So Mr. Keel is thirty-five as well?"

Ann nodded.

"Well, then he's a man young enough to be a lovin', hard-workin' husband who can give you plenty of children and old enough to know a good woman when he sees one and not waste any time in reachin' out and grabbin' hold of her," Cricket said. "You go on and set your sights on Mr. Keel if you want to, Ann. He's as handsome as anything and does right well for himself with his farmin' and cattle."

Vilma exhaled an exasperated sigh, but she didn't say another word. Cricket had made her point to Vilma—made more than one point that day, in truth—and it had nearly worn her to the bone.

"The quilt is so beautiful, Ann!" Marie exclaimed once more. "Mr. Keel will love it, I'm sure. And it will certainly brighten up his farmhouse."

"Yes," Vilma agreed, taking her place as an ally and friend instead of playing the devil's advocate. "I'm sure Mr. Keel will truly appreciate the new quilt. And I suppose the age difference between the two of you isn't all that shockin'. I mean, now that I think about it, my daddy is eleven years older than my mama, and they're as happy as if they were already livin' in eternal paradise together."

Ann blushed and began to refold the quilt. "Well, I just hope he'll like the quilt."

"He'll adore it, Ann," Cricket assured her friend. Sighing with relief that at least their four choices as to who to do kind things for that week had been made, Cricket reiterated, "So, we've got Mr. Keel gettin' a new quilt. Mrs. Maloney is gettin' her teapot, Hudson Oliver is gettin' the biggest and best surprise of his life, and Heathro Thibodaux is finally gettin' properly welcomed to Pike's Creek." She looked to Vilma, asking, "What are our assignments then, Vilma?"

Vilma thought for a moment, dipped her ink pen in the inkwell at her feet, and said, "Well, since I have the best penmanship, I'll write Mrs. Maloney a little note to go with the teapot. But I do think Ann should write the note to go with the quilt for Mr. Keel."

"Anything else?" Marie prodded. "What should Cricket and I do?"

Vilma smiled. "Build up your reserves of courage and determination, I would think."

"Fine," Cricket agreed. "Then if we're finished plannin' for Friday, I'm just dyin' to strip my clothes off and get to swimmin'!"

"Me too!" Marie giggled, taking the ribbon from her hair and beginning to unbutton her blouse.

"And I am not wearin' my corset this time," Cricket announced. "I was wet to the skin for two days last time."

"Do you mean we should go swimmin' in just bloomers and camisoles?" Vilma gasped with an expression of horrified astonishment.

"I absolutely do," Cricket confirmed with a giggle.

"Me too," Ann added. "After all, no one comes out here...not ever."

"Well, whether they do or not, I just don't know if it's proper to—" Vilma began.

"Oh, Vilma, please," Marie whined. "We're hot, and this old house is so stuffy. No one is gonna catch us. Let's just have some fun for once without you naggin' on and on at us. All right?"

Cricket giggled as she watched Vilma huff and puff for a few more seconds, until at last she conformed, "All right then. Bloomers and camisoles it is. But if we get caught, I swear I won't ever forgive you all."

"We won't get caught," Cricket assured her. "Nobody's around close. And certainly not in the heat of the day like this."

"Fine then," Vilma said, laying her pen and pad down on the floor. "Last one to the swimmin' hole is an old maid!" Leaping up from her chair, Vilma laughed as she bolted out the door of the old Morgan house.

Cricket giggled with amusement as she followed Marie and Ann out of the house. As all four girls raced for the Morgan swimming hole, Cricket's frustrations, fatigue, and worries seemed to scatter—dissolved somehow by the warmth of the sun and the beauty of the day.

She could smell the cool water of the swimming hole as they neared—was delighted by the scent of warm summer grass, green cottonwood leaves, and wild summer roses. She thought for a moment that perhaps the roses had only grown wild since the Morgan house had been abandoned. Perhaps, and even most likely, they had been planted long ago by loving hands that had cared for them for ever so long. Perhaps they had once been pruned back or trained to cling to a bright white wooden trellis. But now they'd grown wild for years and years, and though they may have missed the tender hands that once cared for them, Cricket imagined that their existence in lingering freedom now inspired them to bloom all the more fragrantly.

Cricket splashed into the water just after Ann and Marie. Vilma was already wading up to her neck out farther from the shore. The water was so cool and refreshing! The warmth of the sun was ambrosia to Cricket's soul, and she turned her face heavenward, allowing the sensation to calm her. As she dipped her head back into the water, she exhaled a sigh of reprieve. She wasn't quite sure what had caused her to feel so bothered before—perhaps all the chores her stepmother had demanded she finish up or all the planning and coaxing for their Friday night shenanigans—perhaps anxiety for what might or might not happen between Marie and Hudson Oliver on Friday. But whatever had taken her tranquility from her, Cricket felt serene in that moment at least.

As she listened to the birds in the trees and the laughter of good friends—as Marie, Ann, and Vilma splashed and played in the water—Cricket thought there could be nothing so beautiful in all the world as the bright blue, cloudless sky above and the feel of the cool water rinsing her cares away.

CHAPTER TWO

Heath had half a mind to just slit Conqueror's throat when he finally found him—slaughter him up and have himself a tasty beef supper. The bull was turning out to be a heap more trouble than ex-Texas Ranger Heathro Thibodaux had counted on. Still, he thought of the roll of paper money the rancher over in Thistle had paid him for Conqueror's stud service and figured the bovine rascal was worth the trouble in the end.

Heath was just glad old Fred Elmer had seen Conqueror heading toward the Morgan place—glad the stubborn bull hadn't headed off toward Ralph Burroughs's herd the way he'd done the week before. Not that Ralph Burroughs would have minded Conqueror consorting with his cows free of stud fees. But since Heath had quit rangering, he'd need every dollar his small herd of cattle and farm would allot him. He had plenty of money held up in secret, but a dollar was a dollar when a man was looking down the long, lonesome road of life.

Heath swore under his breath as he saw Conqueror's hoofprints in the soil. Yep—the bull had changed his mind and was heading straight for the Burroughs place.

"Well, come on, Archie," he said, spurring his buckskin to a trot. "Let's get ol' Conq back home before Ralph Burroughs gets some calves he ain't paid for out of it this time."

It took more than an hour to head Conq for home and get him into the small corral. By the time the bull was secured once more, Heath was hot, tired, and cranky. The heat of the day was beating down on him like fire and brimstone, and all he could think of to cool himself off was a dip in the old Morgan swimming hole. Nobody used the old swimming hole. The fact was the whole place was abandoned—house, barn, and swimming hole. As he rode Archie toward the swimming hole, Heath grinned. He liked the seclusion it allotted, and once summer had hit hot and dry, he'd taken to swimming three or four days a week. There was nothing quite like being alone out there in the cool water—listening to the birds in the trees and enjoying the modest summer breeze that would waft by every once in a while.

Heath dismounted, loosely tethered Archie's reins to a cottonwood, patted the horse on the flank, and mumbled, "You have at that new grass there, boy."

Tossing his hat to the carpet of soft, green summer grass under the tree, Heath unbuttoned his shirt and was just unbuckling his gun belt when he heard voices—female voices.

Stripping his shirt off, wadding it up, and pitching it over to join his hat, Heath walked toward the swimming hole—all the while making sure he was well hidden by the brush. What he saw when he managed a good view of the water through the trees and bushes made him chuckle.

Four young women were playfully splashing around in the water, entirely unaware that anyone was near—especially a man. Glancing around, he saw their discarded shoes, stockings, petticoats, and dresses scattered over a couple of fallen trees nearby. The mischief in him considered snitching their clothes for a moment—hightailing off with them and leaving the girls to figure on how to make it back to town in nothing but their underwear.

Still, Heath knew better, and he wasn't near mean enough to do such a thing to four little innocents—no matter what everyone in town thought. And all he needed was one more reason for folks to think he wasn't worth a wad of mud.

So he paused, listening to the girls' happy prattle and their careless giggling. It was, after all, a heavenly sound—female happiness. He missed it—missed hearing his sisters chirping away as they brushed their hair each morning and readied for the day. He exhaled a heavy sigh, wondering if he'd ever see Fanny and Clara Jean again.

But Heath pushed thoughts of his family to the back of his mind—reminded himself of what he'd done—or rather, what he hadn't done.

"Marie King…this time next month, you and Hudson Oliver will be standin' right there in front of Vilma's daddy sayin' your vows!" he heard one of the girls giggle.

"We will not!" another girl said, splashing water at the first.

"Yes, you will!" a third girl countered. "I won't rest until I've seen your weddin', Marie…until I've seen Hudson Oliver whisk you away in his arms and carry you over the threshold of the house the two of you will share forever."

Heath frowned a bit—studied the third girl who had spoken. Oh, he knew her name well enough—Magnolia Cranford—"Cricket," as everyone in town called her. He knew who all four girls were, in fact. He'd recognized them right off. After all, it was his job to know people, to watch them, to know their business. At least, it *had* been his job—and old habits died hard.

These four Pike's Creek girls were thicker than fleas in a cat's right ear. Furthermore, he was ninety-nine percent certain it was these four girls that were the little do-gooders in town—always leaving cookies on somebody's front porch or making rag dolls and gifting them in secret to all the little girls in town.

He smiled with triumph, realizing he'd found their hideout. He'd always suspected that, whoever the group of secret do-gooders in Pike's Creek, they must've had a meeting place, like a bunch of rustlers or bank robbers—somewhere they could plan their do-gooding in secret. It made perfect sense that they'd use the old Morgan place. The rumor around town was that the old house was haunted by the ghosts of two boys who had drowned in the swimming hole some years back. Heath felt his eyebrows arch in admiration for the girls, if for no other reason than that they obviously dared to beat back their fears of specters and drowning to find themselves an outlaw hideaway of sorts.

"For Pete's sake, Cricket!" the fourth girl rather scolded. "You're so dramatic. A month? There's no way Hudson and Marie will be married in a month. Well, a month ain't even long enough for a proper courtship."

Heath shook his head. Yep. He could always spot this one coming a mile away—the preacher's daughter. She always walked like she had post shoved up the back of her dress. Stiff as a board and twice as plain.

"Well, I don't care," the Cranford girl said. "I want Hudson and Marie married in a month. And once I've got Marie all tucked in with Hudson, I'll go to work on Ann and Mr. Keel. And once that's taken care of...I'll work on you, Vilma Stanley!" The Cranford girl laughed and splashed water at the preacher's daughter.

The Cranford girl. Heath considered her for a moment. Fact was, he'd considered her before. There was something about her—a strength and determination he admired, but from afar. She was a pretty thing too. He grinned thinking how opposite her manner of walking was from the preacher's daughter. While Vilma Stanley walked stiff and straight like she was tied to a post, the Cranford girl had a rather enticing little swing to her walk. The other two girls in the swimming hole were the Burroughs girl and the King girl—both pretty girls and both with little waggles when they walked. But it was the Cranford girl who had always captured Heath's attention whenever she passed him in town. She was dangerously attractive in some way and put him in mind of...

He'd lingered too long—allowed his thoughts to drift to absurd venues. And besides, he figured if he had come up so easily and unseen on the Pike's Creek girls, so could someone else—someone with far more malicious intentions than he could ever imagine. The girls needed a warning—needed to know they should be more careful and wary. The world wasn't all sugar and cinnamon anymore. Not that it ever had been, but Heath knew firsthand just how ugly it could be—especially for pretty young girls with innocent minds and bodies.

"You girls enjoyin' that swim?"

Though Cricket only gasped with surprise as a man stepped from the brush and into view, Ann and Vilma squealed at having been so startled.

"Oh my stars and garters!" Vilma exclaimed under her breath. "It's Heathro Thibodaux!"

And indeed it was Heathro Thibodaux. Cricket's mouth gaped as she stared at the only half-dressed man standing on the bank of the swimming hole, studying them unabashedly.

"I heard there were a couple of drownin's awhile back out here," he said, still studying them.

"That's right," Marie answered—the mama bear in her character showing up quick as a whip. "What of it?"

Cricket glanced to Marie, as astonished as ever at her brazen courage.

Heathro shrugged the broadest, bronzest shoulders Cricket had ever seen and said, "I'm just wonderin' if it's a wise thing...you girls bein' out here all alone like this."

"Well, it looks like you were plannin' on swimmin', Mr. Thibodaux," Marie challenged. "Why is it unwise for us but all right for you?"

"Because no one would mourn me if I drowned, Miss King," he answered. Aiming an index finger at Cricket, however, he added, "But Pike's Creek would be mighty brought down if one of you pretty little fillies was lost."

Cricket held her breath as the extraordinarily handsome man seemed to study her for a moment. She took a step backward, ensuring that the deeper water covered her to at least her shoulders. He was unfairly attractive—simply sinfully good-looking! His piercing blue eyes seemed threatening as he stared at her—menacing but hypnotically intriguing at the same time. Cricket had never seen him without a hat before, and she marveled at how his dark brown hair was nearly the same color as her own. The strong set of his squared jaw was only further emphasized by his two or three days' whisker growth, and if his superbly handsome face wasn't enough make a girl blush, his long legs, broad shoulders, and bronzed muscular chest and stomach were. Vilma was right: every woman in the county was sweet on Heathro Thibodaux, and for well-substantiated reasons.

"The fact is it just ain't safe for you girls to be out here swimmin' in the nude the way you are," he added.

"Nude?" all four girls exclaimed in unison.

"We are not swimmin' nude, Mr. Thibodaux!" Cricket vehemently defended.

But Heathro quirked a disbelieving eyebrow. "Then you all just come on out and prove it," he dared. "I mean, looks to me that by the pile of clothes over there on those fallen logs…you girls are swimmin' in the nude."

"We have plenty of clothin' on," Vilma assured him.

But the ex-Texas Ranger shrugged. "Well, then…I suppose you girls don't mind if I go ahead and join you…bein' that you've got plenty of clothin' on and all."

Four simultaneous female gasps ensued as Mr. Thibodaux unbuckled his gun belt, dropped it to the grassy bank, and then began to unbutton his britches.

"No! N-no, no, no!" Cricket stammered. "We…we were just finishin' up our swim, Mr. Thibodaux. I-I'm sure you'd like some peace and quiet…so we'll just be on our way, if it's all the same to you."

Heathro grinned, folded his muscular arms across his muscular chest, and said, "All right. I'll just wait for you girls to come on out then."

Cricket felt herself blushing—the heat on her cheeks emanating from within her body feeling much hotter than what the bright sun was providing on the outside.

She glanced to Marie. Her face was as red as a radish as well, as were the faces of Ann and Vilma.

"You got us into this, Magnolia Cranford!" Vilma scolded in a perturbed whisper. "Now you can just think of a way to get us out!"

"What's the matter?" Heathro asked from the bank. "I thought you girls had plenty of clothin' on. What's the harm in gettin' outta the swimmin' hole with me watchin' then?"

Cricket looked to Ann and Marie for support, but they were as caught in the trap as she was. Frantically she tried to think of something—anything that would get them out of the swimming hole without Heathro Thibodaux seeing them in nothing but their soaking wet (and no doubt nearly transparent) underthings.

"Um...we, um..." Cricket stammered.

Oh, Heath was loving it! It was all he could do to keep from laughing. He'd caught them all right—caught these young innocents of Pike's Creek without any kind of retreat.

"Well?" he urged, almost losing his determination not to laugh. "Are you gonna get out or what? It's hotter than hell out here, and I'm goin' for a swim...alone or with company."

Again he began to unbutton his britches, unable to keep a low chuckle from escaping his throat when the preacher's daughter closed her eyes and began reciting the Lord's Prayer in a whisper.

"Wait!" the Cranford girl called out. "Will you give us your back for just a moment, Mr. Thibodaux? Please?"

Heath grinned. "Why, of course, ladies. Of course. My mama would be ashamed if I weren't gentleman enough to allow you young ladies the chance to—"

"Thank you!" the four girls exclaimed in unison as Heath turned around.

He smiled as he heard the wild splashing behind him as the girls made for the bank—the sound of the preacher's daughter calling the other girls to repentance as they scrambled out of the water and to their clothes.

"You girls have a nice afternoon now, you hear?" he called as he heard them retreating faster than a tomcat with a firebrand tied to its tail.

Chuckling to himself, Heath stripped off his britches, wadded them up, and tossed them aside. He began to strip off his underwear too but figured he'd better play it safe—just in case the mischievous young ladies of Pike's Creek decided not to retreat all the way back to town.

Heath didn't waste any time. Diving into the swimming hole, he bobbed up, leaned back, and began floating. The sensation was refreshing—cool and soothing. He closed his eyes and just floated, letting the sun warm his face while the water cooled the rest of his body.

He sighed, thinking that old Conq would surely be the death of him. He couldn't believe how stubborn the creature was—not to mention strong. He'd have to do something to reinforce the corral fence, that was for certain.

But suddenly, Heath's musings over Conqueror scattered as a vision of the four young women he'd found at the swimming hole leapt into his mind. He frowned as that vision led to another—a far less pleasant and a deeply haunting vision—a vision of a group of other young women that were not so unlike the girls of Pike's Creek. Only the images of the faces of the girls lingering in his mind now were gruesome—images of what they'd looked like lying dead on the canyon floor, their bodies broken and bleeding—their eyes fixed on the blue sky and blazing sun overhead—their dead, open eyes.

Heath grimaced as the memory of the blood still trickling from one of the girl's cracked skull lingered. The visualization of the trail of blood trickling over the rocks of the canyon floor like a crimson stream would haunt him his entire life long. Heath knew it would—and he was glad. He deserved to be haunted—deserved to have an ever-present reminder of his weakness and failing eating at his mind for eternity.

Opening his eyes, Heath held his breath and dove beneath the water's surface once more. When he bobbed up again, he wiped the water from his eyes and surveyed the landscape around him. He wondered how everything could still look so green and fresh and lovely. How could the world still hold such beauty when such evil and ugliness existed in it as well?

It was a question he couldn't answer in that moment. And anyway, his head hurt from thinking on the past. With a heavy sigh he swam to the bank and pulled himself from the water to stretch out on the cool green grass.

He heard Archie whinny, and he grinned. Archie was a good horse. And even though Conqueror was a pain in Heath's rear end, his shenanigans made life a whole lot more interesting.

The sky was a beautiful blue above, and a meadowlark was whistling somewhere nearby. The soft summer breeze in the cottonwoods stimulated the cicadas in their branches, and Heath closed his eyes, letting the soothing music of one of God's most interesting insects lull him to reprieve.

He grinned as he lay in the grass, listening to the cicada chorus. The Pike's Creek girls had looked like they'd been caught robbing a bank when he'd stepped out of the bushes. And as he continued to think on the incident, he began to remember the conversation he'd overheard.

"So the King girl fancies Hudson Oliver, does she?" he whispered aloud to himself. "And did I hear it right, or am I imaginin' they said that Burroughs girl is sweet on Cooper Keel?"

Heath chuckled then sighed. "Well, at least they got good judgment in character. Maybe that'll make up a bit for the bad judgment in swimmin' in their underwear." Raising his voice a bit, he called, "Ain't that right, Archie?"

The horse whinnied its affirmation, and Heath continued to bask in the sun on the bank of the swimming hole—trying not to be disturbed by the fact that he kept wondering whom the Cranford girl was sweet on.

"Good night, Daddy," Cricket said, pressing an affectionate kiss on her father's cheek.

"Good night, sugar," Zeke Cranford said. "You sleep tight now, you hear?"

"I will," Cricket assured him. "Good night, Ada," Cricket said, placing a quick kiss to her stepmother's cheek.

"Good night, Cricket," Ada said, smiling. It was obvious she was pleased with Cricket's gesture.

As Cricket smiled at Ada a moment before heading down the hall to her bedroom, she reminded herself of how hard it must be for Ada—being a mother to a daughter who was only six years younger than herself.

The truth was Cricket had been fairly mortified when her father had announced to her months before that he planned on marrying the new schoolteacher, Ada Hatley. Ada was only twenty-five years

31

old, but the entire town of Pike's Creek had considered her an old maid when she'd first come to town. Yet the moment handsome Zeke Cranford (the most sought-after widower of Pike's Creek at the time) had announced that he planned to marry the old maid schoolteacher, everyone began noticing how young Ada was.

In fact, Cricket herself had been very unwilling to see Ada as anything much more than a peer when her father first began courting her. For pity's sake, Ada could more easily have passed as her sister than her stepmother.

Still, Cricket wanted nothing more than to see her father happy again. It seemed he hadn't been truly happy since her mother's death several years before. And if Ada Hatley could put the hop back in her daddy's step, then Cricket would learn to accept it.

Accepting Ada as her stepmother had proved to be more difficult than Cricket had assumed, however. Add to it the fact that Cricket was used to having all her father's attention before Ada, and had to learn to give up most of that attention after Ada, and things had been somewhat uncomfortable around the Cranford house for the first couple of months.

But everything was becoming more and more comfortable between Ada and Cricket—even if Cricket considered Ada's never-ending chore lists a bit too extreme at times. Besides, Cricket secretly enjoyed the fact that all the other men in Pike's Creek silently envied Zeke's having scooped up Ada for his own.

Furthermore, the moment Heathro Thibodaux moved to Pike's Creek—well, Cricket Cranford was more than merely glad that her father had snatched up Ada Hatley and carried her over their threshold. Cricket was forever thankful in fact that her father had married Ada *before* Heathro Thibodaux had come to town. No doubt Ada would've been as smitten by Heathro as every other woman was, had she not already been in love with Zeke. Furthermore, Ada was beautiful—a real dark-haired, blue-eyed beauty! Cricket figured that of any woman in town, Ada would've had the best chance of catching Heathro's eye. Ada might just have managed to lasso Heathro for her own if she hadn't already been married to Cricket's father.

Cricket frowned. Thoughts of Heathro Thibodaux being snatched up by any woman always made her feel a bit sick to her stomach. Oh, certainly she knew the day would come when he would marry someone. In truth, it was probably a miracle that he hadn't been roped in by some woman's feminine wiles already. But until the day came that the handsome ex-Texas Ranger was legally wed to another woman, Cricket was determined to dream of being the one to lasso him and tether him to her porch.

"Heathro Thibodaux," Cricket whispered aloud. She liked the way Heathro's name felt on her tongue—smooth and sweet like a delicious secret. As she'd done every night for months before drifting off to sleep, Cricket let her thoughts linger on the handsome newcomer to Pike's Creek.

He was, without question, the most handsome man Cricket had ever seen—or even imagined, for that matter. In fact, the first time Vilma had seen Heathro, she'd called him a "tall drink of water" and said staring at him was more refreshing than swimming naked on a summer Sunday afternoon. Considering how stiff and perfect Vilma was, her scandalous description of Heathro Thibodaux was even more significant.

As Cricket lay in the soft comfort of her bed, continuing to let her mind nest on thoughts of how truly wonderfully attractive Texas Ranger Thibodaux was, she giggled, thinking that looking at him *was* more refreshing than swimming naked on a summer Sunday afternoon. He *was* a tall drink of water—far taller than most of the other men in town—and his shoulders were as broad as the state of Texas itself. Sky-blue eyes, bronze skin, square jaw, and dark hair—and that smile! In truth, Cricket had only seen Heathro Thibodaux smile three or four times, but each incidence was something she'd never forget. His smile was bright and white, and the gold tooth he owned on the upper-right incisor of his smile only embellished the richness of it.

That one tooth. Cricket's smile faded as she thought of it. Oh, no doubt the flash only added to the splendor of his smile. Yet it also served as a reminder to anyone who had ever read or heard of what had happened in Texas one year before. No doubt it was a powerful remembrance to Heathro Thibodaux himself—a visual indication of true barbarity, pain, and loss.

In that moment, Cricket wondered—when Heathro looked in the mirror each morning and saw that tooth, did he think of eight dead girls buried in the bottom of a bleak and barren canyon? Did he think of the eight dead girls that he, for no fault of his own, had been unable to save? After all, the outlaws who had cracked Ranger Thibodaux's tooth, beat him nearly to fatality, shot him, and left him for dead were the same outlaws who had murdered the eight girls he'd been trying to save. Cricket was certain the poor man never once saw that tooth in his head without thinking of those girls. It was no wonder he'd quit rangering.

Though Cricket had spent many a night thinking of Heathro Thibodaux, of the horror of what he'd been through, this was the first night she'd ever wondered about his tooth—the tooth she found so perfectly embellished his already stunning smile. This was the first night she'd wondered what he thought about it.

Quickly she crept from her bed and to the chest at the foot of it. Raising the lid, she carefully shuffled through the many treasures she secreted there until she found the one she wanted to study again in that moment.

Sitting down on the floor, Cricket unfolded the newspaper clipping she'd managed to squirrel away from behind the saloon when a cowboy had tossed it in the garbage barrel a year ago.

"*Abducted Young Women Found Murdered*," she read aloud in a whisper. Cricket had read the story many times. Yet each time she read it over again, a horrific sympathy for all that had happened to Heathro Thibodaux the summer before swelled inside her.

Sunday last, Texas Rangers found the bodies of the eight young women abducted from Turner Bend one week previous. All had succumbed to death. The eight promising young women of Turner Bend, having been abducted by a heinous band of outlaws one week previously, met their death on the rocky bed of a canyon, having been pushed over the canyon ridge ledge while tied together at hands and feet. Near the bodies of the dead young women, Texas Rangers found one of their own, Ranger Heathro Thibodaux, clinging to life, but only just.

Shortly after the Texas Ranger posse set out in search of the abductees, Ranger Thibodaux argued that the band of outlaws was traveling with the girls to New Orleans, while other members of the posse insisted the miscreants were mapping Mexico as their destination. Ranger Thibodaux broke from the posse and tracked the outlaws and their young female prisoners in a solitary manner. However, when he came upon the outlaws and their victims, he was but one man against ten and was beaten, shot, and left for dead. Barely conscious and unable to move to assist the eight abducted young women, Ranger Thibodaux watched helplessly through swollen, bloodied eyes as the outlaws discussed the matter of his arrival. It was decided among these evil abductors of innocence that if one Texas Ranger was near, then a full posse would soon follow. Thus, Ranger Thibodaux, wounded and slipping in and out of consciousness, witnessed the most gruesome of acts as the outlaws murdered the eight Turner Bend innocents.

"They tied their hands and feet," Ranger Thibodaux reported, "tethered them together loosely, and pushed them over the rim of the canyon."

Ranger Thibodaux suffered a broken arm, a broken leg, broken ribs, a broken hand, a cracked tooth, three gunshot wounds, and various bruising and lacerations. He was unable to assist the Texas Ranger posse as they identified and buried the eight young women from Tuner Bend.

While recovering from his injuries in San Antonio, when asked if perhaps it may have been better for the Turner Bend young women had he not come upon the outlaws at all, Ranger Thibodaux answered, "I would rather see those girls dead on the floor of the canyon and know their souls are safe in the arms of the Lord than to live my life knowing those outlaws had reached New Orleans with the girls alive. They're far safer in death."

Witnesses report that many who heard Ranger Thibodaux's response spat on him, calling him a coward and a devil. Yet with rumors of white slavers operating in Texas and the New Mexico Territory, there are many who support Ranger Thibodaux's estimation.

Regardless of whether Ranger Thibodaux was amiss in his actions and opinions, the township of Turner Bend mourns for those eight bright and beautiful blossoms that were lost. They were and are: Minnie Edwards, aged 16 years; Hattie Campbell, aged 17 years; Dora Murphy, aged 18 years; Ruth Wallace, aged 18 years; Hazel Palmer, aged 16 years; Charlotte Berry, aged 17 years; Pauline Elliott, aged 15 years; and Dorthia Gilbert, aged 15 years.

Cricket exhaled a heavy sigh discouragement and pain. She shook her head, brushing the tears from her cheeks as she folded the clipping and returned it to its place in the old wooden chest at the foot of her bed.

It was all so unbelievably horrific, so painful, so heinous! She thought too that Ranger Thibodaux had been right: all eight of the girls who had died were free from their pain and misery, safe in the glories of heaven. And yet their families were left to mourn them—to drown in a grief that even ever-sympathetic Magnolia Cricket Cranford could not imagine.

And what of Heathro Thibodaux? As always, it was Heathro that Cricket felt most sorry for. What a burden it must've been to bear—to know that he was correct in his estimations that the white slavers meant to take the girls to New Orleans. But because none of the other Rangers had believed him, every girl had died—and Ranger Thibodaux had helplessly watched as they had.

With another exhaled sigh of near despair, Cricket crawled back into her bed. She closed her eyes and listened as the fragrant evening breeze of summer caressed the leaves of the trees outside her open bedroom window. She could hear the crickets underneath the back porch as they played their soothing song—hear the croaking of the bullfrogs along the banks of the stream and the melodic tinkling of Mrs. Maloney's wind chimes in the distance. She inhaled deeply the aroma of the breeze, of fresh-from-the-oven bread that someone in town was baking—the sweet scent of the summer grasses, wildflowers, and the mellow bouquet of the small herd of cattle that Mr. Burroughs had driven to town in order to load onto the train the next day.

And yet it wasn't until an image of Heathro Thibodaux settled into her mind that she was able to stop more tears from trickling over her temples. At lease he'd lived. The girls—all eight of the Tuner Bend girls—had died. But at least the world hadn't lost Heathro Thibodaux too.

Cricket thought of the plans she and her friends had made earlier in the day. She thought of how delighted Mrs. Maloney would be when she opened her door Friday night to see the beautiful teapot Vilma had sold her hair to purchase sitting on her front porch. She thought of Mr. Keel. Even a lonesome man would appreciate a new quilt—especially one so lovingly stitched as the one Ann had made for him was. She thought of Hudson Oliver and how, in one way or the other, his life would never be the same once Marie had confessed her feelings. And she thought of Heathro Thibodaux—thought that if anyone in Pike's Creek deserved to be welcomed to town, deserved a kiss, then it was the heroic young Texas Ranger who had at least tried to save the abducted girls of Turner Bend.

Cricket pictured him then—the way he'd appeared earlier in the day as he'd stood on the bank of the swimming hole. A body would never know just by looking at him that he owned such a past. Muscular and strong, handsome, and alluring, he looked nothing like a man who had endured the horrors that he had.

The crickets congregated under the back porch abruptly stopped their song. Cricket knew her father must've gone out to close the barn doors for the night. Still, it wasn't long before the musicians for which she was nicknamed began to play once more.

"Play on, my dear ones," Cricket whispered. She smiled a moment as she thought of the day her father had explained that he and her mother had begun calling her Cricket when, at the age of four, they had begun to wonder if she would ever stop talking. As crickets played incessantly, it seemed Magnolia Cranford prattled and chirped with full the same vigor and consistency.

"Play on," she whispered again. "Sing me to sleep. Drive away this sad feelin' my heart is achin' with." She brushed one last tear from her temple as she turned on her side, fluffed her pillow, and sighed. "And play a pretty song for Mr. Thibodaux too please. He more than earned the right to be soothed by your gentle melody."

CHAPTER THREE

"You gonna drop in on Mrs. Maloney, Cricket?" Zeke Cranford asked his daughter.

"Beg your pardon, Daddy?" Cricket asked as the heat of guilt rose to her cheeks. Quickly she thought back over the past few days. Had she let something slip concerning the plans she, Marie, Ann, and Vilma had to gift Mrs. Maloney the teapot? The four girls liked to perform their acts of anonymous kindness…well, anonymously. And as far as Cricket knew, her father didn't even suspect it was she and her friends who periodically scattered joy to others under the cloak of darkness. Yet she must've said something that indicated to her father she was involved. How else could he know about their plans where Mrs. Maloney and the teapot were concerned?

Zeke looked up from his plate of bacon and eggs, smiled at Cricket, and answered, "Well, it's Friday. Don't you usually drop in on the ol' gal on Friday?" He looked back down to his plate, stabbed a bit of eggs with his fork, and added, "Fred Elmer says he seen her limping a bit yesterday, and I was just wonderin' if all was well with her. So I thought since you usually visit with her on Fridays—"

"Oh! Oh yes!" Cricket exclaimed as understanding and reprieve washed over her. "Yes, of course I plan to visit her today." She giggled a sigh of relief and said, "You about gave me a fit of apoplexy, Daddy. For a minute there I thought…"

Cricket closed her mouth tightly, but it was too late. As always, she'd said too much.

"You thought what?" Zeke asked.

"I thought…I thought you were gonna tell me some terrible sad news about Mrs. Maloney or somethin'," she fibbed.

"Nope," her father assured her. "But then again, limpin' ain't never a good thing. So you be sure you inquire about it today when you're visitin' her, all right?"

"I will, Daddy," Cricket promised. "I surely will."

"You're still gonna help me with the washin' this afternoon, aren't you, Cricket?" Ada asked then.

Cricket was somewhat crestfallen by Ada's already asking her to do chores before she'd even had a chance to finish her breakfast. Still, turning to Ada, she forced a happy countenance and answered, "Yes, Ada. I'll be back to help with the wash by noon. Would that be soon enough?"

Ada grinned and sighed—almost as if she'd been expecting to be slapped across the face and hadn't been. "That'll be just fine, Cricket. Thank you."

Cricket smiled sincerely then, for she felt sympathy for Ada's struggles welling in her own bosom. How difficult it must be for Ada—trying to find the balance between being so young herself and yet nestled in the position of having a stepdaughter old enough to be her peer. The thought briefly crossed Cricket's mind that perhaps she, Marie, Ann, and Vilma should let Ada join them for their shenanigans once in a while. After all, Ada was nothing if not kindhearted—and to the very core to boot.

Still, she quickly abandoned the idea. Their secret shenanigans were something that had to be kept secret. The incidents of spreading joy and happiness she and her friends organized would cease to have the enchanting effect they had if everyone in town were to find out who was doing them. And Cricket knew how completely Ada confided in Zeke. There wasn't anything on the face of the earth or in the clouds of heaven above that Ada would keep from Cricket's father—and it was as it should be.

Cricket turned her thoughts to executing the mischief planned for that night. The truth of it was Cricket had been jumping-jittery all week long! It seemed that not an hour ticked by that Cricket wasn't going over the strategies of accomplishing her particular deeds in her mind—her plan to see Marie and Hudson Oliver in each other's arms and her plan to properly welcome Heathro Thibodaux to Pike's Creek. In fact, every time she thought of Heathro Thibodaux and her promise that she would kiss the handsome, heroic ex-Ranger, a wild sort of frightened excitement leapt in her stomach. For one thing, she honestly wondered if she really could successfully muster the courage she would need to kiss Mr. Thibodaux when the time came. And for another, she began to envision that he might shoot her where she stood when she did.

"Have you seen that ornery bull Heathro Thibodaux come by?" Zeke asked.

"What?" Cricket breathed, startled by the fact that her father would mention the name—the very subject of her worried thoughts.

"Yes, I have," Ada answered. "It was out and about the other afternoon, and Mr. Thibodaux had quite a time gettin' it on home."

Zeke chuckled. "I can imagine he did." Shoving another piece of bacon into his mouth, he added, "But a cattleman over in Thistle told me just how much he paid for Thibodaux's bull's services awhile back…and I'm guessin' all the trouble that bull causes is well worth it where money's concerned."

"You know," Cricket began, scooting her chair back from the table, "I think I'll just run on over to Mrs. Maloney's house right this minute. That way we can know for certain that she's well enough…and I can be back long before noon to help with the wash, Ada."

Zeke Cranford's brow puckered a bit. Cricket seemed a bit more hoppy than usual. He was fairly certain some kind of tomfoolery was churning around in her mischievous little mind. Of course, it hadn't escaped his attention that she was always a little less settled whenever Heathro Thibodaux's name was mention.

Zeke grinned. Ah! The agony of young love! He sure was glad he was past it. He looked to Ada and smiled. She was a beauty, that was for certain; inside and out, Ada was a beauty. She was just what Zeke had needed, and he thanked the Almighty every night for putting her in his path.

Returning his attention to Cricket, he said, "Sounds like a good plan there, pumpkin. You tell Mrs. Maloney me and Ada say hello... and to let us know if she needs anything. Anything at all, all right?"

"I will, Daddy," Cricket said, rising from her chair and placing a quick kiss on Zeke's face.

"I'll be back as quick as I can, Ada," Cricket offered with a smile.

"Thank you, Cricket," Ada said, returning the smile.

Zeke grinned. The two women in his life were beginning to find a comfortable place with one another. It was another blessing he silently thanked the Almighty for.

Cricket was out the kitchen door and down the back porch steps quicker than a rabbit with a red fox on its heels. Once her daddy had made mention of Heathro Thibodaux, Cricket had been overcome with an urgency to escape. She'd been thinking so long and so hard about Pike's Creek's newest bachelor that she was afraid she'd burst at the seems and start spilling all her private thoughts about him to her daddy and Ada if she lingered any longer!

It was so very difficult to keep such things bottled up. It wasn't healthy either, or so Mrs. Maloney claimed. And although Mrs. Maloney was right—it did feel better to confess secret feelings and worries to a friend—Cricket sometimes wondered if the old gal had simply used the fact to coax information out of Cricket in a weak moment or two. Yep, Maymee Maude Maloney was the one person on the face of the earth who could weasel just about anything out of Magnolia Cricket Cranford. As she walked toward Mrs. Maloney's house, Cricket shook her head, giggling with amusement—because it was absolutely true! Once Mrs. Maloney got Cricket to talking, there was no stopping Cricket from saying just about anything or answering just about any question.

In fact, the only thing Cricket had managed to keep from Mrs. Maloney since the first day she'd rather accidentally ended up sitting on her front porch for a visit was the fact that Cricket knew exactly who the do-gooders of Pike's Creek were—the fact that Cricket herself was the ringleader.

Maymee Maloney had been the very person (at last) who had helped Cricket to understand her father's growing adoration for Ada. Mrs. Maloney had helped Cricket to accept Ada into the family—into her deceased mother's role. It had been Mrs. Maloney who had counseled Cricket in times of frustration and despair. It had been Mrs. Maloney who had comforted her, laughed with her, teased with her, gossiped with her, and taught Cricket more than any one woman could ever imaginably teach another.

Cricket adored Maymee Maloney—simply adored her! And she liked the way Mrs. Maloney referred to her as Magnolia instead of Cricket. It made her feel grown up and refined somehow—even for the fact that she rarely kept her shoes on when she was at Mrs. Maloney's house or that she rarely laughed quietly when in her company. Still, Cricket liked to be called Magnolia, even though no one else seemed to call her that—other than Vilma when she was scolding, that was.

"Good mornin' there, sweet Magnolia!" Mrs. Maloney called as Cricket hurried up the front porch steps of the Maloney house.

"Good mornin', Mrs. Maloney," Cricket chirped as Mrs. Maloney reached up from her seat in her front porch rocker and gathered Cricket into a warm embrace.

"My, don't you look chipper already today," the elderly woman laughed. "Have you come for a visit already?"

"Yes, ma'am," Cricket assured her friend. Taking her designated seat on the old tree stump stool in front but to one side of Mrs. Maloney's porch rocking chair, Cricket added, "I just couldn't wait to get out of the house and come see you today. I hope you've had your breakfast already."

"Oh, hours ago, darlin'! Hours ago," Mrs. Maloney assured her with a smile.

Cricket's smile broadened. She like the way Mrs. Maloney's eyes smiled with her mouth—the way they looked like little half-moons of delight. The old gal's blue eyes had faded to nearly gray with so many years of seeing so much life, but that didn't make them sparkle with pure merriment in life any less.

"Daddy said he heard you were limpin' a bit a few days back," Cricket began. "Are you all right?"

Mrs. Maloney rolled her eyes with exasperation. "Land sakes! A body can't get away with anything in this town," she sighed. Her smile did not fade, however, and she continued, "I just twisted my ankle a bit, that's all. It's all healed up nice now. Even the bruisin' is goin'."

"Well, how did you do that?" Cricket asked. "You weren't runnin' a footrace with those Burroughs boys again, were you?"

Mrs. Maloney laughed and shook her head. "Oh, goodness no! I was just doin' a little waltzin' in my parlor and stepped wrong."

Cricket's eyebrows arched with curious delight. "Waltzin'? With whom, may I ask?"

"With none-of-your-nevermind, Miss Magnolia," Mrs. Maloney teased.

"Mrs. Maloney!" Cricket playfully exclaimed. "Have you got a beau? Have you been entertainin' a gentleman in your parlor of late?"

But Maymee Maloney simply tossed her head and laughed with pure glee. "Oh, don't I wish it, Magnolia. Don't I wish it."

Cricket had grown wise to Maymee Maloney's weaseling ways, however—and they were twofold. Not only could Mrs. Maloney weasel anything out of Cricket, she could also weasel her way out of not giving a straight answer to any question she chose not to answer.

"I'm not lettin' you off this time, Mrs. Maloney," Cricket giggled. "Who is this mysterious beau you were waltzin' with in your parlor that found you with a turned ankle?"

Mrs. Maloney grinned—her eyes grinning too. "Oh, just Nobody," she answered. "Nobody MacGee. That's what I call him…Nobody MacGee. Nobody has been my waltzin' partner since the day I lost my darlin', sweet Mr. Maloney. Yep. Me and ol' Nobody…we kick up our heels like nothin' you've ever seen when the urge comes over us."

Cricket's heart pinched with sadness for Mrs. Maloney's loneliness— for the loss of her husband, even though it had been long ago. She knew she couldn't dwell on the subject or she'd be reduced to tears of sympathetic sorrow, loss, and loneliness.

"Well, you tell Mr. Nobody to watch his feet next time you all are sparkin' in the parlor then," she teased. "He's got to be careful with a delicate, well-mannered lady like you."

"We weren't sparkin', Magnolia," Mrs. Maloney corrected with good humor. "We were only waltzin'."

"Mm-hmm," Cricket said, feigning suspicion. "Oh, I'm sure you were."

Cricket and Mrs. Maloney both erupted into giggles for a moment. And when they each finally drew a breath, sighing with the contentment that comes of having been distracted by lightheartedness, Mrs. Maloney asked, "And how are things with Ada? Are the two of you gettin' to know one another a little better?"

Cricket nodded. "Yes...I think so," she answered. "And I see now that I was bein' selfish and silly. I don't know why it took me so long to start to understand."

"Well, don't spend any more time worryin' about why it took so long. Just spend the time buildin' your relationship with Ada from here forth," the wise old woman counseled. "I think that someday you'll find her to be one of your truest and most loyal friends."

"Maybe so," Cricket mumbled.

"Meanwhile, I saw that tall drink of water that ruffles your bloomers in at the general store yesterday," Mrs. Maloney said, having lowered her voice to nearly a whisper.

"And who might that be?" Cricket asked, blushing and feigning ignorance.

Mrs. Maloney smiled and giggled a bit. "That Mr. Heathro handsome-as-the-day-is-long Thibodaux, that's who."

"Hmm," Cricket said with a shrug. "I suppose that's nice."

"Well, he's a lot more fun to look at than a hound's hind end, I can tell you that."

Cricket nodded and quietly mumbled, "Mmm-hmm."

"That reminds me...Me and Mr. Maloney had us a hound dog once that had a little patch of white hair shaped exactly like a heart situated right under his tail on his hind end." The old woman began to chuckle. "Mr. Maloney named him Valentine, and that ol' hound slept at the foot of our bed for near to twelve years before he died." She sighed and shook her head. "Old Valentine. I hadn't thought of him in so long."

Cricket smiled. "A heart right under his tail?"

"Yep," Mrs. Maloney said with a nod. "I was forever and always scoldin' Mr. Maloney about liftin' up that dog's tail to show folks the heart. It just wasn't proper."

Cricket began to giggle again. Mrs. Maloney was more fun than anything! Suddenly Cricket's excitement swelled so warm and enchanting in her bosom that she thought she might burst with delighted anticipation—knowing that, that very night, the elderly little darling would receive the pretty teapot from the general store window.

"Anyway, as I was sayin', I saw your Mr. Thibodaux in the general store yesterday," Mrs. Maloney continued, having remembered her previous train of thought. The woman was impossible to distract.

"He's not *my* Mr. Thibodaux," Cricket corrected. "In fact, I hear tell the Widow Rutherford has nearly got him roped in." The thought of Anastasia Rutherford winning the affections of Heathro Thibodaux caused all the pleasure Cricket had known a moment before to dissipate entirely.

"Oh, she's tryin' all right. I'll give her that," Mrs. Maloney began. "But it's gonna take more than a pretty lasso to tether that boy to any woman's porch."

"A pretty lasso can tether any man to a woman's porch, Mrs. Maloney, and you know it." Cricket felt somehow defeated—almost depressed.

Mrs. Maloney nodded. "Sometimes that's true…and sometimes it ain't," she said. "And anyway, Anastasia was in the general store the same time as me and Mr. Thibodaux, and he didn't do more than nod and mumble a greeting when she said hello to him." Mrs. Maloney frowned and seemed thoughtful. "I think those goin's-on last year just did that man too much damage."

Cricket sighed and shook her head. "I don't understand why he seems to bear the guilt of it all," she said. "He was the one who was right when the rest of the posse was wrong. It wasn't his fault he had no help."

"Oh, but a good man always thinks he should've done more… could've done more…even against impossible odds."

There was quiet for a moment, and Cricket tried to divert her own thoughts from Heathro Thibodaux and his past—from Heathro Thibodaux at all!

But it seemed Maymee Maloney wasn't about to let that happen. "Why don't you lasso that man for yourself, Magnolia?"

Cricket rolled her eyes with humiliation and exasperation. "Oh! Of course!" she exclaimed with friendly sarcasm. "And then I'll just become President of the United States and live forever too, while I'm at it!"

"Oh for Pete's sake," Mrs. Maloney scolded. "Lassoin' a man ain't anything as difficult as becomin' President of the United States." She smiled and shook her head. "Sometimes I wonder what on earth goes on in that mind of yours."

"Says who?" Cricket asked, perking up just a bit—for she could see the mischief in Mrs. Maloney's smiling eyes, and it always cheered her.

"Says me," Mrs. Maloney answered. "In fact, why don't you just run on over to his house one night, rope him up good, tie him to a chair, and go about *convincin'* him that you're the woman he's always wanted?"

Cricket laughed, shaking her head with amused disbelief. "You make the most scandalous suggestions sometimes, Mrs. Maloney!" she exclaimed. "And what do you mean, go about convincin' him, anyway? What could I possibly do to convince him to want *me*…even if he was tied to a chair?"

But Mrs. Maloney only laughed, her gray eyes so radiant with misbehavior that Cricket thought surely stars had been plucked from the heavens and placed in her head where her eyes used to be. "Oh, let's save that for another time," she said. "For now, why don't you tell me what all is goin' on with your daddy and Ada. Did Ada finish puttin' up all that strawberry jam she was workin' on?"

Cricket smiled and nodded. She knew Mrs. Maloney had said all she was going to say on the subject of Heathro Thibodaux being tied to a chair and how Cricket could convince him to want her. She was a sneaky little thing—and Cricket loved her all the more for it.

When Cricket, Marie, Ann, and Vilma had first decided to begin their do-gooding shenanigans, they decided that everything mysterious and secretive was easier to go about veiled in the concealing cloak of night. Thus, they had therefore decided they'd have to be literally cloaked as well. Going about their do-gooding with only the moon and starlight as their guides was certainly helpful at hiding their identity, but they had all agreed they would need something more—costumes of a sort.

It had been Cricket who had first offered the suggestion of rounding up old camisoles, shirtwaists, bloomers, and petticoats and dying them black. Vilma had been mortified at the suggestion, of course—or at least she'd pretended to be (though Cricket knew that the preacher's daughter secretly relished the chance to run around town in a set of black underwear—it fulfilled her unspoken desire to rebel). Marie and Ann had heartily agreed at once, however, Marie explaining that the black would help them blend into their dark surroundings while do-gooding and Ann offering that it would put to good use their old, too-worn clothing.

And so, one rather dreary winter morning, Cricket, Marie, Ann, and Vilma set about dying old undergarments. By the next evening, they were dressed head to toe in their proper do-gooder apparel and flitting around Pike's Creek scattering joy to others by means of leaving cookies on porches, dollies on little girls' window sills, and even apple pies in barns for the widows and widowers in town.

For months and months the girls had enjoyed their shenanigans—and so had anyone and everyone who had been a lucky victim of them. And so, as Cricket pulled on her black stockings in preparation for the shenanigans they had planned for Mrs. Maloney, Mr. Keel, Heathro Thibodaux, and Hudson Oliver, she smiled at the memory of that very first night of mischief. She'd never known such excitement and pure gladness as she knew in making others smile and lightening their hearts—even if only for a moment.

Logically, however, as she pulled her black shirtwaist over her black camisole, her excitement turned to nervous anxiety as she thought again of her chosen task for the evening—Heathro Thibodaux. In truth, she was still silently wondering how in all the wide, wide world she would ever find the courage to do what she'd promised to do! Welcoming him to Pike's Creek was easy enough—but to kiss him? If Cricket were to be honest with Ann, Vilma, and Marie, she would confess that she wouldn't be sure whether she could muster the gumption to actually kiss the man until the very moment presented itself! Of course, she couldn't confide the truth of it in her friends. After all, she was the strong one—the fighter.

Cricket knew, as did her friends, that every one of them was a fighter. There wasn't one among them who would ever back down from doing right or from pushing on through whatever trial crossed their paths. But the fact remained that Cricket owned the greatest sense of responsibility—felt compelled to defend, protect, encourage, and help the others. And most of the time Cricket was willing. But each and every time she thought about kissing Heathro Thibodaux, not only did her arms and legs break into gooseflesh but her stomach also churned into such chaos that she thought she might vomit!

But there was no time to be fearful. Merry mischief was afoot, and as Cricket finished dressing and quietly crept out of her father's house by way of her bedroom window, the cool night air and wonderful aroma of burning cedar in warm hearths sent an overwhelming exhilaration riveting through her! Four people would drift to sleep with smiles on their faces—or at least in their hearts—after Cricket and her friends were finished with their shenanigans that night. Well, Mrs. Maloney and Mr. Keel would feel lighter-hearted. Cricket wasn't so sure about Heathro Thibodaux. Furthermore, she knew that Marie's confession to Hudson Oliver, accompanied by her plead for him to remain in Pike's Creek, would no doubt find Hudson Oliver unable to sleep or settle down for that matter. Still, in her soul Cricket knew Hudson would stay—that he already cared deeply for Marie. And so she soothed herself in knowing that at least three of the recipients of their do-gooding would benefit.

The stars were bright, twinkling overhead like tiny beacons, and the moon was beautiful in its brilliance, like a wafer of silver in the night sky, as Cricket made her way to meet Ann, Marie, and Vilma at the old lean-to just outside of town. The soothing aria of the crickets mingled with the gentle summer breeze in the trees seemed the music of heaven, and the fragrance of lilac and honeysuckle wandered on the air like a delicate, feathered perfume.

"There you are, Cricket. Finally!" Cricket heard Vilma whisper as she reached the old lean-to.

"I'm sorry, everyone," Cricket apologized. "Daddy and Ada were up longer than usual tonight. I had to fib a headache to get away to my room."

"It's fine, Cricket," Marie said. "We were just talkin' about who we should do first...Mrs. Maloney or Mr. Keel."

"Mrs. Maloney," Ann and Vilma chimed in unison. They looked at one another and smiled.

"Ann is still nervous about the quilt for Mr. Keel, and I don't want us to accidentally damage the teapot somehow," Vilma explained. "So is that all right with you, Cricket? If we deliver Mrs. Maloney's teapot first?"

"Of course," Cricket affirmed. "Why wouldn't it be?"

"We thought maybe you'd want to deliver Mr. Thibodaux's gift first," Ann explained, "so that you wouldn't have wait to—"

"Oh! Oh, I'm fine with waitin'...truly," Cricket interrupted. She was glad it was dark. Perhaps the other girls hadn't noticed her radish-red blush or nervous agitation.

"Then we'll do Mrs. Maloney first," Marie confirmed. "Then Ann will give Mr. Keel his quilt and—"

"Then Ann will leave Mr. Keel's quilt on his porch," Ann interjected.

Everyone giggled, and Cricket felt sorry for Ann. She knew that leaving the quilt on Mr. Keel's porch was nearly as frightening for Ann as the idea of stealing a kiss from Mr. Thibodaux was to her—even if they were apples and onions.

"Right," Marie giggled. "Then Ann will leave Mr. Keel's quilt on the porch, and then it will be Cricket's turn...and last of all mine." Marie moaned with anxiety, and Cricket felt the call to strength in her heart—as ever she did.

She placed her hands firmly on Marie's shoulders. "This is the night, Marie," Cricket whispered as the delicious anticipation of adventure mingled with her own anxiety in her bosom. "This is the night you will win Hudson Oliver for you own!"

"Yes, Marie," Vilma said, taking Marie's hand and offering a squeeze of encouragement. "After tonight, there will be no more wonderin'. After tonight, you'll know how Hudson feels."

Ann took Marie's free hand then, grasping it between both of her own. "Hudson loves you, Marie. All of us know it. Even you know it! And now it's time for the two of you to quit horsin' around and get on with it."

"That's right, Marie," Cricket said. But when she saw the doubt beginning to darken Marie's sapphire eyes, she knew her friend needed more. "And just think...by the end of tonight, you'll know just what it feels like to have Hudson Oliver kiss you!"

"Y-you mean, I'll know what it feels like to kiss *him*," Marie stammered. "What if he—"

"He won't," Cricket interrupted before Marie could swell her own doubt. "Once your lips touch his...I know Hudson Oliver will be like bread dough in your hands, Marie. There's no way possible that boy won't have you in his arms makin' love to you right there for all the stars to see! I know it. I do."

"It's true, Marie," Ann said. "I know it too."

"And me," Vilma added.

Cricket wondered for a moment why it was everyone assumed that Marie's challenge for the evening required so much more encouragement than hers did. In truth, wasn't it far and away different for Marie to confess her heart and offer a kiss to the young man she'd loved nearly all her life than it was for Cricket to walk up to a nearly complete stranger and steal a kiss? But naturally the moment passed as

Cricket reminded herself that only her pride was at risk, while Marie's entire future was what teetered on the edge.

"He loves you, Marie," Cricket assured her friend once more. "I know he does."

Marie grinned, sighed, and nodded. "All right. All right. Then let's get to Mrs. Maloney's and spread some sunshine, shall we?"

"Yes!" Cricket giggled, throwing her arms around Marie's shoulders and hugging her tightly. Ann and Vilma joined the embrace, and the girls giggled with excitement.

As they made their way toward Mrs. Maloney's house, Cricket again took a moment to admire the beauty of the stars and moon in the night sky. All would be well, she thought to herself. Mrs. Maloney would cherish her teapot, Mr. Keel would be warm in not only the comfort of a new quilt but the knowledge that someone was looking out for him, and Hudson Oliver would finally have the door to confessing his own feelings flung wide open by Marie's courage.

As for Heathro Thibodaux and his welcome to Pike's Creek—there was nothing to do but wait until the moment arrived and hope that the brooding ex-Texas Ranger wasn't startled into shooting the girl who meant to welcome him to town by stealing a kiss.

CHAPTER FOUR

Cricket clamped one hand over her mouth to keep from squealing with amusement as she, Ann, and Marie watched Vilma quietly tiptoe up Mrs. Maloney's front porch steps. Her delight was nearly euphoric. Oh, how thoroughly Mrs. Maloney would love the teapot! No teapot in the world had ever been or would ever be so treasured and cared for. Cricket felt a pinch in her happy heart—painful gratitude for Vilma and her sacrifice for Mrs. Maloney's sake. Oh, certainly Vilma's hair would grow back. But Cricket knew how vain Vilma Stanley was about her beautiful auburn hair. It was truly a heartfelt and humble forfeit.

"I'm so excited I think I'm gonna cry," Ann whispered.

"Hush, Ann," Marie gently scolded, wiping a tear from the corner of her eye. "You'll have me bawlin' like a calf if you start."

Cricket blinked away the moisture in her own eyes as she watched Vilma carefully situate the teapot on Mrs. Maloney's front porch. She bit her lip with impatience as Vilma took entirely too long in placing the accompanying note just so on its spout.

"Oh, she's gonna get caught," Marie groaned. "She always draws it out so dang long!"

"It's part of her way of doin' things," Cricket whispered. "Remember when we were in school and her cat died?"

"How could we ever forget?" Ann sighed with mild exasperation. "Standin' out in the rain in the dead of night...all four of us bawlin' our eyes out over that silly cat."

"Herman," Marie offered quietly. "His name was Herman."

"Oh, believe me, Marie," Ann giggled. "I'll never forget his name *or* the two hours of standin' in the rain bawlin' over him."

"Shhh!" Cricket suddenly shushed. "She's gettin' ready to knock on the door."

Simultaneously, Cricket, Marie, and Ann dropped to their bellies in the cool, sweet-scented grass across the street from Mrs. Maloney's house. There was the echo of Vilma knocking on Mrs. Maloney's front door on the air and then the comical sight of Vilma hightailing herself across the street to join the others.

Cricket couldn't help but laugh as she watched Vilma—all dressed in black underthings, leapfrogging across the street like a bullfrog with a firebrand at his behind.

"Here she comes!" Ann giggled. "Look at her go!"

Marie laughed so hard she snorted a little and sent Ann and Cricket clamping their hands over their mouths to ensure Mrs. Maloney wouldn't hear them sniggling with overpowering mirth.

"It's done!" Vilma panted as she plopped down on her stomach in the grass next to Cricket. "Do you think I knocked loud enough? I think the ol' gal has trouble hearin' sometimes. Daddy said she slept clean through his sermon last Sunday."

Cricket smiled when Marie leaned over, whispering in her ear, "Well, then half the congregation in Pike's Creek must have trouble hearin'…'cause the snorin' durin' her daddy's sermon last week was nearly deafenin'."

"Shhh!" Ann whispered. "The door's openin'!"

Sure enough. Cricket's eyes widened with wild anticipatory excitement as Mrs. Maloney's front door swung wide to reveal Mrs. Maloney standing just inside, dressed in a gingham nightgown and holding a lamp in one hand.

"Hello?" the elderly woman called into the darkness of night. "Who's there?"

"Oh, look down, woman! Look down!" Vilma whispered with impatience.

Almost as if Mrs. Maloney had heard her, the lovely old woman glanced down, spying the teapot.

Mrs. Maloney gasped—placed a hand to her bosom. "What in tarnation?" the girls heard her exclaim. Mrs. Maloney set the lamp down on the porch and picked up the teapot. "Oh! Oh, it's you!" she said to the teapot. "It's you. It really is you! Oh, how I've watched you for so long…but…what's this?"

Nobody breathed as they watched Mrs. Maloney unfold Vilma's note. They could hear her sniffling as she read—saw her wipe tears from her eyes.

"Thank you!" Maymee Maude Maloney called from her front porch out into the night. "Thank you, whoever you are! It's beautiful. So much more beautiful than it was when it was a prisoner at the general store! I promise to cherish it all my life. Thank you!"

Cricket wiped the tears from her cheeks as she watched Mrs. Maloney pick up the lamp and disappear into her house, closing the door behind her. She began to cry all the more savagely, however, when she saw Vilma collapse facedown in the cool summer grass and begin to sob.

Marie and Ann were as soppy as Cricket and Vilma, and it took several long minutes for any of the four black-shrouded do-gooders to recover their emotions.

Red-eyed and with tear-streaked cheeks, the four young ladies of Pike's Creek gathered themselves and started out for Mr. Keel's home.

"She really will love it, won't she?" Vilma asked, taking Cricket's hand as they walked.

Cricket smiled, wiped a fresh tear from her cheek, and nodded. "More than anyone in all the world ever could," she affirmed.

"I feel warmed and happier now," Ann said, stepping in beside Cricket, tucking her quilt under one arm, and taking her other hand.

"Me too," Marie added, clasping Vilma's free hand.

"I don't even miss my silly hair," Vilma added.

Cricket squeezed Vilma's hand with admiration and affection. "You're very brave and givin', Vilma," she said. "One day you're gonna burst out of whatever those invisible tethers are that keep you so wound up and be who God meant you to be."

Vilma squeezed Cricket's hand in return, but the new tears in her eyes kept her from speaking.

They walked silently for a time along the backside of the business buildings of Pike's Creek, each lost in her own thoughts. Though she didn't know what Marie or Ann or Vilma was thinking exactly, Cricket supposed their thoughts mirrored her own—that she wished she could spend more time doing lovely, kind things for folks in secret. It was what she felt she was meant to do, and she was glad for her companions in it.

"Just look at that moon," Ann said as they strolled along toward Mr. Keel's house and barn. "Just like a new silver coin hung high in the sky."

Cricket smiled, touched by the way she and Ann often thought of things similarly.

"And the stars!" Marie whispered in awe. "No wonder folks cast wishes at them. They truly twinkle like they're trying to speak to you… don't they?"

"Well, I wish they'd speak to me," Ann said then. "I wish they'd tell me whether or not Mr. Keel will think this quilt is the silliest thing or be glad he has it to keep him warm in the winter."

Mr. Keel's house was in view, and Cricket could see a lamp burning in the kitchen window. "Well, maybe when he opens the door and finds it tonight, you'll know, and the stars won't need to tell you," Cricket whispered. "Now let's quit talkin' and creep over behind that big lilac tree there by the kitchen door. It should hide us pretty well, don't you think?"

Quietly the girls made their way to the large lilac tree that grew to one side of Mr. Keel's back porch. Oh, it was so fragrant! Lilacs abloom was one of Cricket's favorite fragrances in all of heaven and earth.

"I'm havin' second thoughts about this," Ann nervously whispered as they carefully settled behind the old lilac tree.

"No second thoughts are allowed, Ann," Marie reminded. "You know that."

"But this is different," Ann quietly argued. "I mean, who in their right mind gives a widower a new quilt? And in the middle of summer to boot?"

Cricket reached out, taking Ann's hands in her own. Forcing her friend to look at her, she encouraged, "A kind, compassionate sort of woman who sincerely cares for him and worries about his comfort." Cricket smiled. "There isn't anything in all the world more cozy and comfortable than a soft, new quilt…even in the summer. Especially if a body wants to sit outside awhile and enjoy the cool evenin' air once the sun has gone down. Right?"

Ann smiled. "Right!" she agreed. "And after all, if Mr. Keel's beddin' is anything close to as worn out and needin' mendin' as his underdrawers are, then he surely needs a new quilt."

"His underdrawers?" Vilma exclaimed.

"Hush, Vilma!" Marie scolded. "He'll hear us out here if we don't stop chatterin' away like flock of magpies."

Vilma rolled her eyes, dismissing Marie's scolding. "Oh no, he won't. And besides, I want to know how Ann came by the knowledge of what condition Mr. Keel's underdrawers are in."

Cricket giggled. Vilma Stanley could find scandal about to erupt in anything.

Ann shook her head with amusement and whispered, "All you gotta do is take a look at his laundry when it's out on the line, Vilma. His underdrawers are truly a sight to behold. Holey knees, safety pins where buttons oughta be on the trap doors. It's nearly indecent."

Vilma grinned and arched a suspicious eyebrow. "Seems to me a body would have to be pretty close to a pair of underdrawers to see such detail as that."

"Well, there ain't nothin' wrong with lookin' at a man's underdrawers, Vilma," Marie interjected, smiling and winking at Ann.

"I suppose not," Vilma agreed. "As long as the man isn't wearin' them at the time."

"Oh, for Pete's sake, Vilma," Marie groaned. "I swear! You get so wound up about the simplest things and then don't bat an eye about things that are truly scandalous."

"Shhh," Ann whispered. "Let's just get on with it, girls. We've got a lot yet to do tonight, and if we stand here talkin' any longer, I swear I'm gonna fraidy-cat it and run off before I have a chance to deliver the quilt."

"Well, then go on, Ann," Cricket prodded. "Just sneak on up to Mr. Keel's front porch, drop the quilt and the note, and then knock on the door. It's that simple."

"Yeah. Then run for your life and get back here with us before he opens the door," Marie giggled.

"Maybe you'll even get a glimpse of those ratty underdrawers of his again, Ann," Vilma playfully teased. "Makes sense that the man would already be strippin' down for the night. It's near ten o'clock."

Marie and Cricket rolled their eyes and exchanged grins. Vilma Stanley—preacher's daughter one moment, scandal of Pike's Creek the next.

Ann inhaled a deep breath, exhaling it slowly. Fretfully she rubbed her hands together.

"I can do this," she mumbled to herself with a firm nod of her head. "If my daddy managed to survive Gettysburg, then I'll manage to survive this." She looked to Cricket with an expression of impending doubt and added, "Right?"

"Right," Cricket assured her.

"It's just a quilt, Ann," Vilma said. "It's not like you're proposin' marriage."

Marie took Ann by the shoulders—stared into her eyes. "Do it, Ann. Do this, and then you'll know that all autumn and winter your handsome Mr. Cooper Keel will be warm and cozy beneath a quilt *you* stitched for him."

Ann nodded, reached down, and gathered the carefully folded quilt, with handwritten note pinned to it, into her arms. "I'm goin'. I'm really goin'."

And she did! Cricket smiled and dropped to her knees behind the large lilac tree. Marie and Vilma dropped down too, all three girls parting various lilac branches in order to view Ann's admirable bravery.

"There she goes," Marie began to narrate in a whisper. "She's up the porch steps...and silent as a mice. She's puttin' the quilt down—"

"Oh, for heaven's sakes, Marie!" Vilma whined. "Me and Cricket both have two good eyes in our heads."

Marie wrinkled her nose at Vilma and then looked back to Ann. "She's movin' the quilt a little closer to the kitchen door…"

Cricket giggled when she heard Vilma puff a breath of exasperation.

"She's movin' toward the door," Marie continued. "She's…she's…"

"She's gonna get caught if she doesn't hurry up! What's she waitin' for?" Vilma whispered.

"She's diggin' in her petticoat pocket," Marie answered.

"What in tarnation for?" Cricket asked. What could Ann be doing? The quilt and note were perfectly placed on the front porch—right in front of the door where Mr. Keel would easily spot them. What could she be lingering for?

Marie laughed quietly. "It's a little jar," she said. "I know what she's doin'. I've seen her do this a million times."

"Well, I haven't. What is it?" Vilma inquired.

"It's a little jelly jar," Marie explained. "She's gonna put one of those little candles her mama makes inside the jar and light it. That way Mr. Keel will see the quilt right away. *And* there'll be a pretty little embellishment too."

Cricket smiled—sighed with admiration and approval. If there was one thing Ann was, it was a master of making the simplest things resplendently beautiful.

"She's so good at things like that," Vilma mumbled.

"Yep," Marie agreed.

"She brought matches too?" Cricket asked as she saw Ann draw a small box of matches from her petticoat pocket.

"Shhh!" Vilma and Marie scolded in unison.

"I swear…that girl thinks of every little detail," Cricket whispered.

She continued to peer between the lilac branches with Marie and Vilma as Ann struck a match on the sole of her shoe and lit the small candle she'd placed inside the little jar. Instantly the tiny golden flicker of light the candle produced kindled Mr. Keel's back porch with a warm and comforting glow.

"She'll have to be quick now," Vilma noted aloud.

Cricket knew Marie and Vilma were holding their breath, just as she was, as they watched Ann rap firmly several times on Mr. Keel's kitchen door. They gasped, giggling quietly as Ann leapt from down from the porch as gracefully as a doe and headed for the lilac tree.

Ann Burroughs looked just like a little pixie skipping through the night as she reached the lilacs and hunkered down behind it with the others.

"What if he's not home?" she asked in a whisper.

"Shhh," Cricket soothed. "He's home. We all saw the lamp glowin' in the window. He wouldn't leave it burnin' if—"

"Shh! He's openin' the door!" Vilma exclaimed.

Again Cricket held her breath as she saw the kitchen door of Mr. Keel's house swing in—watched Mr. Keel himself step out onto the porch and quickly look from one side to the other before his attention was arrested by the jar and candle at his feet.

"Oh my!" Ann breathed.

Quickly Marie clamped one hand over Ann's mouth to keep her quiet as four sets of young female eyes widened to the size of turkey platters.

Cricket smiled as she glanced to Ann. Ann had been exactly right—Mr. Keel's underdrawers were some of the shabbiest imaginable. Furthermore, they were only bottom underdrawers, not long johns. Held secure at the waist by a drawstring, Mr. Keel's topless underdrawers not only nicely revealed his kneecaps through the holes in them but allowed four of Pike's Creek's most mischievous young women a view of his muscular chest, shoulders, and arms.

Cooper Keel was known as one of the hardest-working men in Pike's Creek—and it showed by means of his anatomy. Even for the dark, Cricket could see that Ann's cheeks were as red as summer roses.

"Who's there?"

The sound of Mr. Keel calling out into the darkness startled the girls to further breath-holding.

But he didn't pursue his questioning any further. He simply reached down, picking up Ann's beautiful quilt. He frowned as he lifted the note a little, and Cricket saw his lips move as he read his name on the front.

Picking up the jar and candle, Cooper Keel grinned, chuckled, turned, and disappeared into his kitchen, firmly closing the door behind him.

"Come on!" Cricket said, taking Ann's hand and pulling her away from the lilac tree and farther from Mr. Keel's house.

Once the girls were out of earshot of Cooper Keel's house, all four erupted into triumphant and gleeful laughter.

"That was wonderful!" Marie exclaimed. "Did you see his face, Ann? Did you see it? He was thrilled with the quilt!"

Ann smiled. "He did seem to like it, didn't he?"

"He loved it, Ann!" Cricket confirmed. "I've never in all my life seen Mr. Keel smile like that. Never!"

"Did you see his face?" Marie repeated. "Ann, you made Mr. Keel smile…warmed his heart. I mean, did you see his face?"

"Did she see his face?" Vilma interjected. "Who had time to look at his face?" It was only then that Cricket noticed Vilma still wore an expression of pure astonishment.

"What do you mean, Vilma?" Cricket asked.

Vilma shook her head as if trying to pull herself from a daze. "Well, I apologize, Ann," she began, "for teasin' you about bein' sweet on Mr. Keel. I mean…he may be as old as your daddy, but I bet your daddy doesn't look like that without his shirt on. I know mine doesn't."

Marie and Cricket nearly fell to their knees, overcome with amusement at Vilma's continued flabbergasted expression.

"He is well-formed, isn't he?" Ann said, smiling. "But then again…I already knew that."

"What?" Vilma exclaimed.

"Oh, stop!" Marie laughed, trying to catch her breath. "Stop! I can't laugh this hard anymore! My back is achin' already!"

"Wait a minute," Vilma said, however. "What do you mean you already knew Mr. Keel was well-formed, Ann Burroughs? How could you possibly know he looked like…like *that*?"

Ann arched a triumphant brow, grinned with harmless gloating, and announced, "Because I saw him swimmin' naked at the ol' Morgan swimmin' hole four Sundays ago, that's how."

Cricket gasped with abrupt surprise. "What?" she giggled. "You're just teasin' us, right, Ann?"

"Nope," Ann responded, however. Looking to Vilma, she added, "And close your mouth, Vilma. It isn't at all becomin' to walk around with it gapin' open like an old bear cave."

"H-how naked was he, Ann?" Marie asked. Even Marie King appeared flabbergasted—and that was a rarity indeed.

Ann laughed, shaking her head—tickled at having astounded everyone. "Only as naked as he was just now, ladies," she confessed. "He was just wadin' around in the swimmin' hole...about waist deep. I didn't see anything my mama wouldn't want me to."

"Well, thank heaven for that, Ann Burroughs!" Vilma breathed at last. Placing a hand to her bosom, apparently to still her startled and chagrinned heart, she exhaled a heavy breath. "I thought sure you'd been ruined for life, girl. For pity's sake, don't scare me like that."

Cricket's smile broadened when Ann winked at her with achievement. It didn't take much to rattle Vilma, but Cricket was sure Vilma would still be rattling long after they'd finished their shenanigans and returned home. It was magnificent!

"Now let's just move on to somethin' else," Vilma suggested, fanning her still-blushing face. "We shouldn't be nestin' our thoughts on half-naked men, now should we? Let's just move on with the evening. I believe Mr. Heathro Thibodaux is next on the list. Isn't that right, Cricket?"

And just like that, Cricket's profound amusement in Ann's having flustered Vilma to the core vanished.

CHAPTER FIVE

"He rides home this way every night," Cricket whispered. "I can see him through my bedroom window. Every night at about ten, he passes our house on his way home. Then he heads along the old fence line, stops, and waters his horse at this trough out here behind the general store...then disappears into the night."

When no one else responded to Cricket's explanation of how she happened to know where Heathro Thibodaux would be that night, she turned to see three familiar faces—each donning an individual expression of being rather thoroughly entertained.

Marie's long-lash-shaded eyes were narrowed, emphasizing the sly, insightful, knowing expression of a fox that Cricket recognized all too well. Ann's pretty blue eyes were wide with admiration and delight, just as they always were when she felt deep approval of something Cricket said or did. And Vilma, as always when she felt she'd uncovered something Cricket would rather she not know, arched her eyebrows so high with triumphant understanding that Cricket thought they might leap right off her forehead if she strained them any further.

"What?" Cricket asked, feigning ignorance. Of course she knew the girls found unmeasured humor in the fact that she knew Heathro Thibodaux's evening routine so meticulously. But she wasn't about to let on that there just might be something a little obsessive about it.

"Well, *that's* mighty convenient," Ann said, winking an understanding, pretty blue eye at Cricket.

"My, yes," Vilma added with a giggle.

"So what's our plan then, Cricket?" Marie asked, eyes still narrowed with her signature clever-as-a-fox expression. "Are we just gonna lie in wait, snatch him off his horse when he passes, and tie him up so you can have at him like a kitten to cream?"

Everyone giggled, and Cricket rolled her eyes with exasperation—yet smiling too, for it was a little strange that she knew Heathro Thibodaux's evening path so well. She also knew that if it had been Marie describing Hudson's habit, she'd be teasing Marie instead of Marie teasing her. It was all in good fun between friends, and Cricket knew it.

"No," she answered. "I thought we'd wait until he stops to water his horse and then…and then I'll carefully approach him and…and…"

"And kiss his guts out!" Ann exclaimed.

Marie and Vilma laughed, and Cricket rolled her eyes again. "No, Ann Burroughs. Don't be a ninny-knickers. When he stops to water his horse…I'll…I'll carefully approach him and welcome him to Pike's Creek…just as any other neighborly folks would do."

"Well, I doubt that someone like, say, Mr. Keel would welcome Mr. Thibodaux to town in that way, Cricket Cranford," Vilma teased. "But Widow Rutherford just might."

Cricket straightened her posture, gritting her teeth with determination to not let Vilma or the existence of Widow Rutherford get under her skin.

Ann came to Cricket's defense immediately of course with a scolding response. "After Cricket is finished welcomin' Ranger Thibodaux to town, he won't even remember Widow Rutherford exists."

"That's right," Marie strongly confirmed. She put a comforting, encouraging arm around Cricket's shoulders and said, "You do it, Cricket. You kiss his guts out so he won't ever look twice at Widow Rutherford again."

Vilma shrugged. "Unless he thinks Cricket *is* Widow Rutherford. How ever will he know who is kissin' him if you insist on wearin' that ugly old mask, Cricket?"

Everyone was struck silent—for Vilma did have a valid point.

Over the past week, as Cricket had considered how she would find the courage to not only approach Mr. Thibodaux and welcome him to town but also steal a kiss, she'd come to the conclusion that she would only be able to muster the necessary gumption the task required if she disguised herself. It was one thing for Marie to confess her heart to Hudson Oliver. They'd known each other forever, and, besides, Cricket knew Hudson cared for Marie already. But to waylay Heathro Thibodaux—to steal a kiss from him when he didn't know Cricket from a mangy old mutt—it was apples and onions.

Therefore, Cricket had settled on masking herself a bit in order to conceal her identity. She'd taken a long strip of black cloth left from the new mourning dress Ada had helped her make, fashioned it into a mask by cutting two holes for her eyes, and determined she would simply tie the length of cloth at the back of her head.

Yet now that she stood near the watering trough behind the general store, she realized that for all the courage the anonymity of wearing the mask helped inspire in her, Heathro Thibodaux could well assume that the female bandit who was about to kiss him was indeed the Widow Rutherford! Or any other woman in town, for that matter.

"Vilma's right!" Cricket exclaimed in near panic. "I don't want him thinkin' it was Widow Rutherford who welcomed him to town. He might set out to courtin' her or some such awful thing!"

Marie glared at Vilma, and Ann scolded, "Vilma Stanley! You do beat all!"

"But she's right," Cricket reiterated. "What if—"

"Everybody in town, including Mr. Good-Lookin' Ex-Ranger Man, knows Anastasia Rutherford would never do anything as impulsive or courageous as to ambush him at an old waterin' trough and smooch him straight on the mouth," Marie assured Cricket. "He won't ever in a million years think it was her, Cricket. Don't let your backbone melt now."

"She's right," Vilma agreed with a nod. "Marie's right. Everybody knows Widow Rutherford would never do anything the likes of this, Cricket. I'm truly sorry. I didn't mean to put doubt in your mind. I was just thinkin' out loud and—"

"Well, stop thinkin' at all, Vilma," Ann scolded. "If you please," she added as a softener. Turning to Cricket, she encouraged, "Remember…

we can do anything we set our minds to do, Cricket. Don't you always tell us that?"

Cricket exhaled an exasperated sigh. "Yes…I do." Sighing once more, she straightened her mask and mumbled, "I surely do…dang my own self."

"Shhh!" Marie whispered. "I think I hear someone comin'."

Cricket held her breath and listened. Yes—the rhythm of a horse walking at a slow pace.

"I think it's him!" Ann breathed.

Cricket was simultaneously elated with anticipation and scared to death! Heathro Thibodaux would probably strangle her right then and there—drown her in the watering trough—pull his pistol and belly-shoot her. Yet her next thought was, *But what if he doesn't?* What if he accepted her kiss and let her be on her way? The not knowing was invigorating to an intensity Cricket had never before experienced.

Carefully peeking around the old oak tree behind where the girls had hidden themselves to wait, Marie breathed, "I think it's him. Right there. Isn't that his horse comin' this way?" Marie looked to Cricket.

Anxiously, Cricket peered out from behind the tree into the darkness. Nodding, she whispered, "I told you all. He's as regular as a mornin' rooster."

"Get down, girls," Ann instructed.

Each girl dropped to her belly in the grass beneath the oak—everyone but Cricket.

"Now don't lose your gumption, Cricket," Vilma quietly urged. "Just take a deep breath and do what you've come here to do…which is to show Marie King how it's done, right? That's all."

"I'm already losin' my gumption, Vilma," Cricket rather growled as she watched Heathro Thibodaux dismount, allowing his horse to water at the trough. "This is not an easy thing to do," she whispered to herself.

"Go now, Cricket!" Marie prodded. "Now! Before he leaves!"

Cricket inhaled a deep breath, attempting to muster as much courage as her fighting spirit could. She watched Heathro a moment longer, goose bumps breaking over her arms and legs, and she thought of what a dream-borne pleasure would surely come from feeling his lips pressed to hers.

"I figure…if I hop up onto that old trough, my face oughta be about just level with his…and that's when I'll do it. I'll just jump up on the old trough, and…and then I'll do it." She looked to Vilma, Marie, and Ann for reassurance. "Right?"

"Right," they all whispered with synchronized nods of encouragement.

Cricket's brow puckered, and she bit her lip. Fear was quickly taking over, but she knew Marie must confess her feelings for Hudson that very night—and if Cricket's courage spurred Marie's, then she must do what she'd promised to do.

As she took her first quick steps away from the protection of the oak and the security of friendships, Cricket thought perhaps her heart leapt up into her ears and was doing battle with her eardrums. It was pounding like a locomotive, and she was certain it was just as loud. She thought she might actually faint for a moment with anxiety. But with each step toward Heathro Thibodaux, she continued to breathe— continued to remain conscious.

"Heathro Thibodaux?" Cricket called as she neared him. She didn't want to startle him into shooting her before she'd even had the chance to try to kiss him. But her heart nearly stopped when the handsome Texas Ranger looked up, catching sight of her. He was *so* handsome!

She paused for only a moment and then continued toward him.

"Yeah?" he asked as she reached his position and carefully stepped up onto the old watering trough. She balanced by straddling the trough and placing one foot on either ledge of it.

Her courage instantly began to wane as the beautiful man looked her up and down from head to toe and back, grinning with obvious amusement. "What's all this?" he asked.

Oh, his voice was like some beguiling, mystic spell! Low and clear like the wind through a canyon—warm and enthralling like the feel of the fingers of the same wind through Cricket's hair the time she'd ridden Ann's black thoroughbred, Harley.

"I…I've come to welcome you to Pike's Creek, Mr. Thibodaux," Cricket stammered. "O-officially, that is."

Heathro Thibodaux smiled as he again studied Cricket from head to toe. "Have ya now?" he chuckled.

"Yes, sir," Cricket confirmed. "I figure that no one has ever properly welcomed you…a-and that someone should have…so I'm here to do just that."

Though the only illumination afforded in the darkness was provided by the moon and starlight, it glinted on the gold of his upper-right incisor a moment as he smiled, dazzling Cricket and causing butterflies to hatch in her stomach.

"Is that so?" he asked, still smiling. "And just how do you mean to welcome me to Pike's Creek, sweetie? You gonna rob me or somethin'?"

"No, sir. Not at all," she assured him, still fascinated by how alluringly handsome he was. "You've been chosen to receive reassurance, Mr. Thibodaux…friendship and warmth of community."

"Oh, is that right?" he asked.

"Yes, sir," Cricket assured him, summoning every shred of bravery she never thought she could wrangle.

"And what is this gift?" the once Texas Ranger inquired.

Swallowing the lump of apprehension that had gathered in her throat, Cricket answered, "Why, a-a kiss, Mr. Thibodaux."

Quickly reaching out and taking hold of the front of the black vest the man wore, Cricket pulled him to her before her courage evaporated altogether—and holding her breath, she pressed a warm and rather lingering kiss to his lips.

The kiss lasted only a short time—mere moments. Yet Cricket knew that should she live to be three hundred and thirty-seven years old, her heart would never soar to the heavens on wings of pure rapture the way it had the moment she'd felt the touch of Heathro Thibodaux's lips to hers!

His lips were softer than she'd imagined they would be—smooth and titillatingly balmy. She fancied, during those mere moments that she kissed him, that he did not in any way deny her kiss. Certainly he did not recognizably return it, but at least he didn't push her away at once. At least he didn't draw his gun and shoot her in the guts.

As Cricket ended the kiss she'd given Mr. Thibodaux, she found she was breathless—rather unsteady on her feet.

Using her grip on his vest to steady herself where she stood on the trough, she managed to somehow whisper, "Welcome to Pike's Creek, Mr. Thibodaux."

Cricket didn't expect anything in return for her having offered a brave kiss to the Texas Ranger. Maybe a nod—a quiet, "Thank you." But what she did not expect, however—what she never imagined would happen—was the manner in which the man so quickly turned on her.

A quick gasp escaped her as, instead of offering his thanks for her welcome, Mr. Thibodaux promptly caught Cricket's wrists in his hands. He was all the more intimidating as he leaned closer to her, glaring at her as he spoke.

"You girls need to be a little more careful about what you're playin' at, sweet pea," he said almost threateningly. "You all run around town in the dark wearin' nothin' but your bloomers and gettin' into all sorts of mischief. Well, I'm afraid that one day mischief is gonna sneak up behind you and bite your sweet little fanny, darlin'."

As intimidated and near frightened as she was by Mr. Thibodaux's unexpected reaction to her neighborly offering of support, Cricket's temper was even more piqued.

"First of all, how do you know what we're up to or when we've been about it?" she asked. "And second, we only do kind things for people…to remind them that they're cared for and important. We don't do anything malicious or unkind."

"Well, first of all, missy…just because I don't ranger no more don't mean I'm not still wary and keepin' my eyes on the things around me. And I understand that your intentions are good—I really do." Cricket fancied his grip on her wrists only tightened as she struggled a little to try and free herself. "But you girls ain't seen what I've seen in this world," he continued. "It ain't every man that would allow one of you all to hop up on a waterin' trough and kiss him the way you just did me…and then let it go at just that."

Cricket rolled her eyes, sighed with exasperation, and blushed with humiliation. It was obvious Heathro Thibodaux didn't share the same vision of community and brotherly love that she and her friends did. It was obvious his previous career and experience had hardened him and harnessed him with a suspicious nature—and her temper softened a little, causing a smidgen of her exasperation to flee her being.

"Oh, for pity's sake, Mr. Thibodaux," Cricket rather scolded. "This is Pike's Creek you're livin' in now. What in the world could ever happen here? There's not a man in this town that would…that would take advantage of our kindheartedness."

"You're sure about that, are ya?" he asked as the frown on his handsome brow deepened.

"Of course," she assured him.

"There's not one man in this town that you don't trust?" he asked again.

"Not one," Cricket answered with full confidence.

"Are you willin' to bet your *life* on that?"

Cricket frowned again as Mr. Thibodaux's grip tightened at her wrists—as his eyes narrowed and his gaze fell to her mouth.

"M-my life?" she stammered, suddenly overwhelmed with a mixture of emotions—mingled fear and exhilaration. "What on earth do you mean?"

"I asked you if you're willin' to bet your life on the fact that there ain't one man in Pike's Creek who would take advantage of your *kindheartedness*, girl," he growled.

"W-well, yes. I mean no…not my *life*. I-I mean…yes, I guess," Cricket stammered. "I don't think any man here would—"

"That's just it," he interrupted. "You girls don't think. You run around town, doin' kind things for folks…but you never stop to think whether or not all folks are gonna be kind to you in return. So now it's up to me to teach you a lesson."

Somehow, and quick as a rabbit too, Heathro Thibodaux pushed Cricket's arms around to her back, anchoring her wrists tightly in one strong hand, as his other hand roughly took hold of her chin.

"Say hello to the one man in Pike's Creek that you better not ever bet your life on, little blossom bottom," he mumbled a moment before his mouth ground to hers.

Cricket winced, a quiet squeal of distress sounding in her throat as Mr. Thibodaux pulled her against him, slipped his hand to the back of her head, and physically commanded her to submit to the hot, wet kiss he was forcing to her mouth—to her *mouth*, not just to her tender and quickly bruising lips.

Yet Cricket was grateful for her quick wit and instincts, as well as her gift of sympathy, for they whispered to her not to fight him—that the more she fought the Texas Ranger and his ravaging kiss, the more he would endeavor to dominate her in proving his point. And so she quit struggling, quit trying to pull her face away from his. And when she did quit struggling, she immediately sensed not only his frustration but also the softening of his assault on her. In fact, in the very last moments that his open mouth endeavored to more gently mingle with hers, Cricket felt a wild quiver of pleasure race over her spine.

His dominating kiss ended, and he released his hold on her as he growled, "Still willin' to bet your life on me, girl?" he growled. Wagging a scolding index finger at her, he warned, "You girls settle this mischief down before you find yourselves in real trouble one day."

But Cricket, left utterly confused and torn between lingering delight and dazed distress, felt abruptly weak-kneed and began to teeter where she stood straddling the water in the trough.

"Now get down from there before you fall and hurt yourself," Mr. Thibodaux said, reaching over to take hold of his horse's reins. "And you girls quit this runnin' all over like a bunch of—"

Cricket teetered to her left—tried to regain her balance by leaning back. She was unsuccessful, however, and felt her knees buckle and her body begin to fall—even for the fact that Heathro Thibodaux hollered, "Hold on!" as he reached out and tried to grab hold of her. But he wasn't quick enough, and Cricket gasped as she tumbled backward into the water of the trough.

The splash of her landing was enormous and startled Ranger Thibodaux's horse. The horse reared, and Heathro soothed, "Whoa there, Archie…whoa." Immediately he reached into the trough, taking hold of Cricket's arms and hauling her out.

"Are you all right, girl?" he asked. He seemed genuinely concerned, but Cricket didn't want his concern. She was too humiliated—too disappointed by the outcome of her "welcoming him to town."

"I'm fine," she tersely answered, tears filling her eyes. "Just fine." Scowling at him as she wrung water out of her petticoats, she said, "Welcome to Pike's Creek, Mr. Thibodaux. I hope it suits you."

Then, crossly flicking water at him, she turned and marched back toward the oak tree where she knew kindhearted friends would be waiting for her.

"Cricket!" Ann exclaimed as Cricket reached the tree and began wringing more water from her petticoats. "Are you all right? We couldn't hear a thing the two of you were sayin' to one another." She bit her lip as she studied Cricket for a moment, adding, "But we heard the splash well enough. Did you slip or somethin'?"

They hadn't heard the conversation? Cricket thought. Not one word of the exchange between her and Heathro?

"You couldn't hear us?" she asked, unbelieving.

"Nope," Marie confirmed with obvious disappointment. She grinned then, however—her foxish, sly grin—and said, "But that was sure some welcomin' kiss you gave him. I thought we were gonna be waitin' here all night before it ended."

Cricket glanced back over her shoulder toward the watering trough. Her heart sank to the pit of her stomach with miserable disappointment when she saw that Heathro Thibodaux had already mounted his horse in preparation to leave. She heard him growl, "Yaw!" and watched the horse break into an immediate gallop.

"So?" Vilma prodded. "What did he say? Was he mad or glad? For Pete's sake, Cricket, you've got to tell us everything! We couldn't hear a whisper!"

Full realization washed over Cricket then. They hadn't heard the scolding Heathro Thibodaux had given her—hadn't clearly seen the kiss. From where the girls stood behind the old oak, it must've looked like Cricket simply kissed Heathro, that he'd accepted it, and therefore that the kiss had extended far beyond anyone's expectation.

She looked to Marie and saw the hope shining in her foxish eyes—the hope that if a near total stranger had accepted a kiss from Cricket, then surely Hudson Oliver would not spurn hers. And she knew what she must say.

"He thanked me for welcomin' him," Cricket lied.

"He did?" Marie exclaimed. The hope was welling so thick in Marie that Cricket could almost smell it.

"H-he did," Cricket continued. "He said that he was grateful for the welcome, and…and once I started kissing him…he kissed me back."

Ann's blue eyes widened with wild enthusiasm. "Was it…was it simply wonderful, Cricket? Kissing him? Did it make you feel…well…wonderful?"

Cricket forced a smile as she stripped the wet mask from her head. "Well, if you want me to be entirely honest…"

"Oh, definitely!" Vilma assured her, smiling with impatient anticipation.

Cricket's smile broadened as it became more natural and not so feigned. "Then I'll say it this way. I have never in all my life experienced anything the likes of what just happened between me and Mr. Heathro Thibodaux!" It was the truth after all. She had answered Ann's question with complete honesty. Good or bad, blissful or frightening, Cricket's moments of kissing Heathro Thibodaux truly had been like nothing she'd ever known.

Cricket's three friends squealed with delight, giggled, and threw their arms around her in warm embrace.

"How marvelous, Cricket," Ann giggled. "You did it! You kissed him! No matter what happens now…you'll always know what it feels like to kiss Mr. Thibodaux."

"Yep," Cricket said as more tears filled her eyes. She felt unhappy, confused, spurned. And yet at the same time, a strange thrill would well up in her each time she relived the moments with Heathro in her thoughts.

"But why did you fall?" Vilma asked. "It's not like you to be so clumsy."

Leave it to Vilma to point out the worst part of the event.

"Don't you know anything about kissin', Vilma Stanley?" Ann asked. She rolled her pretty blue eyes and explained, "When a man kisses you the right way, it makes you dizzy and turns your knees to raspberry jam." Ann looked to Cricket. "Isn't that right, Cricket?"

"Yes…that's exactly what happened," Cricket fibbed, smiling and nodding with rigid affirmation. "I-I was so overwhelmed by the bliss of it all…that my knees wouldn't hold me up any longer. Mr. Thibodaux did try to catch me, but I was already too far gone."

The girls all giggled and sighed, and Cricket was relieved that they believed her. And after all, it was mostly the truth.

But the evening wasn't about Cricket; it was about Mrs. Maloney, Mr. Keel, and Mr. Thibodaux—and it was about Marie and Hudson Oliver. Cricket knew the faster she turned her attention to ensuring that Marie captured Hudson for her own, the more quickly her own poor experience with the ex-Texas Ranger would begin to fade.

"All right then," she sighed. Turning to Marie, Cricket began to unfasten her black corset. "I'm as wet as a rat in a barrel of whiskey. You're changing clothes before you meet up with Hudson anyway…so might I please strip off these soakin' things and borrow yours?"

"Of course!" Marie exclaimed. "But I'm so nervous, Cricket. What if—"

"None of that, Marie King," Cricket interrupted, however. "If I can face Heathro Thibodaux like I just did…then you can confess your heart to Hudson Oliver."

Marie nodded and began to unbutton her own black corset in preparation for changing her clothing.

"Did he recognize you, do you think, Cricket?" Vilma asked as she carefully removed Marie's best dress from the flour sack Marie had stored it in.

Cricket shook her head. "No. No, I don't think he had any idea who I was." That part was the truth. Although she knew Heathro Thibodaux probably suspected just who made up the band of Pike's

Creek do-gooders, she was certain he'd had no idea which one had actually kissed him. After all, in truth Heathro Thibodaux didn't know Cricket from a fly on a pile of horse manure.

Heathro slammed the door behind him. The house was hot. He'd forgotten to leave some windows open while he'd been gone, and the heat of the house did nothing to lighten his flustered and frustrated demeanor.

As he stormed around the house, unlatching every window and throwing the framed panes open wide, he grumbled to himself.

"Silly girls," he growled. "And she just waltzed right up to me in black underwear, kissin' me square on the mouth like I was her baby brother." Heathro stripped off his shirt, tossed it on the table, and plopped down on a kitchen chair. As he tugged his boots off, he continued to vent aloud to himself. "Why, I mighta just tossed her over my shoulder, drug her off to the nearest barn, and gone about any business with her I had a mind to." He paused, sighed, dropped his boots to the floor, and continued, "Not that I woulda ever really done the likes, of course...but it's the principle of the thing. I mean, who does this girl think she is? Walkin' up to strangers and bein' so intimate. I mighta been crawlin' with disease or somethin'. I might be a lunger, for all she knows!"

He turned in the chair, rested his arms on the table, and hung his head—weary from a day of hard work and from scolding the charming girl who had offered him about the sweetest moment he'd ever known.

Still, he knew he couldn't let his hardened guard down, and so he mumbled, "Where were the damsels in distress anyhow? Ain't it the man who's supposed do the flirtin' and scandalous kiss-stealin'? What happened to the days where the *man* hunted out the girl and wooed and won her, I ask you?"

The truth was Heathro felt sick to his stomach—ailing for the way he'd treated the poor little filly who was just trying to do the neighborly thing and welcome him to town. She'd tasted as sweet as honey— sweeter even—and he knew it could've done his soul good to kiss her back all tender and beguiling like a good man would've.

But he couldn't let his guard down even for a moment, so he ranted, "Seems like all the girls around here are either half-neked in the swimmin' hole or runnin' up to strange men and kissin' 'em all the damn time! What kind of a town is this? Don't these people teach their daughters what men can do? What bad men are capable of?"

Heathro closed his eyes as the vision of eight bloodied, broken bodies flashed in his mind—dead young women strewn over murderous rocks when they should've been growing up to be lying in the arms of the men they would've loved and married. He stomach felt worse— threatened to heave for a moment—so he turned his thoughts back to the girls of Pike's Creek, the little do-gooding so-and-sos.

Truth was, the world needed more women like them—more women like the sweet, blossom-bottomed, sugar-mouthed honey that had kissed him.

"Heathro Thibodaux, you dirty son of a..." he began.

He inhaled a deep breath, exhaling slowly to calm himself. It wasn't his fault after all. Someone had to teach those girls a lesson—even if it did mean he'd had to contribute to the loss of one girl's innocence. He thought of how horrified the girl must've been when he forced such an assaulting response to her kindnesses. He hoped it hadn't been her first kiss, God help him. But what else could he have done? She couldn't go around kissing just any man she chose to.

And then he really began to feel nauseated as he wondered how many other men the girl had kissed the way she'd kissed him. Had be been the first and only male newcomer to Pike's Creek that the girl had offered a part of herself to?

As his stomach churned, threatening to empty itself, Heath grumbled, "It's just the damn heat. It's hotter than hell in this house!"

Fairly leaping up from his chair, he stomped to the kitchen door, nearly knocking it off its hinges when he pushed it open, and stepped out into the night. Angrily he sat down hard on the top porch step and inhaled a breath of cool, refreshing air. It did help settle the sickness in his stomach a mite—helped his anger lessen a bit.

Heathro looked up to the sky—watched the stars twinkling and the moon beaming as brightly as a shiny silver coin. He wondered if he'd been the last victim of the Pike's Creek do-gooders that night. He paid close attention to everything around him, and in doing so, he surmised that the girls typically performed four acts of kindness each time they went about their mischief. He wondered who else had been chosen besides him. He wondered if any other men had been chosen— and the thought that there might well have been another man who received what he had perturbed him all the more.

Still, he determined to calm himself. He'd listen up to everyone in town the next day, keep a watchful eye, and discover who else had been chosen and what they'd received.

Meanwhile, the memory of the girl's kiss washed over him, softening him up at last. He swore he could still taste her mouth in his—and it was like sugar. He shook his head, knowing the poor little thing must've been horrified at the way he'd kissed her—practically devoured her.

"That's right, Heathro Thibodaux," he sighed to himself. "You're as mean and offensive as they come."

He leaned back against the porch, closed his eyes, and just tried to breathe normally. But he couldn't quit thinking about the poor little blossom-bottomed do-gooder. And he couldn't keep his mouth from wanting to taste hers again.

CHAPTER SIX

"You can do it, Marie," Vilma whispered. "If Cricket can walk right up to Heathro Thibodaux and kiss him, who she hardly knows from Adam, then you can surely go over there and knock on Hudson's window to summon him out."

"I know, I know," Marie said. She turned to face Ann and asked, "Do I look all right? Is my hair too mussed or anything?"

"You look perfect, Marie!" Ann assured her friend.

"Cricket?" Marie asked, turning to Cricket.

Cricket smiled. Certainly the hurt in her over the experience with Heathro Thibodaux stung as painfully as it had half an hour earlier, but she still smiled—for Marie looked radiant.

"You look lovely, Marie," Cricket said. "Hudson won't be able to take his eyes off of you."

"Yes, Marie," Vilma agreed when Marie turned to Vilma for reassurance. "You look ever so beautiful."

"All right then," Marie sighed, trying to be brave. "Wish me luck, girls. I'm off."

Cricket's heart was beating with such brutal anxiety that she was certain the inside of her chest was bruising. Hudson wouldn't spurn Marie—she was certain of it. Yet there is always that measure of doubt to cause apprehension.

"There she goes," Ann whispered. Since Marie was the one doing the doings, Ann took over as narrator. "She's almost to his bedroom window."

Cricket tried to breathe easily, but it was difficult. She felt Vilma take her hand and glanced over to see the worry on her face as well.

"I just keep tellin' myself that things went just fine between you and Mr. Thibodaux…so they oughta fly like fireworks on the Fourth between Marie and Hudson," she said. "Right?"

"Right," Cricket assured her—though the comparison to what she hoped would transpire between Marie and Hudson was apples and onions compared with what had really happened between her and Heathro Thibodaux.

"She's at the window!" Ann whispered. "She's pausin'. I think she's scared."

Marie glanced back to where Cricket, Ann, and Vilma stood peeking out from around the corner of the Hudsons' barn. She did look frightened—pale as a ghost and close to panic.

"Go on!" Cricket whispered, gesturing to Marie that she should knock on the window. She nodded with encouragement and breathed a sigh of relief when Marie's expression changed to that of determination.

"Here she goes," Ann said. "She's raisin' her fist. She knocked!"

No one drew a breath. They simply stared at Marie standing outside of Hudson Oliver's bedroom window and waited.

Marie glanced back to Cricket, and Cricket gestured that she should knock a second time. Marie did knock a second time, and almost before she'd finished, the window opened wide.

Hudson Oliver himself leaned out the window and asked, "Who's there?"

"It's m-me, Hudson," Marie stammered. "Marie King."

"Marie King?" Hudson repeated.

"Yes. I-I was wonderin' if you might be willin' to come out and have a word with me for a moment," Marie said.

"Sure," Hudson agreed. "I'll be right out."

"B-but," Marie added as Hudson started to turn. He paused and looked at her. "But don't tell anyone why you're comin' outside, all right?"

"All right," Hudson said, smiling. "Hang on. I'll be right there."

Cricket exhaled the breath she'd been holding—heard Ann and

Vilma do the same. She looked at them to see smiles spreading across their faces.

"Well, that was easy," Ann said.

"So far, at least," Vilma added.

"Yeah. It wasn't bad at all," Cricket happily chirped.

"So far, at least," Vilma reminded.

"Always the ray of hope there, Vilma," Ann grumbled.

"Shhh," Cricket hushed. "Here comes Hudson."

They watched as Hudson Oliver—tall, dark, and handsome as a dream—sauntered out the kitchen door and around to his bedroom window.

He smiled when he stopped to stand directly in front of Marie. "Hey there, Marie. What're you doin' out here in the middle of the night?"

"I...I've come to talk to you about somethin'," she answered.

"Me?" he asked, pointing to himself with one thumb. "About what?"

"Well...I-I heard that your family is plannin' on leavin' Pike's Creek," Marie stammered as she gazed up into Hudson's face like a lovesick puppy. Hudson was quite a bit taller than Marie, and Cricket knew Marie must feel intimidated by the way Hudson was staring down at her. After all, Cricket wasn't even the one speaking to him, and *she* felt intimidated just watching.

"Yep," Hudson affirmed with a nod. "The family is movin' to San Antonio. My daddy's mother passed on last month and left him everything she owned...includin' her house and the family business." He shrugged. "So we're headin' out there in a week or so."

"Oh," Marie managed. She dropped her gaze for a moment, and Cricket could feel the fear and trepidation washing over her friend. It was a brazen thing to do: to tell a man you cared for him and beg him to abandon his parents and siblings, especially when Marie wasn't even certain Hudson cared for her. But Cricket was sure—ninety percent sure anyway.

"Come on, Marie. You can do this!" Cricket heard Ann whisper.

Cricket silently prayed that Marie's courage would not fail her.

"Oh, God…don't let her fear win over," the preacher's daughter prayed aloud, however.

"Is that what you came out here to ask me about?" Hudson inquired. "You come all the way out here this late to ask me about when the family is movin'?"

"Yes," Marie fibbed. She recovered quickly, however, and stammered, "Well, n-no. Actually…the truth of it is…"

"Look up at him," Cricket whispered. "Come on, Marie. Just look up at him." Cricket thought her own heart was going to burst with frustration—either break or beat itself to death with the brutal hammering of agony for Marie's sake.

But then Marie did look up at Hudson, and Cricket could see the determination returning to her pretty face.

"Actually, I came to ask you not to leave," Marie confessed, gazing up into Hudson's beloved face. "I-I came to ask you to stay in Pike's Creek…not to go with your family to San Antonio."

Hudson's strong brow puckered. "Why? Why would I stay in Pike's Creek when my whole family is movin' on?"

Cricket feared she might lose the contents of her stomach to heaving caused by apprehension. He'd asked so forthrightly! Just come right out and asked. Cricket wondered whether she would have the courage to answer Hudson with just as much frankness as Marie had to do in that next moment. Would she? Could she do what she had encouraged Marie to do? And was Hudson as dim-witted and unobservant as he sounded? Or was he simply trying to draw a confession out of Marie?

"She's not gonna be able to tell him!" Ann whispered to Cricket. "I don't think she can find it in her to simply—"

"Because I want you to," Marie answered Hudson suddenly.

Cricket felt her eyebrows spring into arches as her mouth dropped open in delighted and relieved astonishment. In fact, she knew her expression was not so different from Hudson's—for the smile that spread across his face was as wide as the Mississippi.

"You want me to stay here?" Hudson asked.

"Yes. I-I want you to stay here in Pike's Creek, Hudson," Marie managed. "I don't want you to go. I want you stay here…because

I…I-I…" She seemed breathless for a moment—took a step back from Hudson.

Cricket held her breath again, whispering to herself, "Do it now, Marie. Now. Don't wait!" She knew that if Marie waited much longer to finish casting her lure—if she waited until Hudson questioned her again—the moment would be lost. She needed to kiss him that moment—that very moment! The anticipation, the desperation for Marie's sake aching in her, was torture.

"She's gonna miss her chance!" Vilma whined to Cricket. Cricket saw the tears in Vilma's eyes and knew Vilma and Ann (who was literally on her knees, hands clasped, head bowed, and whispering prayer) were in nearly as much agony as Cricket was.

Hudson breathed a chuckle. "Well, that's awful sweet, Marie," he said. "But my family needs me to—"

He was interrupted—his sentence hanging unfinished in midair as Marie reached out, taking hold of the lapels of the dark gray vest he wore.

"But I need you more," Marie said, her voice quivering with emotion. "I love you more, Hudson."

Cricket heard Vilma and Ann gasp as Marie then lifted herself on the tips of her toes and kissed Hudson Oliver square on the mouth.

Cricket watched—waited for the lingering kiss to end—waited to see what Hudson Oliver would do. But what he did was nearly as unexpected to Cricket as what Heathro Thibodaux had done. Cricket had hoped Hudson wouldn't spurn or humiliate Marie—hoped he'd be willing to discuss the matter with her. But what actually happened was astonishing.

When Marie ended the kiss, stepped back, and cast her gaze to the ground, Hudson Oliver simply took hold of her shoulders, turned her so that her back was against the house under his bedroom window, and said, "Well, why didn't you say so before, darlin'?" the moment before he kissed her.

And what a kiss it was! Cricket knew her eyes were bugging out like a mouse caught in a dead man's fist. She knew because when she glanced to Vilma and Ann, their eyes were just as bugged out—their mouths hanging just as agape.

"Well…I didn't quite expect this as his response," Vilma whispered as she watched Hudson gather Marie into his arms—watched Marie's arms slide around Hudson's neck as she returned his impassioned kiss.

"I dreamed of it though," Ann giggled. "Oh, look at them! I swear he's settin' her stockin's on fire!"

Cricket smiled as she watched Hudson making sudden and passionate love to Marie—right there under his own bedroom window. "I knew he loved her," she whispered. "I knew it!"

The sight of Hudson and Marie lost in one another's wildly impassioned affections healed Cricket's heart a bit from the sting of what had happened with Mr. Thibodaux. Marie would be happy—happy with Hudson Oliver. They'd be married soon, she was sure of it. And one day, little dark-haired angels would be playing at their feet. Maybe Marie's babies would call her Auntie Cricket. Maybe they'd play with the children Cricket hoped to have one day.

"I feel better," Cricket sighed.

Vilma looked to her, frowning. "Better? How could you feel any better than you already did? The goin's-on between you and that tall drink of water Heathro Thibodaux didn't look much different than what's happenin' right now between Marie and Hudson."

"It was apples and onions, Vilma Stanley," came Cricket's response. "I mean, look at them." She gestured to where Hudson now had Marie pushed back against the outer wall of his house again, driving such a kiss to her that Cricket wondered how on earth the girl could breathe.

"That's love, Vilma," she stated. "That's deep, everlasting, true, true love." She exhaled a sigh of contentment for Marie's sake. "Heathro Thibodaux doesn't know me from a fried turkey gizzard. But Hudson knows Marie. His eyes know her, his heart knows her, and his very soul knows her."

"Looks like his lips know her pretty well now too," Ann giggled.

Vilma returned her attention to Marie and Hudson, sighing as she watched them embracing, kissing—resplendent in the joy of what was obviously mutual adoration. "How perfectly wonderful would it be to have a man love you like that, girls?" Vilma asked.

"I imagine it would be as perfectly wonderful as it looks," Cricket sighed, unable to keep her thoughts from drifting back to the moments with Heathro Thibodaux—unable to keep from wishing the scene between her and the ex-Texas Ranger had been a mirror's reflection of what was now happening between Hudson and Marie.

"Well, I suppose we should leave them to their sparkin'," Ann suggested.

"We certainly should," Cricket agreed. "Let's head home and get some sleep, ladies. We'll leave Marie to being breathless in Hudson's arms and get ourselves to bed."

Ann giggled. "And maybe I can dream about Mr. Keel, and you can dream about your kiss with Mr. Thibodaux, right, Cricket?"

"Right," Cricket answered, forcing a smile.

Ann looked to Vilma. "And since Vilma refuses to tell us who *she* spends her nights dreamin' about…we'll just have to say sweet dreams about whoever he is, Vilma."

Vilma smiled, curtsied, and said, "Thank you, Ann Burroughs. I'm sure they will be very sweet."

With one last glance at Hudson and Marie, who hadn't yet lessened the intensity of their passionate kissing in the least, Cricket turned and followed Ann and Vilma into the night. Another night of mischief was finished, and Cricket felt the familiar descent of her spirits with it. As wonderful and satisfying as it was to do nice things for other people, Cricket always experienced a somewhat melancholy hour or so once the shenanigans were over. For one thing, she was always very tired. But the thing that disappointed her most was that it was over.

Oh, she always perked up after a while—once she'd gotten home, changed into her soft nightgown, and collapsed onto her comfortable bed. Once she'd begun to review the shenanigans over in her mind—to envision the smiles, laughter, and tears of those whose hearts had been lightened—then her feelings of being let down would disappear.

Still, as Cricket made her way back home, quietly climbed in through her bedroom window, and readied for bed, she wondered whether this time her spirits would ever rebound the way they normally did. She thought of Mrs. Maloney—her joyful tears at having found the teapot waiting for her on her front porch. She thought of Mr. Keel and how Ann's quilt would brighten his lonely home and bring him comfort. She thought of Marie, no doubt still locked in the arms of her lover—imagined how blissful she must feel. Yet no amount of forcing her thoughts to linger on the other townsfolk of Pike's Creek who had been touched that night kept them from returning to her experience with Heathro Thibodaux.

At first she thought that the only way her exchange with Mr. Thibodaux could've been worse was if he'd actually pulled his gun and shot her. Yet in the next moment, even that didn't seem more dismal an outcome.

Cricket climbed into bed, closed her eyes, and attempted to go to sleep. But sleep didn't come—only visions of Heathro Thibodaux— only a fascinating tingling on her lips each time she thought of kissing him.

His voice resounded in her mind, repeating the warnings of what men who were not to be trusted might do to innocent girls. Cricket knew his experience the year before—the death of the abducted girls he had been unable to rescue—was what caused him to be so threatening and calloused toward her. The fact was that people made judgments and decisions based on their personal experience—and Ranger Thibodaux's experience where men and young women were concerned had been far, far more than merely tragic. They'd been depraved, heinous, and wretchedly mournful.

Perhaps she should have expected him to be wary, harsh, and reprimanding considering what he'd been through, seen, and felt responsible for. But Cricket knew she could have had no way of knowing it.

She felt so saddened for him. A good man would blame himself for what happened to the abducted girls, even though it was no fault of his and could not have been in any way avoided. Good men were like that. Her father was like that.

When Cricket's mother had fallen from her father's horse and died instantly of a broken neck, Zeke Cranford blamed himself. He had been the one who had purchased the horse, ridden the animal for four years. It was his fault the horse was in the corral in the first place. At least, that was the way Zeke saw it. He never considered the mountain lion that had spooked the horse or the rock that had been where it lay for hundreds of years or the happenstance that his wife's neck would strike the rock when she was thrown. No. To Zeke Cranford, his wife's death had been his fault and his alone.

Cricket knew it was just what Heathro Thibodaux felt. In his mind, he should've been able to kill all those outlaws with his bare hands in one sweeping moment—or grip the arm of the last girl to go over the cliff and save her and the other seven tied to her.

Thus, she began to feel somewhat comforted about his treatment of her that night. He knew true evil and ugliness—had walked hand-in-hand with it—had been beaten, shot, and nearly killed by it. It was no wonder he should warn her to be careful.

Cricket closed her eyes and called up the memory of kissing him—of the moment her lips first pressed to Mr. Thibodaux's. Instantaneously her body erupted with goose bumps, her lips tingling with the fleeting feel of kissing him—with the sudden awareness of the manner in which he had crushed his mouth to hers. However lascivious it had been, the memory of it whisked Cricket to moments of sudden breathlessness. She thought of the true intimacy of the kiss Heathro had forced upon her, and she was suddenly and overwhelmingly distraught that she did not accept it and, in truth, bathe in the wonder of it when she'd had the chance.

Heathro Thibodaux had kissed her—fairly made love to her right then and there while she stood on the watering trough! And she had failed to realize the wonder of it until that very moment.

Yes, he'd scolded her. Yes, he'd threatened her and implied she was ignorant. But the fact remained that, though his intentions were certainly to frighten and horrify her, he *had* indeed kissed her! His lips had taken hers; his mouth had tasted hers. His hand had carefully cradled her chin and cheeks, not brutally pained them as his mouth had worked to discourage her from trusting the men in Pike's Creek.

It had not been a tender, loving kiss he'd forced to her mouth—but it had been his kiss.

Cricket realized then that although it was certainly not the kiss she would've dreamt of receiving from him, still it was Heathro Thibodaux's kiss. He'd kissed her, and that was that. It was what she would choose to remember from that night. Not his harsh manner or reprimanding words. Not his vexation or no doubt painful memories. No. Cricket would cherish the simple truth that, in the end, Heathro Thibodaux had returned her kiss after all.

CHAPTER SEVEN

"Well?" Ann prodded.

Marie was grinning like a mule eating briars. She'd been with Hudson, and it had made her late arriving at the old Morgan place.

Friday night had been epic for many reasons where Cricket and her friends' do-gooding shenanigans were concerned. Of course, for Cricket the evening had been bittersweet. For the four days and nights since she'd kissed Heathro Thibodaux in welcoming him to Pike's Creek, she could hardly think of anything else—her emotions constantly vacillating between euphoria and humiliation.

But for Marie, the outcome of confessing her feelings to Hudson Oliver couldn't have been more perfect. And now Ann, Vilma, and Cricket waited very impatiently to hear what had happened when Hudson informed his parents he wouldn't be moving to San Antonio with the rest of the family.

"Come on, Marie!" Vilma whined. "We've been waitin' on pins and needles all afternoon!"

Marie's smile broadened. "Well, when Hudson told his folks that he was plannin' on stayin' here in Pike's Creek to court me…all they did was ask him to help them move down to San Antonio. They weren't even angry or anything!"

Cricket squealed with delight, clapping her hands together as Ann threw her arms around Marie in an affectionate, happy embrace.

Vilma pursed her lips and exhaled a heavy sigh. "Thank the Lord!"

she exclaimed. "I was so afraid somethin' might happen to interfere. Oh, I'm so happy for you, Marie."

"Oh, Marie!" Cricket giggled. "You are gonna be Mrs. Hudson Oliver before the summer is out. I just know it!"

Marie laughed, looked heavenward, and said, "Oh, I do hope so."

"You will," Cricket assured her. "I'm tinglin' from my head to my toes with knowin' it!"

Vilma smiled and, winking at Cricket, teased, "That's pill bugs tinglin' your toes, Cricket Cranford. You're standin' in a whole mess of them…and that's what you get for always strippin' off your shoes and stockin's the way you always do in the summer."

Cricket squealed—this time with horror—and began hopping around as she looked down at the old Morgan house floor.

"She's only teasin' you, Cricket," Ann giggled. "There ain't any pill bugs underfoot." Ann looked to Vilma and scolded, "You're awful, Vilma Stanley. You about scared her to death."

"Vilma!" Cricket scolded, lightly slapping Vilma on one shoulder. "You gave me a fit of the willies! For Pete's sake!"

"Well, one of these days you're gonna get caught in a predicament without your stockin's and shoes on…and heaven help you when you do," Vilma nagged. "You're lucky your feet aren't covered in slivers and burrs."

"So Hudson's gonna go with his family…just long enough to move them?" Ann asked as everyone returned to Marie and the delicious, romantic love story unfolding between Marie and Hudson Oliver.

Marie nodded. "Mmm-hmm. He thinks he'll be gone about ten days to two weeks." An expression of worry briefly passed over Marie's face, but then resplendence renewed itself there. "But then he'll be back, and we'll just set into courtin', I suppose."

"Oh, Marie," Ann sighed, "it's just all so romantical! I just love hearin' about you and Hudson…all your sparkin' and such."

Marie bit her lip with barely restrained delight and sighed. After a moment, however, she gasped, obviously having just remembered something.

"Oh, but, Ann," she began, "did you tell them about Mr. Keel yet?"

Ann shook her head—blushed the color of Rhode Island radishes. "Did you tell us what, Ann?" Cricket asked.

When Ann only continued to blush, Marie answered, "Did she tell you about what happened with Mr. Keel?"

"No, indeed," Cricket answered, her eyebrows arching with charmed anticipation as she looked to Ann. "Do tell, Ann Burroughs. What happened between you and Mr. Keel?"

"Well, nothin' really," Ann said, tucking a strand of loose hair behind one ear. Cricket smiled—for the pleasure on Ann's face would've been obvious to a blind duck.

"Oh, go on, Ann. Tell them!" Marie prodded. She looked to Vilma and Cricket and added, "And it wasn't nothin'."

"Ann?" Vilma began, "are you holdin' back some scandalous information concernin' yourself and Mr. Keel?"

"No. Not at all," Ann admitted. She began to wring her hands and blush an even deeper hue of red. "It's just that…well…yesterday in town…I was walkin' along to the general store. Mama needed some buttons."

"And…" Vilma prodded.

"And…and I was just walkin' along…when all of a sudden, I hear the most divinely deep, masculine voice say, 'Afternoon, Miss Burroughs.' And I looked to see it was Mr. Keel!" Ann explained breathlessly.

"Oooo!" Cricket cooed with delight. "Did he look right at you too?"

Ann nodded, blushed almost violet, and said, "And he smiled and winked at me! He winked…right at me! He knew it was me he was winkin' at!"

"Mr. Keel?" Vilma exclaimed. "Mr. Cooper Keel…the same Mr. Keel who never smiles…ever?"

Ann nodded. "And he winked! I mean, he truly did wink at me!"

"When Ann told me about it," Marie began, "she said she thought Mr. Keel only winked at her because he thinks she's a nice little schoolgirl. But I told her…no, sirree! He winked at her because she's a beautiful woman who caught his eye."

"That's exactly right," Cricket agreed.

"Definitely!" Vilma affirmed.

"I just thought I might faint dead away with happiness!" Ann sighed. She closed her eyes for a moment, a dreamy smile caressing her sweet face. "I can still hear his voice in my head." She opened her eyes, nodded, and added, "At night...when it's very quiet...I can still hear his voice speaking to me if I listen very hard."

Cricket sighed too, for her heart was fluttering just as if it were a giant butterfly caged in her bosom instead of a vital organ meant to pump her blood. She could feel Ann's joy—and Marie's—and it was wonderful!

"In fact, I was in such a hurry to get here to tell you all about Mr. Keel speaking to me—and the wink—that I rode Harley as fast I could!" She giggled. "I'm sure that horse is wondering what in all the world had gotten into me."

"He's probably hopin' Mr. Keel will wink at you every day...if it means he gets to ride like the racehorse he was born to be," Vilma offered.

"Probably," Ann giggled.

"And surely you're still floatin' on air after that...that exchange between you and Mr. Thibodaux, Cricket," Marie teased. "Isn't that right?"

"Absolutely!" Cricket half fibbed, half told the truth.

"Well, now it's Vilma's turn," Ann suggested. "Who do you fancy in Pike's Creek, Vilma? I've had a smile and wink from Mr. Keel, Marie is about to become engaged to Hudson Oliver, and Cricket will always know what it's like to kiss Heathro Thibodaux. Now how about you? You never have told us who you fancy."

Vilma sighed. "Well, that's because...well, in truth, I just haven't fancied anyone in quite some time." She quickly added, "But I'll let you girls know as soon as I do."

Cricket felt her eyes narrow as she studied Vilma. There was something Vilma wasn't telling them.

When they'd been schoolgirls, it had forever and always been Vilma who had been the one to fall so desperately in love, with a different boy every other month, that Cricket, Marie, and Ann began to wonder if there were something wrong with her. When they were nine years old, Vilma had fallen in love with Isaiah Bentley one week and then turned right around and fell in love with Taylor Samuels the next. After that, for about a month, Marie was certain that Vilma was set on a bad path where men were concerned and would surely end up working as a saloon girl in New Orleans.

But now that Cricket thought about it, Vilma Stanley had not mentioned being in love with anyone in over a year—and that didn't seem right. There was definitely something Vilma wasn't telling her friends. Yet Cricket sensed that they should not press her—not yet.

"Promise you'll spill your secret when some cowboy does steal your heart, Vilma?" Marie asked.

"Of course!" Vilma giggled. "Now…let's sit down and talk about our upcomin' shenanigans, shall we? These things take some plannin', you know."

"Yes, they do," Cricket sighed, pulling up one of the old Morgan chairs and taking her seat. She could see Vilma was uncomfortable, and Cricket was determined to soothe her. "I was thinkin' on makin' a doll for that little Pomroy girl. She seems so sad since Mrs. Pomroy died havin' her baby last spring."

"I think that's a lovely idea, Cricket," Vilma said, taking a seat of her own and picking up her pen and inkwell from their place at her feet. "Now…who's next?"

Cricket inhaled the comforting fragrances of summer—the green pasture grass, wildflowers, trees—everything beautiful nature offered in warm weather. The grass was cool and refreshing to her feet, and she smiled at the way it tickled when it slipped between her toes. Meadowlarks called back and forth to one another from opposing sides of the pasture, and the slight breeze that breathed through her hair now and then caused the leaves to whisper.

Cricket imagined for a moment that they whispered about her— about the scandalous, brazen kiss she'd given to Heathro Thibodaux and the one she'd received in return. But unlike the folks of Pike's Creek, who would've frowned at her and harshly scolded their disapproval, the summer leaves seemed amused or delighted in the knowledge.

She sighed as she thought then of Hudson and Marie. Oh, it was so romantic! Surely they'd be married by the summer's end. And then Marie would spend the autumn and winter wrapped in the arms of her adoring husband—and no doubt beneath a beautiful quilt stitched lovingly by Ann.

"Ann," Cricket breathed as her smile broadened. So Mr. Keel had winked at her, had he? It was wonderful! He'd taken note of her—even not knowing who had gifted the quilt to him. Perhaps Ann would be married soon as well. How delicious that would be to witness. Surely Ann and Mr. Keel would cause more whispering and gossip than even Ada and Cricket's father had when they'd married.

But what of Vilma? Cricket frowned as she continued to meander through the pasture. Vilma was so obvious in so many ways, but not when it came to the romantic feelings of her heart. It was almost as if she was afraid to speak of them—afraid speaking of them would ensure her dreams of whatever man she dreamt of would never come true.

Cricket wondered if it was because Vilma was Reverend Stanley's daughter. Just as Vilma's brother Wyatt was the town imp, always stepping into or causing trouble, Vilma seemed determined to remain a spinster or something—perhaps to balance out her brother's undesirable character. Whatever the reason Vilma was so this way and that about everything, whatever the reason she would never admit to Cricket, Ann, and Marie who it was that made her heart beat faster, Cricket was certain it had to do with the fact that she was Reverend Stanley's daughter.

Mrs. Stanley was a nice enough woman—kind, caring, compassionate. But she was entirely controlled by her husband. She rarely spoke to anyone, unless it had something to do with the church bazaar or Sunday school. Thus, the more Cricket thought it over, the more she determined that Vilma was probably torn between wanting to rebel against her father (for her dominated mother's sake if nothing else) and wanting his approval.

Cricket sighed, thankful that her father was simply a hard-working blacksmith who owned the livery stables. She was certain that being Reverend Stanley's daughter would truly be miserable—on so many levels of misery.

"Run, girl! Get your fanny over that fence!"

The shouting startled Cricket, and she stopped dead in her tracks, frantically looking around her to see who was calling out. Quickly her attention settled on none other than Heathro Thibodaux. He was advancing from her right at a dead run and waving his arm toward the fence.

"Get over that fence!" he shouted.

But Cricket was confused and paused. "Why?" she said—although not loudly enough for even the grasshoppers to hear her.

"Run! He might gore you right through! Go!" Heathro shouted, still running toward her.

Cricket gasped as she heard it then—the mad pounding of approaching hooves—and she knew at once why Mr. Thibodaux was running at her and shouting for her to get to the fence.

She didn't pause to look back over her shoulder, for she knew the bull was there—Mr. Thibodaux's ornery, mischievous stud bull!

Panic washed over Cricket as she broke into a dead run and headed for the fence. It hadn't seemed so far to Mr. Burroughs's fence line moments before, but as Cricket focused her attention on it now, it felt as if it might as well be a mile away.

The thundering of hooves rumbled the ground beneath Cricket's feet, moving closer, and she dropped her shoes and stockings in order that she might run faster.

"Run!" Heathro shouted as he approached. He was nearly to her, but she imagined that even if he intercepted her, there was little he could do to fend off a charging bull.

Cricket reached the fence, reaching out and taking hold of the top rung as she stepped up onto the bottom one, gasping when she felt a strong hand on the seat of her skirt—felt Heathro Thibodaux lift and shove her hard to hurry her over the fence. The ground felt like stone as she tumbled over the fence and landed on the other side. Even for the soft, cool grass she landed on, the fall knocked the wind from her body. Mr. Thibodaux hurled himself over the fence in one smooth leap, landing with a jarring thud in the grass next to her. Cricket blushed with humiliation and quickly rolled over to sit on her sitter as he raised himself from a sprawl and hunkered down next to her.

"Have you lost your hearin', girl?" he grumbled, brushing grass from the front of his shirt. "I thought sure you'd hear that bull chargin' you long before I started hollerin'."

Cricket was not only embarrassed that she'd been caught daydreaming while wandering through Mr. Burroughs's pasture but also wildly unsettled by Heathro Thibodaux's proximity. Other than the night she'd welcomed him to town, she'd never been so close to him.

Thus, her defenses were a bit piqued, and she retorted, "Well, maybe you oughta do a better job at keepin' him penned up, Mr. Thibodaux."

"Well, I admit that goes without sayin'," he grumbled. "But what on earth were you thinkin' on? I swear I hollered at you for five minutes before you finally turned and looked at me."

"I-I was just thinkin' on…things," she stammered. It was then she noticed a sharp pain in the bottom of her right foot. Reaching down, grasping her foot, and studying the large, long splinter lodged in the arch, she moaned, "Ouch!"

"Let me see it," Mr. Thibodaux demanded.

Without waiting for her to show the injured foot and splinter to him—without even waiting for her to consider whether she should— he reached out, gripping her ankle in one hand and raising her foot to investigate it.

He frowned. "Ooo…that is a nasty splinter. It's shoved way down in there too."

"Wh-why was he chasin' me so hard anyway?" she asked as she tried once to pull her foot away from him. But he held tightly to her ankle. Oh, Cricket knew she should be thoroughly mortified at having a man take hold of her naked ankle—horrified at his investigating her bare foot the way he was. But she wasn't. In truth, she was entirely fascinated by the way goose bumps were breaking over her arms and legs. She was so affected by his touch that the pure delight of his handling her caused her to reflexively try to pull her ankle from his grasp once more.

But Heathro tugged back, frowning as he continued to study the splinter. "I don't know," he mumbled. "He don't usually charge." He glanced up from her foot then for a moment, grinned, and said, "Maybe he mistook you for a pretty little heifer he wanted to consort with."

His smile broadened when Cricket blushed, gasping in astonishment. "That was entirely inappropriate, Mr. Thibodaux," she forced herself to scold—more out of knowing she should than really wanting to.

She caught sight of the gold top incisor at the right of his smile as he laughed. She could've sworn the sunlight caught sight of it too, glinting it with a flash of sparkle for a moment.

"If you don't quit wrigglin' around like a worm, I'll show you something inappropriate that'll really ruffle your britches, Miss Cranford," he said as he drew a small knife from his boot. "Now hold still."

Cricket's mouth gaped open in astonishment at his even more inappropriate remark. But being that his knife was at the sole of her foot, she didn't dare scold him. Instead, she held her breath as she watched him use his thumb and the blade of his knife to begin working the long splinter out of the bottom of her foot. She really should reprimand him—or at least ask him to explain what he meant—what the *something* inappropriate was that he'd show her if she didn't quit wriggling. But the splinter was causing her pain.

"Ouch!" she squealed as he gave one final tug, slipping the splinter from her foot at last.

"There now," Heathro said, frowning once more as he studied the wound. "Just scrub it out good when you get home, and it oughta be fine."

Cricket's eyebrows arched in marvel as Heathro proceeded to spit on her foot and fiercely rub his saliva into the wound with his thumb.

"Y-you just spit on me," Cricket stammered—though she found it peculiar that the action didn't disgust her. In fact, she felt an oddly delighted giggle bubbling in her throat and struggled to keep it there.

"Yep," he affirmed as he wiped the sole of her foot on his knee. "I don't know why," he began, grinning as he glanced up to her, "but spit always soothes a wound for some reason, don't it?"

Cricket couldn't stifle the giggle in her throat any longer, and it tumbled from her mouth as she said, "So you're claimin' your spit is medicinal somehow, Mr. Thibodaux?"

Heathro chuckled. "You bet. That's what I'm known for...medicinal spit."

He studied the bottom of her foot again, and Cricket bit her lip in an attempt to control the smile begging to spread across her face. His hand was so warm and strong where it gripped her ankle. She knew she shouldn't enjoy his touching her so inappropriately—but she did!

"Yep," he sighed, releasing her foot. "It'll hurt for a while. But like I said, a good scrubbin' will clean it out good enough, I reckon," he instructed as casually as if he were explaining how to fry an egg in bacon drippings.

Mr. Thibodaux sat down in the grass and stared at her for a long, silent few moments. "Seems to me I see you runnin' around barefoot more than I do with shoes on," he said at last.

"W-well, I like to be without shoes," she awkwardly explained. "They make me feel so confined somehow...and I just have to take them off. I just don't like shoes, if you must know."

He nodded, arching his eyebrows with an expression of understanding.

She'd had nearly forgotten about the bull—until it butted its head against the fence, startling her. She growled a little as she frowned at the animal. It responded by puffing a breath at her, sending tiny beads of bull mucus into the air to lightly spray her face.

"And I don't like your bull either," she exclaimed, squeezing her eyes closed and grimacing at the feel of the bull's nose moisture on her face.

"Oh, he ain't so bad once you get to know him," she heard Heathro chuckle.

She felt something wiping her face and opened her eyes to see him offering a handkerchief to her. "Sorry about that," he said, flashing the dazzling smile the sun liked to kiss. "I think he likes you. Ol' Conq don't blow his snot on just anybody."

"I'm flattered," Cricket mumbled with sarcasm.

"I could moisten that hanky up with some of my medicinal spit if you like there, Miss Cranford," he teased.

"No thank you, Mr. Thibodaux," she said. "I'll be fine."

Cricket was thoroughly disconcerted by the way the aroma of leather clinging to the handkerchief caused her stomach to flutter for some reason.

Heathro Thibodaux stood and leapt back over the fence, taking hold of the big bronze ring in the bull's nose. "I'll admit, he's got a mean streak of mischief runnin' in him." He chuckled to himself and added, "But I suppose that's why he's so good at what he does."

"And what's that?" Cricket asked. Oh, she well knew that Mr. Thibodaux's bull was a stud bull. But for some reason, the mischief in her wanted to see what Mr. Thibodaux would answer. Would he tell her bluntly and rather improperly exactly what the bull's purpose was? Or would he work his way around just coming right out and saying it?

Cricket smiled, pleased when the ex-Texas Ranger simply answered, "He makes me a lot of money, Miss Cranford. That's what he's good at."

She watched as Heathro tugged on the ring in the bull's nose, forcing the animal away from the fence and in the opposite direction.

"I suppose I should thank you for warnin' me he was comin' at me, Mr. Thibodaux," she offered. "And for removin' that nasty ol' splinter."

"I'm sorry he went after you in the first place, Miss Cranford," he said with a nod. Reaching down into the pasture grass, he picked up Cricket's shoes and tossed them over the fence to her. "You have a good day now, all right?"

"You as well, Mr. Thibodaux," she offered with a smile.

Cricket watched him go—watched the sinfully handsome Heathro Thibodaux swagger through the pasture, leading his naughty bull behind him. She must've sighed a dozen times with pleasure as she gazed after him for a long while. But finally, she turned and started back toward town.

She wasn't ready to settle into evening chores with Ada yet, so she determined she'd pay a short visit to Mrs. Maloney. Cricket had been so impatient to visit the old gal—to see if the subject of the gifted teapot arose. She'd planned to wait a few more days, maybe even until her regular Friday afternoon visit, but she was too eager to see just how much Mrs. Maloney was enjoying the pretty teapot Vilma Stanley had sold her hair for.

As she meandered toward Mrs. Maloney's house, Cricket thought how odd it all seemed—she and Mr. Thibodaux sitting in the grass, having just barely outrun a charging bull and talking like nothing else had ever happened between them. She was certain then—certain that he did not know it had been Cricket Cranford who had kissed him only a few nights before. Surely if he had known it was she, he would've continued the angry scolding he'd given her that night. But he hadn't. He'd simply spoken to her as if he'd never in a thousand years suspect it was she who'd kissed him—she who he'd kissed in return.

Brutal or not—forced in anger or not—the fact remained that Heathro Thibodaux had kissed Cricket Friday night. Cricket rolled her eyes in humiliated exasperation with herself at having referred to his spit as "medicinal." Yet the thought traveled through her mind that the moisture in his mouth that had blended with hers Friday night when he'd kissed her so forcefully was the same that had soothed the bottom of her injured foot. She blushed, wondering why the thought was somehow thrilling to her instead of offensive.

"So then I opened up the door…and what was sittin' right there on my front porch but this beautiful little teapot," Mrs. Maloney chirped as she and Cricket sat in her kitchen. She sighed with admiration as she studied the teapot sitting on a doily on her silver tea tray.

"Unbelievable!" Cricket gasped, shaking her head with contrived disbelief. "Someone just…just left it there?"

"Yep," Mrs. Maloney confirmed. "The only way I even knew it was meant for me was because of the little note that came along with it."

"There was a note too?" Cricket asked. "How intriguin'." She smiled. "Maybe you've got yourself a secret admirer, Mrs. Maloney."

But Maymee Maude rolled her eyes and puffed a breath of skepticism. "Not a chance, Magnolia. And besides, I've got Nobody to keep me company."

Cricket giggled. "Ah yes! Mr. Nobody MacGee…your secret beau."

"Oh my, yes!" Mrs. Maloney exclaimed. "Why…just the other day he was over for supper, and, my oh my, did we converse!"

"About what?" Cricket loved Mrs. Maloney's good-natured sense of humor. Of course she felt bad that the elderly woman had only an imaginary male companion to talk to at supper, but it seemed to make her happy enough.

"Oh, everything under the sun and more, honey," the old woman answered. Her eyes twinkled like the stars as she spoke. But suddenly, Mrs. Maloney reached out and took Cricket's hands in her own. "But let's talk about you," she said. "Have you roped that handsome ol' Texas Ranger in for yourself and convinced him you're the one he wants?"

Cricket laughed, shook her head, and answered, "Of course not! Don't be silly." However, she paused, smiled with triumph, and said, "But I'll tell you what I did have a hand in."

"Mr. Hudson Oliver and Miss Marie King sparkin' out behind the Olivers' barn every night like a couple of fireflies?" Maymee offered with a wink.

Cricket shook her head, laughing again. "I swear, nothin' in this town gets past you, now does it?"

Maymee shook her head. "Nope. Not much anyway. And I don't know how you did it, Magnolia…but I'm glad you did. I thought those two were gonna see their heads explode if they didn't kiss out some of that attraction pretty soon."

"Yes indeed," Cricket agreed. "They are very affectionate…from what I hear anyway."

Mrs. Maloney and Cricket each giggled for a moment—like two little schoolgirls who had just spied their schoolmarm spooning with the mayor.

"But…I still think you oughta tether up Heathro Thibodaux for yourself," Maymee sighed. "He's so good-lookin'! I swear if I were even twenty years younger, I'd tie that boy up, marry him, and have my way with him."

"Have your way with him?" Cricket asked. "What on earth does that mean anyway? And what did you mean when you said I oughta tie him up and set to work *convincin'* him that I'm the one he wants?"

Mrs. Maloney's sparse, silvery eyebrows pursed in a wondering frown. "Well, Magnolia...you *do* know what goes on between married people, don't you? Where babies come from and the like?"

Cricket rolled her eyes with amusement. "Of course! Don't be silly."

But one of Maymee's sparse, silvery eyebrows arched with doubt. "Did your mother ever explain those things to you, honey?"

"She didn't have to," Cricket said with a shrug. "Daddy did. When I was sixteen."

"And what did your daddy tell you...about where babies come from and what goes on between a husband and wife?"

Cricket shrugged once more. "They sleep together...in the same bed. And when the time is right, a baby starts growin' in a woman's tummy. All us girls know about it...even Vilma Stanley."

"Oh, I see," Maymee mumbled.

Maymee was a bit unsettled in her stomach at the thought of Cricket's mother having died when Cricket was so young—before she had the chance to talk to her daughter about the sorts of things that mothers should and need to talk to their daughters about. Maymee Maloney had married her husband when she was just fifteen and without any knowledge whatsoever about the intimate goings-on between husband and wife. If it hadn't been for fact that she'd married such a kind, loving, patient, and understanding man as Butch Maloney, her wedding night—her entire intimate married life, for that matter—might have been thick with self-doubt and a constant feeling of embarrassment rather than the joy borne of true, loving passion. When the time came for Cricket to marry, Maymee wouldn't let the risk of astonishment and lack of understanding drive even the smallest wedge between Cricket and whomever she chose to marry. Maymee would prepare her herself—just as she'd prepared her own daughters. After all, she loved Magnolia Cranford like her own child.

"But why are you askin' me that?" Cricket asked, interrupting Maymee's thoughts of maternal responsibility toward Zeke Cranford's girl.

"Oh, nothin' all that serious," Mrs. Maloney answered—though Cricket was certain the old woman was once again weaseling out of telling her something. "Just that you oughta kiss him the way he needs to be kissed."

Cricket's eyes narrowed with suspicion. "You're leavin' somethin' out, aren't you?"

"Anyway, as I was sayin', there it was…this teapot, just sittin' on my front porch like it belonged right there all along," Mrs. Maloney said.

CHAPTER EIGHT

"Ada," Cricket began, "do you think you and Daddy are gonna have any babies?"

Cricket smiled, amused as Ada knocked over the bucket of clothespins at her feet.

"Well...well, I don't really know," she stammered, blushing so bright a pink it looked as if she'd been out in the sun too long without a bonnet or hat. "Why would you ask?"

Cricket shrugged. "I was just thinkin' on it...how fun it would be to have a little brother or sister to dote over and cuddle." And it was true. Cricket *had* been thinking on it—ever since her conversation with Mrs. Maloney the week before.

When she and Mrs. Maloney had been sitting at Mrs. Maloney's kitchen table talking about the teapot and Mrs. Maloney had, once again, brought up the idea that Cricket should rope up Heathro Thibodaux and convince him she was the one for him—well, it had been plain obvious that Mrs. Maloney was leaving something out. Cricket knew darn well that the old gal had weaseled her way out telling Cricket *something*, but she didn't quite know what—and it had been bothering her ever since.

"Well, I was just thinkin' that since you and Daddy share a bed now," Cricket carefully treaded, "that it only makes sense...bein' that you're so young and all...that a baby oughta be bakin' in the oven about now. That is all that's involved, isn't it? Just the fact that you're married and sharin' a bed? Nothin' else is required...unless I'm mistaken."

Ada was still blushing, but she smiled, tossed her head with a pretty laugh, and said, "Oh, Cricket! You know there's more to it than just sharin' a bed." But Ada paused, looking inquisitively to Cricket. "Don't you?"

Cricket shrugged. "Well, that's all Daddy told me. That when a man and a woman get married, they start sharin' a bed, and then suddenly there's a baby inside you."

Ada put her hands on her hips, frowning. "Is that all Zeke told you? That's it? Nothin' more?"

"No...that's it," Cricket admitted—though she was one hundred percent sure now that Mrs. Maloney had certainly weaseled her way out of saying something important.

Ada puffed a breath of exasperation. "I swear, that man! He's as dumb as an ox sometimes!"

"I'm guessin' he left somethin' out," Cricket offered, more curious than ever.

"Yes, he left somethin' out!" Ada exclaimed. "He left everything out! Why, if my mother hadn't told me what she did before I married Zeke, I woulda probably passed out cold on my weddin' night when..."

Ada stopped herself, but it was too late. She looked at Cricket, tears filling her eyes as she suddenly realized that Cricket had been very young when her own mother had passed away. There hadn't been a woman around to tell Cricket the intimate details of...of intimacy. Ada knew that in marrying Zeke—a darling, charming man who was obviously uncomfortable when speaking to his daughter on certain subjects—the responsibility for such things as maternal advice and comfort had fallen to her. But she'd never imagined she'd have to explain to a girl nearly her own age exactly how the human race proliferated.

Still, Ada wasn't at all sure that hanging out laundry was the proper time and place to explain things to Cricket. And besides, Ada had some time. Cricket wasn't being courted by anyone—or even interested in anyone as far as Ada knew. Therefore, she'd think on it awhile—figure out just what to say to Cricket in explaining intimacy between husband and wife, and how and when to tell her.

"I'm guessin' it's somethin' I should be hearin' from my mama, Ada," Cricket said, smiling with understanding. "So it's not your fault. And we can talk about it later."

Ada smiled, feeling somewhat relieved.

But then Cricket laughed. "After all, what more can there be to it than what Daddy already told me?"

Once more Ada tripped over the clothespin bucket, sending clothespins scattering through the grass beneath the clothesline.

"Not so much, I suppose," Ada giggled nervously, blushing anew as she bent to gather up the clothespins.

Cricket's eyes narrowed with suspicion. She determined that maybe growing up in a tiny town like Pike's Creek had kept her ignorant of certain details of life, and she wondered for a moment—was it a good thing or a bad thing?

Either way, she'd find out what she wanted to know. If her Daddy or Ada wouldn't tell her, she'd eventually wiggle it out of Mrs. Maloney, one way or the other.

Sighing, Cricket looked up into the beautiful blue of the summer sky overhead. A few large clouds were sitting way up high—like big, puffy angels gazing down to guard folks below. A hummingbird zipped in and out of the clothesline, and Cricket and Ada exchanged delighted glances. It was simply a lovely day—a perfect day—and Cricket couldn't wait to finish hanging out the laundry so she could race to the old Morgan house to meet the girls.

After all, she hadn't told them about being chased by Heathro Thibodaux's bull yet—about how Mr. Thibodaux applied medicinal spit to her injury and threatened to show her "something inappropriate." Furthermore, the Olivers were packed up and ready to head down to San Antonio, so Cricket was certain Marie was a mess of tears and worry.

She wondered whether Ann had received any more winks and smiles from Mr. Keel and if Vilma were going to be in a jovial mood or one of her self-righteous, call-everyone-to-repentance moods.

All in all, there was so much to talk about with the girls. And so, too impatient to linger any longer, Cricket gave up gazing into the lovely sky and began to hurriedly pin up the rest of the clothes she and Ada had finished washing. Mischief was waiting for her at the old Morgan place, and it looked to be a fine day for swimming too!

❦

"And then he kissed me once more," Marie sniffled. "One more long, lingerin' kiss before he climbed up into the wagon seat and drove off into the mornin' sun."

"He'll be back, darlin'," Ann soothed, placing a comforting arm around Marie's shoulders.

Cricket winced at the pain her own heart was feeling for Marie's worry and sadness. Marie and Hudson had been nearly inseparable since the night they first kissed their loving confessions. She knew it was a horrid thing to anticipate ten days before Hudson returned—at least ten!

"He gave me these," Marie said then. Brushing tears from her cheeks, she held up her left wrist and tugged at the sleeve of her shirtwaist to reveal the most beautifully crafted silver and turquoise bracelet Cricket had ever seen. Not that she'd seen many, but she'd seen similar jewelry on the wealthy woman who occasionally disembarked from the train for a short stretch of the legs before continuing on to Santa Fe.

Vilma gasped and studied the bracelet closely. "Marie, it's beautiful! And so expensive!"

Marie smiled halfheartedly. "It is beautiful, isn't it? There's a turquoise pendant laid in silver hanging from a silver chain and matching earrings as well...but I left them at home. I was afraid to wear them all together—afraid I'd lose them or somethin'."

Cricket took Marie's hand and admired the bracelet. It was a thick cuff of silver, very intricately designed, with a large oval piece of turquoise inlayed in the center of the band. It truly was the most astonishing piece.

"Well, Hudson certainly has been observin' you, Marie," Cricket giggled. "That's for certain. I wonder how many times he saw you standin' over the jewelry case in the general store wishin' after pretty things."

And it was true! Just as Ann loved her black thoroughbred, Harley—just as Vilma loved pens and inkwells—Marie King loved jewelry. She nearly had bracelets coming out her ears, being that her parents gifted her one every Christmas. But even Cricket had never seen the like of Hudson's gift up close. It was truly beautiful and unique—just like Marie King herself.

"I hope he's safe…that he hurries home to me," Marie sniffled.

"He'll be safe," Cricket assured her. "And he'll be home soon and sparkin' your stockin's to catchin' flame before you know it."

Marie nodded and forced a smile. Unexpectedly then, as she stared at Cricket, she began to giggle. Almost instantly her giggle turned to laughter.

"What's so funny?" Cricket asked, giggling herself simply because Marie's laughter was so contagious.

"I'm sorry, Cricket," Marie breathed, continuing to laugh with merriment. "But the vision of you sittin' there on your fanny in the grass with Heathro Thibodaux spittin' on your foot and rubbin' it in… oh, I just wish I could've seen that!"

"Me too!" Ann exclaimed, breaking into her own trilling giggle. "And you didn't even have time to think on the fact that he placed his bare hand on your fanny to push you over the fence!"

"On the seat of my skirt, Ann! Only on the seat of my skirt!" Cricket corrected, still giggling over her friends' amusement.

Even Vilma was laughing. "I told you, Magnolia! I told you that runnin' around without your stockin's and shoes would find you in a predicament one day."

"Yes, you did, Vilma Stanley," Cricket happily admitted. "But if it was meant to find me in a predicament, I'm so glad the predicament it found me in was with Heathro Thibodaux and his medicinal spit!"

The girls burst into laughter, tears rolling from their eyes. Even Marie's tears had turned from those of sadness to those of mirth.

"Oh, you all do my very soul so much good!" Vilma panted. "I swear, no one on earth makes me laugh like you girls do."

Cricket was only able to nod her agreement, still too overcome with a fit of giggles she thought would see her rolling on the floor in another minute.

"Well, well, well…looky what we have here, boys."

All four girls looked to the doorless threshold of the old Morgan house, their laughter ceasing abruptly. There in the doorway stood no less than seven or eight scroungy-looking men—all with pistols drawn or rifles aimed directly at them.

"Someone's helpin' us along today," the man who stood in front of the rest said as he stepped into the room. The other men followed him in, still keeping their guns leveled at Cricket, Ann, Marie, and Vilma.

"Who are you?" Vilma ventured.

"Why…we're just men of business, darlin'," he answered as he began to circle the girls as a group. "Just men out and about lookin' for things to sell."

Instantly a vision of the newspaper article hidden in the chest at the foot of Cricket's bed flashed through her mind. Were these men white slavers? Were these the same men that had killed the eight girls for whom Heathro Thibodaux had nearly given his life in trying to save? Whether or not they were, it was obvious their intentions were neither friendly nor kind.

"Help! Help us!" Cricket managed to shriek a moment before the man's dirty, rough hand covered her mouth from behind.

"You hush, girl!" the man growled in her ear. He held a pistol to her head. "You hush! And if any of you others have any ideas of runnin' or hollerin' out, I'll put a bullet right through your pretty little friend's head here."

Another man stepped forward, leveling his rifle at Marie. "Now, you girls come on outside with us. You do just as we say, and we won't kill ya."

The man with his hand over Cricket's mouth ordered, "And bring that thoroughbred with us. He'll fetch a nice price." Chuckling—his rancid breath hot against Cricket's ear—he added, "But not as nice a price as you, darlin'. No, sirree. Not as nice a price as you."

"Of course I'll come with you, Cooper," Zeke Cranford assured his friend. He patted Cooper Keel twice on the back and added, "The more people that's lookin' for your niece, the faster we'll find her and bring her home."

"What's goin' on, Zeke?" Ada asked, drying her hands on her apron as she stepped out onto the front porch.

"It's my niece," Cooper Keel answered. "My brother's daughter, up in Thistle…they can't find her."

"What?" Ada gasped.

"My brother don't know if she run off with a boy she was sweet on, fell into a ravine, or if it's somethin' else," Cooper explained. "But they can't find her, and it's been more than a day. I just got a telegram askin' me to come up and help search for her."

"Cooper's asked me to go, honey," Zeke explained to his pretty young wife. He hated to leave Ada and Cricket for any length of time—but he knew Cooper needed the help. "I hope that's all right."

"Oh yes, Zeke! You have to go. You must!" Ada exclaimed with sincerity. "You all have to find that girl!" Ada ran a hand over her head in nervously smoothing her hair. "Why…she could be layin' out there in the wilderness hurt…or somethin' the like." Ada looked to Cooper. "Go now, Cooper. You and Zeke go. Don't waste any more time."

"Thank you, baby," Zeke said, quickly kissing Ada on the mouth. He looked to Cooper. "Let me get saddled and get my rig, and I'll meet you over at your place."

"Thank you, Zeke," Cooper said with nod. Looking to Ada, he smiled. "And thank you, Ada."

"Of course, Cooper," Ada said, forcing a smile. "No need to thank anybody for anything. You boys just be on your way. You find your niece, you hear?"

"Yes, ma'am." Cooper Keel touched the brim of his hat and nodded to Ada.

"You and Cricket…don't be worryin' the way the two of you do whenever I'm gone," Zeke told Ada. He kissed her once more and then hurried down the porch.

"Oh, we will worry, Zeke," Ada whispered as she watched him head toward the livery. "We will worry."

Ada frowned. She was already anxious. She felt a shiver of unease travel through and hugged herself, rubbing her arms to dispel the unpleasant goose bumps erupting there.

Glancing around, she wondered where on earth Cricket had run off. But she quickly remembered Friday—the day Cricket visited old Maymee Maude Maloney and then ran off to who knows what mischief with Marie King, Ann Burroughs, and Vilma Stanley.

Ada sighed, feeling somewhat comforted in knowing that with Cricket either visiting Maymee Maloney or off wading in the creek with her friends, she wasn't alone. And besides, Pike's Creek was a nice town with nice people in it.

Having decided her prickly goose bumps and strange anxiety were caused by Zeke's leaving and nothing else, Ada turned around and went back into the house. She did hope Cricket didn't linger too long with her friends. It wasn't that there was choring to do—just that Ada had begun to truly enjoy Cricket's company. They were becoming friends—at last.

CHAPTER NINE

Heath slowed Archie to a slow walk when they reached the row of ancient willows lining the west side of the creek. He knew Archie enjoyed the cool, fresh caress of the green-leafed willow branches as they swept over his head and haunches as much as Heath did. There was something soothing about tree shade and the touch of a leaf to hot summer skin. Archie whinnied, and Heath smiled.

"All right, you lazy piece of horsehide," he chuckled as he dismounted and allowed Archie to drink from the cool water of the stream. "And save some for the rest of us, boy."

Heath hunkered by the creek bed, plunging one hand into the cool water and raising a cupped palm of refreshment to his mouth. "Ahhh!" he sighed. "It's good, ain't it?" He scooped a few more mouthfuls of fresh water to his lips and then removed his hat and ran wet fingers through his hair.

He was near the old Morgan place and could see the dilapidated roof rising above the tree line a ways upstream. He shook his head and frowned, wondering whether the four young ladies from Pike's Creek who had pulled that little "welcome to Pike's Creek" prank on him more than a week before were somewhere nearby, plotting their next do-gooding activities. Still, he couldn't maintain his frown for long—not when the memory of that girl's kiss was on his lips—not while he was still torn between the guilt he owned for so ruthlessly kissing her in return and the pleasure he'd relished while doing it.

Yep. That little blossom bottom had really rung his bell the week before. He'd had a hard time thinking on anything else since.

In an effort to divert the course of his thoughts, Heath looked downstream instead of upstream for a moment. It was a butterfly of a day—bright, fresh, warm, green, and colorful. Even the bank of the creek seemed calm and happy. At least up to the point where there'd been something to muddy it up.

"What done that, I wonder?" he said out loud as he stood and strode to the place where the grass and flowers had been disturbed.

Heath's frown returned as he studied the ground—looked across the stream to see even more disturbance there. The disordered wet mud and grass on Heath's side of the creek had been made by boots and shoes—many pair. As he looked behind him, he could identify at least six or seven different men's boot prints on the bank of the creek—and what looked to be three or four different sets of women's shoes. One shod horse as well.

A familiar and unwanted anxiety rose in him as his mind ran back a year to a similar scene he'd come across. Not wanting to think about it, he sloshed his way across the creek to the other bank and followed the multiple sets of prints a ways. Not too far from the creek, nestled in a clearing located in the center of a group of trees, Heathro Thibodaux found what he'd hoped he wouldn't—what he'd silently prayed he wouldn't. There in the grass and dirt of the clearing, numerous hoofprints now joined all the boot and shoe prints. Furthermore, as he reached down and touched the horseshoe print of the horse that had crossed the creek with the group of people, he realized the horse was a thoroughbred.

There was only one thoroughbred in Pike's Creek, and it belonged to Ralph Burroughs—or rather his daughter. Heath studied the ground only a moment more. Then he stood and ran back to the creek, across it, and to Archie.

Mounting in one smooth leap, Heath yelled, "Yah!" and sent Archie off on a mad gallop toward the old Morgan place.

He didn't need to be told, and he didn't need more evidence. Texas Ranger Heathro Thibodaux knew exactly what had gone on near the creek. But if he was going to convince the men of Pike's Creek to raise a posse, then he knew he better damn well be certain they had enough evidence.

As he reached the Morgan place and dismounted, Heath was not surprised at what he saw. There'd been a scuffle all right. It was obvious by the prints in the dirt. And it looked like the outlaws had had to drag at least one girl out of the house; he could see the drag marks in the dirt leading away from the old threshold and out into the yard.

"Dammit!" he growled as he mounted Archie once more.

The Texas Rangers had hunted down and hanged all the outlaws who had killed the eight girls they'd stolen the summer before. But where one outlaw hanged, it seemed three more sprouted from the hanging tree on which his corpse was left to rot.

Heath knew exactly who had been taken too—the four silly but well-meaning girls who prowled around town in their black underwear every few Friday nights. Heath had often wondered how the citizens of Pike's Creek could be so blind to exactly who the little do-gooders were. But then again, not everybody had the sharp eye or training he had. Furthermore, maybe some folks did know that it was the Cranford, King, Burroughs, and Stanley girls doing it all. Maybe they just chose to keep their mouths closed about it for the same reason Heath did— because they were sweet girls, doing sweet things in a world that needed a whole lot more sweet in it.

He had to raise a posse and get after them. From the looks of the dirt and dried mud, the outlaws had a day on him at least. Heath knew there were good men in town—good men who would believe him. At least, he hoped they would.

As Heath and his horse galloped toward town, the beauty of the day was lost to him. What did willow branches and cool water mean? Blue sky and green grass, for that matter? Heath Thibodaux knew exactly what the outlaws had in mind for the girls of Pike's Creek, and it made his stomach churn. He thought again of the sweet, innocent, kindly offered kiss he'd returned with brutality. What he wouldn't give to take it back—to kiss that girl again the way she deserved to be kissed.

He growled as he rode, sick at heart, enraged, and with the taste of a kiss he'd desecrated in his mouth.

Heathro Thibodaux arrived in Pike's Creek to find nearly every resident of the town holed up in the church. Heath learned that Zeke Cranford and Cooper Keel had headed up to Thistle earlier in the day to look for a girl that had gone missing there. So when Cricket Cranford had not come home for supper the night before, her stepmother, Ada, had gone to the King, Burroughs, and Stanley residences looking for her. Naturally she'd found three sets of other concerned parents, and the missing girls' fathers had ridden out in search of their daughters until the sun set. They'd returned home with no information, and thus everyone in the town was alerted and had gathered at the church in order to coordinate search parties.

Reverend Stanley was in charge, of course. Heathro could hardly stomach the preacher. He liked preachers as a rule. But he did not like the Reverend Edgar Stanley. The preacher of Pike's Creek seemed far too arrogant, self-important, and downright bossy to be a good man of the cloth. He rubbed Heath Thibodaux the wrong way at every turn.

In fact, as Heath stood leaning against the back wall of the church, listening to the reverend openly criticizing Ralph Burroughs and Clifford King for refusing to wait to go searching for their daughters that morning until the town had been called together, Heath's stomach turned one too many times. It appeared almost as if the self-centered preacher were burning daylight just to buoy ego. But daylight was precious, and Heath needed help—whether he liked it or not. The past had taught him a hard lesson in that.

"I hear there's a girl missin' over in Thistle," Heath called from the back of the church when Reverend Stanley paused for one brief moment.

"Mr. Thibodaux," the reverend greeted rather coolly as Heath strode up the church aisle to the podium.

"Yes, there is a girl missin'," Ada Cranford answered as Heath turned to face the congregation.

"Thank you, Mrs. Cranford," Heath said with a nod as he stepped in front of the podium, blocking Reverend Stanley from the townsfolk's view.

"I'm afraid that a missing girl in Thistle confirms what I know happened to your girls here," Heath began. "There's white slavers in the area, and they're gathering up girls to sell."

Gasps and groans, shouting and crying commenced.

"You don't know that, Thibodaux!" the preacher shouted. "How dare you come into my church and—"

"Well, unless I'm mistaken, preacher…this here is the Lord's church, not yours," Heath growled as the townsfolk settled a bit. "Furthermore, I'm tellin' you that these girls are in the hands of white slavers. I've seen their tracks outside of town. Seems to be eight or nine of them at least…and I figure they took the girl in Thistle and all four of ours too."

"And how can you be so sure it's these…these…outlaws that have our Pike's Creek daughters?" the preacher argued. "Who are you to be makin' these kinds of conclusions from some tracks?"

The Pike's Creek folks gathered in the church had gone silent—listened—waited for Heath's response.

"How can I be sure? You mean other than the fact that Ralph Burroughs's thoroughbred—the one his daughter rides—other than the fact that thoroughbred is with them?" Heath growled. "Well, I'll tell you how. I'm a Texas Ranger, Stanley…still papered up, badged, and legal. And I've had experiences you cannot imagine! Experiences nobody ever should have to imagine. And I am tellin' you here and now, this is white slavin'! Do you understand what I'm tellin' you? These girls are gonna be sold into brothel life if they're lucky! We have to get our men together and get after these outlaws. I figure they've probably got sixteen to twenty hours on us already."

"White slavers? Here? In Pike's Creek?" Reverend Stanley still doubted.

"And one of them is your daughter, preacher," Heath added.

"Well, if a posse is needed—" the preacher began, but he was stopped short by the hard, resounding slap of Ada Cranford. Heath hadn't seen her approach, but he sure heard her slap the preacher.

"You've kept us waitin' here all mornin', Edgar!" Ada Cranford cried. "How dare you doubt this man! How dare you doubt the word of man who is familiar with just this kind of atrocity!"

Ada turned to Heath. "Will these white slavin' outlaws hurt our girls before they sell them, Mr. Thibodaux?"

Visions of the bodies of the dead girls strewn over the rocks at the bottom of a canyon leapt to Heath's mind—all the pain of the beating he took, the gunshots to his body, the tooth broken out of his head. But there was no time for guilt or pain—no time for reflection on failure.

"They...they'll keep them as *unspoiled* as possible, Mrs. Cranford," he answered. "But if we don't track them down—"

"You men quit sittin' around lookin' at each other like a bunch of dumb dogs!" Heath looked to see Maymee Maloney standing at the back of the church. "Posse up with the one real man left in this town, and find our girls!" she cried, dabbing at her eyes.

"I need to ride up to Thistle and bring Zeke home," Ada Cranford said.

"I'll go with you, Ada," Maymee offered. "We can take my surrey and team." Looking to Heath, she asked, "Sh-should someone ride out and look for Clifford and Ralph?"

"It would take too long, Maymee," Heath began, "us not knowin' where they are. The ladies in town can explain everything when they return...and then they can set out to meet up with us."

Heath was rather surprised when it was none other that Reverend Stanley's son who asked, "What do we need to do first, Mr. Thibodaux?"

Other men nodded in agreement with Wyatt, and Heath said, "Saddle up. Bring enough supplies for several days. Get to it now. We're leavin' here in ten minutes or less," he ordered. Heath glared at Edgar Stanley. "You comin' along to help save your daughter's virtue... maybe her life, preacher?"

"You best be right, Texas Ranger," Edgar growled. "If you make a fool of me, I swear I'll—"

But Edgar Stanley couldn't finish his sentence—not from where he sat on the floor rubbing at his sore jaw once Heath's fist had met with it.

"I'm leavin' now," Heath growled, "with or without you, preacher."

❦

"We're just stoppin' long enough for you ladies to take care of your necessaries," Heck informed them. "No lingerin'. We gotta ride."

"But we're so tired," Vilma informed the leader of the gang of outlaws who had abducted Cricket and her friends from the old Morgan place the day before.

"We're so tired, what, girl?" the outlaw asked.

Vilma tried not to cry, straightened her posture, and said, "We're so tired, Mr. Alford."

Heck Alford smiled. The sight of his yellow teeth and red gums churned Cricket's stomach. His hair was long and black—greasy as a skillet after frying fish. His beard was long too, hanging nearly to his chest.

"Well, that's more like it, redzee," Heck chuckled. "You show me a little respect, and I'll make sure you benefit for it, darlin'. You all have five minutes to take care of your business, instead of just three."

Quickly, Cricket and the other girls dropped to their knees next to the stream, cupping water in their hands and frantically drinking.

"I'm so thirsty!" the girl named Pearl exclaimed. Pearl was from Thistle, and Cricket and the others had learned she was the niece of Ann's own Mr. Keel. The outlaws had taken her the day before they'd abducted Cricket and the others from Pike's Creek.

"I'm so dry from not havin' enough to drink, I don't even think I can make water this stop," Jinny said. Jinny was from a town a day's ride from Thistle. So was a girl named Nina. Jinny and Nina were sisters and had been abducted a day before Pearl. All this Cricket had learned during the brief stops the outlaws made in order to water and feed the horses and girls.

Cricket was terrified—perhaps not as trembling and uncertain as she had been the first few hours after having been taken from the old Morgan place, but terrified nonetheless.

Ann and Marie were strong, but Cricket saw the fear in their eyes as well. Of all the girls, Vilma was the only one who had attempted to speak to the dirty band of outlaw white slavers. Cricket wondered if her courage stemmed from the fact that she was somewhat red-haired (auburn-haired people were considered red-haired, after all) or if her brazenness had something to do with her being a preacher's daughter. Maybe her faith that no harm would come to her if she spoke to the men was stronger than Cricket's and the others'. Then again, maybe she was just a fool. Whatever the reason, Cricket was glad that outlaw boss, Heck Alford, had taken to Vilma for some reason. Vilma's bravery in speaking to Heck and the others had found the girls with longer breaks from riding and more jerky and hardtack at mealtime.

"You!" one of the men shouted. Cricket looked up from her place kneeling on the creek bank to see the man Heck called Patterson looking at her. He was an ugly man—uglier even than Heck—with dirty blond hair that hung near to his waist and a filthy beard full of crumbs and other unidentifiable things that Cricket guessed had probably originated in his nose.

"Me?" she asked—though she knew he was speaking to her.

"Yes, you," he grumbled. "Take that little one with you when you go to do your business," he said, pointing to Nina. "I don't want you chatterin' with them other friends of yours." He looked to Marie and Ann then. "That goes for both of you too." He pointed to Ann and instructed, "You take the one from Thistle." Looking to Marie, he ordered, "And you take that other one there." He pointed to Jinny and then leveled his rifle at Cricket. "Now get goin'. You all ain't got all day."

Taking Nina's hand, Cricket helped her to stand. Glancing around, she spied a piñon tree not too far off. It was small but wide and would provide a little privacy.

"Come on, Nina," she said. Glaring at Patterson, she mumbled, "Be a gentleman and turn your head this time please."

But Patterson only chuckled. "Hey, Heck," he called to his boss. "You were right. This one does have voice in her throat after all. And she seems pretty high and mighty to boot."

"Well, good," Heck said. "It's nice to see you girls are gettin' more friendly."

Gripping Nina's hand more tightly, Cricket glared at Patterson and marched toward the piñon tree. "Just be glad the others aren't close, Nina," Cricket whispered to the younger girl.

"Oh, I am," Nina assured her.

Cricket and Nina quickly tended to the necessaries of life and returned to where the others were already gathering. She exchanged looks of encouragement with Vilma, Ann, and Marie and felt somewhat hopeful once more.

"Now mount up, you hussies!" Heck hollered. "We gotta long ways to go yet today."

Ann began to weep as she watched Heck mount Harley, and Cricket's heart broke along with her friend's. She knew how much Harley meant to Ann—how well she treated the animal—how tenderly. But Heck hadn't quit spurring him since the moment he'd first mounted, and Cricket knew Ann was horrified—not that being abducted by white slavers wasn't terrifying and horrifying enough.

"Wait!" Nina called as Cricket began to mount the horse the outlaws had assigned to her.

"What's the matter, Nina?" she asked.

"I-I hear somethin'," Nina whispered. Suddenly, Nina's horse whinnied and reared. As the animal began to frantically stomp the ground, Nina cried out and leapt backward in trying to avoid being trampled.

"What in the hell is goin' on?" Patterson shouted.

Reaching out and taking hold of the anxious horse's reins, Cricket soothed, "There now. Hush. You're all right," as she stroked the velvet of its nose.

"What is it, Patterson?" Heck hollered as he reined in his horse.

"Oh, somethin' just spooked one of the horses is all," Patterson answered.

Cricket glanced over her shoulder to where the other men waited a little farther off. A wave of renewed terror washed over her. There were seven of them—seven girls who had been taken from their homes and families. Ten men to keep them corralled as they traveled. Or, as Heck had explained in no uncertain terms the day before, ten men who would shoot any girl who tried to escape or ride off.

She thought of Heathro Thibodaux—wished he would come for her—for them. Yet with her next thought, she was glad he wouldn't.

He'd nearly been killed last time he'd tried to stop a gang of white slavers. Furthermore, Heck Alford had told the girls that at the first sign of a posse, he'd shoot every one of them right between the eyes.

Therefore, Cricket didn't know whether to wish for a posse to find them or to pray that Heck Alford, Patterson, and all the others would just drop dead for no reason.

"Ahhhhhhh!"

Cricket startled at the sound of Nina's scream.

"It bit me! The snake! It's a rattler, and I've been bit!" the girl screamed.

Cricket looked to see an enormous rattlesnake coiled up near a large rock next to Nina. The horse that had spooked reared again, pulling its reins free of Cricket's grasp as it began stomping the ground.

"It's a damn diamondback, Heck!" Patterson shouted. The idiot outlaw fired his pistol at the snake but missed, and the snake struck again.

Cricket screamed as she saw Nina crumple to the ground in agony. This time when Patterson fired, the large rattler must've known it was whipped—for it uncoiled, slithering off into the sagebrush nearby.

Heck arrived then, reined in Harley, and asked Patterson, "How big was the snake?"

Patterson shook his head. "Six or seven feet, at least."

"Help me!" Nina cried as she looked at the punctures in her stockings where blood was seeping out.

"You bit more than once, girl?" Heck asked.

"Yes!" Nina sobbed. "Twice! It bit me twice! Oh, help me, mister! I don't wanna die!"

"Well, darlin'," Heck said as he drew his pistol, "I sure am sorry to hear that."

Cricket screamed as the sound of the gunshot echoed in her ears. She could hear the other girls scream—heard them begin to sob. But she couldn't move; she couldn't breathe. She could only stand there in the middle of nowhere—staring in horrified disbelief as Nina slumped to the ground. She was dead.

❧

"I sure hate that we lost one, Heck," Cricket heard Patterson say as the outlaws sat around the fire after dark that night.

"Aw, she was dead the moment that diamondback bit her, boy," Heck grumbled. "You know that as well as I do. And she woulda slowed us down anyhow."

"That's a might lotta silver to lose though, boss," said a man Cricket had heard Patterson call Frank. "It shore is a shame."

"You think we could pick up another girl along the way, Heck?" another man asked. "You know…to make up for the one we lost today?"

But Heck shook his head. "Naw. We don't wanna venture too close to any town now, boys. We just need to head straight for New Orleans. Six girls will do us fine. We'll make a wagonload of money off them. 'Specially that redhead and that purty one they call Grasshopper, or whatever it is."

"Cricket," Patterson offered. "They call her Cricket."

Heck and the other men laughed. "Well, she didn't chirp one word before today…so's it puts me to wonderin' how in the world she got a name like that."

The men chuckled, and Cricket wiped the tears from her cheeks. She couldn't think of anything but Nina. Every time she closed her eyes, all she could see was Nina's body dropping to the ground—the way they'd left her just lying there with no protection—no grave or even rocks to keep the buzzards away. The outlaws hadn't even taken the time to close her eyes—and it was all Cricket could think about.

She tried to block out the sounds of the outlaws' conversation—tried to ignore the discomfort of her hands and feet being bound. She tried not to hear the other girls weeping—trying to gasp quietly as they sobbed with sorrow for Nina and fear for their own lives.

Closing her eyes, Cricket inhaled the warm aroma of cedar smoke, of evening grass, and of the beads of dew that were already starting to gather on its tender, green blades. She tried to imagine her daddy and Ada, wrapped in each other's arms and kissing the way they did each evening before retiring to their bedroom. But more than anything, she envisioned Heathro Thibodaux—tried to recall the warm, moist, sweet flavor of the driven kiss he'd forced on her little more than a week before. What she wouldn't give to have that kiss at that moment. Oh, she'd thought it was harsh and rather lustful only eight (or was it nine?) days ago. But now—as she lay there allowing the memory of it to bathe her in a moment of escape—she wished for Heathro Thibodaux's driven kiss more than anything! She even wished his danged bull was chasing her through Mr. Burroughs's pasture—that Mr. Thibodaux was hollering at her to get her fanny over the fence and then helping her do it—that he was spitting on her foot and rubbing it in.

Cricket opened her eyes, knowing it did no good to dream of Heathro Thibodaux then. No matter what she did, he wasn't going to simply appear out of nowhere, fight ten men off, and free them.

"Cricket?"

Cricket looked up to see Vilma staring at her. Her face was tear-stained, but her cheeks were dry.

"Yeah?" Cricket whispered.

"I don't wanna be sold in New Orleans," Vilma said.

"Me neither," Cricket answered. "But...but it's better than bein' shot and left to die out here, isn't it?"

Vilma's tears did start fresh again then. "You do know what they plan to sell us for, don't you, Cricket?"

"To be slaves," Cricket wept. "I mean, we fought a war over slavery. Mr. Lincoln freed those people in the South. So I don't understand how on earth we can be forced to do hard labor when we—"

"It ain't that same kind of labor, Cricket," Vilma sniffed.

"What do you mean?"

"I heard Daddy talkin' to mama about some things once," Vilma explained. "Wyatt and I both heard him. These outlaws that do this—these bad men who steal woman and take them to sell in Mexico, New Orleans, and such places—they don't sell them to be slaves workin' in people's homes. They sell them to—"

"Shut up!"

Cricket gasped as she felt one of the men kick her in the seat to quiet her.

"Not another word outta you girls tonight! Do you hear me?" the man growled.

Cricket sniffled as Vilma closed her eyes and wept more profusely. Cricket closed her eyes as well—tried to forget the dust and dirt that clung to her face and arms and hands—tried not to notice the pain of her sunburned nose and cheeks or the dry, stale taste in her mouth. Once more she tried to think of that night in Pike's Creek—the night she'd kissed Heathro Thibodaux and he'd kissed her back. If the morning found her dead and being eaten by buzzards, at least her soul would always remember the feel of being held by such powerful, capable hands as Mr. Thibodaux's—of being ravaged by such a tantalizingly hungry kiss, given by such a handsome and alluring man.

As ever when she thought of Heathro Thibodaux, Cricket's heart ached for the haunting, grievous pain she knew he bore for the sake of what had happened to the girls abducted by white slavers a year previous. And in that moment, she remembered his warning—the warning he'd given her before he'd kissed her. Heathro Thibodaux had warned her about the ugliness in the world—about men like these outlaws whose hands she now found herself in. Was this what God wanted? For Cricket and her friends to learn about the evil that walked the earth, when all they'd tried to do was add beauty to it? No! She didn't believe that. It was just her fear and overwhelming fatigue putting such thoughts in her mind. She needed rest. If she were to have any chance at all to think clearly the next day—to be ever watchful of an opportunity for escape—then she needed to rest.

Once more she smelled the aroma of the cedar wood fire burning—listened to the crickets' summer-night song—and let her mind nest on her memories of Heathro Thibodaux—of their kiss—of their moments near Mr. Burroughs's pasture.

I'll show you something inappropriate that'll really ruffle your britches, Miss Cranford, he'd said as he'd worked to remove the splinter from the bottom of her foot that day. Over and over she let his voice echo through her mind—*I'll show you something inappropriate that'll really ruffle your britches, Miss Cranford*—over and over again, until at last there was nothing but blessed, unconscious dark.

CHAPTER TEN

Heath frowned, gritted his teeth, and tried to remain as patient as possible. He was ready to string up Edgar Stanley in the nearest tree. The man was the most self-centered, self-righteous pile of horse manure he'd ever encountered!

After announcing at the church that he'd be leaving with what men would join him, Heath stormed out. He informed the other men that they would meet out at the old Morgan house within the next thirty minutes to start the search, and then Heath mounted Archie and rode for home. He didn't linger long, however—just long enough to gather a few supplies, his Texas Ranger badge and papers, and a few other little odds and ends something whispered to him to take. Then he was off to the old Morgan place.

Although Heath was glad to see that seven men were waiting for him, including Wyatt Stanley, he was not so pleased to see the Reverend Stanley there as well. The man was trouble. Every feeling in Heathro Thibodaux's gut told him Edgar Stanley was an idiot and not to be trusted.

Still, help was help. Thus, after showing all the men the signs of the struggle out in front of the Morgan house, and then down the creek bank, across it, and in the clearing in the trees, Heath led the posse south, tracking the gang of outlaws and the stolen Pike's Creek girls by their tracks. He silently prayed that the rain would hold off until he found the girls. If it rained and washed away what was left of any evidence he could easily track—well, he wouldn't think about that.

Heath was certain the outlaws were heading for New Orleans. Edgar Stanley and several of the other men argued that Mexico was closer, however. They were doubtful that the outlaw gang would travel farther all the way to New Orleans.

But Heath explained what he believed—what his soul told him to be the truth. There was a man in New Orleans by the name of Jacques Cheval. Over the past several years, he'd built a secret, though massive, empire—selling women of any race, creed, and color into forced harlotry. The year before, while Heath trailed the band of outlaws who had in the end pushed their victims to their deaths at the bottom of a canyon, Heath's previous investigation and his guts had told him those outlaws were headed to meet with Jacques Cheval as well. Still, none of the other, more experienced Texas Rangers had believed him. And though he'd broken off from that posse, ridden off on his own, and was proved to be right, it did no good at all—none.

So Heath didn't argue much with the righteous Reverend Stanley, or the other men that tended to believe Mexico was the outlaws' destination. He figured that as long as he could track the Pike's Creek girls with the evidence left in the dirt and brush along the trail—well, it didn't matter whether the rest of the men believed him. Tracking would lead them to the girls, wherever the outlaws were headed. And so Heath's silent prayers to keep the rain at bay became almost constant as the men traveled.

But even though the good Lord kept the rain from falling that first day, it seemed even divinity couldn't keep Reverend Stanley from trying to prove he knew more than anybody on earth or in heaven.

"The tracks end here," Edgar Stanley announced as Heath dismounted Archie and studied the tracks on the riverbank. "It's obvious they crossed here."

"Not necessarily," Heath mumbled as he stood and gazed across the river.

"If we cross here, we'll find tracks on the other bank," Edgar assured the men.

"Maybe we will, and maybe we won't," Heath said. "But even

if there are tracks on the other side of the river…it don't mean they crossed and headed southwest."

"Of course it does," Edgar argued.

Then, before Heath could even move to stop him, Edgar Stanley charged his horse into the water and began fording the river.

"We need to look around thoroughly on this side some more, before we go off half-cocked assumin' things, boys," Heath growled to the other men. "Don't you all follow him. Even if we find tracks over there, it could be a ruse."

Grinding his teeth with barely restrained anger, Heath slowly surveyed the riverbank. If the outlaws were taking the girls to Mexico, then it was likely they did cross the river right where the posse waited. However, Heath's gut never lied to him—and it was still egging him on toward New Orleans.

As he walked along the bank of the river, searching for any signs of another crossing, a momentary wave of terror broke over him. What if they didn't find the girls in time? What if they did find them, but during the fighting to get them back one or more of them was killed? He thought again of the kiss the girl had given him—scolded himself for being so harsh with her. Of course, he knew that whatever was going on with her now, it was much more harsh than he'd been with her—but that didn't matter. He'd been—he'd been wrong.

"Over here!" he heard Edgar Stanley shout. He looked up, across the river where the self-righteous preacher sat astride his gray mare like some sissied-up French king. "There's tracks! Right here! The tracks pick up right here…then head off into the rocky terrain ahead!"

"Do you see any tracks beyond the rocks?" Heath hollered.

"I don't need to," Stanley shouted back. "The tracks pick up here. They're headed to Mexico."

"No!" Heath shouted. "They're tryin' to fool us. If you can't track them over the rocks, then—"

But Reverend Stanley wasn't about to be proved wrong by some beat-up Texas Ranger who had failed miserably to save the last set of stolen girls he'd tracked.

"You men ford here!" Stanley ordered. "I ain't wastin' any time on a fool's errand."

"But Mr. Thibodaux says it could be a trick," Wyatt called to his father.

Even from where Heath stood at a distance on the opposing side of the river, he could see the fury and indignation on Edgar Stanley's face. His son had questioned him—and in front of the other men. Heath shook his head, knowing that now Edgar's path was set. If Heath found Vilma Stanley standing right downstream, Edgar wouldn't admit defeat now.

"You men ford here," Edgar shouted. "We don't need Thibodaux to track for us." Glaring at his son, he added, "Now, boy!"

Heath stormed back to Archie and mounted. As the other men began to tentatively ford the river—certain, no doubt, that their spiritual leader would never lead them astray in any regard—Heath shook his head.

"You're a fool, Stanley!" he hollered. "And arrogant, egotistical fool! Let's hope I can save your daughter before your arrogance finds her sold into harlotry in New Orleans."

"We'll see you back in Pike's Creek once we've brung the girls home," Stanley hollered back.

But Heath shook his head. "I'll see you in hell first, you selfish son of a..." Heath voice was lost in the wind as he spurred Archie into a gallop downriver—the opposite direction from which Reverend Righteous and the other men were headed.

Cricket gnawed on the piece of flavorless jerky Heck had ordered one of his men to feed the girls at midday. It made her stomach churn—but not as badly as her hunger had made it churn before the man had given it to her. The girls had been allowed to sit together to rest and eat. Heck told them it was because no one had acted up or talked back to him all morning. But Cricket suspected it was so the men could keep a closer watch on them. After all, maybe she, Ann, Marie, Vilma, Pearl, and Jinny were sitting together in a close circle, but the outlaws were simply positioned in a wider circle surrounding theirs.

Cricket glanced over to see Heck stretched out under a tree, his hat tugged down over his eyes, and a quiet snore emanated from his ugly, whisker-ridden nose. Patterson was playing cards with another man behind her. As for the other outlaws, most of them were staring at the circle of girls with wicked grins or talking in low, guarded voices.

"I don't know why they don't just have their way with us and be done with it," Jinny whispered, wiping a new tear from her cheek.

"Because we're worth more when we're…when we're unspoiled," Vilma said. Placing a comforting arm around Jinny's shoulders, she soothed, "They'll leave us be, Jinny. Don't you worry. We'll be safe until we reach their destination. So just try and be brave, and don't live in fear of…of that."

"Of what?" Cricket angrily breathed. "I don't know what it is I don't know…but I don't know somethin'." She leaned toward Vilma. "Last night you told me they don't plan to sell us to be slaves as in cleanin' house and doin' chores. What do they plan to sell us for then?"

Vilma shook her head—rolled her eyes with fatigue and exasperation. "Please do not pretend to be so innocent, Magnolia Cranford," she scolded. "You're the sharpest knife in the kitchen drawer. You know more than any of us put together, so don't pretend you don't know what I mean."

"Well, I don't know what you mean either, Vilma Stanley!" Marie interjected in a hushed voice.

"Me neither," Ann admitted then.

"And I certainly don't understand all this," Pearl whimpered. "There I was…just walkin' along on my way home from my sewin' lesson with Miss Karen, when all at once, they snatched me up!" She sniffled and restrained the tears brimming in her eyes. "And now you and Jinny seem to know somethin' the rest of don't…even Cricket. And that's makin' me more and more fearful by the minute."

"Well, it should!" Vilma grumbled. She looked from Jinny to Ann. "Are you serious, Ann Burroughs? Are you tellin' me that you really do not know what these men have planned for us in the end?"

Ann shook her head, blushing with embarrassment at her own ignorance.

"Marie," Vilma began, "you and Hudson Oliver are, what…maybe two months from gettin' married. Surely you understand all this?"

But Marie just shrugged. "I just thought that since the slaves were freed by Mr. Lincoln, folks down there in New Orleans are just forcin' anyone they can get their hands on into doin' their hard work for them."

Vilma's expression changed from that of doubt to that of complete astonishment. She seemed rattled for a moment, looking from one girl to the next as if she were still unable to believe they didn't grasp everything they should.

At last, looking to Cricket, she asked, "Do you know what a harlot is, Cricket?"

Cricket asked, "Like in the Bible, you mean?"

"Yes."

"Well, it's a bad woman," Cricket answered. "Like a female outlaw or somethin'."

Vilma and Jinny exchanged surprised glances.

"I heard my daddy call that red-haired woman who serves liquor over at the saloon in Thistle a harlot," Ann offered. "Is she a criminal, do you think?"

"I don't know," Marie said. "I never thought about that much." Marie's eyes widened. "Vilma! Are they gonna try and turn us into outlaws?"

But Vilma shook her head. "How can you girls be so naive?" she asked. "You know where babies come from, don't you? What a man does to a woman to…to start a baby growin'?"

"Of course, Vilma," Cricket grumbled. "What do you take us for? Idiots?"

Vilma's expression then changed to daring. "Go on then, Cricket. Tell us how it all works."

Cricket sighed with frustration. She didn't see what babies had to do with outlaws abducting woman. It was ridiculous. Still, in that moment (as in many moments throughout her life before that time), she felt that there *was* something she didn't know—something pertinent to their situation.

132

"Well, you marry the man you love," Cricket began, "and after you're married, you share the same bed with him. And then one day… because you're married…a baby just starts growin' inside you."

"Exactly," Pearl affirmed.

But Marie and Ann looked to one another with puzzled expressions.

"What are you talkin' about, Cricket?" Marie asked. "The doctor gets a baby from another town and gives it to you."

"What?" Ann exclaimed. "That's not true, Marie."

"Yes, it is," Marie argued. "My mama told me all about it when my little sister was born. And again when my brother was born."

But Ann argued, "No. Before each of my brothers was born, Mama just went out for a walk one day, and when she came back, she told me there was baby growin' inside her. Then after those long months of waitin', she went on over to Mrs. Maloney's house, and when she came home, she had a new brother for me. I have three brothers, and it was the same every time."

Vilma's mouth dropped open in astonishment, but Pearl offered, "I heard all three of those too…before I heard a woman in our congregation confessin' to my daddy about how the baby she had *really* came about."

"Your daddy is a preacher too?" Cricket asked.

"Yep," Pearl answered. "And I know what Vilma means now… about these outlaws wantin' us to stay *unspoiled*."

"Well, I don't," Cricket grumbled. "Vilma, if you know somethin' we don't…that we should…you need to tell us. And you need to tell us now. I'm havin' a mighty hard time understandin' how babies have anything to do with us gettin' sold as slaves in New Orleans." Vilma blushed a bit, and it unsettled Cricket even more. "And what on earth is it with you preachers' daughters eavesdroppin' on conversations you ought not hear?"

Vilma inhaled a breath of bravery and nodded. "My mama told me the story about babies comin' from the doctor too," she admitted. "But when me and Wyatt overhead Daddy and Mama talkin' one night… well…we both learned the truth."

"Well then…if we're all so ignorant, tell us the truth too," Cricket begged. Her irritation with Vilma's know-it-all attitude was gone, replaced by fear of what she didn't know herself—fear of what was truly waiting for them at the outlaws' destination.

"All right then," Vilma breathed. "All right. Gather closer," she whispered. Cricket leaned toward the center of their circle, and so did the others.

"The truth of it is, what I'm about to reveal to you girls can either be the most romantic, magical experience of your life…or the very stuff of nightmares," Vilma said quietly. "And we, my darlin's…are headin' for the nightmares way of it."

Heath had slowly traveled nearly two miles downriver along the bank. He hadn't found what he was looking for—evidence that the band of outlaws had ridden in the water downstream instead of permanently crossing the river to head for Mexico. He'd begun to doubt himself. Maybe he'd been wrong. Maybe Reverend Righteous was right. But with every doubt that crossed his mind, his gut churned with encouragement. And if there was one thing Heathro Thibodaux had learned, it was to always trust his gut.

So Heath rode Archie farther downriver, his eyes scanning the bank looking for any signs of disturbance. Doubt was thick in his mind—as thick as certainty was in his gut—and the battle between the two was exhausting. Still, just as his doubt was at its height, he saw exactly what he'd been looking for.

Just over two miles downriver, he saw the tracks—the mud and tracks left by horses and riders as they'd left the water for dry ground. He'd been right! The outlaws were heading for New Orleans to sell the girls into Jacques Cheval's brothels.

He reigned in Archie and briefly wondered if he should ride back and try to catch the other men—but only briefly. Time was too short. He'd surely closed the distance between the outlaws and himself, being that traveling in the river would've slowed their progress considerably. But he couldn't waste any time, not a moment. He had to think of something—some way to save those girls on his own.

His gruesome, tragic experience taught him not to take on the gang alone—not in the conventional way, anyhow. He'd have to think of something else—a way to infiltrate them maybe. Whatever he came up with, he needed to come up with it fast.

Heath looked up when he heard the calls of buzzards then. They were close and circling overhead. He'd been tracking the riverbank too intently to notice them before. But now—now as he watched the ten or twelve buzzards circling, taking turns swooping to the ground to land on some carrion nearby—his heart fell to the pit of his stomach with a nauseating thud.

Not a hundred feet from where he paused lay a body—a body he could see was dressed in a woman's clothing.

He felt the perspiration begin to drip from his forehead and temples. Was it one of the Pike's Creek girls? Was it the one who'd kissed him? He felt guilty for hoping it wasn't, but he did hope it wasn't her—prayed it wasn't. In fact, he hoped it was any of the girls from Pike's Creek other than the one who'd kissed him.

Heath mumbled an apology to the heavens for thinking such a thing and then said, "Go on, Archie. Waitin' ain't gonna change it."

He hollered at the buzzards—fired a shot at the two coyotes waiting in the sagebrush as he approached. Heath could see the animals had been at the body for some time and tried to prepare himself for what the condition of it would be.

"Whoa," he breathed as he reined Archie to stop next to the dead girl. Dismounting, he frowned and felt his heart harden with anger as he hunkered down to study what had once been a living, breathing young woman with her whole life stretching out before her.

Heath's eyes filled with excess moisture, and he thanked God when he saw the girl's hair was blonde. It wasn't the Cranford, King, or Stanley girl. Wiping tears of anger and sadness from his eyes, he sniffed and looked to the girl's feet. The dead girl's hair did have the color of summer grain—not dark hair like the Cranford or King girl or red hair like the Stanley girl—blonde hair like the Burroughs girl. Yet her shoes indicated she wasn't the Burroughs girl. Ralph Burroughs's daughter had been riding her thoroughbred, and Heath had never seen the girl and her horse without her wearing riding boots. Furthermore, he figured the dead girl was too skinny to be the Burroughs girl. Of course, he couldn't be sure it wasn't the Burroughs girl—not for certain—not after the way the buzzards and coyotes had already been at the arms and face. It was a disturbing, gruesome sight, and Heath could only hope the girl had been dead long before nature's creatures had taken to her remains.

Heath saw the blood on the girl's shirt. It wasn't from the animals having at the body. This blood was from the bullet hole somebody had put through her heart. He reached down, tugging at the skirt and petticoats covering her legs. Lifting the girl's right leg, he saw the blood on her stockings from the puncture wounds—two sets of puncture wounds. He nodded as his suspicions were confirmed. On the back of the girl's right calf were two rattler bites. From the space between fang marks, he knew it had been a big snake that had gotten the poor little thing.

Almost desperately, Heath began checking the girl's pockets for anything that might identify her not being Ann Burroughs for certain. Eventually, he found a silver chain around her neck, tucked inside her shirt. An oval locket hung from it, and he opened it to find photographs of a man and woman—nobody he recognized. This girl was not one of the Pike's Creek girls, and Heath mumbled, "Thank God."

He wondered whether this girl had been Cooper Keel's niece who had gone missing from Thistle. Or was it some other poor little thing the outlaws had taken from some other town along their way? Whoever she was, the gang that had taken the Pike's Creek girls had deemed her worthless the moment the snake had bitten her. No doubt they'd shot her simply for convenience—so they wouldn't have to drag along a dying prisoner.

Heath was nauseated, near to vomiting, and sat back on his heels, putting one fist to his mouth until he was certain that the contents of his stomach would stay put. It wasn't the sight of the dead, mutilated body of the girl that sickened him—though the sight of it was certainly something he'd never purge from his mind. Rather it was the fact that he'd been too late to save her. He closed his eyes and visualized the eight other girls he'd failed to save a year earlier. Now the count was nine; he was responsible for the deaths of nine sweet, young innocents.

"That ain't true though," he said aloud. "It wasn't my fault," he mumbled as he yanked at the silver chain around the girl's neck. The chain broke, and Heath put it in his pocket. He'd see that it was given to her parents—if he lived and could find out who she was, or had been. He stood and turned to his saddlebags, retrieving the small, short-handled shovel he always carried when he rode.

Oh, he knew he probably shouldn't linger burying the dead girl, but he couldn't just leave her there like that. The buzzards and coyotes would pick and gnaw her down to the bones if he did. Not that he'd ever want to take her back to wherever she came from—not that he'd even tell her parents, if he had the chance, what condition he'd found her in. But he couldn't just leave her there.

As Heath worked at digging out a very shallow grave and then covering the girl's body with heavy rocks so the animals couldn't get to her, he kept reminding himself that her death wasn't his fault. It was the band of outlaws that had done it. Maybe even the posse that had paused back at the river where the tracks had been found—but it wasn't his. Deep in his soul, he knew that the deaths of those eight other girls a year back weren't his fault either. But someone had to bear the blame; someone had to tether his soul to the fact that it had all happened. And no one else seemed willing to do it.

And so, as he laid the last rock on top of the pile of stones covering the poor girl's mutilated body, Heathro Thibodaux promised himself that she would be the only dead girl he found while tracking the outlaws and the girls from Pike's Creek.

As Cricket lay there in the darkness—as she tried not to hear the outlaws talking and laughing as they sat around the campfire—she thought about all that Vilma had explained to them earlier in the day. First of all, she wondered why folks kept the particulars of how babies came to be such a fortified secret—why they lied about it. After all, it wasn't a game or anything—nothing like letting children believe in Santa Claus to make the merriment and excitement of Christmas more magical. It was how the human race continued to exist, for pity's sake! She was glad, however, that her daddy hadn't made up something ridiculous like a woman just taking a walk and coming back with a baby. In fact, Cricket (knowing her daddy as she did) figured that if it hadn't been for the initial animosity toward Ada that Cricket felt just after the wedding, her daddy may very well have told her the whole truth of it. He knew she'd get married herself someday, and Zeke Cranford never let his daughter step into anything wearing a proverbial blindfold of any kind.

In truth, everything Vilma had described made perfect sense. Even the other girls thought so—Ann, Pearl, and Marie—though Marie had blushed seventeen shades of red when Vilma explained that Hudson Oliver no doubt would know exactly what to do when their wedding night came. "Men seem to be a bit more instinctive, I heard my mama tell my daddy that night Wyatt and I were eavesdroppin'," Vilma explained.

Still, with all that had been revealed about intimacy between a man and woman, a husband and wife—what Vilma explained the outlaws were planning to sell them all for—everything had changed. Even in that very moment, just the memory of Vilma's details caused Cricket's eyes to fill with tears. She thought she'd known fear and dread the night before—but now fear and dread had turned to terror and despair!

Silently she prayed for deliverance from the hands of the evil men that held her and her friends captive. She prayed for freedom and the protection of their virtue. She prayed that one day a man would love her the way Hudson loved Marie—that he would marry her and together they would be not only man and wife but also lovers in heart, mind, soul, and body. In truth, she prayed that Heathro Thibodaux would be that man. After all, Cricket knew she was in the hands of evil. She felt like she might vomit at the thought of what the outlaws had in store for the girls when they reached their destination.

"No!" she breathed as tears escaped her eyes, streaming over her temples as she lay on the hard ground, her hands and feet bound. "No! Let this pass!" she prayed in a whisper. "Let this pass! Get me home somehow, God. Get me home, and let it be Heathro Thibodaux I give myself to one day. Oh, please! Please!"

Midst her quiet sobs, Cricket felt a wave of hysteria begin to overtake her. Vilma Stanley—what a character she was. Cricket giggled and sobbed simultaneously as she breathed to herself, "Leave it to the preacher's daughter to know all there is to know about what goes on between a husband and wife when they share a bed."

Cricket tried to scream as the hand clamped hard over her mouth. She tried to struggle as visions of one of the outlaws not having enough self-control to leave her to her unhappy end of being sold flashed through her mind.

She tried to call for help—but from whom?

"Shhhh!" A man's low voice hushed her. "Settle down, Miss Cranford. Don't fight me, or you'll draw their attention."

Cricket still squirmed, trying to peer up through the darkness to the face hovering over her, his hand held tightly over her mouth. But he placed his head next to hers on the ground before she could see him clearly.

She felt his hot breath on her ear—heard him whisper, "Stay as still as you can. If they see me, we're all of us dead, do you hear me?"

Cricket quit trying to scream—quit struggling—nodded.

"Good girl," the man said. "Now you know me, don't you?"

Cricket shook her head.

"Then look over here at me…but don't move or cry out," he instructed.

The man kept his hand over Cricket's mouth as she slowly turned her head to her right. Instantly, she began to struggle again—to try and struggle *to* him, not away. For there—his body stretched out on the grassy incline above her head—his handsome, beloved face mere inches from hers—was Texas Ranger Heathro Thibodaux!

CHAPTER ELEVEN

Cricket tried not to sob—tried to remain as quiet as possible—but an overwhelming trembling and near hysteria, borne of sudden hope, was so viciously racing through her body she could neither remain perfectly still nor stop her tears.

Heathro Thibodaux removed his hand from over her mouth, and Cricket was able to gasp a deep breath. It settled her sobbing a bit.

She started to speak to him—to thank him for coming and beg him to free her—but he put an index finger to his mouth, indicating she should remain silent.

"There's no posse with me, Miss Cranford," he whispered against her ear.

Cricket knew she should be dismally disappointed with returning hopelessness at what he'd said, but she wasn't. Even for her predicament—even for her fatigue and soreness of body and mind from traveling so roughly—Cricket simply closed her eyes and relished the feel of Heathro Thibodaux's breath on her neck—of his low, soothing voice in her ear.

"But there's hope all the same," he said. "I've got me a plan that I think will stall these sons of…these outlaws until the posse wises up and tracks us here. All right?"

Cricket nodded.

"I need your help though," he continued. "You're the only one of these girls who can help me with what I'm plannin' to do. All right?"

Again Cricket nodded. "Then listen close…'cause I gotta be fast before they spot me."

Cricket's tired, sore body erupted with goose bumps as Heathro pressed his lips to her ear as he instructed, "I'm gonna show up tomorrow mornin'…pretendin' I've been trackin' these men in order to assist them in gettin' to New Orleans to sell you. So no matter what, don't any of you girls let on that you know me, you hear? You tell all these girls to glare at me, spit at me, and act like they hate me as much as they hate these outlaws. Make sure you tell them come first light… so they ain't surprised when I show up."

"But they'll kill you!" Cricket whispered. "They'll kill you for even seein' us! They won't give you a chance to—"

His hand over her mouth and his quiet, "Shhh," quieted her once again.

"They might…but I don't think so," he explained. "I think I've got an ace in my pocket that'll get me into the game. Then we'll play them until that posse gets here."

Again Cricket nodded, and he removed his hand from her.

"But you need to know somethin'," he added. "This plan involves you a bit more than you might like…but it's the best idea I can come up with. So no matter what I do or say, you play along with me, girl. I'll explain better when I can…or maybe you'll just figure it out. But if I take hold of you or somethin'…whatever I do tomorrow…you fight me at first. You fight me as hard as you would if one of these sons of… if one of these devils was takin' hold of you instead of me, all right?"

"Yes," Cricket breathed, new tears trickling over her temples.

"Now I gotta go," he said. "But I'll never be farther away than a few hundred feet until you see me tomorrow mornin'. I won't leave you girls. And I'll do my best to keep you safe until that posse gets here. Do you trust me on that?"

"Yes," Cricket whispered as she wept tears of joy, hope, fear, desperation, and so many others.

"Then I'll see you in the mornin'," he whispered. "Just be strong. Keep these girls strong too."

He was gone. As quickly and quietly as he'd been there one moment, Heathro Thibodaux was gone the next.

Cricket lay trembling, trying so hard to weep softly, but it was difficult—and one of the outlaws heard her.

"Hush up over there, girl!" Patterson shouted. "You ain't got nothin' to be bawlin' over…at least not yet." The men chuckled with amusement at Patterson's vile implications.

Cricket inhaled a deep breath and attempted to calm herself by thinking on the feel of Heathro Thibodaux's lips to her ear, his breath on her skin, and his promise that he wouldn't leave them. Maybe the posse would get there sooner than he anticipated. Maybe the terrifying, miserable ordeal the abductions had caused was nearly at an end!

Whatever Heathro Thibodaux's plan was, it just had to work. It must! Whispering a prayer—even with her hands and feet bound and tethered to the girls resting uncomfortably next to her—Cricket finally drifted off to sleep on the gentle wings of renewed hope.

Marie looked to Cricket, sighing with agitation.

Cricket nodded and mouthed, *Be patient*, as she glanced to each girl in turn.

During their breakfast, she'd explained to the girls what had happened the night before—Heathro Thibodaux's miraculous emergence and what he'd told her. Naturally, all the girls had begun firing questions at her at the speed of gunshot bullets.

The girls wanted to know when Mr. Thibodaux would intercept them. They wanted to know why he didn't have a posse with him. They wanted to know why he'd chosen Cricket to speak to. But Cricket could only repeatedly answer, "I don't know. We have to wait."

Still, it had seemed like hours and hours since daybreak—even though it hadn't been more than thirty minutes. Cricket wanted Mr. Thibodaux to appear as badly as all the other girls did—perhaps even more desperately. Part of her had begun to wonder if she'd only dreamt the encounter with him. She'd dreamt so often of Heathro Thibodaux over the past months that her fatigue made her question her sanity for a moment. Furthermore, though she knew none of them could make the mistake of offering any miniscule clue to the outlaws that he was familiar, she just wanted him to be there with them—with her.

When Cricket had again convinced herself that Heathro had actually been with her—had whispered in her ear, touched her, and promised to be close by until he revealed himself—she began to worry for him, at the profound risk he was taking. It was unfathomable! To ride into a gang of ten armed outlaws? What would he say? How would he approach?

As if heaven itself had heard her thoughts, Cricket heard the cocking of pistol hammers and looked over to see Heck stand up, brush the crumbs of hardtack on his pant leg, draw his own weapon, and gaze off to the north.

"Who's this, boss?" Patterson asked.

Heck frowned. He looked at Patterson as if he'd just uttered the most ignorant sentence ever spoken on the face of the earth.

"Hell, Patterson," Heck growled. "I don't know! Could be Santy Claus."

Cricket tried to keep the beating of her heart at a normal pace, but when she looked up and saw Heathro Thibodaux astride his familiar horse—saw the white handkerchief tied to a long stick he was holding in one hand—she thought for a moment she might leap up and run to him! Instead, she clenched her fists and looked to each of her friends in turn.

Remember, she mouthed. *We don't know him.*

Every girl nodded slightly—ever so slightly—and then returned her attention to the approaching rider.

"What's he doin'?" one of the men asked.

"Looks like he wants to talk," Heck answered.

"Should I shoot him, boss?"

Cricket clamped one hand over her mouth to keep from crying out, *No!* She knew she mustn't make a sound; she mustn't do anything to endanger their would-be rescuer.

Thankfully, Heck answered for her. "No. Let's see what he wants. It ain't just any man who would have the guts to ride up on us all alone like he's doin'." Heck paused a moment and then added, "Still...all you

144

boys keep your aim on this stranger…just in case he ain't as harmless as he looks."

Cricket watched as Mr. Thibodaux rode into the camp. Her heart leapt when he reined in his horse and tossed the makeshift truce flag to the ground.

Heathro smiled and greeted, "Hello there, boys."

"And who might you be, stranger?" Heck asked.

Heathro smiled, causing butterflies to take flight in Cricket's stomach.

"I'm Baptiste Thibodaux," he answered. "And if I'm right, you boys are on your way to meet up with my cousin."

Heck's eyes narrowed. "That would depend on who your cousin is, boy."

Heathro smiled again, the sun glinting on his gold tooth. "That would be Jacques Cheval. You mighta heard of him…especially considerin' that you're travelin' on this way…" Heathro glanced to the abducted girls and added, "And with such lovely companions."

Heck inhaled a deep breath, exhaling it slowly. Cricket held hers. No doubt Heck was trying to decide whether Heathro's story held any water.

"So," Heck began, "you ride into our camp here…alone…claimin' to be Jacques Cheval's cousin…and you're expectin' us to believe you. Is that it?"

Heathro leaned back in his saddle, his smile fading to a triumphant grin. "If you boys want Jacques to buy these girls when you get to New Orleans—and he does pay the highest prices for sweet, unspoiled things like these—then you best not ride into the city without me."

"Why's that?" Patterson asked.

Heathro's smile faded altogether then. "'Cause Jacques's boys will gun you down before you can blink," he answered.

Heck's posture straightened with indignation, but Heathro continued, "Did you all hear about that mess last year? A group of ambitious boys like yourselves tried to get to New Orleans with some white flesh to sell without one of Jacques's men with them. Did you hear how that ended?"

"I heared the Texas Rangers killed 'em," one outlaw offered.

"Naw," Patterson disagreed. "That ain't what happened. It was only one Ranger that showed up...and the way I heard it, he ended up at the bottom of a canyon with a bunch of dead girls."

"Yeah," the other outlaw agreed. "And then the Texas Rangers came in and killed the bunch."

"Only it wasn't the Texas Rangers that killed those poor boys," Heathro told them. He shrugged, smiled, and said, "Well...maybe they was dressed up like Texas Rangers, but it was us...Jacques's boys. Jacques don't like nobody bringin' girls into New Orleans without his say-so. Them other boys...they didn't listen to us when we tried politely explainin' how Jacques does things. They were determined to march into New Orleans and find Jacques for themselves." Heathro paused, his grin returning. "But Jacques says New Orleans was already marched on once by them damn Yankees. He ain't gonna be marched on again by anybody. So if you boys are lookin' to get to New Orleans and make yourselves rich men off sellin' these girls here, then you'll wanna let me help you out a mite."

"You got any proof you're with Jacques Cheval?" Heck asked.

Heathro chuckled. "Do you think I'd be fool enough to ride in here all by my lonesome to talk to you boys if I didn't?"

"Then let's see it," Heck challenged.

Cricket watched as Heathro dismounted and began digging in his saddlebag.

"Now," he began as he withdrew a small satchel, "I'm authorized to give you a little bonus money, if you agree to sell these girls to Jacques when you get to New Orleans." Heathro opened the satchel and withdrew what looked like several social calling cards. He offered one to Heck, then Patterson, and then gave several to one of the other men and nodded an indication that he should distribute them to the others.

"Jacques Cheval owns and oversees the finest brothels in New Orleans. They cater to the richest cliental," Heathro said. "If you agree to sell these women to Jacques Cheval, I'm authorized to hand you one hundred dollars per sale, right here, right now, before we even come close to crossin' into Louisiana."

Heck chuckled. "Jacques Cheval…businessman…Veux Carre, New Orleans," he read aloud. Looking to Heath, he asked, "So you're tellin' me that if I agree to sell these girls to Jacques Cheval, you're gonna give me a hundred dollars right here and now?"

Heathro glanced to the girls, his lips moving as he counted them. "That'd be six hundred dollars. One hundred dollars per head," he corrected. "But that's only if you allow me to help you deliver them safely to Jacques Cheval, and only Jacques Cheval. And if you take the agreement and the money and then try to do Jacques wrong…" Heathro shrugged. "Well, I'll just say it simple. You're all dead men."

Patterson laughed. "We're all dead men?" He looked around to some of the other outlaws and then smiled at Heathro and said, "You're the one that was dumb enough to ride in here all alone with a saddlebag full of money." Patterson leveled his pistol at Heath.

"Careful, boy," Heath threatened calmly. "I rode in here all alone, but Jacques don't send anybody out to do business by himself." Heathro raised an arm. "I bring my arm down in one position, and the others start home to tell Jacques that we've struck a deal and new girls are on the way. I bring my arm down another way…well, let's just say that same bunch of Texas Ranger–type fellows will take care of business for Jacques the way they did last year when that other bunch decided to try and refuse Jacques Cheval's generous offer."

Instantly the outlaws were unsettled. They began looking around as if expecting to find guns at their backs already.

"So what'll it be, boss?" Heathro asked Heck. "You want six hundred dollars in your pocket now…another two thousand in your pocket when we reach New Orleans? Or do you want to die like a duck in the desert here and now?"

Heck studied the social calling card Heathro had handed him—looked him up and down a moment. "You tellin' me that Jacques Cheval himself is gonna pay me that much for these girls?"

"Yep. If they get to him entirely *unspoiled*, that is," Heathro said. "Of course, that's why he always has me travel along."

"Why you?" Heck asked.

"Because I have a way of inspirin', shall we say, *cooperation* from the female sex when I have a mind to," Heathro answered.

Heck chuckled and rubbed his dirty beard with his thumb and forefinger as he studied Heathro from head to toe. "Why? 'Cause you're so pretty and all?"

Heathro shrugged. "Maybe," he answered. "But it's more of somethin' else. I'll share that with you if you agree to Jacques's proposal." Heathro Thibodaux's arm was still raised, and he added, "But my arm is gettin' a mite fatigued here, boss. I'm gonna bring it down. So which way will it be? Do we have an agreement? Or do you want the rest of Jacques's boys to ride on in?"

Heck seemed thoughtful. "Two thousand and six hundred dollars," he sighed. "That's more than I thought we'd get for these mousy little females." He nodded and then offered a hand to Heathro. "You have yourself a deal, Mr. Thibodaux."

Heathro smiled, waved his arm as if waving off a regiment of soldiers, and then struck hands with Heck. "You've made a wise choice, boss. And Mr. Cheval thanks you for offerin' him such a fine and, no doubt, lucrative investment."

Heck nodded, turned to his men, and hollered, "Lower your guns, boys. Mr. Thibodaux here has made us a dolly of a deal."

Heathro handed Heck a wad of paper money, returned the small satchel to his saddlebag, and said, "All right then. Let's get started."

"You mean break camp?" Patterson asked.

"Well, yes…but only after we've started," Heathro answered.

"Started what?" Heck asked.

Heathro's eyes narrowed, and he stared at the girls. Cricket found herself blushing under his piercing gaze, knowing she must look like a wet rat the cat dragged in—wishing she looked as fresh and perky as she did on Sunday mornings before church.

"Which one's the leader, do you think, boss?" Heathro asked.

"You can call me Heck," Heck began, "and what do you mean exactly?"

Heathro walked to where the girls stood, Heck and Patterson close at his heels.

"There's always a leader," Heathro mumbled as he looked Marie up and down. He took hold of her chin and seemed to study her eyes. Marie belligerently pulled her face from his grasp, however, and Heathro chuckled, "Perfect! This one has a little spunk in her. That's just perfect."

Cricket understood that Heathro was not only telling Heck that Marie was a good specimen for his purposes but also letting the other girls know that Marie's reaction to him was just what it needed to be.

He moved to Ann. "Hmmm," Heathro mumbled. "Blue eyes and gold hair. She'll bring a nice price in New Orleans."

"How about I let you see if you can tell who their leader is, Thibodaux?" Heck offered.

Heathro smiled. "Oh, why not give me somethin' a bit more challengin'?" he said. Unexpectedly reaching out and taking hold of Cricket's arm, he laughed, "This one. This one right here. I knew it the moment I saw her. Here's the leader of your pack, Heck. Am I right?"

Heck smiled, nodded, and laughed with amusement. "You bet that's her!" he exclaimed. "This one's been a pain in my hind end since we took her. Sassy-mouthed too."

"Well, then she's the one I start with," Heathro said.

Patterson frowned. "What do you mean? I thought Jacques Cheval wanted these girls unspoiled."

"Oh, she'll still be undamaged when I'm finished with her," Heathro chuckled. "Just a whole lot more cooperative, that's all."

"Don't you touch me!" Cricket growled, wrenching her arm free of Heathro's grasp.

"You see what I mean?" Heck laughed. "She's a pain in the hind end, I'll tell you that."

"Not for long," Heathro said. Quickly maneuvering Cricket so her back was against his chest, his hand clutching her throat, he drew a long knife from his belt and held it to her tummy. "She just needs to understand a few things, that's all."

Marie, Ann, Vilma, and the others began to weep, and Patterson shushed them.

"What're you gonna do with her?" Heck asked.

"Oh, nothin'. Just have a little talk, that's all," Heathro said. "And when we get back, she'll be less of a pain in your behind, Heck. I promise you that. Just give me a few minutes with her."

Cricket struggled and cried, "No! No! Don't let him take me!" as Heathro began to force her toward a large outcropping of boulders.

"Now we don't need no audience, men," Heathro called over his shoulder. "And keep these other girls quiet."

"You think we oughta trust him, boss?" Cricket heard Patterson ask.

"Look here, Patterson," Heck responded. "The man has proof he's with Jacques Cheval, and he put more money in my hands than I ever seen all at once. So I think…"

Heck's words drifted off as Heathro roughly pushed her behind one large boulder.

"Cry out," he instructed. "One more time."

Cricket did as she was told—heard the outlaws chuckling—her friends sobbing inconsolably.

Heathro puffed a relieved breath. "So far, so good," he said. "But this is gonna be rough, Miss Cranford."

Cricket nodded and brushed the tears from her cheeks.

"We're gonna have to muss you up a bit, girl," he said. He looked her over for a moment. "Here," he said, rubbing his hands over her hair to muss it—not that it wasn't already as wild as a tumbleweed. "Now, scratch me here," he instructed pointing to one cheek. "And you need to make sure you draw blood, all right?"

"I-I can't do that!" she exclaimed in a whisper.

She began to cry once more as he took hold of her shoulders, stared into her face with an expression of fierce determination, and said, "You have got to do as I ask, girl!" He took her hand in his, rather brutally squeezing her fingers together as he raised it to the back of his neck. Then he forced her fingernails to pierce his flesh, next drawing her fingers down so that she scratched him.

Instinctively Cricket cried out in horror as she saw the blood on his neck—the tiny bits of his flesh and blood under her fingernails.

Heathro seemed entirely unaffected, however. "Let's see now," he mumbled, frowning as he again studied her. "Let's make this look believable."

Cricket could only stare at her bloody fingernails and fingertips. Therefore, it wasn't until she heard the tearing of the fabric of the front of her shirtwaist that her attention snapped back to Heathro.

"What are you doin'?" she exclaimed, mortified that her neck and left collarbone were now exposed.

"Makin' this look convincin'," he answered. "I told you that already."

He tore her shirtwaist again, exposing her left shoulder as well. Cricket looked down—thought she appeared like she'd been attacked by a mountain lion.

Then Heathro grasped her hands and put them at his chest. "Now tear my shirt. Tear it like you would tear it if you were defendin' yourself from me."

But Cricket shook her head. It was too surreal—too awful! Surely she wasn't hidden behind a bunch of rocks with Heathro Thibodaux instructing her on how to appear as if she'd been assaulted.

"I-I can't," she stammered.

She gasped as Heathro firmly took hold of her chin, forcing her to make eye contact with him.

"Listen to me, Magnolia," he growled. "If you do not help me, we are all dead. Do you hear me? You, me, all the other girls…your friends. I will not let these men kill you girls…and I will not let them get you to New Orleans! Do you understand me?"

"Yes," Cricket managed.

"Then help me, Magnolia," he pleaded. "Do as I say…no matter what. All right?"

Cricket nodded.

"Now," he began again, "if I'm comin' at you…defend yourself."

Roughly he grabbed her around the waist—tried to pull her to him. Every instinct Cricket had begged her to allow him to embrace her. But she understood what Heathro Thibodaux intended to do: he intended to make it appear as if he'd broken the spirit of the girls' leader in order to make her and the rest of the girls more *cooperative*.

"I'm comin' at you, girl," he told her. "What're you gonna do about it? Are you gonna let me have my way with you? Or are you gonna fight me off and try to—"

Cricket struggled—tugged at Heathro's shirt to try and escape him. When she heard the familiar sound of tearing clothing, she stopped. She looked up to find him grinning at her.

"There you go, darlin'," he said as he released her and inspected his torn sleeve and the missing buttons from the front of his shirt—the result of their struggle. "Now," he said, studying her again. "Bite your lips like this."

Cricket watched, frowning as Heathro bit his lower lip and then his other. "It'll make your lips swell a bit, honey," he explained.

She did as she was told, and he nodded with approval.

"Okay...one last little thing here," he said quietly. "Now hold still."

Cricket watched as Heathro rubbed his chin with his thumb and fingers. "Should work," he mumbled more to himself than to her.

Again she was rendered breathless with astonishment as Heathro Thibodaux bent, rubbing his whiskery jaw over her exposed shoulder, her neck, and then her cheeks. It was a chaffing, uncomfortable feeling—but for some reason rendered Cricket covered with goose bumps. Over and over Heathro chaffed the tender flesh of her neck and cheeks with his rough whiskers.

"Bite your lips some more," he told her as he mussed her hair again—swept over her skin with his face one more time.

He held her back from him, nodded, and winked. "Good enough, I suppose. For a start." Pulling her away from the rocks, he forced her hands behind her and began pushing her toward the camp. "If you've got any left in you, now would be a good time for some more tears, sugar."

Oh, there were plenty of tears left in Cricket—plenty! As she stumbled back to camp terrified, hopeful, tired, elated, despairing, and tantalized all at the same, she collapsed in a heap near the other girls when she reached them.

"She looks like hell!" Patterson angrily exclaimed. Looking to Heck, he added, "What's he gonna do? Beat 'em all to submission?"

"Nope," Heathro answered. "Only this one…and I ain't gonna beat her."

Lowering his voice so that the girls couldn't hear him, he nodded to Heck to gather the men. Once they all stood close enough to hear, he began, "She's their leader. We get her restrained a bit, get her thinkin' that I'm gonna cut her a deal with Jacques if she helps us get the others there…well, it makes our trip a whole lot easier, boys."

Heck glanced around Heath to Cricket. "She does look like hell though. What's she gonna look like when we get there?"

Heath smiled and chuckled a bit. "*Cooperative*, my boys. Cooperative and fresh and pretty as a June bride."

"How you gonna do that when you're beatin' on her?" Patterson asked.

"I didn't beat on her," Heath explained. "I kissed her…made her feel desirable and beautiful."

Patterson looked around Heath then. "I still think she looks like hell."

"Well, maybe she does now," Heath countered. "But you wait. She'll warm up to me, and then she'll be as pretty as the summer days are long." Heath frowned, reached out, and tugged at Patterson's disgusting beard. He'd seen stray dogs that looked cleaner—and smelled better. "Listen here. Who do you think those girls are gonna trust? You and this flea-ridden beard? Or me…all cleaned up like a mama's boy for Sunday school? Get rid of this rat's nest, and them girls will take to you more."

Heath's attention fell to something else then. Taking hold of Patterson's arm, he studied the silver and turquoise bracelet he wore—the bracelet he knew Hudson Oliver had given to Marie King. After all, Hudson had bragged to nearly everybody in town about it only a couple of days previous.

"And what's this?" Heath asked, pointing to the bracelet. "It looks like somethin' some little girl's daddy gave to her."

"I got it off that one over there," Patterson admitted, pointing around Heath.

Heath turned, pretending to look from one girl to the other. "Which one?" he asked.

"That taller one with the dark hair and blue eyes," Patterson confirmed.

Heath looked back to Patterson. "Well then, you give it back to her."

"What?" Patterson exclaimed with indignation. "It's worth a lot of coin!"

Heath quirked one eyebrow. "More than that girl's gonna sell for in New Orleans?"

Patterson frowned. "No."

"That's right," Heath said. "So you give that girl back her bracelet, shave off this ratty beard…and those girls will start lookin' at you a whole lot differently than they have up until now."

Heck smiled—chuckled as full understanding overtook him. "You're gonna charm them all the way to New Orleans, ain't you?" he asked.

Heath smiled and nodded. "Now you're catchin' on. When it comes to women, a man gets a lot more cooperation if he feeds them sweet butter and honey instead of horse manure and thistles. Ain't that right?"

All the men understood then—or thought they did. As they smiled and laughed, triumphantly patting one another on the back, Heath exhaled a very slight sigh of relief. These outlaws really were as stupid as they looked—and that meant the girls had a chance of survival.

"Oh, but she got you good there, didn't she?" Heck asked, gesturing to the blood and scratches on Heath's neck.

Heath laughed. "Yep. She's a cat, that one. But nothin' I can't tame, boys. Nothin' I can't tame."

CHAPTER TWELVE

"Well, the trick is," Heath explained as he rode next to Heck, "to make a woman fear you…but at the same time, you gotta make her think she needs you for everything. You gotta make them totally dependent on you. Then, once you've done that, you can pretty much get them to do whatever you want."

Heck chuckled. "So that's your job for Jacques Cheval, boy? You come along and get one of the girls to fall in love with you? That's it?"

Heath shook his head. "Nope. I get them to trust me…make them think I'm on their side and favor them. And it won't work with just any of the girls. You see, you've got to get the strong-minded one who influences them most. You got to get the leader to crawl on into your web and wind her up. You gotta get her under your control…and then you get control of all the rest just because. It's the same way it works with herdin' cattle…even soldierin' for that matter. You see what I mean?"

Heck nodded, thoughtful.

The truth was Heath wanted nothing more than to draw his knife and slit the outlaw's dirty throat—shoot him or beat him to death would work too. But he knew better. He was one man, and he'd tried the direct approach before and ended up watching eight innocent girls die for it.

So he swallowed the vile taste in his mouth that gathered there each time he looked at Heck Alford (or any of the other outlaws), plastered on a smile, and continued, "Now, I can tell this one here—

this one they call Cricket—she's gonna be a tough little cat to tame. But I figure, judgin' from the fact we're gonna have to make camp somewhere and hole up through this rain probably for the rest of the day and through the night…I figure I can have her right where we need her to be by mornin'."

Heck looked up. "What rain?" he asked. "I see the thunderhead… but it's far out in front of us."

"Not for long," Heath explained. "It's gonna rain like hell all afternoon. But I know a place up here not too far where we can dig in and wait it out—as long as the river don't flood too high anyway."

"So you know this trail purty good then, I guess," Heck observed.

"Like the back of my hand, brother," Heath said with a nod and a smile.

And it was true. Heath had lost track of the times he'd followed the white slavers' trail to New Orleans. Many times he and his fellow Rangers had been successful in tracking outlaws down and returning young, innocent girls to their families fairly unscathed. But not the last time he'd followed it. Nope. Not that last time he'd followed the old trail—alone anyhow.

"So he doesn't hurt you at all?" Pearl quietly asked Cricket.

"No," Cricket whispered.

"But…but you always look so tousled, swollen-lipped, and chaffed when you return," Pearl noted. "And you hardly have any seams left hangin' together on your shirtwaist."

"I know," Cricket admitted. "But trust me…he's just playin' these men. He's waitin' for the posse to catch up with us. He thinks they can't be more than a day behind now."

"But it's been two days already, Cricket!" Pearl exclaimed as she began to weep.

"Hush up there!" Patterson hollered at them from behind. "You girls just ride and keep your mouths shut."

"Don't worry, Pearl," Cricket quietly encouraged. "Ranger Thibodaux knows what he's doin'."

"That's right," Vilma said from the other side of Pearl. "Don't you lose faith, hope…and your endurance."

Pearl glanced behind them, however—to where Marie and Ann rode on either side of Jinny. "But Jinny's lookin' worse and worse. She hasn't been herself since…since they murdered her sister," Pearl reminded Cricket—and quite unnecessarily.

"I know," Cricket sighed with worry. "I know."

"I said shut up!" Patterson shouted. "Single file now, girls! If you're gonna gossip like a bunch of old hags, then you can't ride next to each other. I done told you all this before! You first, Red," he ordered Vilma.

Cricket watched as Vilma's face turned as red as a September tomato. Patterson had taken to calling her Red over the last day or two, and it infuriated the preacher's daughter from Pike's Creek.

As Cricket obeyed Patterson's order to ride in single file, she tried to bury the doubt that was growing stronger and stronger in her. No doubts lived in her about Heathro Thibodaux (Heath, as he'd asked her to call him during their time together the day before). None at all. Heath would give his life before he'd give up on trying to free them. Cricket was as sure of that as she was of the air she breathed. But it was the hope of the posse from Pike's Creek being close behind that she was beginning to doubt more and more.

For two days, Heath had taken hold of Cricket, dragged her off to a secluded place, and pretended to "rough her up a bit." He'd explained to her the pile of horse manure he was feeding the outlaws—that he was winning her over so that she would cooperate with them and convince the other girls to cooperate as well. The idea was that Heath appeared to be breaking Cricket, much the same way a cowboy broke a new mare.

Each time the group stopped for a meal or to see to necessities, Heath had whisked Cricket away and spent the brief time they were together mussing up her hair, rubbing his whiskery face over hers to chafe it, and creating an appearance that he had been "sparking with her," as he put it. Furthermore, Cricket's part had been to seem more and more docile in his company—even smile at him and offer the facade of growing fond of him. And she'd played her part well. Heck,

Patterson, and the others would always chuckle triumphantly whenever Heath would return Cricket to the other girls, leaving her with a wink, a dazzling smile, and a flattering word.

Heath's plan was working too. The outlaws were less fierce, less violent toward the girls. Patterson had even trimmed his smelly rat's nest of a beard and returned Hudson's bracelet to Marie. Of course, Cricket had explained to Marie that she must be more tolerant of Patterson now—lead him into a false sense that she liked him more than the other men because of his kindness toward her.

Naturally Marie had nearly vomited when Cricket had explained Heath's plan and why Marie must be nice to Patterson, but Marie was strong, and she did as Heath encouraged. As a result, all the girls had noticed that Patterson wasn't quite as wary of them as he had been before.

As for Cricket's trysts with Heath, overwhelming guilt was beginning to mingle with all the other emotions raging through Cricket—because she relished every moment with him! Certainly Cricket's secluded encounters with the unlawfully handsome Heathro Thibodaux were nothing but a facade—a ruse created for the sake of fooling the outlaws into keeping them away from the girls as much as possible until the posse arrived. But no matter how often she reminded herself of the truth of it all, Cricket could not keep from bathing in blissful wonder of owning Heath's attention—of knowing his touch, no matter how unwillingly rough it may have been at times, as he attempted to make her appear as if he'd "been havin' my way with you," as Heath explained—and of hearing his voice as he instructed her on what to do next.

In fact, as Cricket rode on, pondering over all that had happened between them—the conversation, the plotting, the mutual hope that the posse would come—she was astonished at how well she felt she'd come to know him. In only a few minutes spent together several times a day, Cricket had begun to see into Heath's soul. She saw his pain at having lost the girls the year before—the guilt that threatened to consume him—and the strength he mounted in order to keep it from doing so.

The sound of Jinny coughing startled Cricket from her thoughts for a moment. Glancing back to Jinny, she could see how pale and frail-looking the girl had grown since the death of her sister. Silently Cricket prayed Jinny would not become too ill—for she feared Heck wouldn't pause any longer in killing Jinny than he did in killing her sister if he thought he couldn't make a profit from selling her.

Thoughts of Jinny and her sister Nina drew Cricket's mind back to the first day Heath had entered the camp. He'd taken Cricket off to some secluded place five different times that day. Each time Cricket would return looking more meek and cooperative than she did the time before—as he instructed. It was part of Heath's plan to outmaneuver the outlaws.

But it was the final "tryst" they'd had that first day—it was those moments that Cricket's thoughts lingered on now.

"Tell me about the dead girl," Heath had begun. "The one I found snake-bit. I buried her a bit, by the way."

Instantly Cricket had begun to sob—to tremble with remembered horror and painful grief racing through her—her own grief, but also Jinny's. So bitter was her sobbing, so violent her gasps for air, that Heath had pulled her into the comfort of his strong, protective embrace.

Stroking her hair, he'd soothed, "It's all right now. That little girl isn't in pain anymore. She's in the arms of the Lord and free from misery. It's only us left behind that are feeling so guilty and sorry for her…missin' her." He paused a moment, allowing Cricket to cry into the softness of his shirt. Once she'd settled herself a bit, he'd repeated, "Now tell me what happened." Keeping her safe against him, protected by the capable power she could feel in the firm, solid contours of his muscular chest beneath his shirt, he urged, "You don't need to go on about it too long, but I do need to know what happened. A rattler got the girl…then what?"

Cricket nodded. "Yes…a snake bit her. A big one. It bit her twice."

"And they shot her because they knew—"

"Heck shot her!" Cricket cried. "He didn't even try to save her… didn't even show a morsel of compassion or carin'! He just shot her and forced us to leave her there without buryin' her or sayin' a few words or anything. Her poor sister…Jinny. That's Nina's sister."

"Nina was the girl who died."

"Yes," Cricket whispered. A strange sort of panic began to overtake her then. Her trembling increased, and she felt like she couldn't draw a regular breath. "It w-was my fault!" she sobbed. "I had been the one to be with her just a minute or two before! I should've known when the horse reared that somethin' was wrong…b-but we were all so frightened and tired. I should've…I should've stayed with her…made her walk in front of me. I-I—"

But Heath interrupted her with a firm, "No. No, that ain't true at all. That girl's death is on the heads of these outlaws, Magnolia. Do not take this on yourself when it was no fault of yours."

Cricket had looked up to Heath then—gazed into the mesmerizing blue of his eyes, studied his lips far longer than she'd intended—desperately wanting to run her palm over the square line of his jaw for some reason.

"B-but you know how I feel," she told him. "You know why I blame myself. If anybody in the world understands, it's you."

Heath frowned, inhaled a deep breath, and nodded. "I do. I surely do. And I know you must think I'm a hypocrite for tellin' you not to blame yourself when I still blame myself for those eight girls last year. But this is different."

"No, it's not," Cricket assured him. "Not to me."

He nodded again, knowing she was right. Then he released her from his embrace, taking her face between his hands as he looked directly into her eyes.

"Now listen," he began. She quivered as he brushed tears from her cheeks with his thumbs. "You girls are doin' real good with all this… especially you. I'm sorry I'm havin' to be so rough on you, but you can see that this is workin' pretty well, right?" Cricket nodded—studied the contours of his unbelievably handsome face. "These men are some of the most ignorant I've ever seen…thank goodness. They're believin' all this hogwash I'm feedin' them. It's like shootin' fish in a barrel." He smiled, chuckling a bit, and Cricket felt her own lips curve upward a little. "You just keep puttin' up with me handlin' you so harshly and then seemin' to be nicer and nicer to me, and we'll make it through this. That posse has got to be closin'. We travelin' slower than molasses uphill in January, for Pete's sake. All right?"

"Yes," Cricket said with a nod.

He inhaled a deep breath, exhaled it with a note of discouragement and regret, and said, "Then come here, Magnolia. I need to scratch you up a piece again before I send you back."

Cricket nodded once more—even smiled—for the truth was that she didn't mind when Heath scratched her up a bit by rubbing his whiskers on her cheeks, over her mouth, and down her neck. Sure, it was somewhat uncomfortable and left a smoldering rash on her flesh for twenty or thirty minutes afterward, but it was almost intimate in nature—and Cricket enjoyed that it was.

As Heath began to slowly brush her face with his chin, a question that had been bouncing around in Cricket's head all day long suddenly popped right out of her mouth. "Where did you get all that money… the six hundred dollars you gave to Heck?" she asked.

Heath paused in chafing her, his beautiful blue eyes brightening with mischief as he gazed at her a moment, and then said, "Didn't I tell you that ornery old bull was worth all the trouble? You can thank ol' Conq for that."

Cricket's eyebrows arched in astonishment. "That bull made you six hundred dollars?" she exclaimed.

Heath nodded. "A whole lot more than that, in truth."

"Goodness sakes!" Cricket breathed in exclamation.

"Goodness sakes is right," Heath mumbled, brushing his whiskers along the length of Cricket's neck.

And "goodness sakes" *was* right! At the sound of Patterson nagging Vilma again, Cricket's attention was drawn back to the fact that she was a prisoner, riding astride a horse and on her way to New Orleans to be sold. Yet even so, goose bumps rippled over her arms and legs at the memory of Heath's face sweeping her own—of the capable manner in which he held her arms as he endeavored to make her appear ravaged.

It was morbid—perhaps insane—to be thinking such romantic thoughts of Heath Thibodaux when the circumstances were so dire for him, Cricket, and all the other girls. Yet Cricket wondered if perhaps it wasn't her mind's way of actually keeping her sane in the end. If Heath hadn't found them—if he hadn't had the courage to begin the farce that found him able to accompany the group—then certainly the circumstances would be entirely void of hope.

Thus, why not daydream about him? Cricket asked herself. Why not escape the reality of their grim prospects and fill her mind with the sorts of things she'd filled them with days before, only days before, when she'd been an innocent, carefree young woman, stealing a kiss from the man her heart was drawn to?

"I guess you was right, Baptiste," Heck said, shaking the rainwater from his sopping hair and beard.

Cricket grimaced, thinking she'd smelled wet dogs that didn't stink as bad as these wet outlaws did.

"Yep," Heath confirmed. "I knew the moment I saw that thunderhead this mornin' that we were in for it. And we can't travel in this. The dry creek beds around these parts fill up with so much fast-movin' water, a body can get completely swept away to drownin'. It's best just to wait it out here."

"I'm glad you knew this place," Patterson said. He shook his head. "I don't know where we woulda holed up otherwise."

Heath hunkered down and rubbed his hands together in front of the blazing fire in the hearth. "Well, I've ushered a lot of women through here for Jacques," Heath said. "And knowing where to hole up can save a man's life sometimes." He glanced to the girls all huddled in one corner of the large, albeit dilapidated old house. "It can save his goods too."

Heck frowned. "I don't know. That one there…that Jinny?" he said, pointing to Jinny. Cricket glared at him, protectively putting an arm around Jinny's shoulders as Heck mumbled, "She ain't lookin' too rosy in the cheeks anymore. I sure as hell hope we don't lose another one."

"We won't," Heath assured him. "She's just tired…worn out from the travel. These girls ain't used to it…so it's probably good this storm hit. It kind of forces us to let them rest a mite."

"I suppose," Heck sighed. He shook his head. "But I don't want no posse catchin' up to us…not when I'm only a week away from collectin' two thousand dollars." He paused, frowned, and looked to Heath. "You really think Jacques Cheval will pay me…uh…us that much?"

"Absolutely," Heath said with a firm nod. "At least that. And I know what you mean about losin' time and maybe riskin' a posse bein' at our backs. But believe me, it'll be better to deliver these girls to Jacques all rosy-cheeked and healthy than it would be to show up with them lookin' like starved cattle."

"I can see that," Heck agreed.

Cricket had been listening so intently to the conversation between Heath and Heck that she didn't notice one of the other outlaws, a man called Boone, had managed to settle himself to standing right beside her. Heck had told his men to keep their distance from the girls—especially since Heath had arrived. But Boone was a drinker, and often defiant.

"What you starin' at there, Miss Violet Eyes?" Boone asked her.

Cricket ignored him. She could smell the liquor on his breath. And besides, she was supposed to be enamored of Heath—which she truly was, of course. But Heath had instructed her to appear as if she were depending on him for everything.

"I asked you a question, girl!" Boone hollered unexpectedly. "And when I ask a question, you better answer me!"

Cricket cried out in pain as Boone pushed the lit end of the cigar he'd been smoking against the tender flesh of her body just above her left breast and below her left shoulder.

"Boone!" Patterson shouted. "What the hell are you doin'?"

Patterson was on Boone in an instant, but the wound on Cricket's skin could not be undone. Tears streaming down her face, she looked to the burn. It had already begun to blister and hurt something terrible.

"What the hell?" Heath roared as he strode across the room, laying out Boone to sprawling on the floor in one swift punch before hunkering down to assist Cricket.

His eyes met hers, and she saw the regret, guilt, and self-blame in the deep blue of his eyes. "What the hell is wrong with your man there, Heck?" he shouted. "Patterson…get me some flour…now!"

"Yep," Patterson agreed as he headed out the door to the supply wagon.

"Boone!" Heck shouted. "You stupid, dimwitted dunce! I told you not to touch these girls…not a one of them!"

"She wouldn't answer my question, boss," Boone explained, struggling to his feet.

I'm sorry, Heath mouthed to Cricket, frowning with his own pain and anger. Raising his voice, he said, "Well, Heck…Jacques don't like imperfections. I'd say your idiot man there probably just lost you a hundred dollars…more if this burn gets infected."

"Is that so?" Heck asked.

Cricket recognized the evil expression of fury in Heck's eyes. She'd seen it once before—the very moment he'd killed Nina.

"No!" Cricket screamed only an instant before the shot rang out—an instant before Boone dropped to his knees.

"B-but, boss," Boone stammered as he put a hand to his belly and looked at the blood the gunshot wound left there.

All the girls screamed, breaking into tears as Heck fired again—this time hitting Boone in the head and causing his body to fall limp and lifeless right next to Cricket.

"I-I brung the flour," Patterson ventured as he stepped back into the old house and offered a small sack of flour to Heath. Patterson gulped as he looked at Boone, lying dead on the floor, and then to Heck, who had already reholstered his pistol.

"Give me that," Heath growled, snatching the flour sack from a stunned, mouth-agape Patterson. Tearing it open, Heath scooped out a handful of flour and quickly tossed it onto the cigar burn.

Cricket was astonished at how soothing the flour was the instant it touched her wound. She wiped the tears from her cheeks, even though more followed.

Rising to his feet, Heath flung the sack of flour back to Patterson—

who barely caught it and inhaled a bit that puffed from the sack when he did.

"Dammit, men!" Heath shouted. "Every scratch on these girls… every lost hair, every bruise will cost us money! How can I get that through your thick skulls? This here…this burn…" He pointed to Cricket. "That's gonna cost us dearly…especially me! I'm the one Jacques trusts to get these girls to him! Not only does somethin' like this come outta your pay, but it comes outta mine!"

"Well…at least we got one less man to share the earnin's with now…so don't it all even out?" one man asked.

"What? You think Heck or me hasn't already thought of that, boy?" Heath growled. "We could shoot every one of you dirty dogs and keep these girls and the money they'll bring all to ourselves. But that ain't the plan…and it don't show no integrity. None at all." He strode to the man who'd suggested that Boone's death was a benefit. Taking him by the collar, Heath threatened, "Why don't we just have Heck shoot you too? Then there's even more money for the rest of us, boy!"

The man gulped, and Heath released him with a violent push. He turned to Heck then, removed his hat, and raked his fingers back through his hair.

"Heck…we can't have this," he said. He leaned closer to Heck, lowered his voice, and added, "And of course, who does that idiot decide to hurt…but the very woman we need to cooperate with us. I'll be lucky if I don't have to start all over with her now."

"I'm sorry, Baptiste," Heck sighed. "I shoulda cut Boone loose long ago. His drinkin' always got him in trouble." Heck paused, glancing around Heath to Cricket. Cricket glared at him, wiping more tears from her eyes. "But what will you do with her? Do you really think we lost our hook over this?"

"I don't know," Heath said, shaking his head. "I don't know…and I won't know until I've…" Heath turned and looked to Cricket. "You feelin' okay, sweetheart?" he asked.

But Cricket shook her head. She wasn't sure what answer Heath wanted her to give, but judging from the conversation between him and Heck, he wanted doubt to settle back into Heck's mind—wanted him to wonder whether Jacques Cheval would still pay him top dollar for the girls.

"Wonderful," Heath growled. He shook his head, turning his attention back to Heck. "We cannot lose the cooperation of these girls, Heck. You've seen how much easier it is when we have it."

"But what're we gonna do then?" Heck asked.

"Start over, I guess," Heath sighed. He looked to Patterson. "Patterson," he addressed the newly shaven outlaw.

"Yeah?" Patterson asked.

"You and Heck...you stay close to these girls tonight," Heath instructed. "Don't let any of the other men near them."

"Well, sure thing," Patterson agreed. "But what about you? Where're you gonna be?"

"Startin' over," Heath said as he reached down, taking hold of Cricket's arm and pulling her to her feet.

"Cricket!" Ann cried out. "What're you gonna do with her?"

"I'm gonna see to her wound for one thing, darlin'," Heath answered. "And she and I are gonna have us a little chat."

All the girls began to weep then—huddled closer together.

"But don't you girls worry none about your little Cricket here," Heath added. "I'm gonna take real good care of her tonight."

Cricket felt it was her cue to struggle—and she did so.

"Now hold on there, honey," Heath said, taking her arms and holding them behind her back. "You'll be just fine. Don't I always take care of you?"

Cricket ceased in struggling—pretended Heath's holding her hands at her back was painful, even though it wasn't.

"Give these girls some extra water, Heck," Heath instructed as he pushed Cricket toward the door. "And keep those other men away from them tonight. I want them to get some sleep. Those bags under their eyes ain't doin' nothin' to make any of them more becomin'."

"I hear ya, Baptiste," Heck agreed. "You boys bunk down!" he ordered his men. "Let's get some shut-eye. We're gonna need to ride like hell when this rain breaks."

Kicking the door of the house open with one foot, Heath dragged

Cricket out into the rain. "Keep those girls warm and safe, Heck!" he hollered over his shoulder. "I don't want none of us losin' another nickel off any of them!"

"Oh, we won't," Heck assured him. "I'll make sure of that."

The rain was torrential! Cricket could hardly breathe as Heath led her to an old barn located not too far from the old house.

Once inside, Heath closed the barn doors and drew the bolt. The windows had no shutters remaining, but there was still plenty of shelter from the rain.

"Hold on here a minute," Heath mumbled.

Cricket watched as Heath cleared a space on the dirt floor directly in the center of the barn, dragging a small metal watering trough to the place. Quickly gathering dry straw and other pieces of discarded wood, he tossed them in the small trough along with an old milking stool he'd found abandoned in one corner. Then, taking a small tin from his pocket, he opened it to reveal several stick matches—and before long, a fire burned warm and comforting in the trough.

"Here," he said, leading her to the fire. "Warm up good before you catch cold."

Cricket nodded and began to warm her hands.

"Well, Heck sure don't stop to think about killin' somebody, does he?" Heath grumbled as he stripped off his soaking shirt, wrung it out, and hung it over a stable wall. "He didn't blink an eye at shootin' his own man to death right there in front of all the others."

Cricket wiped the tears and rain from her face and breathed, "Nope."

He removed his hat, tossing it to join his shirt and shaking the rain out of his hair. "Well, it's one less man I'll have to worry about killin' if that posse don't show up pretty soon, I suppose."

Cricket tried not to stare at him—but it was difficult being that he was standing right next to her only half dressed. She thought of the day he'd come upon her, Ann, Marie, and Vilma swimming in the swimming hole. She'd been alarmingly unsettled seeing him in such a state then, but this moment was even more disconcerting! Heath

Thibodaux was so close to her she could feel the heat coming off his body as surely as she could feel the heat from the fire.

She wanted to turn to him, throw herself against him, and beg him to hold her. But she didn't. She wanted to confess that it had been her, Magnolia "Cricket" Cranford, who had stolen a kiss from him not so long ago—though it seemed like forever in that moment.

"Now, let me see that burn," Heath said, taking her arm and turning her to face him. He grimaced as he studied it. Cricket's breath caught in her throat as he reached out, gently pressing the tender flesh around the wound with his fingers. "I shoulda brought that bag of flour with us," he mumbled. "The rain washed off what I put on there before."

"It's f-fine," Cricket stammered. His touch was thrilling to every sense she owned! Never in a million years should he ever be allowed to touch her bare skin the way he was—especially where he was—she knew it. But there was no part of her that wished for him to stop.

"It's bad," he sighed. He frowned as he studied her face. "We'll have to keep a sharp eye on it…make sure it doesn't start showin' signs of infection." He growled. "I wish had some of that ointment I keep at home for burns and such."

Cricket felt a wave of hysteria bubbling up inside her as Heath's fingers continued to touch her near the wound. "I-I suppose…I suppose we could try some of that medicinal spit of yours," she giggled. She couldn't think what had come over her. Nothing whatsoever was amusing about their situation—nothing. But suddenly the memory of their moments in the pasture—of Heath tending to the splinter in her foot, of actually spitting on it—somehow it all seemed so carefree and funny.

She was surprised when, instead of a reprimanding word or even glance from him, he chuckled a little. "My medicinal spit," he said. He shrugged then, adding, "Well, why not."

Reaching down and retrieving a knife from his boot, Heath lifted Cricket's skirt to reveal the not-so-dusty-as-the-rest, upper ruffle of her petticoat. Using his knife, he swiftly cut a small piece of the fabric.

"Well, here goes," he mumbled, moistening the piece of cloth with his tongue and dabbing at the burn a bit.

168

Cricket was rendered stiff as an oak! She couldn't move—for she was entirely stunned, as well as enthralled, by Heath's gesture.

"Hmm…needs a bit more than that," he said to himself.

Cricket gasped then as he bent, pressing his tongue to the wound for several moments.

He repeated the action once more, saying, "Well, I don't know if that'll help it heal…but at least I got the cigar ashes out of the wound. It should heal better that way."

It was too much—all of it. Being forcibly dragged from the old Morgan house, Nina's murder, the rough travel and lack of food and water, Heathro Thibodaux appearing so soon after Cricket had wished for him to appear, the times since spent in his company as he endeavored to make Heck believe he was charming her into his will. It was all too much for her to fully comprehend in that moment, and she began to sway as dizziness started to overtake her.

As everything began to spin faster and faster, Cricket felt her knees buckle—felt powerful arms keep her from crumpling to the ground.

"Hey! Hey there, darlin'," Heath said, supporting her body with one arm as he gently patted her face with the opposite hand. "Don't you black out on me. Stay with me. Come on now, Magnolia…fight that faint."

Cricket felt Heath lift her into the cradle of his arms—felt him lay her down on a soft bed of straw. Her body ached with fatigue, and she moaned as it relaxed. She hadn't fainted—at least not completely—but she'd weakened enough that her mind was swimming.

All at once she felt the urge to giggle—to laugh. And as the giggles in her came fizzing up into the air, she reached up and placed her palm against Heath's warm cheek.

"Hey," Heath said. "Come on now…come back to me here, sugar," he coaxed.

Cricket smiled and giggled, for she was blissful in seeing Heath poised above her the way he was—his handsome brow furrowed with concern.

She giggled again. Then all at once, her tears returned, and she was weeping.

"Do you know what my first thought was when those men took us?" she asked in a whisper.

"No," Heath answered. "What was your first thought there, honey?"

Cricket felt her lower lip quivering with emotion. "I-I thought…I thought, 'Well…at least I have my shoes on,'" she answered.

His smile—Heathro Thibodaux's beautiful, dazzling, gold-embellished smile. It was the last impression Cricket's eyes discerned before darkness swallowed her.

CHAPTER THIRTEEN

"Hey," Heath said, taking Cricket's face in one hand and moving her head back and forth in an attempt to revive her. She just couldn't take all the fatigue, fear, loss, and pain of body and mind anymore—and he understood why. It was no wonder her mind sought reprieve desperately enough to faint. He figured the cigar burn had finally been the straw to break the camel's back, and she'd needed a few moments of unconsciousness.

"Wake up now, honey," Heath said, gently patting her soft cheeks. "Don't give up on me now." He grinned, breathing a sigh of relief as he saw her eyelashes flutter a little. "There you go, Magnolia. You just come on back to me here. We've got some things to plot out still."

Cricket's eyes opened a little, and she seemed to stare at Heath as if trying to recognize him. Oh, but she was a pretty little thing! Heath had noticed her the very day he'd moved to Pike's Creek. He'd kept his distance, of course, being that he was who he was—and what he was. But he'd always admired her from afar, wishing he'd had the worthiness to approach the little spitfire bundle of mischief. His smile broadened as her eyes opened wider, revealing the violet tinge that drew him in like a siren's song.

"Are you all right?" he asked. He could tell full consciousness was washing over her, for the fear suddenly returned to her beautiful eyes, accompanied by a deep blush of embarrassment at having awakened to find herself cradled in one of his arms as she sat in his lap on the ground where he'd settled with her when she'd fainted.

"I'm so sorry," she whispered. She tried to sit up but was obviously overwhelmed with dizziness and collapsed against him.

"You've got nothin' to be sorry for, sugar," he soothed her. "Take a minute or two, and let your mind catch up with your body, all right?"

Cricket wanted to take far more than a minute or two! She was sitting in Heath's lap, held snuggly against the warm, solid contours of him, his arms gently embracing her. Why on earth would she ever want to leave?

And then she remembered all that had transpired just before she'd fainted—his tending to the cigar burn, his encouraging her to tell him what her first thought was when they'd been captured. How ridiculous she must've sounded! How ridiculous she must look!

The realization that she looked like a tattered, mangy kitten without a home—and the fact she'd actually told him that her first thought when Heck and his men took them was that at least she'd had her shoes on—was too humiliating.

Pushing herself from his arms to sit on the ground in front of him, she said, "You must think I'm the biggest imbecile to ever walk the earth."

But Heath simply smiled and asked, "Why would I think that?"

"Well, I look just like one, for starters," she answered, attempting to smooth her tousled hair. "And second...who in their right mind would be worried about havin' their shoes on or not while bein' abducted?"

He laughed, and the sound settled her anxiety a bit. "I think it was a very good thought, Magnolia. Can you imagine what this trail woulda been like for you if you hadn't had your shoes on?"

His amused smile was contagious, and Cricket couldn't keep from grinning herself. "I suppose you're right."

Heath was silent for a moment then—stood and strode toward one of the windows. He seemed thoughtful for a long while but finally said, "This rain...it ain't gonna let up until nightfall at least."

"And it's a good thing, right?" Cricket ventured. She stood on still weak and wobbly legs and joined him at the window. "It gives the posse more time to catch up to us."

"Not if it's got them holed up somewhere too," he sighed, "which I've no doubt that it does." He was pensive again for a moment and then turned to her and said, "And your little friend Jinny…she ain't gonna make it if somethin' don't give in soon."

The thought of Heck shooting Jinny the way he'd shot Nina and Boone caused nausea and panic to well in Cricket's stomach. "But what can we do? As soon as she looks too weak to ride or sell, Heck will just—"

Her words were silenced as Heath reached out, covering her mouth with one hand. "No," he growled. "I ain't gonna let that bastard kill another girl."

He dropped his hand from her mouth, and Cricket stammered, "B-but how…how will you stop him from killin' her if she—"

"Tomorrow will be mucky, muddy, and miserable," he said. "If that damn posse hasn't shown up and Jinny doesn't look any better by the time we stop to make camp tomorrow night, then…then I'll just have to get you girls out of here by myself."

"But you almost died last time you didn't have help!" Cricket exclaimed.

Heath looked to the lovely, brutalized girl standing next to him. He felt his brow furrow in a deep frown. "Don't you mean last time I tried to do somethin' like this myself, every one of them died?" he asked.

"That wasn't your fault," she answered. She was serious. He could see the sincerity in her violet eyes—beautiful eyes that were once again brimming with tears. "I-I read a newspaper article about it," she began. "You told that other posse they were goin' the wrong way. I'm guessin' the same thing happened in Pike's Creek…or at least somethin' similar." He looked away from her as his own emotions rose to the surface. "Furthermore, I don't know why he isn't with you. I've been afraid to ask…but my daddy would've come with you if he could've. Somethin's wrong. That's why my daddy's not here. I'm right, aren't I?"

Heath turned to her then, taking her by the shoulders and staring at her. All this while—all the time since he'd showed up—Cricket had been worried about not only her own safety, the safety of the girls with her, and even Heath's safety; she'd also been worried about her father too?

"He ran up to Thistle to help Cooper Keel look for—" he began.

"Of course! He went up to Thistle to help Mr. Keel look for his niece, Pearl!" she finished for him as tears tumbled down her cheeks. "So he's fine! Daddy is just fine! He just wasn't in town when we were taken!"

Heath was surprised when Cricket threw her arms around his neck, hugging him tightly and giggling.

"That's why he didn't come with you! That's why!" she breathed with relief. "Hudson was already gone with his family…movin' them to San Antonio. Marie knew that…but I couldn't figure why Daddy didn't come with you…not until now."

It was reflexive, Heath's returning her embrace—that's all it was. As his arms wrapped around Cricket's soft, sensuous form, Heath couldn't keep from pulling her tightly against him—from pressing his face to the top of her head and reveling in the gentle feel of her hair. But it was only a reflex—a natural response to an embrace—wasn't it?

But even as he tried to convince himself he was only responding as any man would to having the lovely Magnolia Cranford throw her arms around him, Heath knew he couldn't truly fool himself. He'd wanted to have her smile at him, embrace him, and much, much more than that since the very moment he'd first seen her months before. It was just something he didn't dare allow himself to admit—even to himself.

After all, a man didn't just see a woman across a room or a road or in the general store one day and instantly know she was the one he'd been looking for his whole life—the mate meant for his body and his soul. That sort of horse manure only happened in fairy tale books—the kinds his sisters Clara Jean and Fanny used to read to him when he'd been a little boy. Heath frowned, thinking he was lucky Clara Jean and Fanny hadn't turned him into a sissy altogether with reading such stories to him and forever dressing him up in dresses, stockings, and bonnets just to amuse themselves.

His attention was arrested as Cricket suddenly gasped, however—stepping out of his arms and away from him a bit.

"Oh, I'm so sorry," she apologized, blushing red as a ripe apple in autumn. "I-I was just so relieved to know that Daddy is all right and…" She paused, swallowed hard, and looked up to him once more. "But I don't want to see you get hurt tryin' to get us away from these men. Even without Boone, there are still nine of them."

"Well," Heath began, feeling cold and somehow alone since the moment she left his arms, "they will shoot Jinny if they think she'll die along the trail anyway. And I couldn't live with that. So I figure that if that posse don't track us down by tomorrow evenin'…then I have to try to get you girls outta here. In the end, I don't think these outlaws are stupid enough to kill the only things that will make them some money…that bein' you girls. And if they kill me…" He shrugged. "Well, at least you'll know I tried my best to—"

This time it was Cricket's hand over Heath's mouth that silenced. "Don't say it!" she cried in a whisper. "I won't have you killed on account of me or anybody else. We girls are tough. W-we can make it until the posse finds us…even Jinny. I'll see to her…take care of her. We won't let Heck know she's ailin' and then—"

"Heck already knows she's ailin', Magnolia," he interrupted. "And if we wait any longer, hopin' for a posse that might never come, more of you girls might die. I can't have that. I can't have any more deaths on my shoulders."

"It wasn't your fault last year!" she told him. Stomping her foot hard on the ground, she fisted her hands and said, "I read the account of it all. You did everything you could. It wasn't your fault. It was the fault of your ignorant counterparts…the men who didn't believe you because—"

"All right, all right," he said, taking hold of her shoulders in an effort to calm her. "I see this won't be an argument I'll ever win."

"No. It won't," she affirmed.

Heath grinned, obviously amused by Cricket's determination.

"Well, I suppose we'll just move on then…and start plannin' how we're gonna get you girls away from these outlaws tomorrow night if that posse doesn't show," he said.

"I suppose so," Cricket agreed.

Oh, how desperately she wanted to be in his arms again—held close against the protection of his warm body—feel his breath against her hair. It would seem ridiculous to anyone if she ever confessed she'd begun to fall in love with the haunted Heathro Thibodaux from the moment she first saw in him the general store all those months ago—but it was true. It was a secret Cricket kept closely guarded in her own heart, a secret she'd never shared with anyone—not her father, her friends, or even old Maymee Maloney. Certainly Ann, Marie, Vilma, and Mrs. Maloney all knew Cricket was wildly infatuated with Heath, but none of them knew the depth of her feelings, the expanse of her desire to be loved by him. They would've thought she was mad if she'd told them the severity of it all. And so she never did—never told anyone but herself.

"I figure we get them drunk, first off," Heath began. "We get them drunk and wait until most of them are asleep. Then I can slit the throats of whoever's left to guard you all, and we'll take all the horses and ride out. Being drunk and havin' no horses oughta do it. They'll never catch us on foot. And then—"

"Slit their throats?" Cricket gulped. "Why not...why can't you just shoot whoever's on guard?"

"And wake the others?" Heath shook his head. "Nope. It's gotta be quiet so the rest of them will sleep through our ridin' off."

Heath's eyes narrowed as he frowned. "You think I'm a monster for bein' willin' to kill them that way, don't you?"

But Cricket shook her head. "No. I think you're our hero for bein' willin' to kill them that way for our sakes."

"I ain't no hero, Magnolia," he said, shaking his head. "I'm just doin' what any man should."

Oh, she wanted to kiss him! Her mouth was so warm and thirsty to kiss him. After all, he was standing right in front of her—closer even than he'd been standing to her when she'd stolen that kiss while balancing on the old watering trough out behind the general store.

In the low firelight, Cricket fancied there was a strange smolder in his blue eyes—an almost alluring, inviting smolder—and it caused the butterflies resting in her stomach to swarm. She silently scolded herself when her admiration of his wildly attractive essence fell to his muscular shoulders, arms, stomach, and chest. She wanted to be held by him— to be free to caress his skin and know the wonderful sensations that would race through her when she did.

But she shook her head, bringing her mind back to reality. "Just tell me what to do," she offered. "I agree with you. If the posse doesn't show and Jinny is worse…then I agree." She looked at him—gazed into his eyes. "I agree that we should try to escape ourselves."

He sighed, nodding with affirmation. "All right then. That's what we'll do."

Goose bumps riddled Cricket's arms and legs as he took hold of her shoulders again.

"Then I'll think on it awhile and give you some details at sun's up. All right?"

Cricket nodded.

"But for now, I best rough you up a bit and get you back in there before someone comes lookin' for us or the others begin to worry," Heath said. "If you're lucky, maybe this'll be the last time you have to put up with all this nonsense." He smiled at her and winked. "How does that sound, darlin'?"

The truth was it sounded horrible! Every moment she'd spent alone with Heath since he'd arrived had been pure wonder for her. Every touch, every glance, every word he'd given her had made her heart soar, even for the despairing truth of their circumstances. The thought of never touching him again, of never feeling the brush of his whiskers to her face or his powerful arms locked around her, was inconsolably sorrowful for Cricket.

"You should probably do your worst this time," she suggested— more out of desperation to have his attention last as long as possible than to convince Heck and the other men that he'd "had his way with her."

"Should I now?" he asked with a chuckle.

"Yes," Cricket assured him as panic began to detonate inside her. Heath could be killed trying to save them. Yet she knew he had to try, knew that it was the sort of man he was—heroic, determined, and strong. Oh, she well knew they could all lose their lives: Marie, Ann, Vilma, Pearl, Jinny—even Cricket herself. But it was Heath's life she worried for most.

His smile faded, and he took hold of her shoulders. She loved the sense of his touch—no matter what manner of touch it was. The warmth of his powerful hands on her shoulders elated her.

"Looky here," he said. Cricket blinked, sending tears spilling over her cheeks as she looked up at him. "You've been so strong, Magnolia. I have never known any other young woman who could've endured what you've had to. We all woulda been dead a long time ago if it hadn't been for you."

"Us girls would be dead if it hadn't been for *you*," she corrected.

But Heath shook his head. "Nope. I ain't the one who got you all this far. You did. And you've had to suffer a lot in doin' it. You've had to tolerate a lot of terrible behavior from *me*. I know that…and I'm sorry for it."

It was Cricket's turn to shake her head. "You're the only reason we're alive. The only reason we're unharmed and have any hope. If the posse doesn't reach us—if we escape and somehow manage to return home—it'll be because of you." She lowered her gaze. "And besides…I don't think I could've lasted this long without spendin' that time with you. You're the only reason I didn't crumble with fear and despair."

"Now that ain't true, and you know it," he gently argued.

"It is true," she assured him firmly.

"Oh, so you liked being yanked around, manhandled, and nearly violated, is that it?" he said, grinning and breathing a tired chuckle.

"You never came close to nearly violatin' me, and you know it," she reminded, rolling her eyes with impatience at his exaggerations.

"Maybe not…but I thought about it," he mumbled, winking at her.

Cricket blushed, charmed by his flirting with her when things were so dismal.

"So…are you ready for one more round with me, honey?" he asked.

"Of course," she answered as more tears drizzled over her cheeks.

"Well, let's get to it then…before you catch your death of cold out here only half dressed in this drafty ol' barn," he teased, caressing her bare shoulder with the back of one hand.

Cricket's heart leapt inside her as Heath's strong, callused hands encircled her neck—his thumbs gently pushing her chin upward as he leaned down, brushing her right cheek with the whiskery warmth of his right jawbone. Just as he'd done on their other pretended trysts together, he then turned his head, brushing his whiskers against her other cheek.

Every organ and vein, every ounce of blood in Cricket's body, was quivering with desire and exhilaration—as well as with fear and anxiety. She felt new tears filling her eyes—tears of regret, heartbreak, and excruciating love for the man she could never belong to. Even if they made it home, even if neither of them were injured or killed, things would never be like this between them—so unguarded, intimate, and dream-borne.

Again Heath caressed the right side of her face with his strong, whiskery jaw and chin. Cricket noted then that his whiskers did not scratch her as harshly as they had on the other occasions. Either his facial hair had grown to a length to soften it, causing it to be less abrasive, or he was not rubbing his face against hers as roughly as he had before. In fact, Cricket realized in the next moment that Heath wasn't being nearly as coarse with her as he had been on the other occasions when performing the task of chafing her face for appearance's sake. With each stroke of his soft whiskers, jaw, chin, or cheek to hers, she realized the gesture had mellowed to a tender but entirely tantalizing caress.

She tried to breathe normally as Heath caressed first one side of her face with his and then the other, each time allowing his chin to gently brush her lips as he alternated. Cricket discerned that if she were the courageous girl she'd once been—even just two weeks before—she might have mustered the courage to purse her lips even just the slightest, allowing herself to softly kiss his chin each time it passed over them. But she had no courage left. She was spent with fighting for her life and the lives of her friends. In that moment, she was weak. There was no bravery in her—not even enough to steal another kiss from Heathro Thibodaux on what might well be the last night of their lives.

Over and over, Heath's face caressed her—repeating the motion of allowing his chin to brush her lips as he alternated one side of his face with the other in stroking her. And then—then when Cricket thought she might literally die from tethering such powerful desire—the rhythm of Heath's caresses changed. All at once, he stopped alternating one side of his face with the other. Instead, the right side of his face stroked hers over and over and over again. And with each consecutive pass, the corner of his mouth would ever so slightly meet with hers. It was as if he were preparing her for something—coaxing her to turn her face a little—for if she did, their lips would surely meet in a kiss.

But Cricket still found her courage was absent. There seemed to be only timidity and fear in her bosom. Yet as tears of heartbreaking regret escaped her eyes, trickling down over her temples, Heath slowly caressed her cheek with his once more, the corners of their mouths meeting as they had before—and then, oh so blessedly, their lips.

More tears fled Cricket's weary eyes as Heath's kiss lingered on her lips. It was a soft, careful, and caring kiss, and it was followed by another—and another. With each consecutive kiss he offered—with each tender kiss she accepted and reciprocated—Cricket's tears were suddenly borne of the wild exhilaration of returning strength beginning to swell inside her.

And when she thought she could never possibly experience a more powerful delirium than the one Heath's tender, lingering kisses were raining over her, he slowly moved his thumbs from where they'd rested beneath her chin to gently press the place just below her lower lip, coaxing her lips to part.

Cricket's knees buckled, and she melted against him as his mouth claimed hers with the driven, moist, and fiery kiss of the abruptly unleashed eruption of passion. Heath caught her in the embrace of his powerful arms, his mouth never separating from hers even for an instant. But she was weak and found herself clinging to him not only because she was desperate to prolong their impassioned exchange of kisses but also because she could not find her own feet for a moment.

As Heath continued to support her—to hold her—to kiss her as Cricket could never have imagined, not in all her wildest dreams of him—she at last managed to slip one hand under his arm, as her other traveled caressively over his opposing shoulder. And then an ounce of strength returned to her, and she rebounded somewhat, clinging to him as he kissed her.

Her mind was on fire—her body as well! She felt as if she couldn't breathe one moment and in the next felt as if so much breath were inside her that she might fly apart. Again and again Heath claimed her mouth with his—kissed with such intensity that Cricket was sure the warm, rich flavor of his kiss was all the sustenance she would ever need again. Over and over Cricket returned Heath's affectionate advances—endeavoring to please him with her answering kisses as thoroughly as his intoxicated her. And all the while tears escaped her eyes to trickle over her temples and cheeks—tears of consuming, feverish bliss.

Heath felt her hand caress the breadth of his shoulder—felt her fingers travel to caress the back of his neck. He quivered as she melted to him—her warm, tender body so welcoming of his physical attentions.

The gesture affected him far more than he ever could have dreamed it would—her simple touch sending his mind whirling and his body into such a state of desire that he began to tremble with restraining it. Again and again—over and over—he endeavored to drink his fill of her kiss, of her mouth, of the feel of her soft, tempting body pressed against his. The sense of holding her in his arms—of having her so willingly there—caused moisture to rise in his eyes, for he sensed he could've won her heart in a different life. If he weren't the failed Texas Ranger burdened with the deaths of eight innocent girls—if he were a good man like her father or Cooper Keel or even the young Hudson Oliver—if Heath had been a man like those, he might have owned the girl he so desperately cared for and craved—the girl in his arms that was accepting and returning his kiss.

Suddenly, Heath's hands gripped Cricket's waist as his mouth ground against hers with a wanton intensity. The moist heat of his kiss moved to her neck for a time, and Cricket wondered if the tears of joy streaming over her cheeks would ever stop. She didn't care if he thought her weak for so easily succumbing to his near seduction. In those moments, there was nothing else in all the world she wanted more than to be in his arms forever—to feel the warmth of his mouth on her skin and against her lips.

Again he embraced her—as if he'd meant to stop kissing her and then changed his mind. His mouth left her neck, finding her lips. Hungry, hot, and entirely unbridled—those were the kisses Heathro Thibodaux demanded, and Cricket's trembling was tempestuous. As her heart beat madly within her breast, as her breath came in ragged sobs spurred by mingled desire and fear, she could sense the desperation in him—the knowing—the knowing that tomorrow might find them both dead, left as carrion for the coyotes, buzzards, and any other creatures that would feed on their corpses.

Cricket gasped as Heath broke the seal of their mouths a moment—long enough to push her back against one of the nearby stall walls of the barn before continuing to near ravage her with such impassioned kissing that Cricket was sure she would awaken at any moment to find she'd only been dreaming of such wonder.

"I'm sorry I couldn't keep you from fallin' into the trough," he mumbled against her mouth. "And I'm sorry I kissed you so wickedly. I shoulda done this instead, Miss Blossom Bottom. I'm sorry."

Taking Heath's handsome face between her trembling hands, Cricket gently pushed until he lessened the strength of his aggression. "When d-did you know it was me?" she asked in a whisper. In truth, she didn't know whether to drop dead with humiliation or spring to the heavens on wings of euphoria.

Heath smiled, stroking her cheek with his thumb as he gazed at her. "The moment the first words came outta your mouth," he answered.

"B-but how did you know it was me?" she asked next.

Heath still held her against the stall wall—his body keeping hers captive there in the barn.

"Well, it's your voice for one," he answered. "I am a Texas Ranger, Magnolia. I'm trained to notice details."

"And you knew my voice well enough to…but you've hardly spoken to me since you moved to Pike's Creek. How could you possibly know—"

He silenced her a moment with a sweet kiss and then said, "Well, all right…I'll confess it. It wasn't just your voice." He smiled, and the firelight flinted on his gold tooth. "It's that sweet little blossom bottom of yours, Magnolia. That little swing you've got to your barefoot walk. It just shows off that little blossom bottom of yours so perfectly. So… the truth is it was your voice, that little blossom bottom of yours, and a few other things. That's how I knew it was you."

"But you were so—" she began.

"I'm sorry," he interrupted. "I-I just know how dangerous some men can be…and I didn't want you girls welcomin' any other men to town like that and findin' yourselves in some kinda trouble."

Cricket nodded, overwhelmed for a moment as the irony of it all washed over her. That night—the night she, Ann, Marie, and Vilma had gone about their do-gooding shenanigans and she'd kissed Heathro Thibodaux—that night he'd been trying to warn her that bad men existed who might do terrible things to young women. And now, there she stood in an old barn—a prisoner on her way to be sold into things she never before knew existed.

"I know what would happen to us if Heck actually got us all the way to New Orleans, you know," she whispered.

"What do you mean? Sellin' you girls into brothel life?" he asked. His eyebrows arched in discomfort then as he added, "Or do you mean you know what…what goes on in a brothel?"

"Both," she admitted.

Heath stepped back and rather uncomfortably rubbed the whiskers on his chin. "When did you learn about all that, darlin'?"

"Vilma told us…and Pearl," she answered. She shook her head a moment, mumbling, "Why is it always the preachers' daughters that know things like that?"

Heath laughed, shaking his head. "I don't know…but it sure seems to be true, don't it? I mean, there was this boy in the town I grew up in. He was the preacher's son…and one day we were all out fishin', and he told us other boys all about this saloon girl he'd seen with the sheriff and that they'd been…"

He paused, looking at Cricket—and she could've sworn Heathro Thibodaux blushed.

She giggled. "What? What did that preacher's son tell you?"

"Nothin'," he said, still blushing. Reaching out, he put his hands at her waist, pulling her to him again.

Cricket went willingly, of course, and he mumbled, "Won't you give me another chance, Magnolia? Won't you welcome me to Pike's Creek one more time and see if I can do a better job of acceptin' it this time?"

The teasing was gone from his expression. Reality had taken him over—the reality that the next sunrise might be his last. Fear began to rise in her again, but Cricket was determined to fight it—at least until she'd known one more kiss from Heathro Thibodaux.

Forcing a smile, she put her arms around his neck and asked in a whisper, "But do you promise not to be wicked in return this time, Mr. Thibodaux?"

He grinned then, pulled her body flush with his, and said, "No," as his mouth claimed hers in a hot, moist, ambrosial kiss of fiery desire.

CHAPTER FOURTEEN

The song of the crickets should have soothed her—and the scent of sage on the cool evening breeze. Yet how could Cricket be soothed by anything—even the memories and lingering sensation of having been held and kissed by the man of her dreams? How could even her memories—knowing Heathro Thibodaux cared enough for her to kiss her the way he had the day before—keep Cricket from the anxious anticipation of attempted escape?

The posse from Pike's Creek had not reached them. And Jinny was much worse than even the day before. Already Heck had told Heath that if she continued to slow them, he would have to "take the loss" and arrive in New Orleans with only five girls. Therefore, Heath had informed Cricket at midday that he meant to get them away from the outlaws that night.

Mingled terror and hope leapt in Cricket when Heath told her. Perhaps they would truly escape! Perhaps all would be well in the end after all.

Earlier that evening, as the outlaws sat around the fire discussing the many different ways they would spend the money they would be paid by Jacques Cheval, Heath had coaxed them into the heavy drinking of premature celebration. Now their heavy snores of intoxication had begun echoing through the night some time before. But Heath hadn't come for the girls yet.

Certainly Cricket knew Heath must silently saddle seven of the horses, and she knew it must be a difficult task. Yet what was taking him so long? She glanced over to see Marie looking at her—her expression conveying that her thoughts were similar to Cricket's. Cricket turned her head to her other side and looked to Ann. She knew Ann was worried about Harley. Heck had treated the horse badly, and Ann only hoped he would trust Heath enough to saddle him without making a sound.

A man the outlaws referred to as Burnette had been placed to guard the girls, and Cricket glanced up to see that he sat slumped back against a tree, snoring nearly as loudly as the others. Perhaps Heath wouldn't have to kill Burnette. Perhaps he would sleep through their escape as Heath hoped the others would. But if he didn't, Heath *would* kill him. Cricket felt sorry for the man. Yes, he was a brutal, robbing, murdering outlaw—but he'd been someone's baby once. She wondered for a moment what had set him on the path to evil.

Cricket startled a little as Heath suddenly appeared at her feet. Quietly she sat up, as did Ann and Marie, and then Vilma, Jinny, and Pearl. Heath held an index finger to his lips to ensure they did not speak as he drew a large knife from its sheath at his waist and cut the ropes at Cricket's ankles. Quickly he did the same for the other girls, moving then to their wrists and severing the ropes there.

Burnette stirred a little—moaned in his sleep. Heath's gaze captured Cricket's as her eyes filled with tears. She read his mind somehow. Somehow his suddenly sad blue eyes told her that Heath couldn't risk Burnette waking and sounding an alarm. He nodded to her, and Cricket closed her eyes, concentrating on the fact that Burnette had admitted to killing a Texas Ranger and two women while on a rampage of rape and plundering in a small Texas town down south months before with other men. Heath had told this to Cricket—instructed her to tell the other girls—so that when the time came for Burnette to be silenced, they would know his was not innocent blood spilling.

Heath motioned to the girls, indicating that they should not look behind them. And then he quietly crept past them to where Burnette sat.

Heath wiped the perspiration from his forehead. He didn't want to kill the man and paused, wondering if perhaps Burnette would sleep through their escape. Certainly Heath had killed men before—men just like Burnette—wicked men who raped and murdered women, stole from good people, and hurt them. But he still had no desire to kill him.

Yet if he didn't get the Pike's Creek girls and the other two out of there, Heck would kill Jinny come morning. He'd already told Heath that if the girl weren't better by sunup, he'd put a bullet in her head and move on.

Burnette stirred again, and Heath knew he couldn't afford to pause any longer. Burnette had not been allowed to drink as heavily as the others, and he would wake at the sound of the retreating horses—no matter how quietly they walked away from the camp.

And as if Heath's thoughts had summoned Burnette's consciousness, his eyes opened, and Burnette was fully awake at once, opening his mouth to shout the alarm. But Heathro Thibodaux was quick-handed and lethally accurate—and he turned his back on Burnette's as the man's hands went to his cut throat. Heath heard the outlaw's body slump back against the rocks and felt the burden of another death rest on his already heavy shoulders.

Cricket looked to Heath as he returned—watched as he began helping the girls up one by one. She was the last one he offered his hand to, and she took it—clasping it hard with gratitude for what he'd done for them.

Without a word, Heath led the girls to where seven horses (including Ann's Harley and Heath's mount, Archie) stood saddled and waiting. He assisted each girl in mounting, lifted Jinny into her saddle, and nodded at her in questioning if she were stable enough to ride alone. He mounted his own horse then, pointed in a northern direction, and gestured that Ann and Harley should begin the quiet procession. He'd explained to Cricket (and she to the others) that Ann, being the best rider, would lead them out of the camp initially, while Heath would bring up the rear after each girl was safely away.

Follow the river, Heath mouthed to Ann, and she nodded. Ann walked Harley quietly away from the camp. Marie followed and then Vilma, Pearl, and Jinny. But Cricket paused—not wanting to lose sight of Heath.

Go, he firmly mouthed to her. *Now!*

Cricket did as he demanded and reined her horse to step in behind Jinny's.

As they left the camp, Cricket was overwhelmed by a feeling of euphoric hope. They would be free! They would go home, and all would be well.

She looked back to see Heathro, having reined the remaining horses together, urge his horse to follow them, and she smiled. Yes! They would be free! The drunken outlaws would sleep through their escape and wake to find no horses and the party of girls and their hero already hours away, and entirely out of reach.

Cricket gasped, however, as Jinny was suddenly overcome with a fit of coughing.

"What the hell is goin' on?" Cricket heard Patterson shout.

"Ride!" Heath shouted. "Make that thoroughbred run, girl!"

Instantly Ann urged Harley into a gallop, and the other horses followed suit. Heath had instructed Ann to stay near the river for two reasons. The riverbank on this length of the trail was clear of trees, large brush, and rocks. It meant the girls could ride fast with only the full moon as their light; they could ride fast and not worry about faltering horses. Also, if they followed the river, it would lead them back to a place that would be familiar: the fork where the Pike's Creek posse had chosen Mexico and Heath had chosen New Orleans. From there, every girl knew the way back to Pike's Creek, so they would not be lost.

Cricket heard gunfire and shouting—saw several barebacked horses race past her. She could not leave him! She would not leave Heath, and she reined her horse in and turned it back toward the camp.

"Ride!" Heath shouted, however, as he rode toward her.

Cricket nodded as she quickly took in the scene behind Heath. Intoxicated outlaws were tumbling this way and that, reaching for their gun belts, scattered horses, and even their trousers in some cases.

Heck was the only one who stood shouting after them—firing his pistol at them.

Cricket heard a bullet whiz past her ear, and she turned her horse once more and shouted, "Yah!" as she dug her heels into its sides. The horse whinnied and leapt into a gallop.

Heath was almost right beside her—shouted to her, "You keep ridin' no matter what happens to me!"

He turned in his saddle, firing in the direction of Heck. Then he reached out, slapping Cricket's horse on the flank to speed its pace. He raced past her and then Jinny, Pearl, Vilma, and Marie. He slowed his pace once he was assured that all the girls were riding well. No doubt Ann and Harley were far ahead. Harley was fast, even for a thoroughbred, and Ann rode him well and confidently.

Heath slowed his horse only enough to fall in place behind Cricket, and though Cricket could still hear gunfire, she knew that in the darkness—as well the fact the outlaws were all drunk—the outlaws' chances of hitting the broad side of a barn were almost impossible. And so she rode—Cricket rode as fast as her horse could carry her. The rhythm of Heath's mount's stride behind encouraged her. She fancied her heart was beating in time with Archie's pace, and she smiled a little.

"It'll take them awhile," Heath shouted from behind her. "But they will come after us! They'll round those horses up and ride. So you girls keep ridin' no matter what happens. You ride those horses into the ground if you have to!"

And they did! They rode for hours—not always at a gallop, for they didn't want to drop their horses dead in their tracks so far from home, but they did ride hard and fast. It was close to midday when Heath finally allowed them to stop and take their rest for a few minutes.

The horses were winded and thirsty. And as the girls cupped their hands, dipping them into the shallows of the river and drinking the cool, revitalizing water, the horses drank their fill as well.

Heath barely paused for a drink, for he was wary—watching the trail behind them for signs of the outlaws' advance.

"We can't rest long," he told the girls. "They won't rest much at all. They'll want you back." He growled, swore, and removed his hat, raking a hand through his hair. "I can't believe I dropped that rope tied to the rest of the horses! If I hadn't, they wouldn't have a hope of ridin' after us."

"Heck was shootin' at you," Cricket reminded him.

But Heath shook his head as if it made no difference. "You girls take care of any necessities you might need to now...'cause we ain't stoppin' again for a long while...probably not until nightfall at least."

He looked back to the trail behind them, obviously anxious and on guard. Cricket wondered how long it had taken the outlaws to catch their horses, saddle up, and get after them. Probably not very long, she knew. They were still in danger. Heath was still in danger. In fact, it wasn't until that moment that Cricket consciously thought on a terrible reality. If the outlaws caught up with them, she, Marie, Ann, Vilma, Pearl, and maybe even Jinny wouldn't be killed. They were still worth money to the bad men. But Heath—Heck wouldn't pause in killing Heath.

Frantically she told the others to prepare to leave again soon. They must ride fast. They had to; Heath's life was the cost if they didn't!

"How're you feelin', honey?" Heath asked Jinny once they'd stopped for the night.

"A bit better, Mr. Thibodaux," Jinny answered, smiling at the handsome Texas Ranger.

Heath placed the back of his hand to her forehead and smiled. "Well, you ain't feverish...and that's a good sign, ain't it?"

Jinny's smile broadened, and she blushed under Heath's gaze.

A wave of jealousy washed over Cricket as she watched Heath with Jinny. Naturally she inwardly scolded herself with great severity. It was ridiculous to be jealous—especially considering the fact they were all running for their lives. Furthermore, perhaps Cricket had shared some fantastically romantic moments with Heath—their time in the old barn still seeming to her more like a dream than an experience that she'd actually lived. But that didn't mean she had any claim on him or that he wanted any claim to her. Heathro Thibodaux had done what was necessary to rescue them—that was all.

Yet as Cricket watched him talk with each young woman in turn—place the back of his hand to each girl's cheek in a gesture of offering comfort and encouragement—she wondered whether being abducted had somehow twisted her mind, for she wanted nothing more than to own every second of Heath's attention.

"And how are you holdin' up, Miss Blossom Bottom?" Heath asked, hunkering down in front of the log on which Cricket sat at last. Instantly—with just one utterance—Heath had vanquished all of Cricket's irrational feelings of a moment before.

"I'm fine," she answered, returning his smile.

Heath winked at her and said, "Yes, you are, honey. Very fine."

Cricket blushed, and he reached out, placing his palm to her cheek a moment, allowing his thumb to caressively travel over her lips once.

"Try to get some sleep," he said as he stood. "I'm thinkin' a day and a half more...and we oughta be home."

Cricket nodded. Heath had explained to her the day before that he figured they were two and a half days from Pike's Creek. The girls had been with the outlaws longer than that as they traveled, but that was because the wagon and all the horses traveling slower had taken more time than the return trip would.

"All right," she agreed. "But what about you?"

"I'll be fine," he told her. "I don't think those idiots will travel at night...but I need to keep watch just in case."

"Mr. Thibodaux!" Ann called then.

Heath and Cricket both looked to Ann. She was hurrying toward them carrying something in one hand. Her smile was as wide as the Mississippi, and her eyes twinkled with excitement.

"Look what I found in Harley's saddlebag!" she gleefully squealed.

"What's that?" Heath asked.

Cricket watched as Ann offered a wad of paper money to Heath—the six hundred dollars he'd given Heck as a bonus for agreeing to sell the girls to Jacques Cheval.

Heath chuckled. "Well, what do you know? I forgot all about that."

"Here," Ann said, taking Heath's hand and forcing the money into it. "At least you got this back."

"Maybe you can use some of it to buy Cricket a new shirtwaist to replace the one you nearly tore off her when you arrived," Vilma teased.

Heath smiled, reached out, and lifted a shred of fabric hanging from Cricket's sleeve. "Yeah. I guess this one has seen better days." He frowned then, leaning down to study the cigar burn below Cricket's shoulder. "How's that burn healin' up?"

Cricket quivered at the memory of Heath applying his medicinal spit to the burn the night it happened. "It's fine. It blistered yesterday, and I guess the blisters burst while we were ridin' or somethin'. It hurts, but it's fine," she answered.

"Good," he said. He looked up then to see the girls had all moved to surround him. "What?"

Marie was the first to kiss him.

Stepping up to Heath, she said, "Thank you for comin' for us, Mr. Thibodaux. You saved our lives." Cricket's eyebrows shot up into arches as she watched Marie King place a thankful kiss to Heath's lips.

"W-well...we ain't outta the woods yet, darlin'," Heath stammered.

Ann approached next. "It wouldn't matter if we all dropped dead right here and now...without ever makin' it home, Mr. Thibodaux. You're still our hero and savior." Ann raised herself on the tips of her toes and placed a kiss to his lips as well.

Heath blushed, and Cricket wondered why she wasn't jealous. Just watching Heath place a hand to each of the other girls' cheeks had disturbed her a moment ago—but for some reason, the thankful kisses her friends were offering now didn't.

"Thank you, Mr. Thibodaux," Jinny said then. "I would be dead already if it weren't for you." Jinny glanced away a moment, brushing a tear from her eye. "I heard Heck tell you he was gonna kill me this mornin' if I still looked sickly. So thank you for takin' me away from him." She kissed Heath and stepped back as Pearl stepped forward.

"I know exactly what those men had planned for us, Mr. Thibodaux," Pearl said. She took his face between her hands, pulling his head to hers and placing a grateful kiss to his lips.

It wasn't until Vilma approached him that Cricket felt a frown pucker her brow a little. One never knew exactly what was going on in the mind of Vilma Stanley, and for some reason, Cricket was on edge—though she hadn't been when the other girls kissed him.

Cricket gritted her teeth a little as she watched Vilma reach up and slowly, rather caressively, bury her fingers in Heath's hair above his left ear.

"Thank you," Vilma whispered. "I thought I'd used up my endurance...and then you appeared."

Just as Cricket had feared, Vilma's kiss wasn't quite as innocent, nor quick, as the kisses from the other girls had been. When Vilma pressed her lips to Heath's, she lingered a moment—and a moment was too long for Cricket's temperament. Oh, naturally, Cricket didn't say a word when Vilma finally released Heath and stepped back from him—but inside she was nearly seething.

In fact, Cricket was so distracted by her unsettled feelings within that when she glanced to the group of her friends standing near her, wearing expressions of expectation fixed on her, she simply asked, "What?" It took her a moment, accompanied by Ann's and Marie's nods toward Heath, for her to realize that they all expected her to offer him a kiss of recognition as well.

Heath was also looking at her—grinning with knowing amusement.

"Go on, Cricket," Marie whispered through barely parted lips.

Summoning the guts of a Roman gladiator, Cricket turned to Heath. She couldn't keep from returning his smile. He was too heroic, wonderful, and provocatively handsome not to smile at.

Approaching him, though she felt ridiculous attempting to offer any comparable thanks to what he'd just received five times over, she nodded and said, "Yes. Thank you, Mr. Thibodaux. For our lives...for our virtue and for—"

But she had no opportunity to finish her thanks—for in an instant, her face was held tightly between his hands, and he kissed her firmly on the lips. His second kiss was less forced, softer, moister, and playful.

"You're welcome," Heath said, releasing Cricket nearly as quickly as he'd pounced.

Cricket blushed as she looked to the other girls to see them all smiling with delight—even Vilma.

"But like I said," Heath began then, "we have a long way to go before you girls are safe at home. So rest while you can now…and for just a few hours." His smile had faded, replaced by an expression of concern. "I don't think we should wait until mornin' to head out again. Heck and his men are gonna be after us like the devil chasin' an escaped sinner from hell."

The girls nodded or mumbled their understanding and began to settle on the ground with the blankets Heath had had the foresight to roll to each saddle rig. Cricket was the last to settle. She was worried for Heath. He needed sleep just like the rest of them. And anyway, how on earth would he keep watch in the dark?

Heath noticed Cricket staring at him, nodded toward her blanket, and said, "Go to sleep." Then he sauntered off into the darkness, down the trail in the direction from whence they'd come.

Exhaling a deep breath, Cricket stretched out on her blanket, closed her eyes, and tried to relax. The soft sound of the river as it slowly flowed through the summer night allowed Cricket to imagine she was being rocked. The songs of the summer crickets and night birds blended perfectly—not so loud as to cause sleeplessness but just full enough to soothe. The night was tranquil and serene. The air was fresh and warm, and the fragrances of nature—of wildflowers and grasses, leaves and sagebrush—mingled, perfuming it to the sweet, comforting scent of nectar.

"Come on, blossom bottom."

Cricket had never in all her life felt so fatigued or had such trouble rising to full consciousness. But someone's hand was on her shoulder. Someone was gently shaking her.

"Come on, Magnolia," Heath said. "We gotta get goin'. Them outlaws ain't far behind us."

"What?" Cricket answered as she struggled to sit up and to complete wakefulness.

"I tracked back a ways…and I can see their campfire," he whispered. "They're too close. And we need to start ridin'."

That was all it took to blast Cricket to her feet.

Quickly the girls gathered their blankets, rinsed their faces, and quenched their thirst with water from the river. Heath had had them all leave their horses saddled and bridled, and as Cricket mounted hers, she whispered an apology for his discomfort.

Heath nodded to Ann, and quietly the girls and their horses stepped into a nearly inaudible departure. Cricket glanced over her shoulder to see Heath nod his reassurance.

They moved along silently for some time—the moon and stars as their only light. Cricket wondered how long they'd actually slept. The moon was still up, and the sun hadn't broken the horizon in the east at all. Her body ached, her stomach growled, and she wondered if she could endure another day and a half of travel.

Yet the constant threat at their backs would keep her moving. She couldn't imagine falling into the hands of Heck and his men again. The thought caused tears to fill her eyes, but she held them back and focused on riding.

They had to make it home—all of them! Cricket had to see her father and Ada again. She couldn't bear the thought of never feeling the warmth of their embraces. Marie had to make it home to Hudson! She had to marry him and have his babies. Ann had to heal and win Mr. Keel's broken, lonesome heart. Vilma had to return and grow out her beautiful auburn hair. Pearl must return to her family in Thistle. As for Jinny—oh, Jinny and Nina's parents must have at least one of their daughters live!

As for Heathro Thibodaux, not only was Cricket more desperate about his safety and life than even her own but she also knew in her heart that every girl he'd taken from the outlaw band must make it safely home—for his sake. She couldn't think of his blaming himself for any more deaths that were no fault of his in the first place.

And so she rode. Cricket rode hard and fast, even for the aching and pain in her body. She clung to hope and prayed for deliverance. No matter what the future held for her—for Heath—for all of them—no matter what, she would fight to her last breath in trying to make sure that they all had a future.

❦

The horses needed the rest. If Heath wanted them to be able to carry the girls as close to Pike's Creek as possible before dropping dead, he had to allow them a little reprieve. They were well watered now and seemed somewhat restored to their strength as they paused grazing on riverbank grasses.

Heath studied the girls a moment from where he stood watching the trail behind them. He shook his head, thinking they all looked like hell had them in tow—thin and sunburnt, dusty, tired, and aching from a ride that would wear out most cowboys. He knew the girls were at the end of their endurance. He knew it—but he also knew they had to press on. Pike's Creek was only hours away. Just a few more hours of riding, and they'd all be safe.

His gaze settle on Cricket—and his mouth watered as he thought of how badly he wanted to take her in his arms again and drink his fill of her kiss. He briefly wondered if he'd ever have the chance to kiss her again—for even if he did manage to usher them home, he knew what would happen. He'd be a hero—for a week or two. And then the townsfolk would begin to resent him for being right about where the outlaws were headed. Old Reverend Righteous Stanley would no doubt *graciously* remind them all that it was God and the Lord who'd returned the stolen girls—and he'd be right. But Heath had had a helping hand in it, hadn't he?

Still, Heathro Thibodaux had been a Texas Ranger long enough to know that gratitude more often than not eventually turned to resentment. The hero who arrived with the prize was often regarded as simply a reminder of the terrible thing that had happened. Whether or not Heath had been the one to choose the right trail, track down the girls, manage to strip them from the grubby hands of murderous outlaws, and save their virtue and lives, Heath knew that in the end the town would dislike him for it. Nevertheless, Heath didn't care about the hypocrites in Pike's Creek. He cared about returning the girls to their families and to safety.

But he knew he was tired and worn too—that his endurance was wearing out. He knew it as soon as he felt the thud of the bullet in his shoulder a second before he heard the repeat of the rifle. Lack of sleep, hard riding, and worry had found him allowing himself to be distracted into thinking—and that distraction had now found him shot in the shoulder.

"Get on those horses, and ride like hell!" Heath shouted.

Leveling his own rifle, he aimed and fired—watched Patterson lurch and grab his chest. Instantly, Heath cocked his rifle and fired again, exhaling a breath as he watched Patterson's head jerk back and the outlaw tumble from his horse.

"Hurry!" Cricket instructed as Heath turned and began running toward them. "Get on your horses! Ann! Head Harley for home!"

As Cricket helped Jinny mount her horse, Heath nearly knocked her over as he reached them.

She gasped in horror, fear rinsing through ever inch of her body as she saw the blood at his shoulder. "You've been shot!" she breathed.

But Heath ignored her. "Here," he said, unloading his ammunition from Archie's saddlebags and tossing it to the ground. Cricket shook her head as Heath then forced Archie's reins into her hands. Cricket's horse was still tethered to a nearby tree, and Heath quickly took control of its reins, turned, and started back down the trail.

"No!" Cricket cried. "You're comin' with us! You are not stayin' behind! I won't leave if you don't come with us!"

As quick as a bullwhip, Heath turned on her, took her chin firmly in hand, and growled, "You will ride, Magnolia! You get these girls home! Heck and his men are too close. You'll never make it if I don't hold them off awhile. So get on that damn horse, and you ride like hell itself is comin' for you! Do you hear me?"

Cricket pushed his hand, however, releasing his hold on her chin and shaking her head. "I won't leave you here. You have two rifles, and I'm a good shot. I'll stay and—"

But Heath turned then to Archie. Patting the horse's velvet nose, he said, "You take this girl home, Archie...and don't you come back, do you hear me?"

Another shot rang out, and Cricket screamed as Heath looked at his arm and swore. "Just a graze," he mumbled.

"You can do what you want to me, Heathro Thibodaux," Cricket said as tears flooded her cheeks. "But I won't leave you!" Angrily she wiped at her tears on her cheeks, wishing her hands weren't trembling so violently and betraying her fear and panic. "I can't leave you!" Desperately she reached out, taking hold of Heath's arm. "Please…just let me stay here with you. If I'm with you…if there're two of us…I'm a good enough shot to help, I promise." As Heath's attention fell to her still trembling hands, Cricket released his arm, clasping her hands together and silently begging them to be still.

Heath stared at her a moment, his beautiful eyes narrowing as he studied her. "You have to lead them on, Cricket," he said. "Somebody has to get these girls home…and somebody has to stay here and try to pick off the bastards that are still followin' you so that you all *can* get home."

"Ann can take them," she told him.

"No, she can't," he mumbled.

Heath growled, "Get on that horse and ride, girl!" He looked up to the other girls, scowling as he saw the obvious fear and weakness beginning to overwhelm them. "You girls ride hard, do you hear me? You ride those horses into the ground if you have to. They've got enough life in 'em to get you all home before they drop. Do you hear me?"

The Burroughs girl nodded—as well as the preacher's daughter and the King girl.

Taking hold of Cricket's arm, he turned her toward Archie. "You stop only to let yourselves and the horses drink…but don't let any of them linger. A couple of minutes—that's it. Do you understand?"

"Yes," Cricket whimpered.

"Now mount up," he ordered, holding the stirrup so she could mount more easily.

"All right," she breathed. Heath exhaled a relieved breath—grateful she wasn't going to fight him about it anymore.

But then Heathro Thibodaux made another mistake. He made the mistake of looking at Cricket just once more—and it was nearly his undoing.

Roughly he took her shoulders, turned her, and pushed her back against Archie. His mouth was at her throat before he'd even realized it himself, knowing the taste of her warm, salty skin. Over and over he kissed her there—her neck, the hollow of her throat—allowing his mouth to savor the sensation of the blood coursing through her veins. Again he kissed the soft, tender hollow of her throat and nearly dropped to his knees in weak, wanton desire when he felt her bury her hands in his hair.

Cricket wondered for a moment if she might drop dead of wanting his kiss to leave her neck and find her mouth. But she didn't—and it did. Heath ravaged her mouth with such wanton, hungry kisses that she couldn't breathe for a moment. But she didn't care to breathe—not if it meant leaving Heath to face what was left of the band of outlaws—not if it meant leaving him at all.

Abruptly, he broke the seal of their mouths. He bent, placing a moist kiss to the burn on her chest—and though under normal circumstances she should've slapped him when he took hold of what was left of the sleeve of her camisole, pulling it down her arm and kissing her shoulder with a ravenous sort of vigor and kissing the place where her arm met her bosom—she didn't.

"Now get on that horse and ride, Magnolia!" he shouted.

Without another word, Heath bent down, taking hold of her left ankle and placing her foot in the stirrup as he lifted her. Cricket swung her right leg over Archie's back and adjusted the reins.

"Don't look back," he ordered when she looked down at him and began to cry once more. "You ride like the devil himself is on your flank, and you get home. You get yourself and these girls home, Magnolia. Promise me you'll do it." Cricket nodded her promise, but it wasn't enough, and he shouted, "Promise me you'll get yourself and these girls home!"

"I-I will," she cried. "I promise I will. But you'll be right behind us, won't you?"

Heath's eyes narrowed, and he nodded once. "Now go," he mumbled. He brazenly lifted her petticoat hem, kissing her squarely on the knee. "Go!" he shouted, slapping Archie on the hindquarters.

Cricket gasped but held her saddle as Archie leapt into a gallop. She heard Heath shouting, slapping the other horses' flanks to get them moving, and she rode—rode toward the tangerine sun hanging high in the western sky.

CHAPTER FIFTEEN

"Come on, Harley!" Cricket heard Ann cry. "We can make it! I know we can!"

Cricket reined in Archie and turned him. The others had fallen behind again. Even Harley was struggling. All the horses were so lathered up it made Cricket's heart ache with sympathy for them. But even though there had been no sign of Heck Alford and his band of outlaws—not for all the hours the girls had been riding—Cricket knew they couldn't stop, not when they were so close to town.

Pike's Creek was no more than two miles. In two miles, they would be home, safe—and she could send someone back for Heath.

She wondered whether he were alive or dead, and the pain of thinking it made her breath catch in her throat. She had to make it back to Pike's Creek—to send help for Heath.

"Come on, girls," she encouraged. "We could walk from here if we weren't so worn to the bone."

"Can we walk the horses at least?" Ann begged through tear-filled eyes as she reined in next to Cricket.

Cricket glanced back beyond Ann and Harley—back beyond Marie, Vilma, Pearl, and poor Jinny. There was no sign of the outlaws—none. She was sure Heath had stopped them—or at least held them off long enough for her and the others to be miles and miles ahead of them.

"All right," she agreed. "Let's walk them home. But let's keep sharp eyes at our backs, just in case..."

"In case Heath wasn't able to—" Pearl began.

"He was able to!" Vilma passionately interrupted, however. "He's still holdin' them off for us…or he's killed them all."

Wiping tears from her cheeks, Vilma began to walk her horse toward town.

"He's all right, Cricket," Marie said as she walked her horse forward as well. "I know he is."

Ann and Pearl walked then, Ann stroking Harley's mane all the while.

It was Jinny that was last. Her horse looked as severely ill as she did, and Cricket wasn't sure the animal could make it the two miles to Pike's Creek even at a walking pace. But Cricket forced a smile of encouragement and led Archie to fall in next to Jinny's horse.

Harley reared up ahead and made a sound like a cough. "He's too spent, Cricket!" Ann called over her shoulder. "I'll kill him if I keep goin'!"

With wild frustration and fear, Cricket watched as Ann dismounted and quickly loosened Harley's saddle cinch.

"Ann! We're so close! You can't stop now!" Cricket cried in near panic.

"I'm not," Ann assured her. "I just won't torture Harley anymore. I won't!"

Cricket watched as Ann used every ounce of strength left in her to push the saddle and blanket from Harley's back. She removed the bit from his mouth and began leading the horse as she slowly walked toward town.

Marie's horse, having seen that Harley was free, simply stopped. No amount of encouragement from Marie would get him moving again. Then without warning, Vilma's horse stumbled. Vilma tumbled to the ground only moments before her horse collapsed, panting for breath as it lay in the cool summer grass.

They were in trouble! The horses were wasting—for Pearl's and Jinny's horses stopped as well. The only horse that didn't stop was Archie. In fact, it was as if Archie knew the circumstances were dire—for in the next moment, Cricket felt her body jerk hard as Archie broke into a violent, reckless sort of gallop toward town.

"I'll send help!" Cricket shouted as she leaned forward in the saddle to make the gallop easier for Archie.

❧

"Zeke!" Ada gasped as she burst through the front door.

Zeke Cranford wiped the tears from his handsome but mournful eyes as he looked up to his wife. The expression of indescribable joy on her face, mingled with her tears, caused hope to leap in his chest.

"What is it?" he asked.

"It's…Z-Zeke! It's Cricket!" Ada sobbed. "She just this moment rode into Pike's Creek…on Heathro Thibodaux's horse!"

Zeke was out of his chair, taking his wife's hand and pulling her along behind him as he stormed out the front door faster than a hummingbird could blink.

"Cricket!" he breathed as he saw his daughter rather tumble from the back of a frothy horse.

"Daddy!" Cricket cried as she ran to him. "Daddy! Y-you have to go for him! Y-you have to go back and help him!" she sobbed, collapsing into his arms.

"Oh, my baby!" Zeke wept into her hair. "Oh, my sweet baby!"

Cricket knew she could not faint or find herself otherwise unconscious, no matter how much her body hurt or how tired she was or even how close to dying from lack of food, water, and shelter.

Quickly she babbled on, afraid that she would drop dead and then no one would know where to find Heath or the other girls.

"Daddy, the other girls…they're just outside of town…about two miles east," she breathed through her sobs. "The horses are failin'… even Harley. Someone has to go for them!" Then, clutching the front of her father's shirt in her weak, trembling fists, she cried, "But, Daddy… someone has to go for Heath! Please! If he's not dead…they shot him twice that I saw! Please…please! Someone has to go for him. He's near the fork…the place where he took the trail to New Orleans and the posse crossed to head for Mexico. Please, Daddy! Please! You have to go get him and bring him home!"

"Shhh, baby," Zeke soothed, stroking Cricket's hair.

"What's goin' on?" Cooper Keel asked, hurrying toward Cricket, her father, and Ada.

"The girls are two miles east of here, Coop!" Zeke exclaimed. "Get some men out there. And then you and me...we're gonna saddle up and ride like hell to get Heathro Thibodaux! He's holed up at the river."

"I w-wanna come with you, Daddy," Cricket stammered. "I-I wanna come with you to find Heath, Daddy! I can't stay here and wait...not knowin' if he's alive or dead! He saved us, Daddy. All alone he saved us!"

"What's happenin'?" Reverend Stanley asked as he and others from the town hurried over.

"You coward!" Cricket screamed. Pulling herself from her father's arms, she flew at Vilma's father, slapping him hard across one cheek and then the other. "You coward! You let him come for us all by himself? You didn't believe him? Even after what happened to those other girls? You're a coward! You and all the men who followed you to Mexico instead of listening to Heath!"

Cricket moved to slap Reverend Stanley once more, but her father bound her in his arms to keep her from doing so.

Still, binding her arms didn't bind her tired, frightened, angry tongue. "Your own daughter was out there—Vilma! Bein' dragged with the rest of us to be sold! And you didn't follow Heath? How long did it take you to realize you'd taken the wrong trail, Reverend Stanley? We waited for the posse to come...waited and waited. And then when we knew Heck would kill Jinny...w-we escaped!"

"She's mad with fatigue and trauma, Zeke," Edgar Stanley said. "I forgive her for the rage...and the abuse."

"Forgive me?" Cricket screeched. Cricket struggled in her father's arms, and when she couldn't break free to slap Vilma's father again, she simply spit at him, feeling triumphant as she saw him wipe her saliva from his lips.

"Cricket," Zeke whispered in a low, comforting voice. "Settle down, baby. Settle down. We'll send some folks out to get the girls, all right? And me and Cooper Keel will go for Ranger Thibodaux ourselves. Shhh. Settle down now. Daddy will take care of it from here."

Turning Cricket away from the vile Reverend Stanley, Zeke pulled Cricket to Ada. "Ada," he began, "you keep Cricket at home with you here. Just help her bathe. Feed her some broth…only broth…and see if she'll drop off to sleep."

"But I wanna go with you, Daddy, please! I have to know if he's alive or dead! I have to see him! I-I can't live if—" Cricket cried.

"Shhh," Zeke soothed as he wiped the tears from her cheeks. "I'm sure he's fine, baby. That man's tougher than most. Shot up or not, I'm sure he's fine. You just stay here and keep Ada company while Coop and me ride out and bring him home, all right?"

"He saved our lives, Daddy," Cricket wept. "All by himself he came, and he risked bein' killed. He stayed with us…made sure none of the rest of us died…only Nina…and th-then he saved us. You have to bring him home, Daddy. Please!"

"I will, baby. I will," her father promised. "Now you go with Ada, honey," he said, taking her shoulders and directing her to Ada. "I'll go for the Heath…and you just keep Ada company for me, all right?"

Cricket's tears began anew as Ada embraced her, shushing softly into her ear and stroking her tangled hair.

Zeke was infuriated—purely infuriated! Turning to Edgar Stanley, he said, "You said you lost the tracks at the river…and had the posse head to Mexico even though Heathro Thibodaux said different."

"It was obvious they'd gone toward Mexico, Zeke," Edgar defended himself proudly. "By the time we lost the trail to Mexico, it was too late anyway. If even we had gone back to the other trail—the one Mr. Thibodaux took—we couldn't have tracked them long. The rain had washed any tracks left by the girls, their captors, or that arrogant Texas Ranger. I thought—"

But Edgar Stanley didn't have the chance to explain what insipid thoughts he'd had after that—for Zeke Cranford laid him out in the street of Pike's Creek before he could.

"Come on, Coop," he mumbled to Cooper Keel. "Let's get this town headed in the right direction for once."

❦

Once Zeke had led a group of men, women, and wagons out to find the girls east of Pike's Creek—once he'd talked to the girls a bit and learned a few more details of what had happened to find Heathro Thibodaux holed up somewhere trying to keep a band of white slaving outlaws at bay—he and Cooper Keel had ridden off in search of what was left of the young and heroic Texas Ranger.

Cooper had embraced his niece awhile, assuring her that all would be well. And though Zeke had told Coop he'd be glad to head out on his own, Cooper's niece, Pearl, had begged her uncle to go too—to try and find the man who had saved their lives.

"I'm sorry I had you up in Thistle and thereabouts for so long, Zeke," Cooper hollered as they rode. "If we woulda been there when Ada and Maymee had arrived lookin' for us…we could've already been on the trail after the girls."

But Zeke shook his head. "No. It ain't your fault…or mine. How could we possibly have known that while we were out huntin' for your niece, my girl had been taken and that idiot preacher of ours was leadin' everybody astray? No. We were gonna ride out tomorrow mornin', Coop. It was all we could've done considerin' how long it took us to get back to Pike's Creek today." Zeke choked on the overwhelming emotion settled in his throat. He coughed, adding, "I'm just glad to see my baby girl is still alive. I thought sure she wasn't. I owe Heathro Thibodaux a far greater debt than I can ever repay…even if we do find him still alive."

"Amen!" Cooper agreed.

Spurring their horses, Zeke and Cooper rode far into the night, following the river the way several of the girls had indicated.

Along about midnight, they came upon a sight that even their wildest imaginations couldn't have conjured. As the moon and stars shone brightly in the midnight heavens, Zeke Cranford and Cooper Keel found Heathro Thibodaux—or at least what was left of him.

❦

"Please come inside, Cricket," Ada begged. "You need some rest. Just for an hour or two and then I'll let you come back out here and wait."

Ada wiped a tear from her cheek. "I'll even come out and wait with you, all right?"

But Cricket shook her head. "No. I'm not leavin'. I'm not leavin' until Daddy rides in with Heathro Thibodaux either sittin' a horse…or draped over one." She buried her face in her hands—in the soft, white handkerchief Ada had provided for her once the other one had become so drenched with Cricket's tears that it was no longer useful.

Ada nodded with acceptance. Settling herself in the rocking chair next to Cricket's on the front porch, she followed Cricket's gaze, staring out into the dark, dark night.

Ada sensed there was far more to Heathro Thibodaux's rescuing the girls of Pike's Creek, and the two girls from elsewhere, than Cricket had spoken of. The girl was obsessed—entirely consumed with knowing what had happened to him—with hoping he was alive.

Naturally Ada and Zeke both knew Cricket was somewhat sweet on Heathro—that she had been sweet on him since the day he moved to Pike's Creek. But this was different. This wasn't just gratitude for the man who had rescued her, and it wasn't infatuation. It was something far more, and Ada wasn't about to press Cricket—either for more information on her feelings concerning Heathro or to abandon her post on the front porch watching for his safe return. Until Cricket actually passed out from crushing physical and emotional fatigue, Ada would let her wait for her father to return—let her wait for her father and Heathro Thibodaux. Quietly Ada prayed, however, "Let Zeke come ridin' in with Heathro sittin' a horse and not draped over one. Please, Lord. Please."

It was quiet in Pike's Creek—even quieter than it had been the night before when Heath had allowed the girls to rest alongside the river for a time. There were the usual sounds to soothe Cricket—the lowing of cattle and calves in the distance, the hum of the crickets in the grasses and cicadas in the tree branches. There was also the sound of Ada's rocking chair creak-creaking on the front porch next to Cricket's.

As always in summer, the air was fragrant—filled with a perfume blended of green and growing things like honeysuckle and wheat in the fields. The temperature was not too cool and not too warm. It was perfect—the temperature dreamed of when winter nights were cold and kitchen floors frigid in early spring mornings.

Everything was just as it had been only a week before. Nothing about Pike's Creek seemed different to Cricket in the least—nothing except everything. Everything seemed different—changed. Or was it Cricket that had changed? As she began rocking in her own rocking chair, matching the slow, easy rhythm of Ada's, Cricket knew that she had, indeed, changed. Terrible, terrifying experiences did change a person. Stories had always told her that; losing her mother had taught it to her firsthand. But now Cricket knew something else changed a person as well: love—the wild, impassioned, frenzied love of falling *in* love. And Cricket had been falling *in* love with Heathro Thibodaux for months.

As she'd sat on the porch for nearly the entire twelve hours since her father and Cooper Keel had ridden off in search of Heathro—since the good people of Pike's Creek had retrieved Marie, Ann, Vilma, Pearl, and Jinny from east of town—Cricket had considered all she'd been through with the others. It had changed her somewhat. No doubt it had changed them all. As for Cricket, she wondered how long it would be before she wouldn't be frightened each time she strayed too far from her father's house. She wondered if sugar would taste as sweet in Ada's cake frosting as it had before and if she'd still be able to outrun Heath's ornery old bull if she ever happened on him running loose in the pasture again. She wondered if she'd still want to plan mischievous shenanigans to go about with her friends—wondered if she'd ever be able to think of any to plan again.

And in the darkness of night, as she waited for her father to return—as she waited to know the fate of the man who had saved her, cared for her, kissed her as only a dream could've kissed her—Cricket concluded that, yes, she had experience that had stripped away some of her innocence. But she'd survived it, and she knew that from there on, yes, she would be a bit more wary and easily startled for a while whenever venturing away from the house. But she also knew that Ada's cake frosting would taste far sweeter than ever it had before, that she'd still be able to outrun Heath's bull if the need ever arose. And she knew that more than ever before she would find profound joy in plotting mischievous plans of do-gooding shenanigans with her friends.

The only thing Cricket was uncertain of was whether she would drop dead of a broken heart if her father rode into town with Heathro Thibodaux's body wrapped in a blanket and draped over the back of a horse. In that moment, she thought that, though she could endure most anything on earth that didn't bleed her life from her, she was not sure she could endure Heath's death.

"Someone saw to Archie, didn't they, Ada?" Cricket asked, suddenly needing to distract her thoughts.

"Yes, Cricket," Ada answered with a smile. "He's been brushed, rubbed, watered, and well fed. Mr. Burroughs says that he'll be fine."

Cricket smiled a little. "Good. Good. He's an amazin' horse."

"Yes," Ada agreed softly.

Cricket thought of something then—though she didn't quite know why the matter popped into her head at that moment. Still, it made her smile, and she thought she might be able to bring a smile to Ada's lips as well.

"Ada?" Cricket began.

"Yes?" Ada's eyes lit up like fireworks. Cricket knew it was for the sake that she hoped Cricket was feeling better. "Remember the day I asked you whether or not you and Daddy were gonna have any babies?"

Cricket almost giggled when she noticed that the tempo of Ada's rocking was faster suddenly.

"Yes," Ada admitted. "What of it?"

"Well, I just thought it might ease your mind to know that you don't have to explain everything to me anymore," Cricket answered. "I know all about it now."

Ada's rocking came to an abrupt stop. Cricket looked to her to find her sitting perfectly still—eyes wide as supper plates, pale as a sheet, as if she'd only just seen a ghostly apparition.

"H-how do you know all about it, Cricket?" Ada ventured, her lower lip quivering as her eyes filled with tears. "Did those men…those outlaws…did they…"

Cricket gasped as realization of what Ada must be thinking thumped her. "Oh no! No, no, no, Ada! Nothin' like that! Mr. Thibodaux made sure—"

"Mr. Thibodaux?" Ada exclaimed as a dainty hand leapt to her bosom. "Did Mr. Thibodaux…did he…did he show you—"

"Oh, heavens no!" Cricket desperately interrupted, blushing from the hairs on her head to the tips of her toes. "No! I just meant…I-I…" She'd meant to relieve Ada's mind, not horrify and frighten her. "I just meant that you don't have to worry about bein' the one to explain to me all the parts Daddy left out when it comes to what *really* happens for babies to be born. Vilma told us while we were captive. Vilma and Pearl, anyway."

Ada brushed a stray tear from her cheek, smiling with relief and giggling a little. "Oh, good. You about gave me a fit of apoplexy, Cricket. There for a minute I thought you and Mr. Thibodaux had…" Cricket blushed as Ada sighed again and smiled. She patted Cricket lovingly on the knee. "Well, though I'm quite sure Vilma Stanley knows the particulars of it, I'm *very* sure that she does not know the most important details of…the reasons…the importance of…I'm sure she does not know, bein' that she can't possibly have the experience…I'm sure she does *not* know the emotional aspects of what goes on between a husband and wife who are truly, truly, and deeply in love when… when…"

"When what?" Cricket asked. She was astonished at how quickly Ada's cheeks had gone from whitewash to roses.

But Ada's attention was suddenly arrested by something else. "Cricket? Do you hear riders?"

Cricket held her breath. She did hear it—the sound of horses approaching from the darkness. Leaping to her feet, she dashed off the porch, surprising even herself with having the vitality left to dash anywhere.

Ada was at her side in an instant, and Cricket reached for her hand, grasping it for support. In silence they stared together into the darkness—listened as the approaching clop-clop of horses and riders grew nearer.

"Daddy?" Cricket breathed as she began to discern the outline of a man astride his horse—a large man—a man who sat his saddle exactly as her father did.

She started to run to him, but Ada gripped her hand tight—grabbed her arm and stayed her. "Wait, Cricket. Only wait."

Cricket's eyes were so full of tears they burned like they were aflame. Her breath was so ragged she was more softly panting than breathing.

At last her father was near enough that when the sun suddenly broke the horizon in the east, she saw him clearly—saw Cooper Keel riding just behind him. Her breath caught in her throat as she saw then that her father and Cooper led eight other horses at their backs. Eight horses—and each saddled horse had an outlaw's body draped over it.

Yet as a fresh, new ray of sunshine suddenly beamed across the heavens, Cricket collapsed to her knees when she saw that following the eight horses laden with eight corpses was one more horse—a horse with a rider sitting slumped in its saddle—a rider far more handsome than any other man to ever walk the earth! There, riding into Pike's Creek—a white bandage at one shoulder, weary and dirty, but fully, beautifully, and miraculously still alive—was Heathro Thibodaux.

CHAPTER SIXTEEN

"Well, of course I know who stitched this quilt, Cooper Keel,' I told him," Maymee Maloney said as she poured another cup of cherry and blueberry tea for Cricket. "I told Cooper, 'There's only one woman in town that stitches this perfectly…and that's Ann Burroughs,' I said." Mrs. Maloney offered Cricket another pastry and continued, "And I'll tell you one thing. I have never in all my years of knowin' Cooper Keel seen a smile spread across his face the likes of what the mention of Ann Burroughs coaxed out. No, sirree. Never! And that's countin' the years his wife was alive and with him…God rest her soul."

Cricket smiled, trying not to reveal how perfectly delighted she was that Cooper Keel had inquired of Mrs. Maloney concerning the quilt he'd had left on his doorstep weeks before—or how further delighted she was that Mrs. Maloney recognized Ann's unusually beautiful quilt stitch and told Mr. Keel.

"Well," Mrs. Maloney rambled on, "when I saw the size of that smile on his face and the twinkle that jumped right down from the stars above to land in his handsome eyes, I asked Cooper right then and there…just flat out asked him if he had any, you know, *aspirations* where Ann Burroughs was concerned."

Cricket's eyebrows sprung into hopeful arches. "And what did he say?"

Mrs. Maloney paused, grinning a purely mischievous smile. She picked up her cup of cherry and blueberry tea, took a long, slow sip, and set the cup down again.

"Well?" Cricket urged. "You have to tell me what he said!"

Maymee Maloney leaned closer to Cricket. "Well, when I asked Cooper Keel if he had any of those aspirin'-to-woo-a-woman thoughts where Ann Burroughs was concerned…do you know what he answered me?"

"What?" Cricket giggled, in agony with curiosity.

Mrs. Maloney smiled. "He said, 'Hell yes, Maymee Maloney! I plan on marryin' that girl one day!' That's what he said." Mrs. Maloney's made an expression of firm pointedness. " 'Hell yes,' he said. Right here in my house." Mrs. Maloney was quick to add, "But don't you go tellin' Ann nothin' about it now, Cricket. You let things unfold the way they're meant to unfold, you hear?"

"Yes, ma'am," Cricket sighed. She picked up her teacup and inhaled the delicate aroma of Mrs. Maloney's own blended cherry and blueberry tea. "I won't say a word. Not one word."

"You best not," Maymee reiterated. "Love is a delicate thing. One false move or interference can really pop out a spoke."

"Yes, it can," Cricket mumbled, sipping her tea and trying not to think of the only thing that was ever on her mind—the only person that was ever on her mind—Heathro Thibodaux.

"And Hudson Oliver and Miss Marie King?" Mrs. Maloney began. "I hear the date is set for August…at long last."

Cricket nodded. "Yep. August nineteenth! Oh, I'll sleep better once those two are finally married."

"*You'll* sleep better?" Mrs. Maloney asked, giggling. "Why's that?"

Cricket shrugged. "I don't know. Maybe because it's been so very long in comin'…or because I just know those two were meant for each other." She shrugged again. "I don't know. I just want them married, that's all."

"And what about yourself, sugar bean?" Mrs. Maloney ventured. The old woman placed her elbows on the table and leaned across it toward Cricket. "Why won't you just tie that Heathro Thibodaux up in a chair and seduce the livin' life out of him, darlin'?"

But Cricket shook her head—even as tears welled in her eyes. "I-I can't. He…he…I-I think he remembers bad things when he looks at me now."

"Oh, bull roar, girl!" Mrs. Maloney gruffed. "I've seen the two of you…walkin' around each other like you think nobody notices that invisible attraction connectin' you to one another." She slapped the table with one hand. "I'm tellin' you that boy is yours for the takin', Magnolia." She leaned back in her chair, the mischievous grin returning to her face. "What went on out there between you two, honey? Somethin' did, I know it. Every one of you girls has told the story over and over. You all got taken by Heck Alford and his gang of outlaws. They was headin' for New Orleans when along come Heathro Thibodaux. He tricks ol' Heck into believin' he's workin' for some brothel man, rides along with you all for a few days…and quick as a mouse, you all are on your way back to Pike's Creek." Mrs. Maloney's eyes narrowed as she studied Cricket with suspicion. "Only thing is, there's a few things I keep hearin' repeated. 'Cricket helped Mr. Thibodaux,' for one. 'While Cricket and Mr. Thibodaux were away from the group' is another."

Cricket shrugged and shook her head. "I-I helped plan it…the escape and all. He told me I was the strongest and that he knew I would do as he told me."

"Did he now?" Mrs. Maloney chuckled. "Hmmm. Well," she sighed, "at least Hudson and Marie are on their way to wedded bliss. Looks like Ann will be followin' shortly. And word is Wyatt Stanley suddenly has his eye on you."

Cricket's stomach churned. "Wyatt Stanley is a mousy, manipulative idiot," she mumbled.

"I agree," Mrs. Maloney said with a nod. "So why don't you stomp on that little mouse of a Stanley man and tie Heathro up to a chair—"

"And have my way with him," Cricket finished with a giggle. "I know, I know." It was time to change the course of their conversation. Thus, Cricket asked, "And how's ol' Nobody MacGee doin' these days, hmm?"

Mrs. Maloney's smiling eyes lit up. "Oh, me and old Nobody…" She slowly shook her head for dramatics as she said, "We've been doin' some sparkin' that would make Marie King and Hudson Oliver blush."

Cricket burst into laughter. "Then that *is* some might passionate sparkin'!"

"Mmm-hmm!" Mrs. Maloney affirmed. "Why, my mouth just takes to waterin' at the very thought of it! Do you know what I mean by that, sugar?"

Cricket blushed a little and glanced down to her teacup—but nodded.

"Mmm-hmmm. I thought you might," Mrs. Maloney mumbled. "I just thought you might."

Later that afternoon, as Cricket slowly meandered home from her visit with Mrs. Maloney, she tried to think about anything but Heath. She tried to concentrate on the little set of ragdolls she was finishing for Shanny Lou Harty and her little sister Marianne. Shanny Lou and Marianne had been Cricket's choice for the Friday night shenanigans she, Vilma, Marie, and Ann had planned. It would be their first night of shenanigans since Heath had gunned down Heck Alford and the rest of his gang. But, of course, even the plans for Friday night couldn't keep Heath from her mind.

Cricket stepped off the dirt road and into the soft, cool grass. It felt better on her bare feet, and she squinched her toes several times, relishing the feel of the green grass blades between her toes.

"Hey there, Cricket!" Mr. King called as he drove his wagon past.

"Hey, Mr. King!" Cricket returned with a smile.

Mr. King nodded and winked at Cricket, and she felt warmed and comforted inside.

She looked up and around her. Mrs. Stanley paused before entering the general store when she caught sight of Cricket. The preacher's wife smiled and waved, and Cricket smiled and waved back. It seemed that, since the day Cricket had slapped her husband silly, Mrs. Stanley could not smile and wave often enough at her. Reverend Stanley had said nothing about the incident—well, not really. He'd given a sermon two Sundays later, concerning how one could always know who the better man in life was by who was turning the other cheek and who was delivering the blow.

Zeke Cranford had nearly laid out Edgar Stanley again right then and there in the church, but Ada placed a hand on his thigh, instantly calming him.

Cricket didn't feel much like returning home yet—and for two reasons. For one, she didn't look forward to dusting and oiling the furniture the way she and Ada had planned. And for another reason— she was still trying not to startle at the sudden appearance of her own shadow.

Naturally, she hadn't slept well since returning from being abducted. But it was the near constant sensation of insecurity and fear that accompanied her that bothered her most. In fact, in the two weeks since Heath had saved them all, Cricket had taken to forcing herself to walk out to Mr. Burroughs's pasture—and even to the old Morgan house, but only once. Each time she wandered too far from home, Cricket would nearly be panic-stricken with anxiety—and she was determined not to let fear win. She was the fighter, and she continued to fight.

And so Cricket meandered along, pausing to squinch the grass between her toes, to pluck a honeysuckle bloom and savor its sweet nectar, or to simply gaze up at the sky and remind herself that all was well. Nearly all, at least. It wasn't long before Cricket found herself at the fence surrounding the very pasture through which Heath's bull had chased her.

Sighing, she sat down in the grass—in the very spot where Heath had pulled the splinter from her foot and rubbed his medicinal spit onto the wound. As Cricket closed her eyes, the euphoric memory of the night in the abandoned barn washed over her—of Heath caring for the cigar burn on her chest with the same medicinal spit he's used to soothe her foot.

Goose bumps raced over every inch of her body as she bathed in the returning sensations his kisses that night had rained on her. Heath owned her from that moment on. He'd owned her before that moment—long before! Didn't he know he did? Didn't he care that he did?

Two weeks they'd all been back. Two long weeks in which Cricket had hardly seen Heath—and when she had seen him, he'd only smiled at her as a strange sort of distant, hollow look rose in his beautiful blue eyes. He'd said, "Hello," on three occasions—"Good afternoon, Miss Magnolia," on two others—but nothing else. Cricket had unwillingly at first begun to understand that what had transpired between them had been borne of fear, desperation, and need. Though her heart was as solidly gripped in Heath's hand as it had been all along, his seemed to have flittered from her.

Perhaps men were different. Perhaps men didn't feel as deeply or with the excruciating intensity that women did. Those were often Cricket's thoughts—that perhaps what had been heavenly to her had only been a passing thought for him. Yet she didn't truly believe that. It's just what she told herself when trying to console herself.

She was thankful that none of the other girls inquired about it—about what they'd witnessed the moments before Heath had forced Cricket onto Archie's back and sent her home. Not even Vilma had asked what had gone on between them during the occasions when Heath had dragged Cricket away from the outlaw encampment to "have his way with her." It was as if everyone knew that Heath had done what he'd had to do to free them—everyone but Cricket, that was. Cricket still wanted to believe there was more to what they'd shared—especially in the barn—than just the dictates of necessity.

In truth, Cricket's heart was broken. In truth, she found her way to being alone several times a day, simply so she could release the tears and sobbing that begged for release. She wanted Heath to love her! She wanted to marry him! She even wanted to share his bed—and that was saying something if everything Vilma and Pearl had revealed about intimacy between men and women were true.

As she sat in the grass there near the pasture fence, Cricket realized that she was alone and could cry. Throwing herself onto the cool summer grass, she was instantly overtaken with tears and sobbing—not because of what had happened between she and Heath during her abduction but for what hadn't happened since. Marie would marry her lover, Hudson. Ann would marry Cooper Keel—Cricket felt it in her very soul. Even Vilma would one day reveal to her friends who she loved, stand before her idiot of a father, and be wed, and then flee as fast as her new husband could carry her away from Reverend Stanley and to a new and beautiful life. But Cricket was beginning to think that her dreams had already been granted as having come true. Perhaps the passion she'd shared in the barn that night with Heath was the end of it. Perhaps the moment he'd taken hold of her—so possessively taken hold of her and nearly ravaged her there in front of her friends before setting her adrift astride Archie's back—perhaps that moment had been the end of her dreams coming true.

For a moment, Cricket sat up straight. "I'll just snatch him away, tie him to a chair, and…and have my way with him," she said out loud. She was determined to do it. She truly was—and for nearly two minutes—long enough to stand up and begin willfully marching toward Heathro Thibodaux's house. And then her determination was vanquished—vanquished by the same fear and anxiety that drove her to force herself to farther from home than was comfortable—the same fear and anxiety that haunted her dreams—that often found her calling out in the middle of the night—calling for Heath.

Ada paused, glancing sideways to where Heathro Thibodaux stood thumbing through a pile of work gloves in the general store. Ada was not the most courageous woman to ever be born. But when the ones she loved most were suffering, it then that an unfamiliar bravery often rose in her. And she felt it rising now.

Yet Heath Thibodaux was intimidatingly handsome—even to a woman such as Ada Cranford who was so desperately in love with a man as handsome as Zeke. And so it took Ada several more moments before the unfamiliar bravery nesting in her bosom actually translated to her feet moving her toward Heath.

"Pardon me…Mr. Thibodaux?" Ada began. She gasped a little when the man looked at her, the piercing blue of his eyes having the effect of being able to read her very soul.

"Yes, ma'am?" he mumbled.

"M-may I speak with you for just a moment?" Ada asked.

"Why, certainly, Mrs. Cranford," Heath agreed. "What can I do for you?"

Ada paused a moment—for she had to play the part well. "It's… it's concernin' my daughter, Magnolia." Ada was encouraged when instantly the very of color of the man's face softened at the mere mention of Cricket's name.

"Is she all right, ma'am?" he asked. The concern was not only blatantly obvious on his face but also evidently deep. "She went through so much. I-I worry that…that it mighta scared her more than folks think."

"Well, that's exactly what I wanted to speak to you about, Mr. Thibodaux," Ada ventured, feeling more confident. There was something she didn't know—something Cricket hadn't revealed about everything that had transpired during the girls' victimization and Heath's rescue of them.

"What's that, ma'am?" he asked—though she could see that his guard was up now.

"She's not sleepin' well," Ada answered—and truthfully. "I don't think she rests more than an hour or so at one stretch."

Heath frowned and nodded. "I suppose none of the girls are," he offered. "And it's probably to be expected. Don't you think?"

He was asking Ada—truly, concernedly asking Ada whether she thought the girls being restless at night was a reasonable effect of what they'd been through. It was touching. There he stood—a tall, strong, handsome, virile man, looking as anxious as a puppy somehow.

"Well, yes…I do," Ada answered. Heathro Thibodaux seemed somewhat relieved. "But it's not so much her restlessness at night as it is the fact that…that…"

Heath's frown deepened with concern. "The fact that what, ma'am?"

Ada lowered her voice and responded, "The fact that she wakes up screamin'…screamin' for you, Mr. Thibodaux."

He was undone! Ada could tell by the astonished expression on his face, the way the color drained from his cheeks, and the tiny beads of perspiration that instantly appeared on his forehead.

"Well, I…I-I," he stammered. "I suppose that's because I-I was the one that found her, ma'am," he barely managed. "You know…the person who ended up helpin' her out in her time of need. Wouldn't it be natural for her to call for help…for her to call me for help?"

Ada tried not to smile, but something was sinking into her understanding at last—something concerning Cricket and this handsome Texas Ranger.

"But you see, Mr. Thibodaux," Ada whispered, "Magnolia…she isn't callin' for help when she cries out—not necessarily anyway. She's just callin' for you."

He was rattled—rattled beyond any point Ada had expected to see him rattled. Rather nervously he stroked the dark mustache and goatee, which, Ada had previously noticed, perfectly complemented the strong contours of his face.

"Well, Mrs. Cranford," Heath began, "I'm truly sorry. I don't like hearin' that. All this time I thought Magnolia…that bein' back home safe and sound with you and Mr. Cranford…I thought that's all she wanted."

"Did you now, Mr. Thibodaux?" Ada asked, knowingly arching one eyebrow.

"I mean, I didn't intend to end up in there with them outlaws hauntin' her dreams every night," Heath restated.

Ada couldn't withhold her smile any longer. "Mr. Thibodaux," she began, "you and I both know that you were hauntin' Cricket's dreams long before those dirty outlaws took her, now don't we?"

"W-we do?" Heath stammered. The man truly looked stunned! Truly appeared to be ignorant of that fact Cricket was in love with him!

"Of course we do," Ada answered. "Now, why don't you do somethin' so that Cricket can start gettin' a good night's sleep again, hmmm?"

With a triumphant smile, Ada turned and left Heathro Thibodaux standing in the general store looking like someone had just scooped his good sense out with a spoon.

As she walked back to the house, Ada sighed. At last! At last she'd been able to figure it all out. Of course, she didn't know exactly what had happened between Cricket and Mr. Thibodaux during the days they were in the hands of the outlaws—but she knew something had. She'd known it from the moment Cricket returned but just hadn't quite figured what to do about it. Until she saw Heathro Thibodaux saunter into the general store twenty minutes ago.

Ada hurried home, racing up the porch steps and into the house. "Zeke! Zeke?" she called. She giggled when he appeared in the doorway of the parlor.

"What's all this, darlin'?" Zeke asked. "Are you all right?"

"I'm fine!" Ada breathed, pressing her body against her husband's as she ran her fingers through his hair.

Zeke chuckled and smiled at her—smiled the smile that told Ada she was about to be swept away on the blissful waves of passion. "Why…yes, you are, darlin'," Zeke mumbled. "Yes, you are."

CHAPTER SEVENTEEN

"Girls," Vilma began in her most determined, preacher's daughter's voice, "we have all agreed that we cannot let our fears allow us to miss the Cornfield Chase tonight."

Ann and Cricket glanced to one another, exchanging nods of encouragement.

"Therefore, let us gather our reserves and get over to Marie's daddy's cornfield…and try not to look as unsettled as we feel," Vilma added.

Cricket moaned with anxiety, however.

"Magnolia Cranford!" Vilma scolded. "You cannot let fear—"

"It's not that, Vilma," Cricket interrupted.

"Then for Pete's sake, what is it then?"

But Cricket didn't want to hurt Vilma's feelings. "It's just that… well, I-I—"

"Cricket doesn't want to be caught by your brother, Vilma," Marie blurted. "She's not afraid of the Cornfield Chase because of…of what happened to us. She's afraid of bein' caught by Wyatt."

Cricket winced, preparing herself for the fire-and-brimstone reprimand she knew would be coming from Vilma at any moment.

Wyatt Stanley had been nearly relentless in his pursuit of Cricket for the past couple of weeks since Heathro Thibodaux rescued the girls. He'd nearly driven her mad with wanting to court her, trying to hold her hand, or touching her in any manner possible. And now the annual Cornfield Chase was upon them, and Cricket couldn't face the possibility of being caught by Wyatt. Certainly she'd dreamed of being caught by Heathro Thibodaux, but everyone in town knew Heathro Thibodaux was about as likely to involve himself in the Cornfield Chase as he was to wear a bridesmaid's dress to Marie's wedding!

Cricket opened her eyes, relaxing her grimace when, instead of spewing out a lecture, Vilma began to laugh. Ann looked to Marie with an inquisitive expression, and Marie returned a similar expression to Ann.

"What on earth is so funny, Vilma?" Marie asked.

"Cricket's been worried all week that she would offend you by tellin' you that Wyatt is the last man on the face of the earth she would ever want to kiss!" Ann expounded.

Vilma laughed awhile longer and then drew a deep breath and said, "Magnolia Cranford! Did you really think I wouldn't understand?" she asked. "Why...my brother Wyatt is an idiot! I can't truly believe any girl would actually want to kiss him—especially one that's been kissed by Heathro Thibodaux the way we've seen him kiss you." Vilma giggled, sighed, and shook her head. "In fact, I'll help you avoid Wyatt myself. I happen to know he's gonna be hidin' in the west side of the Mr. King's cornfield. You just stay to the right, and you'll be fine."

Cricket smiled and sighed with relief. "You really aren't mad at me, Vilma?"

Vilma shook her head, rolled her eyes, and said, "Of course not." Suddenly there were tears in Vilma's eyes, and she unexpectedly reached out, taking Cricket's hands in her own. "Cricket, I know I'm difficult. I'm so torn all the time between who I really am and who my daddy demands that I be. But you...you're you no matter what. Abducted by outlaws, kissed in such a manner by Heathro Thibodaux that I thought he was gonna whisk you away to his bed right then and there..."

Cricket blushed—heard Ann gulp and Marie giggle.

"And yet," Vilma continued, "we come home, dirty and starvin' and hurt and battered...and you're still you. You're still worried about whether or not Shanny Lou and Marianne have baby dolls to play with." Vilma paused, wiping tears from her cheeks. "Everything that happened...and nothin' about you changed, Cricket. But I changed... and I needed to."

Rising to her feet, Vilma motioned for the other girls to join her. Ann took one of Vilma's hands as Marie took the other. Then Cricket stepped in with them, joining hands with Marie and Ann to complete their circle of surviving friendship there beneath the old oak tree where not so long ago they'd plotted to welcome Heathro Thibodaux to Pike's Creek.

"Let's go, girls," Vilma said. "Let's go to the Cornfield Chase, toss our cares to evening summer breezes, and agree to kiss whomever captures us with no regrets. All right?"

Everyone nodded—even Cricket—though, in truth, her plan was to not get caught at all!

Every year, Clifford King held the Pike's Creek Cornfield Chase out in his cornfield. It was one of the most anticipated events of the year for the adolescents and young adults of the town. Every unmarried boy or man above the age of sixteen would hide in the cornfield on either side of a triangular wedge Mr. King would leave open each year when planting. Every unmarried girl or woman over the age of fourteen would then gather together in the wedge, choose a cornrow, and begin walking it. For the luckiest girls, it would be the boy or man they were most sweet on that would capture them in their cornrow and steal a kiss. Once someone had been kissed, the boy doing the kissing would loudly shout, "My ears are itchin'!" and everyone would scatter in the cornfield, selecting another row and hoping to be caught.

In years past, the Cornfield Chase was just about Cricket's favorite evening of the year—just above Thanksgiving Day but below Christmas Eve. In years past, Cricket had had kisses stolen by nearly every handsome young man in the county—including Hudson Oliver the year she was sixteen. But she found herself wishing she were like Marie—engaged and in charge of the refreshment tables waiting in Clifford King's barn—engaged to Heathro Thibodaux.

Oh, she could almost imagine it—Heath smiling at her as she arranged cookies and pie slices on dessert plates. But Cricket shook her head to try and dispel her romantic thoughts. It had only been the desperation of the situation that had found her in Heath's arms in the barn that day. It was what she had told herself every hour of every day since her return. She knew it was something she must accept—though she also knew she would never fully accept it.

"Let's go!" Marie giggled, dropping Cricket's hand but keeping hold of Vilma's, pulling the girls along as if playing snap the whip. "It'll be fun, Cricket!" she called.

"Maybe Heathro Thibodaux will even be hiding in the cornfield somewhere," Ann offered with encouragement.

"Maybe," Cricket said, forcing a smile. It would be fun—surely it would. It had always been fun before. Why should this year be any different? As long as Wyatt Stanley didn't get ahold of her, all would be well—or at least so Cricket told herself.

Mr. King began banging on the bottom of his wife's best stewpot with a large wooden spoon. It was the signal—the start of the Cornfield Chase.

While Vilma fairly bolted into a cornrow she'd selected, Ann and Cricket waited. "Just stay to the right, remember?" Ann reminded Cricket.

Cricket nodded, smiled at Ann, and offered, "Maybe Mr. Keel is out there hidin' in the cornfield somewhere right next to Heathro Thibodaux."

Ann smiled nervously, giggled, and said, "Maybe," a moment before she dashed into a cornrow.

Suddenly fearing that Wyatt Stanley might easily spy her if she stayed out in the open much longer, Cricket hurried into a cornrow on the outer boundary of the cornfield.

She exhaled a sigh of relief as she quietly walked the cornrow in the direction of the barn. Cricket figured no one would choose the outrows—they never did—and she could just meander along until she reached the end of the field. Then she could slip into the barn, pretend she'd been caught once or twice, and then spend her time visiting with Marie and Hudson.

"Hey there, blossom bottom."

Cricket startled, her mouth dropping open in astonishment as she saw Heath step from the neighboring cornrow into the path she'd been walking. Instantly she was rendered breathless—merely at the sight of him standing there before her. He smiled, and the moonlight glinted on his gold tooth, the stars seeming to have taken up residence in his smoldering blue eyes. All her feelings—her so carefully guarded love for him, her desire to be in his arms, the fear and anxiety she'd been battling since they escaped the outlaws—all of it mingled to make her insides feel like milky cornmeal mush.

"Hello," she managed to respond.

Heath moved toward her, and she instinctively took a step back. His presence was overpowering! She'd somehow forgotten just how overpowering.

"So," he began, "how're you doin'? You holdin' up all right, darlin'?"

"I'm f-fine," Cricket stammered. "And you? Are y-you well?"

Heath nodded, taking a step toward her again. "I'm fine too."

"Oh, good," Cricket said, forcing a smile. She couldn't keep her hands from wringing, no matter how hard she tried. Every inch of her body was trembling. Every essence in her wanted to be in his arms—to smell the wood smoke on his shirt and the lingering scent of leather mingled with it.

"I saw your stepmama in the general store yesterday," Heath said.

"Oh?" Cricket asked, attempting to appear calm.

"Mmm-hmmm," he confirmed. "She told me you haven't been sleepin' too well, sugar. Is that true?"

Cricket shrugged—was rendered paralyzed as well as speechless for a moment as her attention rested on his mouth. She moistened her lips, wishing she could relive the moments in the barn two weeks before.

"Um…um…I suppose we're all a little wound up yet, aren't we?" she managed.

"Maybe," he said. "Maybe." He stepped closer to her—so close she could've reached out and taken hold of his arm. She could've drawn herself against him. "But somethin' about it has been eatin' at me ever since."

"Really?" she asked.

"Ada says you wake up in the night callin' my name, honey," he revealed. "Is that true, Miss Blossom Bottom?" He reached out, taking hold of her arms and slowly pulling her closer to him. "Do you wake up at night because you're havin' nightmares about me, Magnolia? Or because you want me to be there with you?"

Cricket shook her head. "I could never have nightmare about you," she breathed. "I-I just start to wake up, and I feel so frightened and alone and I-I…"

"What can I do for you, darlin'?" Heath asked. His voice was low and alluring—as if he meant to bewitch her somehow.

"Nothin'," she breathed. "I'm fine. I mean…I'll be fine. I'm sure you're tossin' and turnin' here and there too, right?"

"Those men that took you…those men are all dead, Magnolia," he told her. "You know that, don't you? They can't hurt you now. They can't even endeavor to scare you now."

"I know that," she said. And she did.

"Then what's keepin' you sleepless at night, honey? What's got me interferin' in your dreams?"

Cricket shook her head. "You don't interfere with them," she confessed. "You're just…you're just there. You're in them."

Heath grinned. "Am I," he stated more than asked. "And what am I doin' in your dreams, Magnolia?"

"You make me strong," Cricket breathed as his hands gently encircled her neck. A tear escaped her eye, traveling over her temple as she felt him place his thumbs just under her chin in exactly the manner he'd done every time he'd meant to chafe her face with his whiskers when they'd been traveling with the outlaws, waiting for the posse that never came. "B-but…but…" she stammered.

"But what, darlin'?" Heath asked as he bent, caressing one side of her face with the whiskers on his chin.

"But when I start to wake up…you're not there…and I suddenly realize that I'm tired of bein' strong," she confessed. "I just want to be the weak one for once. I don't want to be the fighter, the leader. I can't be strong anymore…not without you there…and I wake up screamin' for you."

Again he brushed her cheek with his whiskers and then turned to her other cheek, brushing it in the same fashion. He smelled so masculine and strong—so familiar and comforting—like wood smoke and leather—cedar bark and fresh prairie sage.

"I'm just tired of…of…" she stammered breathlessly.

"You're tired of bein' the one everybody else looks to in order to judge whether or not you girls weathered that storm and came out with your wits still about you?" he finished for her.

"I-I never truly feel safe anymore," she managed in a whisper. "I never feel safe unless I can see you…and know you're near," she confessed.

She felt him breathe a sigh into her hair. "That's 'cause I'm the one who helped you girls get away, that's all," he mumbled. "That's all it is."

Heath was wrong, but Cricket wouldn't argue with him.

"You are the strong one, sugar," he said quietly into her hair. "And you'll be fine. It might take a while, but you'll be fine."

"It's the only reason you chose me," she whispered. "It's why you chose me instead of one of the other girls, isn't it? Just because you knew I was strong. You knew I was the one strong enough to do what you needed done in order to help us. You told me so yourself. That's the only reason you chose me."

Cricket's tears flooded her cheeks. She knew it was true in that moment; she always had. Yet in the depths of her heart—where she hid her most desperate of wishes—she'd hoped he'd chosen her because he'd favored her. But in truth, she'd known all along that Heath Thibodaux had chosen her for her strength.

"You were and are the strongest of all those girls," Heath confirmed—and Cricket was sure she heard her own heart breaking. "I woulda been a fool to trust all our lives to any of the others." He brushed her face with his—his hands still encircling her neck—his thumbs still resting beneath her chin.

"But," Heath continued, "I chose you mainly because I figured…I figured if somethin' went wrong…if it came down to it and I could only save one of you girls…then it sure as hell was gonna be you, my little blossom bottom."

As Heath repeated the all-too-familiar gesture of caressing her face with the side of his whiskery jaw, Cricket's body melted to his. Her mouth began to water at the memory of his hot, moist kiss—began to water for the mad want of it again.

"Do you think the corn out here in Clifford King's field is sweet, darlin'?" Heath asked in a whisper. When Cricket didn't respond, he mumbled, "Well, you just give me the chance, and I'll let you taste somethin' that'll put this corn to shame."

Cricket's knees buckled as she felt Heath's thumbs slide up over her chin, tugging it a bit, coaxing her lips to part. As his mouth claimed hers in a smoldering, moist kiss, Cricket's arms tightly wound about his neck, pulling her body flush with his. Her heart was beating with such a mad rhythm it seemed she could actually feel the blood coursing through her veins. Heath's kiss was so powerful—so delicious—and so wonderfully familiar! She'd been desperate for it—craving it since the moment their last kiss had ended—starving for his mouth to be melded with hers. And now it was hers once more.

Heath's hands moved to her waist, his strong fingers and thumbs digging into her ribs as his mouth hungrily ground to hers. He kissed her so vigorously, with such demand of reciprocation, that Cricket gasped a little as she realized she was leaning back so far she was near to losing her balance altogether.

At the sound of her discomfort, Heath instantly broke the seal of their mouths. "Did I hurt you?" he asked, his breathing labored with restraining passion.

"No," Cricket assured him. She kissed him—took hold of the front of his shirt, fisting it in her hands as she endeavored to pull him to her once more. She kissed him again, slipping her arms around his neck and pulling her body against his as his hands went to her waist—the strength of his arms lifting her off the ground as she drove a wanton kiss to his inviting mouth.

Suddenly, however, Heath set her down again.

Breaking first the seal of their mouths and next their embrace, Cricket smiled when he grumbled, "A man can't get nothin' done in a damn cornfield"—and then swept her up in his arms and made his way toward the escape.

"Kiss me," Heath demanded in a growl as he set Cricket on her feet again, pushing her back against the outer back wall of the Kings' barn. He gazed at her a moment, his eyes traveling over her face admiringly as he smiled at her. "In those dreams you've been havin'," he mumbled in a low, provocative voice, "do you ever kiss me in those dreams, Magnolia?"

Though she blushed, Cricket couldn't keep the revealing smile from spreading across her face. "Maybe," she teased.

Heath smiled, gently caressing her throat with the back of one hand. "Then kiss me the way you kiss me in your dreams, darlin'. Kiss me that way."

Cricket smiled as she felt a familiar mischief rising. It made her feel strong and happy—brave—as brave as she'd been the night she'd hopped up on the old watering trough, dressed in nothing but her black underwear, to steal a kiss from the brooding ex-Texas Ranger Heathro Thibodaux.

Taking hold of the front of his shirt, she pulled, maneuvering Heath so that he stood against the wall and she stood before him. He smiled, and Cricket giggled. Quickly she glanced around, her attention falling to an old crate abandoned nearby. Quickly she pulled the crate over, placing it in front of Heath and stepping up onto it.

Taking his face between her hands, Cricket stoked the soft whiskers that formed the handsome goatee surrounding his mouth. Heathro Thibodaux was purely the stuff of fantasy—of dreams and myth and miracle.

"Are you gonna stand there and stare at me like I'm just a lemon drop in the candy jar in the general store?" he asked as his strong hands settled at her waist. "Or are you gonna kiss me the way you've been dreamin' of kissin' me?"

"Hold still, and I'll show you," Cricket whispered.

Oh, Cricket may well have started the kiss—she may well have been the one to press her mouth to Heath's, endeavoring to affect him as he'd never been affected before—but it wasn't long until Cricket was back against the barn wall once more as Heathro Thibodaux bathed her in such a passion that it threatened to set Clifford King's barn on fire.

Wyatt Stanley frowned as he watched the Texas Ranger enjoying his fill of Cricket Cranford's affections. There they were—right there at the back of the King barn—so wrapped in each other's arms it was difficult to discern whether there was one body or two lingering in the cover of darkness.

When he'd seen Heathro Thibodaux carrying Cricket out of the cornfield and toward the privacy of the barn back, he'd initially feared Cricket had been hurt. But it didn't take long for him to discern what was really transpiring, and it infuriated him—because Wyatt Stanley wanted Cricket for himself. Not that he had any profound passion for her—not that he even loved her to any degree. But it was for a different reason he found himself constantly seeking out Cricket—dreaming of owning her.

The day the abducted girls had returned—the moment he'd seen Cricket Cranford slap his father not once but twice—scream at him, spit on him—Wyatt knew he had to have her. Reverend Edgar Stanley hated nothing more than being disrespected, and Cricket had certainly disrespected him. Thus, Wyatt wanted her. He planned to marry her—have *her*, the woman his father loathed more than any other in the world. Wyatt wanted *her* to bear his father's grandchildren.

Yet there was more to the anger that was igniting in him as he watched Heathro Thibodaux drink himself to intoxication on Cricket's no doubt ambrosial kisses. Wyatt knew that his sister, Vilma, had herself been in love with the young Texas Ranger for months. If Cricket Cranford were to win Heathro Thibodaux, then Vilma could not.

Still, Wyatt knew he must be wise—even as sly as a fox stalking its pray. If he wanted Cricket, if Vilma wanted Heathro, then he must be clever—very clever.

Silently Wyatt slipped back into the cornfield. He would honor several fortunate young ladies with his very adept kisses and then return to the barn with all other players of the Cornfield Chase for refreshments. The rest would wait until tomorrow. Nothing would change before tomorrow. After all, it wasn't like Heathro Thibodaux could entirely have his way with Cricket there behind Clifford King's barn—could he?

CHAPTER EIGHTEEN

"You'll never guess who I saw sparkin' out behind Clifford King's barn last night durin' the Cornfield Chase," Wyatt began.

Vilma rolled her eyes with exasperation. She loved Wyatt because he was her brother, but most of the time, she didn't really like him very much. For one thing, he was the worst gossip in town—always embellishing things as well. It was bad enough listening to him when he was telling the whole truth, but it was plain annoying to have to listen to him when he was making up things to add into his tales. But since Vilma was up to her elbows in kneading bread dough, she was trapped.

Therefore, with a heavy sigh, she asked, "Who, Wyatt? Marie and Hudson? That's nothin' special. They spend half the day sparkin' and the other half just gazing into each other's eyes like a couple of lovesick calves."

But Wyatt's smile was more than just triumphant: it was arrogant too. Vilma shook her head, knowing that he really must've caught somebody in a compromising situation this time.

"Nope," he said proudly.

Vilma rolled her eyes once more and unwillingly asked, "Who then?"

Wyatt leaned forward in his chair and, lowering his voice, answered, "Cricket Cranford and Heathro Thibodaux."

All at once, Vilma wasn't so disappointed in Wyatt's information after all. As a truly happy smile spread across her face, she exclaimed,

"Really? Oh, that's wonderful! That's wonderful!" Vilma was so glad inside, she was sure her heart was swollen up to the size of a harvest pumpkin.

But Wyatt frowned. "You're happy about that? What's wrong with you, Vilma? I thought you were sweeter than sugared honey on Heathro Thibodaux!"

Vilma shrugged. "I am…or was," she admitted. "But not anymore. I'm free of a lot of things now, Wyatt. I have a better idea of who I am…or at least, who I want to be."

Wyatt was perturbed; his scowl was proof of it. "So you ain't the least bit jealous that it was Cricket that ol' Texas Ranger chose to go sparkin', rather than you?"

"Not at all," Vilma assured him. "I'm just glad the two of them finally got around to it again. Why, they've both been so miserable since…"

Vilma stopped herself, however. She'd revealed too much. What had happened between Heathro Thibodaux and Cricket the day Heath had stayed behind to defend them from the coming onslaught of outlaws—what Vilma and the other girls had witnessed of the passion that erupted between Cricket and Heath—it was private, a secret. Though Vilma didn't know exactly what had gone on between their hero and her friend each time Heath had drug Cricket away, telling Heck Alford that he meant to make her more cooperative, she did suspect there was a bit of intensity sparking between them. Vilma felt that her suspicions were well justified when she'd witnessed the way Heathro Thibodaux had nearly devoured Cricket right there in front of all of them. And she was glad. Cricket was the kindest, most caring woman Vilma had ever known—and Heath was the most heroic and handsome. It made sense they should be together.

"Since what, Vilma?" Wyatt asked. "Since what?"

Vilma silently scolded herself for speaking so unguardedly to Wyatt. She'd opened a jar of mustard this time—she knew it!

"Since what?" Wyatt pressed again. His eyes narrowed. "Somethin' went on between them while you all were captive, didn't it? Before he saved you all, he had himself a taste of what them men in New Orleans would be missin' out on by way of Cricket Cranford, didn't he?"

"Heavens no!" Vilma exclaimed. "Pull your mind outta the saloon, Wyatt Stanley."

Wyatt shrugged. "Then tell me what went on," he demanded. "If you don't…then my imagination will make up what I don't know."

Vilma was frightened now, truly frightened. Wyatt was an imp sometimes—an imp not to be trusted. And yet she couldn't have him strutting all over town, spreading half-truths and rumors.

"If I tell you," she began, "you have to swear that it won't leave this room, Wyatt."

"I swear," Wyatt agreed—but she didn't trust the naughty smile on his face.

"I mean it, Wyatt," Vilma reiterated. "If I confide in you the details of our horrid, terrifyin' ordeal…if you ever speak a word of it to anyone…"

"I won't, Vilma," Wyatt assured her. "I swear it. It'll be between me and you only. Always, Vilma."

Vilma inhaled a deep breath. She still didn't trust her brother, but she knew it would be worse to allow his imagination to run wild.

"When Heathro came for us," she began, tears filling her eyes at the memories of the horror of her captivity, "when he came, he had to pretend he worked for a man in New Orleans…a man who buys women in order to…to keep money comin' into his brothels."

"Mmm-hmm," Wyatt prodded.

"Heath was able to infiltrate the band of outlaws…figurin' the posse from Pike's Creek would catch up with us soon enough."

Wyatt frowned. "But it didn't…because our father is a fool."

"Yes," Vilma said. "Anyway, Heath infiltrated the gang…explained that in order to make us girls more cooperative, he needed to win over Cricket…because he suspected she was our leader of sorts."

"Win her over?" Wyatt asked, quirking one eyebrow.

"Yes," Vilma continued. "Heck Alford believed Heath…probably because Heath handed him six hundred dollars as a promise that Jacques Cheval would buy us when we reached New Orleans."

"Six hundred dollars?" Wyatt exclaimed. He whistled with admiration. "Where does an ex-Texas Ranger get money like that?"

"Anyway," Vilma continued, already wishing she hadn't told Wyatt about the money, "Heath began takin' Cricket with him to a secluded place several times a day. And when he returned to us, she always looked a little more ruffled...and as if she'd been...been..."

"Ravaged?" Wyatt offered, smiling.

"Seduced," Vilma corrected. "I have no doubt they spent their time together talkin'...plannin'. Cricket always had instructions for us when she returned...things Heath had told her to tell us. Even the last night we were captive—the night before Heath took us from those men— even that night, it was Cricket who told us all the details of the plan... how Heath intended to get the men drunk, slit Burnette's throat, and ride away with us." Vilma paused a moment, smiling as she stopped kneading the bread dough. "I remember how Cricket looked when she came back to us that night. Her eyes were on fire with joyfulness... even for the desperation of our circumstances." Vilma nodded. "And judging from the appearance of her face and lips...that was the night Heath really had his way with her." She looked to Wyatt, quickly adding, "With a long while of sparkin' is all, Wyatt. Just sparkin'."

"How many times did the man take Cricket for some...instruction, Vilma?" Wyatt asked.

Vilma shrugged. "Several times a day...and once before we were tied up for the night."

"And now they're sparkin' out behind Clifford King's barn, are they?"

Wyatt chuckled, and even for the bread dough stuck to her fingers, Vilma reached out, firmly taking hold of his wrist. "Heathro Thibodaux and Cricket Cranford saved my life, Wyatt!" she growled. "Don't you dare to do anything that would harm them...or their reputations in this town. Do you hear me?"

Wyatt frowned. "I wouldn't do nothin' like that, Vilma, and you know it." He yanked his arm out of her grasp and glared at her. "You know I wouldn't."

"Do I?" Vilma asked with suspicion. "If you speak a word of this to anyone, Wyatt…I swear to you I will pack up my things and leave Pike's Creek. I'll leave you here to deal with Daddy all on your own."

Wyatt's eyes narrowed. "I can pick up and leave anytime I want to, Vilma. I can leave too. So what kind of a threat is that?"

"It's not a threat," Vilma told him. "It's a promise. And anyway, you don't have the means to leave town. You've never saved a penny from any money you've earned. And I have. I have plenty of money to leave. So don't you dare to try to hurt Cricket and Heath. Because I will leave you if you do."

"I ain't gonna say a word, Vilma," Wyatt growled. "You're just assumin' they was sparkin' all that while anyway. You never actually saw it the way I did."

Vilma wasn't about to make the same mistake twice, so she responded, "You're right. I never did see Heath kiss Cricket. I'm just speculatin' on what I *think* happened." She returned to kneading the dough, careless of whether her hand had picked up some dust or something when she'd grabbed Wyatt's arm.

"Well," Wyatt sighed. "I suppose we'll just wait and see what happens. Maybe Heathro Thibodaux's conscience will start naggin' at him, and he'll make an honest woman of Cricket."

"There's no need for him to make an honest woman of her, Wyatt!" Vilma shrieked in an angry whisper.

But Wyatt only laughed and stood up from his chair, pinching a piece of bread dough from Vilma's breadboard and popping the dough into his mouth. "Say what you want, Vilma Stanley…but you didn't see him gnawin' at her like a bear to a honey hive the way I did. No sirree."

Wyatt left the kitchen, still chuckling to himself—self-righteous in what he thought he knew.

Anxiety washed over Vilma as she wondered whether she should tell Cricket what happened. Or perhaps she should tell Heath. Angrily punching the dough, she decided she would tell Cricket—that very afternoon. Vilma, Marie, Ann, and Cricket were set to meet out by the old oak tree to finalize their shenanigan plans for the coming Friday night. She'd tell Cricket what happened with Wyatt then. She'd tell

Cricket and Ann and Marie. There was more safety in numbers, after all.

❦

"Don't worry, Daddy," Cricket assured her father, handing him the reins to his horse. "Ada and I will be just fine here alone. Those men trapped in the mine over in Lyman need your help. But you and Mr. Keel make sure Hudson don't get boxed in the mouth or somethin'." Cricket giggled, adding, "Because Marie would be devastated if she had to go a whole week long without sparkin' with him."

Zeke smiled. Cricket seemed so much better. Just over the course of the past couple of days, she seemed happier—less anxious. There was sparkle in her eyes that Ada had confided to Zeke she was fairly certain Heathro Thibodaux had put there. And if Ada were right—and she always was—Zeke was glad of it.

"Are you sure, sweetheart?" Zeke asked all the same.

"Yes, Daddy," Cricket answered. "I'm just gonna run on over to Mrs. Maloney's for a nice, long visit this afternoon, and then Ada and I are gonna put up some blackberry jam for you. How does that sound?"

"Sounds sweet," Zeke chuckled. He sighed. "All right then. I'll be back in a couple of days." He still paused, remembering what had transpired the last time he'd left Ada and Cricket alone.

His eyes must have spoken the words his mind was thinking because Cricket smiled, raised herself on her tiptoes, and kissed him on the cheek, saying, "Those outlaws are dead, Daddy. Nobody is gonna steal me away this time. You go on and help those men. All right?"

"All right," Zeke sighed. He reached out, gathering Ada into one arm and passionately kissing her. She tasted like plump, ripe blackberries, and he moaned, "Mmmm," as he ended their kiss. "You taste so good, honey."

Ada blushed, kissed him quickly on the cheek, and said, "You go on...before I decide to drag you back in the house and...and..." Glancing to Cricket, Ada blushed, finishing, "Before I decide to drag you back in the house and put you to work on those blackberries waitin' in the kitchen."

Zeke laughed and mounted his horse. "You two stay out of trouble this time, you hear?"

His girls giggled, exchanged glances, and clasped hands. "We will," they chimed in unison.

As his anxiety settled somewhat, Zeke spurred his horse toward Lyman and the men trapped in the mine cave-in there.

Cricket sighed a sigh of contentment, even as she watched her father ride away. She wasn't anxious about his leaving—not that day. For one thing, she was still walking on air—for the warm euphoria inside her caused by sparking with Heathro Thibodaux at the Cornfield Chase lingered like a sweet summer breeze.

She watched as Cooper Keel, Hudson Oliver, Clifford King, and Ralph Burroughs joined her father in the distance. Heathro was planning to ride over, once he'd corralled his ornery, trouble-making bull again. Of course, Cricket wished Heath wouldn't go. She wished he'd just stay in Pike's Creek. In truth, she wished he'd carry her to Clifford King's barn again—drench her in his passionate kisses—for the rest of her life!

"So?" Ada began. "You haven't told me anything about how the Cornfield Chase went. Did you have a good time?"

Cricket blushed and nodded. "Yes, I did, Ada." She looked to her loving stepmother and friend, adding, "Thanks to you."

"Me?" Ada asked. Cricket thought it was a good thing Ada had never tried to become an actress—for she had no gift for acting. "I don't know what you're talkin' about, Cricket. Truly."

"Hmmm. Don't you?" Cricket asked. She was certain it was Ada's revelation to Heath that Cricket had been calling out for him at night that had spurred him on to seeking her out at the Cornfield Chase. Why he'd paused for two weeks before that, she wasn't sure. Perhaps Heath had been thinking the same types of things that Cricket had—that it was only the trauma of the circumstances surrounding her abduction and his saving her that found her so willingly in his arms. She wasn't sure. But whatever the reasons that had kept her and Heath apart since returning from bondage, it seemed they had been vanquished by Heath's brief conversation with Ada.

"Not at all," Ada sighed. "Well, I'm off to start preparin' those blackberries. You tell Maymee Maloney that I said hello. All right?"

Ada turned and almost skipped back into the house.

"I will," Cricket called after her. Her smile broadened as gladness for the fact she and Ada were becoming close fluttered in her.

Turning and starting toward Mrs. Maloney's house, Cricket gazed up into the blue summer sky. There weren't many clouds nearby, but a thunderhead was smoldering in the south. Still, there seemed plenty of time to wander a bit and enjoy a visit with Mrs. Maloney.

Cricket sighed with contentment as she meandered toward Maymee Maloney's house. She smiled as she neared the quaint little house of her friend, for she heard birds gleefully twittering in the trees and caught the tinkling sound of the wind chimes hanging on its front porch as she approached.

Mrs. Maloney was waiting for her in a rocking chair on her front porch and greeted, "Well, there you are, sweet pea! I was wonderin' when you'd meander on over this mornin'."

Cricket giggled. Oh, how she adored the elderly woman! Mrs. Maloney was not only a cherished friend but also an invaluable tutor, a counselor, a comfort, and a guide—in truth, Cricket's blessed and beloved mentor.

Cricket dashed up onto the porch, stooping and placing an affectionate kiss on Mrs. Maloney's weathered, velvet-soft cheek.

"Well, aren't we just a perky little persimmon this mornin'?" Mrs. Maloney laughed as Cricket plopped down in the rocking chair next to her. Cricket unlaced her shoes, removed them, and began stripping off her stockings. "And what's that I see?" Maymee asked, closely studying Cricket's face and neck.

"What?" Cricket asked, wondering if she'd inadvertently smeared blackberry juice on herself while helping Ada that morning.

"Why, Magnolia Cranford!" Maymee gasped. "Is that whisker chafin' I see there around your mouth?" Cricket blushed seventeen shades of pink and red as Mrs. Maloney continued to tease. "Were you out sparkin' at that Cornfield Chase last night?" The old woman laughed again, her light blue eyes twinkling with merriment. "Or did you finally tie that handsome Texas Ranger to a chair and have your way with him?"

Cricket smiled and giggled then. Tucking her stockings into her shoes and tossing them aside, she answered, "I didn't tie him up to a chair." Blushing, she added, "I didn't have to."

Maymee Maloney rocked back in her chair, looking to the heavens, raising her arms, and hollering, "Hallelujah! Somethin' excitin' is finally happenin' in this drowsy old town!"

"Shh!" Cricket playfully scolded in a whisper. "It was just a little sparkin', Mrs. Maloney. It isn't…it's not serious."

"The hell it isn't, girl!" Mrs. Maloney exclaimed. "I've been waitin' a month of Sundays for you and that handsome hunk of manflesh to quit prancin' around it all and just have at it the way you've both been wantin' to for months."

"Oh, but I don't think he—" Cricket began.

"Oh, don't you start now," Maymee interrupted, shaking her head. "If it was up to you and Ann Burroughs and all your innocent naïveté, it'd be a miracle to see another baby born in this town."

"What? What about Ann?" Cricket asked. She was wildly curious. She hadn't seen Ann since Mr. King had pounded on his wife's stewpot the night before to start the Cornfield Chase. Of course, Cricket hadn't seen anybody until long after the chase began. She and Heath had spent near to three hours behind Clifford King's barn, either sparking or conversing. And when Cricket had finally peeked into the barn while all the other folks were enjoying pies, cookies, and punch, Ann Burroughs had been nowhere to be found.

Mrs. Maloney's eyebrows arched with triumph. "Well, let's just put it this way, shall we?" she began. "Ann Burroughs…when she dropped by this mornin' to offer me an extra spool of thread she'd found in her sewin' basket…well, she was nearly as bright-eyed and chap-faced as you are."

"Ann?" Cricket asked. "But she's sweet on Mr. Keel! Who would Ann be sparkin' with last night?" Cricket gasped as it struck then. And

241

as Mrs. Maloney nodded with affirmation, she asked, "Do you mean to tell me that Mr. Keel captured Ann in the cornfield last night?" Cricket was delighted—beyond delighted—she was ecstatic!

"Captured her in the cornfield and Clifford King's pumpkin patch and under that old oak tree behind the general store," Mrs. Maloney confirmed. As Cricket giggled with pure merriment, Maymee added, "*And* Cooper Keel was over to speak to Ralph Burroughs this mornin' before the men left for Lyman. Ann's mama told me just fifteen minutes ago that Cooper Keel asked Ralph's permission to court Ann…with the intentions of marryin' her before fall."

Cricket clapped her hands together, squealing with delight. "How marvelous! Oh, how perfectly romantic!"

"Yes," Mrs. Maloney sighed. "It seems everything is workin' out just fine." She paused for a moment, and Cricket noticed the expression of concern that quickly crossed her face.

"What is it?" she asked.

"What's what, honey?" Mrs. Maloney responded, feigning ignorance.

"Somethin' just crossed your mind, takin' the wind right out of your sails. What was it?"

"Oh…oh, nothin'," Maymee fibbed, trying to weasel out of telling Cricket what her thought had been.

"Tell me!" Cricket demanded. "Tell me, or I'll howl at you all day like a hound with a treed raccoon."

Maymee paused—seemed thoughtful for a moment. "I'm…I'm just not sure I should tell you what I'm thinkin'," the old woman admitted.

"Well, why ever not?" Cricket asked. "You can tell me anything… and you should tell me if it's somethin' that's worryin' you…or somethin' you think I should know."

Mrs. Maloney nodded, sighed, and smiled. "You're right, honey. You're right. So I'll just ask you straight out…are you in love with Heathro Thibodaux? Or just awful, awful sweet on him?"

Cricket's eyebrows arched with surprise. She certainly hadn't expected such a serious, forthright question from her normally playful friend.

"You're askin' me to confide my greatest secret to you, Mrs. Maloney," Cricket whispered. "I-I…"

"I just want to be sure there isn't anything on this whole green earth that could take your heart from him, that's all," Maymee explained.

"There isn't," Cricket stated firmly. "Nothin'."

Mrs. Maloney sighed with relief, smiled, and patted Cricket on one knee. "Let's me and you head on into the kitchen for piece of cake and the exchange of a couple more secrets, shall we?"

Cricket smiled and frowned at the same time. Mrs. Maloney wasn't normally so cryptic—sneaky and mischievous, but not cryptic.

"Certainly," Cricket said, rising from her chair as Mrs. Maloney rose from hers.

"Isn't it just the loveliest day, Magnolia?" she asked as she preceded Cricket into the house.

"Yes, ma'am, it is," Cricket agreed as she closed the door behind them.

Once Mrs. Maloney had cut them each a piece of cake, she and Cricket settled down at her kitchen table.

Handing Cricket a fork, Maymee asked, "Have you ever heard the tale of the pied piper of Hamelin, Magnolia honey?"

"Of course," Cricket answered—though she couldn't imagine what in all the world the old tale about rats and a flutist had to do with the price of potatoes up north.

"And what do you remember about it?"

Cricket shrugged. "There's a town infested with rats…"

"Mmm-hmmm," Mrs. Maloney encouraged with a nod. She placed a bite of cake in her mouth, rolling her eyes and sighing with sugar-pleasure.

"And the folks in town can't stand it any longer, so they offer a bag of money to anyone who can get rid of all the rats," Cricket continued.

"And then…" Maymee prodded.

Cricket giggled a little, amused by Mrs. Maloney's random subject of conversation. "And then this man comes along, all dress in patched-up clothes, and he plays the flute…and he tells the townsfolk that he will get rid of the rats if they truly will give him the bag of money."

"Go on."

"All right," Cricket said. "But why am I tellin' you this story in the first place?"

"Because I asked you if you were familiar with it."

It wasn't really an explanation; it was a weasel move on Mrs. Maloney's part. Still, if nothing else, Cricket's curiosity was piqued.

Thus, she continued, "So then a man comes to the town—Hamelin, that's the town. This man comes dressed in pied clothing, and he plays a flute. And he tells the townsfolk that he will rid them of the rats if they will give him the bag of money."

"And what happens next?" Mrs. Maloney asked.

Cricket shrugged. "The townsfolk agree…and the piper plays his flute, and all the rats follow him out of the town and to a river. As he continues to play his flute, the rats all jump in the river and drown… and the town is finally free of the rats."

"But when the piper returns for his reward…" Maymee urged.

"Oh, well, that's the terrible part," Cricket exclaimed. "Not that rats drownin' in a river isn't terrible—not that rats on any occasion isn't terrible. But the most terrible part of the story is that the selfish townsfolk do not give the piper the money they promised! They entirely deny him his reward." Cricket sighed with disapproval.

"What then?"

Cricket took a bite of her cake, smiling as sugar-pleasure flooded her mouth. She swallowed her sweet cake and answered, "Well, the piper feels that the townsfolk are dishonest and not to be trusted. He tells them that he pities their children, for they will grow up to be like their parents…dishonest, lacking integrity, and the like. So one day, while everyone is at church services, the piper returns…and he plays his flute again. And this time the *children* of Hamelin follow the piper, and he leads them away to a glorious paradise where they are happy forever. And though the adults of Hamelin send messengers far and wide to find the mysterious piper—to beg him to bring their children home—he and the children are never found."

"And the moral of the tale is…" Mrs. Maloney urged.

"Always keep a promise…no matter what. Show integrity in the keeping of a promise," Cricket answered, feeling rather proud of herself for knowing the answer. She'd detested the story as a child—found it frightening and sad. But now, even though she still found it frightening and sad, she could see the lesson for its great value.

"Yes. Yes, that is the moral of the story, I suppose," Mrs. Maloney sighed.

Cricket felt her brow wrinkle with inquisitiveness. "Is there more to it then? Somethin' I'm not understandin'?"

Mrs. Maloney nodded, taking another bite of cake and then answering, "I believe so. In fact, I've always thought so, and I think you and I are about to witness the less obvious aspect that story portrays. It's the part that plum disgusts me too."

"What part is that?" Cricket asked, frowning. After all, wasn't the story grim enough with just the one moral to be learned?

"It's what I'm startin' to see in Pike's Creek where your handsome lover, Heath, is concerned, darlin'. It's the same as in the story." She smiled and sighed as she glanced out the window as if remembering the past. "Oh, he was this town's hero, wasn't he?" she breathed. "Handsome with broodin' manner and the tortured soul of a hero. And then what happens? He risks his everything, includin' his life, to go after you girls all on his own." Mrs. Maloney looked back to Cricket, offered a firm nod, and said, "And he saved you—saved your virtue, saved your lives—and everyone in Pike's Creek felt forever indebted to him for his sacrifices and for bringin' our girls home." Maymee breathed a heavy sigh then—a sigh of disappointment in the least.

Suddenly, Cricket understood what part of the pied piper of Hamelin Mrs. Maloney was referring to, and she frowned as anger began to bubble in her bosom.

"Just like when the pied piper piped away those rats," Maymee Maloney continued. "Land sakes didn't this town love Heathro Thibodaux when you girls came ridin' in all livin' and unspoiled!" She slapped her knee with enthusiasm at the memory. "Yes sirree! There he was…all beat up, shot up, bloodied, tired, worn to the bone…our hero! He'd saved you girls from bein' sold to a brothel in New Orleans, saved you from death and things worse than dyin'…and, boy oh boy, did everyone love him!" She paused, slumped back in her rocker, and sighed. "For near to two weeks…and now…"

When Mrs. Maloney paused again, Cricket placed a hand on her knee and asked, "And now?"

The wise woman nodded and continued, "And now, some of the men in this town—the righteous Reverend Edgar Stanley, for one—have started seein' their own weaknesses. They most likely got tired of hearin' their wives go on and on and on, forever and a day on and on, about the magnificent, handsome, young, and strong Texas Ranger who had saved our girls' lives."

Cricket's stomach began to churn with anxiety as complete understanding seeped into her very soul.

"Yes, Heathro Thibodaux had brung you all home," Mrs. Maloney continued. She shrugged and frowned. "But it wasn't anything that any other man couldn't have done by himself—not if Heathro hadn't been the first to think of headin' out toward New Orleans," she said, the sarcasm thickening in her voice. "Why…he should've fired a shot, miles down the river when he found those tracks. If he had, well, surely every other man from town that was ten miles in the opposite direction would've heard the shot, known exactly what it meant, and headed out straight away to assist him." And Mrs. Maloney wasn't finished venting her angry disgust yet. "Why, if Heathro Thibodaux had taken the time to let all the other men in the posse know he'd found those tracks and was hot on the trail…" She forced her expression into one of feigned astonishment and continued, "Then of *course* every other man would've hung his pride out to dry for bein' wrong and followed Heathro in the right direction." Mrs. Maloney nodded emphatically—with such substantial sarcasm apparent in her demeanor that Cricket almost laughed out loud. "And heaven knows that if Heathro had turned around and taken the hours upon hours it would've meant to track the posse down and then so *easily* convince them he was right about those men takin' you all to New Orleans to sell instead of to Mexico…well, pfff! Of *course* all those hours, maybe a whole day long, wouldn't have made a bit of difference in your safety and well-bein'. Why, the men in this town are all so noble and such *fantastic* horsemen, they could've easily made up that day Heathro would've lost."

Cricket expected that Maymee was about to start spewing fire and smoke from her ears! The woman was angry—entirely worked up— but not any more worked up than Cricket was.

"And when it comes to what that boy had to do to get you girls free," Mrs. Maloney began once more, "well…I'm *sure* the men of this town could've just waltzed right in there, shot all ten of them outlaws square between the eyes, and give you girls just the most comfortable escort back to Pike's Creek that any Texas Ranger ever saw." She paused, shook her head, and wagged an angry index finger. "And that's exactly how some of the people in this town are like the people of Hamelin. They've got no lingerin' appreciation or understandin' of what Heathro did for all of us…especially you girls and your families. They've got no lingerin' care for his injuries or the fact that he has to live the rest of his life with the memory of that poor snake-bit girl he was too late to save…with the visions that'll stay in that man's mind forever of havin' to kill ten more men."

Cricket felt her eyes narrow. "Do you really think that what Reverend Righteous and some of the other folks in Pike's Creek think of Heath…do you really it would change the way I feel for him?"

Mrs. Maloney smiled. "Absolutely not, darlin'. I just want you to be prepared for any unkind word you might hear against that honorable young man of yours."

"I wish he were mine," Cricket mumbled, smiling as she thought of his kisses. "I wish I were his."

"Well, it looks to me as though he's been kissin' you like you're his," Maymee giggled with a wink.

Cricket blushed. "I-I probably shouldn't let him kiss me the way I do…or kiss him back the way I do."

Mrs. Maloney scowled, exclaiming, "Why the hell not? He's a good-lookin' man! I doubt any woman would be able to resist him… even if she wasn't in love with him." She enjoyed another bite of cake, sighed, and smiling added, "I wouldn't be able to resist." Pointing her fork at Cricket, she added, "And I wouldn't want to anyhow."

Cricket smiled, relaxing a bit and allowing her anger to subside. She was determined to enjoy the rest of her visit with Mrs. Maloney—determined not to let Reverend Righteous, and anybody else in Pike's Creek who might be resenting Heath's heroics, ruin her lovely day. After all, she'd spent more than three hours in Heath's arms the night before, and the bliss of it was still fresh enough to overpower any harsh feelings Mrs. Maloney's warning may have triggered.

"Now, tell me, Magnolia," Mrs. Maloney began. She smiled—a wildly naughty smile—and asked, "Does that boy taste as good as he looks?"

Cricket laughed, blushed, and whispered, "Even better!"

CHAPTER NINETEEN

Boots in hand, Cricket hurried down the steps of Mrs. Maloney's back porch. She didn't want to disappoint Ada by being late getting home. The blackberries couldn't wait forever.

"And where are you off to in such a hurry, Miss Blossom Bottom?"

The sound of Heath's voice simultaneously startled and delighted Cricket. She turned to the most immeasurable desire and delight of her heart, leaning on one shoulder against the back wall of Mrs. Maloney's house.

"What're you doin' here, Mr. Thibodaux?" she asked. She could feel her heart swelling inside her bosom—knew that the smile on her face was as broad as the sky was wide.

"Oh, I just drop in to check on Maymee once in a while," he said, striding toward her. "She feeds me cake, and we talk awhile. I think she likes the company."

Cricket's eyes widened. "Are *you* Nobody MacGee, Heath?" she asked. Suddenly she wondered whether the Mr. Nobody MacGee Mrs. Maloney claimed was just a pretend friend was actually Heathro Thibodaux—though she knew Maymee must be exaggerating when it came to the sparking she and Nobody did if he were.

"Who?" Heath asked.

"Oh, nobody," Cricket sighed. As she gazed up into Heath's handsome face, she felt like snow that had lingered too long in spring—felt as though every little fragment of her was melting into a warm, delirious puddle.

Heath's grin widened as he studied her from head to toe a moment—from windblown hair to bare feet. Only then did Cricket remember just how tousled and unpolished she must look.

Self-consciously she ran her hand through her hair. "I must look a sight," she mumbled, glancing down at her bare feet and ankles and wincing with humiliation.

"Indeed you do, Magnolia," Heath chuckled. "Quite a sight," he added as he unexpectedly slipped his hands under her arms, pushing her back against the wall of Mrs. Maloney's house. "Just like a ripe sweet cherry...tempting and ready for pickin'," he mumbled as he pressed his mouth to hers in a moist, wanting kiss.

Cricket felt her boots slip from her hand as she met his kiss with pure as much wanting as with which it was applied. Her arms rested on his shoulders as her hands found the softness of his hair, knocking his hat from his head to tumble to the ground and join her discarded boots.

Heath crushed his mouth to hers, sending every sense she owned whirling into blissful oblivion. Yet she owned one final thought that was not of him and his hot, moist, impassioned kiss—and she breathed, "Heath...it's still daytime...and very light outside."

"Yes, ma'am, it is," he said as he placed a soft, wet kiss to her neck just below her ear.

"But wh-what if someone happens by and—" she whispered.

"Quit talkin', woman, and kiss me," he playfully growled as his mouth returned to hers, raining such a rapturous passion over her that all thoughts of anything but him were banished from her bliss-filled body, mind, and heart.

Heath knew now there was no resisting this girl—especially when she appeared in any way more vulnerable and inviting than she usually did. When he'd come upon her barefoot and windblown outside of Maymee Maloney's house, every ounce of self-restraint he'd owned the moment before had vanished. Well, almost every ounce of self-restraint.

Magnolia Cranford was like some peddler's tonic claiming to cure all ills. Only his sweet little blossom-bottomed lover wasn't a bottle of mixed watered-down whiskey and rosewater perfume. Cricket really did cure all ills—all Heath's ills anyway.

He deepened their kiss, an unquenchable thirst for her nearly overtaking him. He could never kiss his fill of her—never satisfy the need to have her soft, curvaceous form against his. She smelled of flowers and grass—and fresh sheets on a summer bed.

"Heathro Baptiste Thibodaux!"

Maymee Maloney's scolding and very maternal exclamation startled Heath enough that he stepped back from Cricket.

"You drag that girl in here if you plan on makin' love to her like that in broad daylight!" Mrs. Maloney ordered. "What're you tryin' to do? Start a scandal? For pity's sake, boy! Seek out some privacy next time."

Heath laughed, "Yes, ma'am," as he swooped Cricket into his arms and hurried up the back porch steps into Mrs. Maloney's house.

Dropping Cricket's feet to the floor just inside Maymee's kitchen, Heath smiled and winced when the old woman firmly slapped him on the seat of his pants and said, "Use your brain next time, honey."

"Yes, ma'am," he agreed, gathering Cricket into his arms and against his body, however.

Cricket was blushing. She knew she was because she could feel the heat on her cheeks. Yet Mrs. Maloney was someone she could trust—someone Heath could trust—and she began to fight her bashfulness.

"Now I'm givin' you children ten minutes alone in my kitchen," Mrs. Maloney said, resting one hand on her hip and wagging an index finger with the other. "Ten minutes and not a second more." Turning toward the parlor, she left them then, calling, "Ten minutes, Heathro! That's all you have, so do your best with the time given you."

"Yes, ma'am," Heath mumbled as he gazed into Cricket's eyes—his own blue eyes smoldering with desire.

"What do you mean pouncin' on me like that?" Cricket giggled as she allowed her arms to slip over his broad shoulders. "You about scared me to death."

"Well, sorry about that, sugar," he said, still grinning at her. "Here…let me offer my sincerest apologies, Miss Blossom Bottom."

Cricket giggled as Heath's lips toyed with hers a moment. He kissed her lightly over and over again, and she knew he was teasing her.

"I'm still waitin'," she whispered as he paused, simply staring at her.

"For what?" he asked.

"That apology you promised to offer," she said, smiling.

"Oh, that," he mumbled as his mouth claimed hers at last.

And claim her mouth he did—over and over and over—until all too soon Mrs. Maloney simply walked back into the kitchen, taking an apron down from the apron hook on the wall and saying, "All right. Ten minutes to the tick." She looked at Cricket and winked. Then, turning her attention to Heath, she said, "Now Magnolia has jam to put up with Ada, and you're supposed to be fixin' that stall door in my barn, young man."

"Yes, ma'am," Heath said, releasing Cricket. Instantly she felt cold and disappointed.

"Run along, Magnolia," Mrs. Maloney encouraged. "You don't want Ada to think you're holed up somewhere with Heath here havin' his way with you."

"Yes, ma'am," Cricket giggled. Quickly she raised herself on the tips of her toes and stole one last kiss from Heath. "Thank you," she told Mrs. Maloney, kissing her affectionately on one cheek before she raced out the kitchen door, retrieved her shoes and stockings, and hurried home.

Maymee arched one eyebrow as she studied Heath. She couldn't suppress a knowing grin, and Heath asked, "What?"

"What?" Maymee exclaimed, slapping Heath on the seat of the pants again with the large wooden spoon she was holding. "Why don't you just tear the girl's clothes off and—"

"Don't give me any more ideas, Maymee," Heath teased. "I've already got too many of my own."

Maymee shook her head, laughing. It was going to be very interesting to watch—to see just how long Heath would take before approaching Zeke Cranford about courting Cricket. She sighed, somehow blissful in her own right at knowing Cricket was in love with Heath, and Heath with Cricket.

Yep. It was going to be mighty interesting indeed.

Heath was distracted as he rode Archie toward home that afternoon—distracted by wondering how on earth he was going to keep his hands off Magnolia Cranford long enough to court her properly. And that was *if* Zeke Cranford agreed to let him do it. Yep, Heath was dangerously distracted. It was why he didn't know he was in trouble until he heard the cocking of several rifles.

Snapping to attention, he glanced around to see Wyatt Stanley, Lash Martin, and Tyler Waller holding rifles on him. He knew Wyatt was a pain in the hind end, but he hadn't ever heard of Lash and Tyler causing any trouble.

"What's this?" Heath asked as his hand slowly slid to his hip.

But Wyatt stepped closer to Heath. "Don't do it, Thibodaux," he threatened. "Lash!" he ordered. "Shoot his horse if he makes another move for his pistol."

Heath frowned and held very still. "What are you boys doin'?"

"Savin' this good, God-fearin' town from the likes of pond scum like you!" Wyatt growled. "Now get down off that horse and lead him on back to the church house."

But Heath paused, saying, "Now look here, boys…I don't know what in the hell is goin' on, but you can't just—"

"I said, get down off that horse and lead him back to the church house, Thibodaux!" Wyatt shouted. "Believe me, after knowin' all that you've done to that poor girl…I'm just lookin' for a reason to blow a hole in your head big enough for me to spit through."

"What girl? What are you—"

Archie reared, almost throwing Heath when Wyatt fired his rifle over Heath's head as a warning.

"All right! All right!" Heath growled as he dismounted and patted Archie's jaw to soothe him. "But you better have a damn good reason for holdin' a rifle on a Texas Ranger, Stanley."

Lash frowned. "I thought you said he weren't a Ranger no more, Wyatt!" he spat.

"He ain't," Wyatt assured him. "He quit after he lost those other girls last year."

"Texas Ranger is a callin' for life, boys," Heath informed them. "Papers and badge…they don't expire."

Lash looked a little rattled, but Tyler and Wyatt glared at him, and he leveled his gun at Archie once more.

"Back to town, Ranger Thibodaux," Wyatt demanded. "Texas Ranger or not, you're gonna do right by that girl."

"What girl?" Heath shouted. "What in the hell are you talkin' about?"

"The preacher will explain when we get back," Tyler said. "Now shut up and walk that horse, mister."

Angry, but not angry enough to get himself shot for a reason he didn't even know, Heath stormed back toward town, leading Archie.

"Two weeks," he mumbled to himself. They'd turned on him in only two weeks. But he shrugged—for he'd seen people turn on a Ranger they felt indebted to in less than that. Still, two weeks wasn't very long. Some folks in Pike's Creek must have mighty short memories.

"And then he says to me," Ada continued, smiling at Cricket, "he says, 'Ada darlin'…when I kiss you, I swear I hear a heavenly chorus start into singin'!'"

"Really, Ada?" Cricket asked, giggling.

"Truly, Cricket," Ada confirmed.

Cricket sighed with contentment. "I just never knew Daddy was so romantic like that."

"Well, most men aren't very affectionate in public," Ada explained. "But I think your daddy's maturity and wisdom give him the confidence to know how important it is to a woman that her lover isn't embarrassed to let people know he loves her."

"Daddy's always been smarter than most folks I've known," Cricket confirmed.

Ada giggled. "Except for when it comes to tellin' his daughter how babies are made."

Cricket and Ada both burst into laughter—mirthful at the thought of Zeke Cranford weaseling out of telling Cricket the whole truth of it.

Their laughter was instantly exchanged for startled gasps when Maymee Maloney suddenly burst in through the kitchen door.

"Magnolia! Ada!" she panted as she leaned against the wall. "Oh, you have to get on over to the church now! Right now! They've got a gun to his head. And you know how stubborn that boy is…as stubborn as any leathery old mule I ever did see! They'll shoot him! Or hang him! I'm convinced they will!"

"Who?" Ada asked. "Who will they hang?"

But even before Mrs. Maloney said his name, Cricket knew who.

"Heath Thibodaux!"

"Heath?" Ada breathed. "Well, why on earth would someone want to be hangin' Heathro Thibodaux?"

Maymee, still struggling to catch her breath, wagged a finger at Cricket. "They think he…they think he…that he bedded Cricket while the girls and Heath were captive. Reverend Stanley is demandin' Heath makes an honest woman of her."

"What?" Cricket squeaked in disbelief.

"Well, I have had enough of this…this horse manure!" Ada said, wiping her hands on her apron, untying it, and tossing it to the table. "And why on earth do these things always happen when Zeke is gone from home?"

Cricket paused for only a moment—only long enough to decide she couldn't afford the time it would take to put on her stockings and shoes.

"Cricket!" she heard Ada holler as she bolted for the door. "Cricket, wait!"

But Cricket was already down the porch and into the street on her way to the church house. As she neared it, she could see Archie tethered to the hitching post out front.

She patted his warm muzzle as she passed him, mumbling, "It's all right, Archie. Don't you worry."

The scene that met her when she stepped into the church was something right out of a nightmare! There he stood—Texas Ranger Heathro Thibodaux, right there in front of the preacher's podium—with Wyatt Stanley's rifle muzzle pressed against the side of his head.

Ann and Marie were crying as they stood listening to Vilma screaming at her father.

"You're so arrogant, Daddy!" Vilma cried. "Wyatt's a liar! You know he is! He's been lyin' since the day he could talk. So why are you believin' him now? Why? I've told you the truth of it! Heathro Thibodaux did nothin' to deserve this! And neither did Cricket…and I think you know it. I think you're just mad, insane with anger and wounded pride because Heath was right about where those outlaws had taken us! This is just your vindictive, angry soul and—"

Everything went silent as Edgar Stanley's backhanded slap to his daughter's face echoed through the church.

"I will not have my town drug down into the depths of immorality!" Reverend Stanley shouted. "Not by the likes of this loathsome sinner… and certainly not by the likes of my own daughter!"

Marie and Ann rushed to Vilma, helping her to her feet—for her father's blow had knocked her to the floor.

"I warned you, Wyatt," Vilma said through her tears. "I warned you."

"I know what I'm doin', Vilma," Wyatt growled. "If you won't stand up for what's right in this town, I will!"

"And what's right in this town, you little weasel?" Ada shouted as she stepped in behind Cricket. "Holdin' a gun to the head of the man we all owe six lives to? To the man who saved our daughters? Your sister, Wyatt?"

"It don't matter who he saved," Wyatt spat. "Not when he stole Cricket's innocence while he was doin' it!"

"Stole my innocence?" Cricket shrieked. "Oh, I hate you, Wyatt Stanley. I've always hated you…and that's what this is all about, isn't it? You not gettin' the attention you want from anybody! Not from me or the other girls in this town…not from your self-righteous daddy!"

Cricket gasped and instantly silenced her venting when, with a nod of Reverend Stanley's head, Lash Martin and Tyler Waller leveled their rifles at Heath's head too.

Cricket looked to Heath with painful desperation. But as his gaze locked with hers, she saw only anger—not fear.

"It's your choice, Magnolia," Reverend Stanley said then. "*Ranger* Thibodaux has agreed to make an honest woman of you. He'll marry you as I have demanded, and eventually this memory of your lustful, lascivious behavior may be forgotten by the people in this town. But you don't have to marry this sinner, Magnolia. If this man took you to his bed against your will—"

"What? No! No! Nothin' was against my will!" Cricket cried. "Because nothin' happened!"

"Are you with child, Magnolia?" Reverend Stanley asked then.

"No!" Cricket cried, looking to Ada for support.

"Zeke will wring your neck with his bare hands for this, Edgar Stanley!" she threatened.

"Edgar?"

Everyone's attention turned to the choir seats. There sat Mrs. Stanley—sitting straight as a board, hands folded in her lap as always.

"Edgar…perhaps we should wait and counsel with Zeke," Mrs. Stanley said timidly. "He is, after all, Cricket's father."

"It doesn't matter who he is, Mrs. Stanley!" Reverend Stanley spat. "What these two sinners have done is an abomination to this town!" He looked back to Cricket. "Either you marry this man, Magnolia…or you're branded a harlot for the rest of your life, and I'll see that Heathro Thibodaux is shot for being a besmircher of feminine virtue. The choice is yours. And as I said, *Ranger* Thibodaux has already confessed the sin and agreed to marry you…so the choice is now in your sinful hands."

"He did *not* confess to it, Daddy!" Vilma cried. "He agreed to marry her to keep her from bein' branded a harlot!"

"I won't hear your voice again, Vilma," Reverend Stanley said calmly. Glancing to Vilma, he added, "From this moment on, I have only one child…a son."

"Oh, Daddy," Vilma breathed, "that's the first truth you've uttered in a long, long time."

But Reverend Stanley ignored Vilma—simply stared at Cricket and asked, "Harlot or married woman, Magnolia?"

"Marry him," Mrs. Maloney said from the open doors behind Cricket and Ada. "Marry Heath, and remove him from danger. Then let your father and the other good men of this town sort it out when they return."

"B-but...I don't want Heath to marry me because someone's forcin' him to," Cricket cried.

Ada and Mrs. Maloney exchanged glances. Then Ada sighed and said, "Marry him, Cricket. I truly believe Edgar Stanley will let Wyatt kill him if you don't."

Cricket turned back to stare at Edgar Stanley—and it was then she saw more than arrogance and pride in his countenance. It was then that she could see the flecks of egotism, conceit, self-importance, and the determination to control in him.

She didn't pause any longer but rather hurried up the aisle of the chapel toward Heath. "I'm s-sorry," she breathed as he stared down at her. His blue eyes were still aflame with seething.

"Come on then, Reverend Stanley," Heath said, turning to face the self-indulgent preacher. "Make her marry me."

Cricket glanced to her right—to where Marie and Ann stood embracing Vilma. They each nodded and attempted to smile—offering her what encouragement they could when there were three loaded guns pointed at Heath's head.

"Dearly beloved," Reverend Stanley began. He looked out over the chapel as if performing a wedding before an entire congregation. "We are gathered here this day to join this man, Heathro Thibodaux, and this woman, Magnolia Cranford, in bonds of holy matrimony."

As tears streamed over Cricket's cheeks, she heard Heathro mumble, "I do," when asked if he took her to be his wife. She wept even more bitterly when she breathlessly answered, "I do," when the wicked Reverend Righteous asked if she took Heath to be her husband.

It couldn't be happening! Surely Heath wasn't being forced to marry her—at gunpoint?

"Then by virtue of the powers invested in me by God and the state,

I now pronounce you man and wife," Reverend Stanley concluded. Looking to Wyatt, he said, "You may lower your guns, gentlemen. They are man and wife now."

Cricket trembled as she watched Heath standing firm and tall next to her. He waited until Wyatt, Lash, and Tyler had lowered their rifles.

Then glaring at Reverend Stanley, he asked, "Didn't you forget somethin', Edgar?"

"And what would that be, Mr. Thibodaux?" Reverend Stanley asked, sneering with triumph.

"You didn't tell me whether or not I can kiss the bride," Heath simply stated.

Reverend Stanley's eyes narrowed, and he studied Heath for a moment, looking to Cricket and then back to Heath. "Very well," he relented. "You may kiss the bride."

"You're damn right I can," Heath growled. "And you be sure to tell Zeke Cranford that it was you who gave me permission."

Cricket gasped as Heath took hold of her arm, turning her to him, pulling her tight against his body, and fairly devouring her with such a sensual, wanton kiss that, even for the despicability of their situation, Cricket's knees turned softer than the blackberry jam she and Ada had been making.

Heath moaned as he kissed her again—more wantonly—with such salaciousness that even though Cricket knew it was for show, goose bumps began to cover every inch of her flesh.

"Might I remind you that this is my father's church, Thibodaux?" Wyatt growled.

Heath broke the seal of their lips then, pausing, his blue eyes smoldering with fury as he stared at Cricket a moment.

"It's God's church, Wyatt," Heath growled as he swooped Cricket up into his arms. "Not your father's."

"Where are you takin' her?" Ada asked.

"Well, I'm takin' her home, Mrs. Cranford," Heath answered. "It's our weddin' night, ain't it?"

"But she doesn't even have her shoes on, Heath!" Marie cried.

Heath grinned and glared at Reverend Stanley once more before saying, "Oh, she ain't gonna be needin' her shoes tonight, honey." Then winking at Ann, Marie, and Vilma, Heath carried Cricket with him as he stormed out of the church and into the street.

None too delicately, Heath hoisted Cricket up onto Archie's hindquarters behind the saddle.

"I'll send your daddy over as soon as he's taken care of all this, Cricket," Ada said, clutching Cricket's hand as Heath mounted Archie and settled into the saddle.

Mrs. Maloney took her hand then. "Trust him, honey," she breathed, smiling. "He's trustworthy, and you know that. So you trust him tonight...whatever happens. Trust him with your heart, my darlin'...with your heart, your soul...and your body."

Cricket's eyes widened as the full understanding of what Maymee Maloney was saying struck her. "Ada," she began in a whisper.

"Hold onto me," Heath demanded, reaching around behind himself, taking her arms, and pulling them around his waist. "Archie's angry...so this is gonna be one hell of a ride home!"

Cricket tightened her embrace as Heath shouted, "Ya!" and Archie lurched into a gallop.

Maymee Maloney smiled as she watched Heathro Thibodaux ride like hell out of Pike's Creek with his new bride. There was a clap of thunder overhead only a moment before a summer downpour began.

"Oh, Maymee!" Ada cried as Marie, Ann, and Vilma wrapped their arms around her and Mrs. Maloney, joining to watch Heathro and Cricket ride away. "They'll get soaked to the skin in this rain!"

But Maymee Maloney's smile only broadened. "Oh, I do hope so," she chuckled. "I certainly do hope so."

CHAPTER TWENTY

By the time Heath reined in Archie in front of his house, Cricket was drenched and trembling—for even though the summer days and nights were warm, the heavy thunderstorms of the high desert were cold.

"Come on," Heath said, dismounting. Putting his hands at her waist, he lifted Cricket down from Archie's back. "Are you cold?" he asked, turning his head to one side and spitting rainwater from his mouth.

"A little," Cricket admitted as her teeth began chattering.

Heath nodded, and Cricket was instantly warmer as he swept her up into the cradle of his powerful arms. Striding with her toward the house, he angrily kicked the door open with one boot and carried her over the threshold into his house.

"Here," he said, letting her feet drop to the floor and keeping his one arm around her until he was sure she was steady again. "I'll get a fire goin' for you before I take Archie to the barn."

"No, no…that's all right," she timidly argued. "I'm fine." But the scowl he gave her made her bite her lip and promise herself not to attempt to ease anything for him.

She watched as he stormed around the small cabin, gathering what he needed to lay a fire. "This is the back of the house," he mumbled. He pointed to the hearth and said, "Fireplace." He pointed to the large, soft-looking bed covered in tattered white quilts on the wall opposite the hearth. "Bed," he told her unnecessarily. "The kitchen and parlor are that way…and the outhouse is over yonder by the barn."

Cricket nodded, even though he wasn't looking at her. She watched as he took a wooden match from a tin on the mantel, hunkered down before the hearth, struck the match, and touched it to the kindling he'd laid there. He blew on the smoldering kindling several times until the fire caught. Then he wordlessly stood, striding to the large wardrobe against one wall.

She watched as he opened the wardrobe doors and began rummaging around inside.

"Here," Heath said, turning to face her and tossing several articles of clothing onto the bed. "You strip out of them wet clothes and put these on. You'll catch your death if you don't. I'll see to Archie while you're changin'."

And without another word, he left by way of the same door he'd kicked in only moments ago.

Standing in the middle of Heathro Thibodaux's bedroom, soaking wet and shivering with cold, Cricket pinched her own arm to make sure she wasn't dreaming. Had Heath really been forced to marry her only a short while before? Would Reverend Stanley really have let Wyatt and the others kill him if he hadn't?

She started to weep again—began to sit on his bed but remembered she was drenched. She didn't know what to do! She felt more confused than she had when Heck Alford and his band of outlaws had abducted her and the others. At least when she had been in the hands of outlaws, she'd known that survival—fighting to stay alive until help came—was her path. But now—now she only knew that the man she loved so desperately more than life itself had been forced to marry her against his will—that she stood in his house not knowing what to do.

Cricket's gaze fell to the clothing Heath had strewn over the bed. She was very cold, and she knew he was right that she might fall ill if she didn't dry off and warm up. She saw a small towel hanging from a hook near the washbasin and pitcher table. Glancing around, she realized there was no dressing screen to ensure her modesty. Thus Cricket surmised that swiftness would be her only ally in that regard.

Seizing the small towel from its hook on the washing table, she began stripping off her clothes. Pantaloons, petticoat, skirt—

shirtwaist, corset, camisole. Quickly she dried herself as well as the small towel would allow. Snatching up the clothes from the bed, she frowned—only a pair of men's underdrawers and a white shirt. Surely Heath didn't expect her to dress in only a pair of his underdrawers and one of his shirts! However, as the realization washed over her that he couldn't possibly have anything else to offer her to wear—and as she also realized that these were Heath's clothes, clothes that he probably wore often, clothes that had clung to his smooth, warm skin—Cricket quite willingly slipped into them.

She laughed a little when she'd finished dressing and caught a vision of herself in the wall mirror opposite the door. She looked exactly like a vagabond—baggy underdrawers barely able to stay at her waist no matter how taut she pulled the drawstring and a shirt that hung down nearly to her knees. Truly she looked ridiculous. And that was the thought that panicked her in that moment.

Heath would return! As soon as he'd tended to Archie, Heath would return and see her looking just like a little ragamuffin! Frantically, Cricket dashed to the wash table, finding a brush there. Pulling the ribbon holding her hair in a long braid, she loosened the full length of her coffee-colored tresses and began brushing it in front of the fire. Her hair was as wet as her clothes had been, and working it to a smooth softness that she was satisfied with was an ordeal.

In fact, Cricket had only just finished brushing her hair when she was startled by the door swinging open—a drenched and dripping Heath stepping into the room.

Heath paused as if astonished—as if he'd forgotten Cricket had come home with him. Slowly he looked her up and down—from head to toe and back again—a deep frown furrowing his brow.

Cricket could tell he was even angrier than when he'd left to care for Archie. She'd thought caring for the horse would surely settle his temper, but he looked more disturbed than he had before.

Heath closed his eyes a moment, removing his hat and wiping the rain from his face and goatee. He silently tried to convince himself that he was only dreaming—that Magnolia wasn't really standing there dressed only in his underdrawers and Sunday shirt. But when he opened his eyes again to behold the woman he loved standing in his bedroom in his underwear and shirt, he shook his head—reminded himself that she'd been forced to marry him. He knew it wasn't Cricket's intention to tempt him—to endeavor to lure him into taking her to his bed. He knew he had to keep his thoughts focused.

But just when Heath thought he'd built up his defenses once more—as he stripped off his rain-soaked shirt and began drying his arms and chest with the damp towel Cricket offered him—she said, "I'm so sorry, Heath."

The emotion in her voice and the new tears on her cheeks were all the evidence Heath needed to confirm that she thought he was angry with *her*—not with Reverend Righteous and his idiot son and friends, not with the good men of Pike's Creek that had ridden off to Lyman that morning to rescue a group of trapped miners, but with her. Cricket thought he was angry with her.

"I'm so, so sorry, Heath," she wept. "I-I didn't know what to do. I really thought they might kill you! I-I..."

Cricket paused in her desperate apology when Heath took hold of the waist of his drenched trousers and said, "You might wanna turn around for a minute."

"Oh!" Cricket breathed, realizing he meant to strip off the rest of his wet clothes.

"And would you toss that other pair of drawers to me?" he asked. "The other pair there on the bed?" he repeated when she didn't move at first.

"Oh," she breathed again. Retrieving the other set of underdrawers Heath had tossed from the wardrobe onto his bed, Cricket stretched her arm behind her in offering them to him.

"Thank you," Heath mumbled, pulling the underdrawers from her hand. A moment later, he said, "You can turn back around now."

Cricket did turn around then—her breath catching in her throat as she saw him standing there in only his underdrawers.

He was rubbing his hair with the small towel in an effort to dry it.

When he'd finished, he tossed the towel into a basket in one corner and looked at her. The rather boyish appearance his tousled hair gave him made Cricket smile.

"What?" Heath asked. He looked at his chest and then down at his underdrawers as if ensuring his modesty. "What's so funny?"

"Nothin'," Cricket said, shaking her head. Her amusement vanished as she watched him rake one hand through his wet hair several times to comb it. Once again he stood before her beautifully bare-chested, handsome as the summer days were long, and more intimidating than ever.

Remembering that she'd been apologizing to him before he'd begun to strip off his clothes, she repeated, "I'm so sorry, Heath. I'm sure it can all be worked out, and I'm sure that…" Her words were lost as emotion choked. "I feel like I can't endure your bein' angry with me. I-I didn't know what else to do! I know Wyatt Stanley…and he would have shot you the second his father allowed. I-I didn't know what to do, Heath!"

But when she looked up, it was to see Heath frowning at her—frowning, yes, but with confusion, not anger.

"You think I'm mad at you, Magnolia?" he asked.

Cricket didn't know what to say. Of course she thought he was mad at her. Certainly he was mad at everyone who had forced him to marry her, but that included her. So of course he would be angry with her too.

"I'm not angry with you, honey," Heath said, striding to her. Taking her by the shoulders, his frown softened. "I'm mad at myself."

"What?" she asked, entirely confused—entirely affected by his touch.

"I mean, sure, I'm mad at that little son of…at Wyatt…at Wyatt and his idiot friends," he began to explain. "And I'm furious to near beatin' the life outta Reverend Righteous. That man needs a good lickin'…more than one." He grinned a bit and brushed a stray strand of hair from her cheek. "But most of all, I'm mad at myself."

"At yourself?" Cricket asked. "Why would you be mad at yourself? For what?"

"For bein' a coward," he mumbled.

He dropped his hands from her, and she felt suddenly cold again.

"A coward?" she squeaked. "When have you ever been a coward?"

Heath inhaled a deep breath—exhaled it slowly. Still looking at her, he answered, "I've been a coward for almost two weeks. I figured all those…those shenanigans you allowed me to heap on you while was waitin' for that damn posse that never came…I figured you'd just endured all that from me." Cricket frowned, and he continued, "We come home, and you seemed so happy to be back with your daddy and Ada. You and Marie, Ann, and Vilma…you all settled right back into doin' the things you used to do. And I figured…that I didn't deserve you anyhow."

Cricket brushed more tears from her cheeks and bit her lip with restraining more emotion as he took her shoulder again, saying, "But then Ada told me in the general store…she told me that you were cryin' out my name in the night. And she said somethin' else—though I don't remember what—and it gave me hope…hope that maybe that first day I came to Pike's Creek and stepped into the general store…" An amused smile spread across his face as he continued, "And saw your little blossom bottom swingin' this way and that as you walked toward me…what Ada said gave me hope. And that's why I showed up at the Cornfield Chase last night and went to work havin' my way with you out behind Clifford King's barn."

Cricket shook her head. It was too much to take in—far too much to believe.

"You're just tryin' to make me feel better about all this today," she whispered. Looking up into the beautiful, sparkling blue of his eyes, she added, "And anyway…even if that's all true…it doesn't explain why you're mad at yourself right now instead of me."

Heath nodded with understanding. "I suppose it don't," he admitted. "But see…me bein' a coward is what found you bein' forced to marry me just now."

"You're talkin' in riddles," Cricket told him. "Just tell me what you mean, Heath," she pleaded.

"I love you, Magnolia," Heath said then. "I started fallin' in love with you that day in the general store. But you know who I am…what

I've seen and done. It hardens a man…scares him away from dreamin' about lovin' the one right woman…and…and askin' her daddy for permission to court her…or to marry her." He released her, ran a hand through his damp hair, and laughed. "And do wanna know the worst of it?" he asked.

But Cricket knew there couldn't possibly be a worst—not if what he'd just said to her were true. Had Heathro Thibodaux really said he loved her? Had he really said, in a manner of speaking, that he wanted to court her—to marry her?

"The worst of it is," he continued, letting his head fall back as he stared at the ceiling, "I almost asked your daddy this mornin'. I was gonna ask him on the way to Lyman…while I was ridin' with him over to help those men. But than that damn bull got loose again, and I had to stay behind and round him up." He looked at her then, and Cricket saw the sincerity in his eyes—the truth—the love.

"So that's why I'm mad at myself, Miss Blossom Bottom," he sighed. "For bein' too much of a coward to ask your daddy if I could marry you a week or more ago."

Cricket smiled; she couldn't help but smile. She smiled and let the tears of joy race from her eyes.

"Really?" she asked in a breathy whisper, pinching her own arm once more to be certain she was awake. "Really, Heath? Are you tellin' me the truth…or are you just really tryin' to make me feel better?"

Heathro Thibodaux grinned. He reached out, taking a strand of her hair and twisting it around his finger.

"Oh, honey…I *know* I can make you feel better," he flirted.

"I know you can too," she flirted in return, blushing from the tips of her toes to the tips of her hair. "But do you mean all that? It wasn't just a story you made up to try and make today seem less…less insane? Y-you're not plannin' on waitin' until my daddy gets back and then makin' this all go away?"

"Sugar, why would I want this all to go away?" Heath asked.

Cricket quivered as he put his hands at her waist—as he slid them to her back, pulling her close to him. With only Heath's loose-fitting shirt between his hands and her skin, his touch was all the more exciting to every sense she owned.

"I really do love you, Magnolia," he mumbled. "Are you truly gonna stand there, knowin' all that has gone on between us…whether spoken or not…are you truly gonna stand there wearin' nothing but my underwear and pretend that you don't already know that?"

Cricket inhaled a deep breath as she fought to build her courage. She thought of what she'd told Marie not so long ago—that if she weren't willing to fight for something she loved—something or someone like Hudson—then she didn't deserve to own it. And how thoroughly, how desperately, and how absolutely she wanted to own Heathro Thibodaux—and wanted him to own her.

Tentatively, Cricket reached out, placing her trembling palms on Heath's broad chest. "Not anymore, I guess," she managed. She looked away from his handsome face, studying the breadth of his shoulders and the smooth bronze of his skin.

Heath chuckled. "Not anymore, huh?" he asked. "So you've known all along that I was in love with you, is that it?"

"No," Cricket answered. "I hoped all along that you would… from the moment I first saw you in the general store that day. Then I dreamed you would…from the moment I hopped up on the stupid waterin' trough and tried to kiss you." She looked up into his eyes then—his beautiful blue eyes so mesmerizing and filled with promise. "Then after that night in the barn with you…that's when I started prayin' you would love me…because I've loved you for so very long, Heath."

Heath gathered Cricket against his warm, solid body. The heat of his skin acted like a soothing balm to her, and she melted to him.

He kissed the top of her head, whispering, "I love you," into her hair.

And she pressed her lips to the warm, bronze skin of his chest, whispering, "I love you, Heathro Thibodaux."

Heath held Cricket there for a time—simply held her—reassuring her of his love with his words and affectionate caresses.

Then, as the fire burned warm and comforting in the hearth—as the sun set and the rain began to fall with a romantic sort of gentleness instead of an angry flood—Heath drew Cricket away from his embrace, asking, "How's that burn healin' up?"

Cricket frowned, puzzled. "Burn?" she asked.

"That burn you got when that outlaw Boone put his lit cigar to you," he explained.

Cricket thought it somewhat odd that Heath should think of the cigar burn in that moment. But she shrugged and answered, "Fine, I suppose."

"Let me have a look at it," he said.

Cricket tried to pull the collar of the buttoned-up shirt she wore down far enough for Heath to see the wound—but it wouldn't stretch the length it needed to. Therefore, she quickly unbuttoned the top three buttons of the shirt, pulling the collar and shirtfront aside to reveal the healed but still pink burn below her left shoulder.

"See?" she said. "It's healin' up just fine." Cricket giggled as she studied the burn a minute. "Must've been that medicinal spit of yours that you…"

Her words were lost when she looked up to see Heath smiling at her with triumph.

"Why are you grinnin' like that at me?" she giggled.

"Well, darlin'," Heath said, sending goose bumps racing over Cricket's arms and legs as he tugged the fabric of his shirt she wore to better reveal the burn, "it's just 'cause you're so conveniently gullible sometimes."

Cricket quivered as Heath bent, placing a soft, lingering kiss to the burn. She gasped as she felt his hand slip beneath the fabric of the shirt to caress her shoulder before traveling to the back of her neck as his mouth scattered lingering, moist kisses at her throat and chin.

"H-Heath," she breathed. "Ada says I don't know as much as I think I do about…about…"

His mouth covered hers, coaxing her, stirring her, exhilarating her until at last she relaxed against him.

"You only need to know that I love you," Heath mumbled against her mouth. "Know that I love you…and love me back, Magnolia. That's all you need to know."

As Heath continued to share loving, impassioned kisses with his wife—as he gently pushed her—gently laid her on the comfortable quilts on his bed—the tender rain cooled the serene summer evening, the fire in the hearth burned tranquil and warming, and Magnolia "Cricket" Thibodaux knew a wonderment in loving that few who walk the earth ever do.

EPILOGUE

Heath had been lying awake for over an hour—reveling in the feel of having the woman he loved sleeping in his arms. He felt freer than he could ever remember having felt before—as if he'd been tied up somehow and Cricket had come along and untethered him. But his body tensed, and his protective instincts leapt in his chest when he heard a horse whinny and a wagon brake set outside.

Gently slipping his arms from around Cricket's soft, warm body, Heath didn't even pause to gaze at her peaceful, contented expression. Memories of Reverend Righteous and his rifle-toting toadies were too fresh in his mind. Quickly slipping on his boots, Heath went to the window, peering out between the curtains as he buckled his gun belt over his underdrawers.

Just outside was a wagon and team that he well recognized, but he wasn't relieved yet. It was Zeke Cranford's team and wagon, and Heath couldn't be certain whether Zeke had come to talk to him or shoot him where he stood.

Glancing back to where Cricket still slept, Heath grinned, figuring she was worth fighting to the death to keep. And so quietly he opened the door and crossed the threshold to meet his fate.

"Mornin' there, Zeke," Heath greeted his father-in-law as he watched Zeke climb down from the wagon seat.

"Mornin', Heath," Zeke greeted with a smile. Zeke chuckled. "I hear you had one hell of a day yesterday, boy!"

Heath puffed a sigh of relief. It didn't look like Cricket's daddy intended to shoot him at least.

"Yeah. A hell of day," Heath agreed.

Zeke studied Heath from head to toe for a moment. Then smiling, he added, "It looks like you had yourself one heavenly night though."

"Z-Zeke…I-I…I want you to know—" Heath began.

"Ooo-weee, boy! You look as weak-kneed as a new fawn on a rowboat!" Zeke interrupted, laughing.

Heath felt himself flush—raked a hand through his hair in an effort to appear more rugged. "Yes, sir…I suppose I do," he sighed with his own chuckle.

Cricket sighed as the sound of laughter intruded on her blissful dreams. She didn't want to wake up—fought it with everything she could. Her dreams had been the stuff of pure fantasy! She'd been dreaming of Heath—dreaming of being kissed by him, held by him, wrapped in his arms as he…

Instantly Cricket's eyes popped wide open. As she stared at the ceiling—at the very unfamiliar ceiling—she realized that she hadn't been dreaming at all! Her mind had only been wistfully reminiscing on what had transpired between her and Heath during the night.

She blushed as she thought about their first night together—as she thought about how deeply she loved him and how entirely he loved her in return.

But as Cricket lay in her wedding bed, resplendent over having married the man she loved, she heard the sound of low laughter again—of her daddy's laughter!

Leaping out of bed quick as a mouse, Cricket crept to the window, peering out through the curtains. Heath was standing outside in nothing but his underdrawers, boots, and gun belt. Her daddy was saying something to Heath, and Cricket breathed a sigh of relief when she saw the smile on her father's face—heard him laugh at something Heath had said.

She puffed another sigh of reprieve as she turned around to face her first morning as Mrs. Heathro Thibodaux.

"Oh no!" she squeaked as she caught her reflection in the mirror across the room. There she stood, wearing nothing but Heath's best Sunday shirt. Her hair was a wild tangle of passion evidence as well. What if Heath invited her father in for breakfast?

As panic washed over her, Cricket clumsily found the hairbrush she'd used the night before and began tearing the knots out of her hair. Once she had it to a manageable, albeit questionably presentable state, she quickly poured water from the pitcher into the basin and refreshed her face. She hurriedly poured water into a glass sitting on the wash table, taking a large mouthful and swishing it awhile before gulping it down and chasing it with another mouthful.

Cricket was just about to check her skirt and shirtwaist (to see if they had dried sufficiently during the night to be worn again) when she heard the door open behind her. Whirling around expecting to see her father, she exhaled a relieved and delighted sigh when she saw only Heath had stepped in.

"That was your daddy," he said, closing the door behind him. "He brought over a trunk of your things that Ada figured you might need."

"Oh," Cricket breathed, suddenly very nervous for some reason. Oh, it was dreamy and marvelous—even comfortable—to imagine herself as Heathro Thibodaux's lover and wife when the moon was out and the fire was crackling warm in the hearth. But there, in the bright light of day, Cricket found herself still wondering if maybe she hadn't just dreamed it all. "Well, that was thoughtful," she added. She nervously cleared her throat, unable to meet Heath's gaze once it had traveled the length of her and caused him to smile. "Ada is so very thoughtful, you know," she added.

Heath chuckled. "Are you nervous, honey?" he asked as he strode toward her.

Cricket bumped up against the wall in trying to step back. "Well… no. I just thought maybe Daddy might be comin' in for a visit with you and…and…"

Heath had her cornered, however. Placing his hands on either side of her head on the wall at her back, he said, "Oh, he ain't stupid, sugar."

Cricket's heart was beating like a rabbit's! Her arms and legs covered in goose bumps.

"He's not?" she breathed.

"Nope. And aren't you glad he didn't shoot me?" he asked, placing a soft kiss to her mouth.

Instantly Cricket's jitters began to subside. "Oh yes!" she breathed. "I'm ever so glad he didn't shoot you, Heath."

Heath smiled and backed away—only a little. "He did beat the tar outta Reverend Righteous though…and Wyatt too. Looks like Pike's Creek will be lookin' for a new preacher. Wyatt and his daddy are already packin' up to move."

"He did?" Cricket asked.

"He did," Heath confirmed. "Seems Ada sent him a telegram over in Lyman, and he rode home late last night, marched right into Edgar Stanley's house, and beat the horse…manure outta father and son. Vilma was already gone. Her mother and her left…moved up to Thistle. Seems Vilma's been correspondin' with some wigmaker up there or some such thing."

Cricket smiled—allowed her arms to encircle Heath's neck. "Is that so?" she asked.

"Yep," Heath answered. "Seems Hudson Oliver and Cooper Keel are tired of all this nonsense too. There's gonna be a double weddin' next week in Pike's Creek. And we're invited."

It was all very wonderful—everything! Vilma escaping her prison of sorts, Hudson and Marie pushing up their wedding date, Mr. Keel and Ann deciding not to fiddle around anymore and join them. All of it was wonderful, just wonderful! But not nearly as wonderful as Heathro Thibodaux.

"So," Cricket began, studying Heath's lips as her mouth began to water for want of his kiss. "A double weddin' next week, is it?"

"Mmm-hmmm," Heath affirmed.

"So…what do you want to do until then, Mr. Thibodaux?" Cricket flirted with her handsome, oh so handsome husband.

"Kiss you, Mrs. Thibodaux," Heath breathed, pressing a soft kiss to her mouth. "Kiss you and hold you…sleep with you in my arms."

"Then kiss me, Heath," Cricket whispered, her violet eyes brimming with happy tears. "Because sometimes I'm still afraid I'm dreamin'."

"You ain't dreamin', honey," Heath assured her with another kiss. "Nope. You ain't dreamin' at all…my little blossom-bottomed…" He kissed her. "Barefooted." He kissed her. "Black underwear-wearin', stranger-welcomin' kiss-stealer," he finished as he kissed her with an incontestable assurance of endless kisses to come. "We ain't dreamin'," Heath promised as he gathered Cricket into his arms and kissed her again…and again…and again…

AUTHOR'S NOTE

Okay, at the risk of having to endure a backlash like I've never endured before, I'm just going to admit something. I'm just going to come right out and say it: I *like* "ly" adverbs! I do! I think the world is missing too may "ly" words these days. And do you know what else I'm going to confess? I like wordy descriptions of things! I like descriptions of nature and physical features of people and places. And I like descriptions of deep emotions and passionate, blissful kisses! I also like exclamation points! A friend once told me that I was like a walking exclamation point—and at first I thought she meant it as a put-down. But then I considered it and thought to myself, "Would I rather be a walking exclamation point? Or a boring old period?" I'd totally rather be an exclamation point!

By now you're probably sitting there going, "What in the world does all this have to do with the price of potatoes in Idaho *or* this book?"

Well, here's the deal—a lot! Over the past year, I've been reevaluating myself. (We middle-aged chicks do that pretty often, you know.) Without boring you with my blah-blah-blah that could go on forever, I simply tell you that one of things I discovered I didn't like about not necessarily myself but my life was the fact that I wasn't enjoying writing the way I used to.

My thoughts began to travel back to a romance novelist I did a book signing with years and years ago. I remember how worn out she was, how stressed and overwhelmed. She didn't enjoy writing anymore—not at all. She had many reasons, but the one that popped out at me during this most recent reevaluation of myself was that she was unhappy because she wasn't writing what she wanted to write! She didn't have the freedoms I've been blessed with. She had a conference room full of editors telling her what to add to her book, what characters to kill off, and so on. But I began to realize that too many times while I'm writing, I start to worry about who I'm going to offend with one of the swear words that aren't even considered swear words when you grow up on a farm—or who's going to be angry because a hero and heroine were kissing while they were standing in a lake. I don't like to disappoint people; it hurts me, worries me, and haunts me like you can never imagine. And yet what I realized was that by not writing true to myself, I was disappointing *me*! And in disappointing me, I disappointed those closest to me—those who love me most, depend on me most, encourage me most, and are the truest definition of family and friends!

Well, as you can imagine, this was kind of a big deal! And it held me up where writing was concerned. I stalled out—totally stalled out. I began to wonder if I ever wanted to write another book. And if I did, *could* I write another book?

To make matters worse, while I was stalled and doubting myself, so many stressful things were going on—some of them wonderful, some of them tragic, but all of them incredibly draining both physically and emotionally.

And so I shelved *Untethered* for a good eight months. I wanted to write *Untethered* the way I wanted to write it because, in the end, it is my story, and I wanted to feel good about it.

Blah blah blah…let's skip ahead. Drama, drama and stress, stress, stress aside, one day I just sat down and decided I was going to finish *Untethered*. Sounds easy enough, right? But not when you sit down, open your master document (which you *thought* was four or five solid chapters) only to discover that all you really had was an outline and one great kissing scene. So what well of motivation do you draw from when that happens? What do you find in your heart to make it fun again? To make you want to write and create and entertain your friends—which is why you started writing in the first place?

So there I was—one great kissing scene and an outline to go on—and nothing coming to me as far as a motivator to write.

I had the characters there—they'd been there from the beginning! There was Cricket, the little do-gooding, barefooted heroine. And of course there was Heathro Thibodaux—whose first name is indeed a conglomeration of some things I adore, such as Lee Majors portraying Heath Barkley in the old TV series *The Big Valley*, Heath candy bars (who can't love that chocolate and toffee number?), and the last name of a good friend, that being "Heath." Heathro Thibodaux was firmly in my mind—as were his uncanny kissing skills.

But I always need more than a good storyline and characters to love. I need a motivator! And whether it's the enthusiasm of doing something for someone else or to simply entertain myself, I need still need a motivator! And let me tell you this—no matter how good Heath was at kissing Cricket, without my motivator I was toast for ever getting them to their own wedding!

And so *Untethered* sat on the proverbial shelf for a month or two more. And then it happened! It's like that old saying, "When you least expect it…" and wham! There it was! Just out of the blue one day, there was my motivator—or to be more specific, my motivators.

And so I ask you this burning question: What do a plunger, the movie *Christmas Vacation*, livestock salt licks, liquid silver jewelry, laughter that nearly causes incontinence, hotel rooms, a plunger, the same plunger again, a black truck, a big silver truck, and my *Untethered* motivators all have in common? The answer is on the dedication page of *Untethered* itself—Danielle and Weezy!

Ah, Danielle and Weezy—angels of mercy, insightful gurus, and cherished, treasured friends! One day as I was reminiscing over something Danielle, Weezy, and I had giggled over, a little light went off in my brain. Actually, it was more like one of those flaming emergency flares! I wanted to do something for Danielle and Weezy that would convey to them the depth of my appreciation and love for their friendship, support, encouragement, loyalty, and inexplicable service to me. And since the thing I used to do as a gift for my friends was to write a book, I decided to write a book for Danielle and Weezy. And that book is the one you just read.

Untethered may have too many exclamation points, and Heath may or may not have his shirt off too often (or not often enough). I didn't bother counting the farm-girl swear words or checking to see whether Heath and Cricket's wedding night moments were too steamy. I simply wrote the book as it played out in my mind—with Danielle and Weezy as my muses. I wrote it for them—for my cherished friends—for all the reasons I began writing in the first place!

I hope you enjoyed *Untethered*—because I truly enjoyed writing it! I'll leave you now with a few little trivia snippets. So until we ride away into another sunset with another handsome hero together—adios, my darlings.

Untethered Trivia Snippets

Snippet #1—If you ever were, or still are, a fan of the Canadian/Disney Channel series *Road to Avonlea* and you think something in *Untethered* tended to remind you of some of those beloved *Road to Avonlea* characters, then go back through the book and highlight names of places and secondary characters. (Tee hee!) It's my own secret little *Road to Avonlea* tribute!

Snippet #2—Mrs. Maloney was my babysitter from the time I was just a few months old until the age of three. She was a kind, plump, elderly lady who used to let me watch *Captain Kangaroo* each weekday morning. She served me wonderful, healthy lunches (though I do remember racing to the bathroom once with a handful of green beans and flushing them down the toilet when Mrs. Maloney was out of the room) and always made me feel safe. I was so little when she babysat me that my vivid memories of her are beginning to fade. But here's one I found the other day in an old thingy I'd printed off twenty or more years ago:

> Mrs. Maloney was an elderly lady who babysat me. I loved her! I can still remember the lay of her house, and I remember watching *Captain Kangaroo* on her big TV. I remember my Julie. She was a little girl my own age—a friend of mine that Mrs. Maloney used to watch as well. Julie and I would flush our green beans down the toilet whenever Mrs. Maloney left the room during lunch. I remember having to stay with Mrs.

Maloney overnight once. I was frightened about being away from my parents for the night even though Mrs. Maloney let me sleep in her bed with her. Thankfully, I had good ol' Muggins to cling to. (Muggins was a soft, plush, yellow, stuffed bunny that became my most treasured possession for a time.) At some point that night, I awoke to find I'd somehow let go of Muggins! I could find no trace of him at first. Panic ensued and escalated as I spied part of Muggins's anatomy sticking out from underneath the slumbering form of Mrs. Maloney! Horrifying! Muggins—smothering to death under my babysitter! I woke Mrs. Maloney and retrieved my dearest Muggins, though it was some time before my breathing steadied and I was able to sleep again.

Snippet #3—Our family loves door-ditching treats and presents! When our children were little, it was one of their very favorite family activities. Most of the time we would light a little votive candle in a jar or candleholder and leave it with our door-ditched items to make them more visible—and more fun!

Snippet #4—The whole "where babies really come from" thread in *Untethered* was inspired by a very enlightening evening my roommates and I experienced at Ricks College long, long ago in 1984.

Snippet #5—Yes. Mr. Keel is named for Howard Keel—who starred in so many wonderful MGM musicals in the 1950s!

Snippet #6—Several descriptions of the moon in *Untethered* were inspired by this something my mother wrote to me in an e-mail while I was working on the book. In fact, if I'm not mistaken, her exact quote may even appear in it. *"The moon is brilliant like a silver wafer in the sky."—Patsy Reed*

Snippet #6—In real life, my friend Weezy Ann rides a black Harley Davidson motorcycle. All four-foot whatever of her!

Snippet #7—In real life, my friend Danielle is a literal connoisseur of southwestern, Native American jewelry. And she wears it better than anyone else I know!

Snippet #8—As of the date of publication for this book, Danielle and Weezy are in possession of the plunger. Whether or not they *know* they have it is still a mystery to me and Kevin!

My everlasting admiration, gratitude, and love…
To my husband, Kevin…
Proof that heroes really *do* exist!
I Love You!

ABOUT THE AUTHOR

Marcia Lynn McClure's intoxicating succession of novels, novellas, and e-books—including *Shackles of Honor, The Windswept Flame, The Haunting of Autumn Lake,* and *Beneath the Honeysuckle Fine*—has established her as one of the most favored and engaging authors of true romance. Her unprecedented forte in weaving captivating stories of western, medieval, regency, and contemporary amour void of brusque intimacy has earned her the title "The Queen of Kissing."

Marcia, who was born in Albuquerque, New Mexico, has spent her life intrigued with people, history, love, and romance. A wife, mother, grandmother, family historian, poet, and author, Marcia Lynn McClure spins her tales of splendor for the sake of offering respite through the beauty, mirth, and delight of a worthwhile and wonderful story.

BIBLIOGRAPHY

Beneath the Honeysuckle Vine
A Better Reason to Fall in Love
Born for Thorton's Sake
The Chimney Sweep Charm
A Crimson Frost
Daydreams
Desert Fire
Divine Deception
Dusty Britches
The Fragrance of her Name
The Haunting of Autumn Lake
The Heavenly Surrender
The Highwayman of Tanglewood
Kiss in the Dark
Kissing Cousins
The Light of the Lovers' Moon
Love Me
An Old-Fashioned Romance
The Pirate Ruse
The Prairie Prince
The Rogue Knight
Romantic Vignettes-The Anthology of Premiere Novellas
Saphyre Snow
Shackles of Honor
Sudden Storms
Sweet Cherry Ray
Take a Walk With Me
The Tide of the Mermaid Tears
The Time of Aspen Falls
To Echo the Past
The Touch of Sage
The Trove of the Passion Room
Untethered

The Visions of Ransom Lake
Weathered Too Young
The Whispered Kiss
The Windswept Flame

CPSIA information can be obtained at www.ICGtesting.com
Printed in the USA
BVOW010327220612

293412BV00002B/5/P